THE *RIVER* VIEW

ALSO BY JAMIE HARRISON

THE JULES CLEMENT SERIES

Blue Deer Thaw

An Unfortunate Prairie Occurrence

Going Local

The Edge of the Crazies

OTHER NOVELS

The Center of Everything

The Widow Nash

THE *RIVER* VIEW

A Jules Clement Novel

JAMIE HARRISON

COUNTERPOINT
CALIFORNIA

THE RIVER VIEW

This is a work of fiction. All of the characters, organizations, and events portrayed in this novel are either products of the author's imagination or are used fictitiously.

First Counterpoint edition: 2024

Library of Congress Cataloging-in-Publication Data
Names: Harrison, Jamie, 1960- author.
Title: The river view / Jamie Harrison.
Description: First Counterpoint edition. | Los Angeles ; San Francisco, CA : Counterpoint California, 2024. | Series: A Jules Clement novel
Identifiers: LCCN 2024010043 | ISBN 9781640096325 (hardcover) | ISBN 9781640096332 (ebook)
Subjects: LCGFT: Detective and mystery fiction. | Novels.
Classification: LCC PS3558.A6712 R58 2024 | DDC 813/.54—dc23/eng/20240301
LC record available at https://lccn.loc.gov/2024010043

Jacket design by Jaya Miceli
Jacket images: mountains © Shutterstock / NFNArts; house © Shutterstock / ArtMari
Series design by Laura Berry
Book design by tracy danes

COUNTERPOINT
Los Angeles and San Francisco, CA
www.counterpointpress.com

Printed in the United States of America

10 9 8 7 6 5 4 3 2 1

For Dan Smetanka and Dara Hyde

People who die bad don't stay in the ground.

TONI MORRISON

The structure of a play is always the story of how the birds came home to roost.

ARTHUR MILLER

CONTENTS

THE *RIVER* VIEW

1 *Maryellen Regrets*

CAROLINE FAIR'S LAST ASSIGNMENT OF 1997 ARrived in a burst of static from Sadie Winton, filling in for the regular dispatcher, and it interrupted a short stealth nap in the patrol car: A woman in the valley was unresponsive, and no officer or ambulance backup was available. One crew was dealing with a heart attack in the Crazies, the other with a rollover on I-90.

Caroline drove south to an expensive ranch on Langley Creek and into a barrage of woe. The Cattons, a San Francisco couple, had opened a guest cabin to a friend—Maryellen Smith, from a rubber-manufacturing fortune—who'd arrived from Jackson, Wyoming, and whose mood was especially ebullient after her husband drove off to stay with his own friends in Blue Deer. Maryellen bought dinner in town for her hosts that night; on the second, she helped cook a bland chicken, drank more than her share of overpriced California chardonnay, and headed to the guest cabin.

The next morning, October 10, would be the last warm day for weeks, and an early riding trip was planned. Despite that, and the front that was moving in—a blue-black fortress coming from the west—the Cattons, who never stayed for winter, didn't check the cabin until ten.

Maryellen did not respond to knocks or calls. Through a window, they could see the telephone receiver on the floor and a foot on the far side of the bed, cramped and white, surrounded by broken glass.

The door was bolted on the inside.

When Caroline arrived, the Cattons were dubious—in fairness people did a double take when they saw her these days—but she managed to force the door to the cabin just as Acting Sheriff Burt Feckler roared up, rallying for the rich, goaded into movement by one of the Cattons' important friends.

Burt poked his head through the door while Caroline determined that Maryellen was very dead, and he headed to the main house with the couple to phone the family. Caroline normally minded when Burt cherry-picked tasks, but she was relieved that someone else would now deal with the hosts' traumatized, self-absorbed incomprehension—how could this have happened? Why in their house? How could Maryellen have trespassed on their hospitality in this way? Maryellen, who did yoga for hours a day and gobbled vitamins—what had been the point?

Caroline was left to deal with the scene, the quiet woman. There was no rush: Maryellen, dead at least since midnight, apparently swallowed all the liquid in a brown bottle of hydrocodone, which was, in a word, overkill. The bottle lay on its side near the bathtub. She was forty, wealthy, beautiful, and—according to the whirlwind of information provided to Burt by the Cattons and the husband, when reached by phone—prone to depression. Though with cause: Maryellen's husband said she'd gone through radiation treatment for breast cancer the year before, and suffered the last of several miscarriages in February, and her beloved father had committed suicide just that summer. The husband told Burt that this was her fourth and by far most successful suicide attempt. Mrs. Catton made cocktails and wept.

Burt was prone to phrases such as "the husband" and "the father" and "the hosts," especially while having cocktails on the job. Caroline heard little else on background, and when she asked for more, Burt held up a hand: he'd let her know what she needed to know. She should stick with the scene.

It didn't matter—Caroline didn't want to think too deeply about the case, and in fact within a few days she'd forget about everything but the body, which would stick with her for years. In the guest cabin, Maryellen left behind a well-tended shell, cheery emails in a nifty PowerBook, an intact bottle of Xanax with the same February prescription date as the empty bottle of hydrocodone, a confounding tray of health supplements, a Smythson diary of parties and self-doubt, a gold- if not platinum-plated trust fund. No note, just Maryellen, who was only a few years older than Caroline, and who'd crawled naked through a trail of her own vomit toward the phone. She'd reconsidered.

When the ambulance guys finally arrived, Caroline could hear them joking with Burt, but they wouldn't in front of her. It was late afternoon by the time she sent the body north for autopsy and drove back to town through a sudden blizzard, feeling like Marge from *Fargo*: thirty-nine weeks pregnant, beset by strange twinges after a long week of shootings, naked artists in alleys, a dementia patient on the train tracks. She typed up her report, handed over her file, and went home. She told Jules Clement about the day while they cooked dinner, and she went into labor at about ten p.m. They had a baby two days later, which was at least a day later than Caroline had hoped.

2 *The First Morning*

SUNDAY

BURT FECKLER WAS FOND OF SHARING HIS THOUGHTS via communiqués on the department board. The Blue Deer *Bulletin* reluctantly gave him a slot on page three for a larger audience.

MESSAGE BOARD TO THE COMMUNITY FROM THE ACTING SHERIFF

> Aug 7, 1998—The Force has received multiple (obviously false) reports from the Public on its tip line about foreigners with masks and guns, sports cars traveling at excessive speeds, unclothed females, et cetera. The Public is advised that Montana Code 45-7-207 criminalizes false reports, and any erroneous and salacious calls will be prosecuted to the fullest extent of the Law. Wasting the time of the Force damages our Community's endeavors, morale, and finances.

The Public, the Community, the Force (normally the Absaroka County Sheriff's Department): Burt loved these words. The first two to mean civilians or amateurs; he used the last with the same ring as Special Forces or SEAL Team. During his largely symbolic stint as boss, Burt labored for hours on his manifestos, which at least provided the sheriff's department staff with a topic beyond iffy arrests and a renovation project that sent decades of files willy-nilly into storage. They all hoped Wesley Tenn, the official sheriff, out on medical leave, would return soon.

The *Blue Deer Bulletin*'s earlier blotter column featured stray animals, drunks, UFO sightings, and unneighborly interactions, but now the county commissioners and local Chamber of Commerce thought the column made the town seem like a deviant Hicksville, rather than what they hoped it would become (Bozeman; a small-business powerhouse; an idyllic, perfectly preserved, high-income bit of the Old West, sans zoning laws). Blue Deer, population five thousand, had a growing share of artsy, worldly émigrés, and for a while, over the summer, citizens who didn't share Burt's kind of worldview put up fake blotters and wanted posters and did what they could to unscrub the city. There'd been an attempt in university towns around the country to bring awareness to violence against women by spraying stencils on sidewalk corners that read A WOMAN WAS RAPED HERE. In Blue Deer, stencils appeared that read A MAN WAS DRUNK HERE, or SOMEONE SOLD A PATCH OF PARADISE HERE, or SOMEONE WROTE ANOTHER BAD NOVEL HERE.

Who knew that all these things weren't true? No one tried for realism—"someone beat a woman here" or "someone lost teeth to meth here" or, in fact, "a woman was raped here"—and the effort for humor lost steam with a spring of flooding and a July of grass fires. Burt, who doubled the arrest rate for minor possession and drunk driving, talked about running as "a real professional" against Wesley in the next election. He went to a big thumper church with billboards on the cancerous outskirts of town, but there were rumors of marital discord and misbehavior, and one of the stencils—A COP DEMANDED A BLOW JOB HERE—was linked to a threatened lawsuit.

Against Burt, who believed might made right.

People really had seen out-of-town men and women with masks in speeding cars multiple times that summer and the previous fall. Descriptions varied—when the lady at the drugstore claimed to have sold a box of condoms to a polite brunette with no apparent clothing under her coat, it did not necessarily conflict with the fishing guide who'd eyeballed a nude in the river, a towel on her wet hair and a flaming-sun tattoo on the small of her back. There were the usual seasonal incidents—the woman in nothing but chaps at last year's Fourth of July parade; the reliable exhibitionists at Eve's Hot Springs; that topless elf in the depot Christmas tree—but this slender woman was seen at least three times during September's late Indian summer, as splayed and open as a person could manage in a tiny sports car, glimpsed like a hundred-mile-an-hour hallucination. Her various chauffeurs happened to be recent Russian immigrants, likable and silly when Caroline dealt with them, in town for vague business opportunities and linked to the kind of minor chaos that offended Burt's sensibilities: bar fights, public urination, dart games with human targets. And why wouldn't there be people from Odessa and Georgia in Montana? All sorts of sketchy money was going into suburb building, ski resort building, restaurants, while dozens of starving, blindingly intelligent Eastern Bloc students flooded into Yellowstone Park, sixty miles south, for jobs with the concessionaire and then found themselves lost and jobless in the fall.

But the chattering class of Blue Deer, the bar-going class, clung to the legend of the Cold War Natasha–style vamp: she was seen again the following May as a blonde, but though the car was moving quickly, all agreed she wasn't a real blonde, and one witness swore that she called out in Russian to him. The local lawyer Peter Johansen christened her Volga Vera of the Vulva (Vera of the Volga Vulva?), and the sidewalk stencils started again, VVV WAS HERE with a vertical line in each V, like a stone age invitation to a fertility rave.

In June, Burt spent a lot of money borrowing a police artist from Billings, who came up with a portrait that looked like Marlene Dietrich, recently sprung from an asylum. People had a field day calling in, identifying sisters and kindergarten teachers. But for some reason, no one linked this woman to the one who'd fired a gun in the Blue Bat the previous fall.

AT SEVEN ON a Sunday morning in early August, Jules Clement's phone rang. This was something he'd mostly managed to avoid since quitting the sheriff's department, but the fucked-up marvel of the moment was that all three of them were asleep, if somewhat askew and in the same room, after a night of Tommy—now ten months old—with a fever.

Jules clamped down on the phone. He and Caroline held their breath; Tommy snored gently. He had a dusty pink fever face, a rime of dried tears on his fat cheeks. Jules slid downstairs and called his mother back.

When Caroline followed him a few minutes later he was sitting in the corner of the living room with the small mutt named Celeste on his lap.

"Are you okay?"

"Yeah."

"What did Olive want?"

Jules lifted a hand, touched his hair, and dropped it again. He was sitting mostly naked in a freezing room, the windows open for the always cool night, before another 90-degree day.

Someone, thought Caroline, must be dead. Which was more or less true, always, of course: she'd only been back at work part-time since April and she'd seen a dozen of them. "Jules," she said, shifting Tommy on her hip.

"My mother wants me to find out how my father died," he said. "I mean how as in everything, if he saw the gun, if he knew it was going to happen, if he knew why. She wants me to go through the files, talk to everyone who was working then, go to Deer Lodge and talk to Patrick Bell and say, 'Hey, Patrick, why'd you shoot my father in the chest?'"

Even Tommy was quiet, listening. Caroline draped a blanket over Jules and said, "Why now?"

"She says she's worried she'll die without knowing what it was like for him. What went through his mind."

"Maybe she had a dream. Maybe it's about the anniversary, or she isn't telling us what the doctor really said. What did you say?"

"I said that these were the last things I wanted to know. That they were unknowable. And she said try."

JULES WAS TALL and brown-haired and skinny, made up of angular, damaged pieces. His nose was not the nose of his childhood, his chin was rebuilt after an experiment in bull riding, and he'd broken the same leg twice. He was thirty-nine years old, and the leg ached in cold weather.

He'd grown up in Blue Deer, an hour north of Yellowstone Park in southwestern Montana, and left for college and a decade of archaeological fieldwork before returning in his early thirties. He was not very good at explaining why he'd come back, but the area was mostly wonderful, and always beautiful: the town was tucked into a curve of the Yellowstone River, surrounded by mountain ranges, crowded with people he mostly loved. It was hot in the summer but with cool nights, cold in the winter but with sunlight.

Before Jules returned to Blue Deer in the early nineties, the thing that people knew about him, the first part of any description, was that his father had been sheriff, and that his father had been murdered. Ansel Clement, son of Henry and Anna, husband of Olive, father of Jules and Louise, purchaser of Beatles and Merle Haggard but closet team Bowie and Bach, died on the afternoon of August 15, 1972, a day after his sixteenth wedding anniversary. Jules remembered Olive and Ansel joking about their hangovers that morning; Jules was out of bed late because it was summer, and he was thirteen, and his only job was mowing lawns.

Every part of Ansel's day was normal until he pulled over a speeding pickup truck driven by a man named Patrick Bell at 4:19 p.m. His body was found five minutes later, lying on the side of the road near his patrol car. Olive wanted to know the truth, but how was that possible, when there was only one survivor. And what was the point? When the call came in, Jules ran down the street behind his mother to the hospital, no one stopping either of them until they reached the stretcher and found a huge red absence below a surprised familiar face.

The memory of his father as an empty rib cage hadn't encouraged curiosity. Caroline talked to Jules about training away the trauma, ways he could distance the scene by seeing it in black and white, or pulling himself back until everything was very small and distant. This ploy was somewhat successful, but it did nothing to bury the noise Olive made in the hospital that day, or the rage Jules felt whenever he thought of the man who made this happen.

And so he tried to not waste more life on the thought of Patrick Bell. After Ansel died Jules ricocheted through school, committing many mostly victimless crimes, doing most available drugs with his best friend, a batshit geek named Larry Grand. Peter Johansen, the lawyer who christened VVV, was a roommate at Michigan, where Jules got a BA, and again in New York, where he earned money at very odd jobs (construction, slicing salmon, social work) while getting a doctorate in archaeology at Columbia, with a specialty in environmental archaeology and human migration. He knew a lot about grave goods and North Africa and the horse tribes of Eurasia, things that had little to do with the contract and private investigative work he did now.

Maybe Jules chose archaeology because it was a perfect profession for facing the enormity and inevitability of death. It caused understandable surprise and anguish for his family and friends when he changed course and joined the sheriff's department as a deputy, even if it all made sense on a Freudian level. He remembered his father as an open-minded, apolitical cop, and the world clearly needed more of them. He would be that person, and he would help the town to become that way.

At thirty-three he made sheriff. At thirty-six, after shooting a man, he quit. He wasn't in the wrong, entirely—the man had killed another officer, and shot Caroline, and would have killed Jules—and he wasn't traumatized. He quit because shooting the man and watching him bleed out caused him no remorse, and he knew he'd never get that song out of his head again.

Why had Ansel died? Why not? Bad things happened all the time to cops and the people they interacted with. Every third or fourth day, some police officer ended up biting the bullet, and a quarter of them probably deserved it; this year's ratio of dead police to the people police caused to be dead would be officially one to five, probably closer to one to ten. But there was no whisper of abuse or revenge in his father's case. Bell never gave any motive beyond bad timing: According to the Bell family, Patrick was rushing home to kill his unfaithful wife. Ansel was in the way.

Jules was an archaeologist again, but in the matter of his father's death, he wanted nothing of the past. All that he could really remember was Ansel's voice, his face laughing, his body moving through rooms, his presence in the front seat of the car or behind Jules in a boat on the river, at the oars. Not enough, but these were pure things. Why mess with them?

AN HOUR AFTER Olive's call, Jules loaded his truck with Celeste and his tools and headed to his office in the Baird Hotel. He drove past houses he'd seen his whole life, eyes twitching with fatigue. Objects took on an otherworldly look, the world seen through the thinner pane and hot brain that comes with hallucinogens or exhaustion. Other cars seemed to move too quickly toward the old pickup, birds and waving branches darting in and out of his peripheral vision, clouds speeding up. He managed to wave to his old music teacher and the kid who'd put up his gutters and a florist he'd slept with in 1984. He didn't wave to his bigoted second cousin or to a woman he'd arrested for meth just before he gave up life as a cop. Celeste turned her head in time with each sight.

A lawn mower sounded through the open truck window like an army of locusts, but the day was lovely, in a ragged sort of way. A pyre of smoke in the foothills, in the general direction of the cemetery, wavered like a warning plume in the wind, and he hoped it was only a slash fire. Half their summers ended in apocalypse now, fire and smoke and despair, but this August was cool and wet after a hot July, and the air was clear.

At a stop sign, beautiful Sadie Winton, who'd just given her notice at the sheriff's department, loped across the street, and Jules smiled back and woke up a little: Sadie would find the missing files for both his archaeological survey at the old county poor farm and for Ansel's death. You could talk Sadie into anything, especially on her way out the door.

Jules parked behind the Baird Hotel, and took the bar door to the empty lobby, Celeste trotting behind. It all smelled of last night's drunks and the day crew's bleach, and he used the banister to pull himself up to the second floor. At his desk, he stared at four mounds of paper—rain-dimpled files for his contract archaeology work, a slender folder for the university class he was supposed to teach in a month, and a messy pile of receipts and bids for the house he was trying to build. His investigative work made up the fourth and largest stack, untouched for weeks: an asset search in a bad divorce, an inquiry from a teacher who thought her mother was being robbed by a stepfather, a search for heirs, and an unfaithful husband who happened to be Caroline's nemesis, Burt Feckler. Jules tried to be discreet about clients; Caroline tried to do the same with police business. But they didn't try that hard.

Jules was more and more troubled by the pettiness of the job, the increasingly tech-tilted methods of investigation. Without an official role, he felt like someone else's personal information was none of his business. Now he pushed the files to the back of the desk and blew at the dust and food crumbs on the surface. He drifted to the window, big pearly cumulus on a dark blue sky, the pigeons on the slate roof of the depot across the street. He took a sip of coffee and brought it down too hard, misjudging.

He eyed the couch in the corner and moved there with some stealth, as if the piles of unfinished work on his desk might see him. He shared this suite with his old college roommate Peter Johansen—cohabiting again—who'd moved to Blue Deer with his wife, Alice, a decade ago, while Jules was still off on digs. Peter never worked Sundays, and it sounded like the housekeepers were still on the fourth floor of the hotel. They rented these rooms above the bar because no one could sleep there at night, given drunks and trains and the deflating joyous noises of the summer. But in the early morning, the streets outside this corner office—the main drag across from the grand former depot, now a museum with a wine store in the luggage building—were wonderfully quiet. And Jules was so very tired.

He lay down, and he stopped thinking about his mother's call, or how far behind he was on his PI work and the archaeological survey of the old poor farm on the flats. He squinched his mind shut to the thought of Caroline still at home with their hot, wailing son. She'd be waiting for the phone to ring with a doctor's appointment, trying not to think about the fragile line separating a mundane ear infection from meningitis, or the piles of work on her own desk.

Jules lay on the couch, hands crossed on his chest as if he were laid out on a bier, or as if Tommy were dozing under his crossed hands and it was necessary to stay utterly still. Celeste curled up at his feet, like a faithful dog on a medieval sarcophagus. Water ran in the third-floor room above, and someone walked back and forth. When the walking stopped, the water kept surging as the finicky asshole upstairs drained and refilled their bathtub to keep the temperature constant.

Jules dropped into a dream of an ocean. He lay in the sun next to a woman who slid a hand down his stomach. He wanted the hand to proceed but something was wrong, something large was swelling out of the water, something horrible was coming, and people were screaming for help.

He woke to horns and *fuck you* from the sidewalk, followed by *fuck you too*. His neck was at a hard angle, and he wrenched it, waking. He screwed his eyes shut again and listened to running feet on the hotel stairs—when did the maids ever run here?—and still the sound of water. He heard the voice of Edie Linders, the hotel owner, pounding on the door, yelling in the hallway: *Jules, help me.*

Jules opened his eyes and tried to understand what he was seeing: a growing lump on the ceiling, a bulging pink spot like something out of Dr. Seuss. Celeste was growling at it. Jules rolled off the couch as swollen drywall descended in a warm, bloody deluge, and ran for the door. He opened it to Edie still screaming, and he followed her upstairs and kicked open the door to room 302.

Where he thought, Holy fuck, it's my neighbor Mac in the bathtub, with just his mouth and nose and open eyes above the surface of the water.

"Oh God," said Edie. "Don't let him die."

They pulled Macalester Selway III, long and soft and floppy in a pair of black boxers, out of the overflowing bathtub. They used pillowcases to tie tourniquets on both of Mac's forearms above the tattered wrists, and pressed a washcloth on his torn throat, and gave him CPR while he spasmed like a dying fish. Just a month before, Jules had wanted to kill this man, and now here he was forcing air into his lungs.

3 *The View from Above*

THE NURSE NAMED MARINA THOUGHT SHE'D RARELY seen such a polite suicide, or such a bad marriage. The stiff-faced wind-up toy of a woman hissing at her husband while the staff pumped his stomach and transfused him was the kind of moment that killed the point of the work. When they pushed the wife out of the ER bay, and she screamed from the hall, the police sent awkward Deputy Sorenson, but he was no match for Elaine Selway, who simply went to the pay phone to call the acting sheriff.

After a few minutes of Burt Feckler howling into Marina's soft, unreadable face from four inches away, she left him to the doctor she most disliked and went outside to smoke a cigarette. She was ready to go back to a war zone, a refugee camp, anything but this.

SAVING SUICIDAL MEN was the sort of thing Jules hoped to stop doing when he resigned from the department, but his severely mixed feelings about Mac Selway mostly stemmed from a lawsuit.

Jules and Caroline planned to build a house on a slice of land on the Yellowstone River at Blue Creek, on the north end of town just as the river turned east, near the site of a ghost town called Doris, which had been one of the first settlements in the area. No one knew if Blue Creek had given Blue Deer its name—Jules had always heard the name had to do with a rotting deer—and no one had a good explanation for what about the creek had been blue. Hornblende at the bottom, shifting from green in the right light? The winter mood of the settlers of Doris or the banished Crow? The name likely came from the spring that was the creek's source, once used for ice before the town was abandoned in favor of the site that became Blue Deer when the railroad came through in 1882.

Doris was abandoned, and its land became cheap. In about 1900, Jules's family—farming Swedes trying and failing to learn how to ranch—owned a string of islands and land on both sides of the river. After the islands mostly washed away and the riverbank was reconfigured by floods, their remaining small wedge was marooned without road access, used only for float camping and feral middle school games that centered on the last of the old town foundations, and later on for drinking and sexual conquest. The Clements would wade across Blue Creek from the closest access or park a car on Lewis Street and sneak in and out through the surrounding property, owned for decades by a little old lady with the genial name of Suzette Whipple, who had a chain of title to some vague portion of the land that traced back to Joachim Rosenfalter, husband of the town's namesake, the original Doris. Suzette was Mac Selway's mother-in-law, and Mac and his wife, Elaine, had recently built a massive new house on the parcel, across a clearing from Suzette's modest fifties bungalow.

The year before, when Jules and Caroline first returned to town after a year of traveling, they'd floated to the land with their friends Alice and Peter and set up tents.

It was the week before Mother's Day and the timing was appropriate: Alice had a baby named Clare in a sling under her coat, and Caroline was pregnant. They looked for morels and made a lot of noise, but the Whipple-Selways didn't seem to care. They all watched surreptitiously while Suzette and her daughter, Elaine, padded grimly back and forth between their two houses, having a vaporous, passive-aggressive argument, and Mac read in a lawn chair and drank heavily. Alice was fascinated by the old shed Mac had renovated (without permit), which had once housed Doris's kosher butcher.

Peter was more interested in the river's changing location and the original boundaries of the Clement family parcel, and a few nights later, after Alice found two early maps of Doris, they all crashed around in the thickets on the river side of the Whipple-Selway houses, keeping to the undeeded land. They used Mac's studio as one fixed point, and that night Jules sketched out a series of drawings, a regression. You could flip through and watch the river move backward in time, filling in the old channel, adding sand and soil and rock to the Clement parcel. In the last, based on one of Alice's tattered maps, a stubby lane led from Lewis Street to the parcel: though the modern town grid stopped at O Street, there had once been a P, platted in 1895 but never constructed. This sixty-foot wide legal right-of-way sliced through the center of Suzette Whipple's land, nearly clipped Elaine and Mac Selway's new white mushroom of a house, and landed on a half acre of eminently buildable Clement lots.

Suzette Whipple disagreed, called a lawyer, and pulled out her own old maps, and things went downhill. Mac and Elaine, who everyone knew were just trying to reach a trust fund payout before divorcing, at least seemed united in something.

NOT ANYMORE. WHILE Jules was pushing mucus out of Mac's chest, flipping him on his side, trying not to notice the older cut marks on his arms, Edie wailed that Mac was one of her new investors. He needed a new place to live, a new business. He needed a new life entirely, or at least that was the plan, and Edie very much needed his cash to keep the Baird Hotel afloat. Blue Deer was mostly a wage-earning town, and it was not easy to own and renovate a 1902 hotel with ten-thousand-dollar January heating bills. This was presumably the point in selling apartments to rich men like Mac Selway and Ivan Luneau.

After the paramedics hauled Mac away, Jules squished around his ruined office. He dragged other furniture away from the buried couch, spread his files—dappled by the tremendous papier-mâché wave of bloody water and plaster—around the periphery of the room to dry out, and then thought: carry on regardless. He cleaned off his monitor, the printer, the telephone, and tried Ed Winton's number. Ed had been hired by Ansel Clement as a deputy in 1968, and Ed knew everything. While the phone rang Jules started to type:

> Aug 9, 1998
>
> Warden Listernik—I'm sure you're aware of the fact that I resigned as sheriff of Absaroka County three years ago. I returned to archaeology, and I'm also working as a private investigator, but I am writing now with a personal concern.

Another hang-up. Ed's wife, Shirley, had dementia.

> My mother, Olive Clement, has been increasingly troubled by questions about the murder of my father, Ansel Clement, by Patrick Bell. To that end, I'm writing to request an interview with Mr. Bell . . .

He tried dialing again, and this time, in the slight pause after Shirley answered, Jules managed, "Shirley, it's Jules Clement. I really, really need to talk to Ed. It's about my father."

"Well, I hope Ansel is working overtime, too."

Shirley hung up again, and Jules threw the phone.

HE COULDN'T GO home to change his clothes—if Tommy was napping, Caroline would kill him for making noise. He'd patted himself reasonably dry, exited via the Baird Hotel fire escape (not for the first time) with Celeste tucked under an arm, and squelched back across the parking lot to his truck. Outside, clouds spun and did not notice his pain.

He headed northeast of town, zigzagging up the rough dirt road from the river to Tokent Flats, only a half mile from Blue Creek if you were a bird but about twenty minutes if you were a demoralized human. He didn't notice a streak of missed blood on his elbow until he was within sight of the poor farm, where he was finally going to begin a field survey, even though a county car dump still covered the site. A big red Land Cruiser was parked near Jules's lean-to, the hood covered with maps and bags, Peter Johansen and Ivan Luneau sitting next to it on the last surviving wall of the poor farm, drinking wine out of jelly jars.

Ivan was an immigration lawyer from Denver, and they all often drank wine together, but this was a little early, even for a weekend. "What's the occasion?" asked Jules.

"I thought you said you'd be up here early," said Peter, looking amused.

"I planned to," said Jules. "I had a difficult morning."

"We know," said Ivan. He pointed to a wrapped burrito. Jules finally understood he was one of the excuses for the bottle of good wine and pile of Mexican takeout on the hood of Ivan's car: they'd come in sympathy. How could they not know? Ivan owned the half floor of the Baird above Mac, and Edie, panicking about insurance, would have found Peter. They were all Peter's clients.

"You're drinking at ten in the morning because of Mac?"

"Well," said Peter, "the hospital called, but it's also true I turned in that brief Friday. And we're going to drive up to harass Clusker, see what new bullshit he can spin about Marvel, make sure he's not going to pave paradise."

Jules had managed to forget Peter's first capital punishment case, on behalf of a Guatemalan who'd hit a bigoted Gardiner butcher in self-defense but a little too hard, for a little too long. It was a masochistic case to take, almost as brutal as sorting out Cavendish Clusker's ownership claim to the ghost town of Marvel, or Mac Selway's unpleasant marriage. "How do you feel about the brief?"

"Not good." A pause, but then Peter rallied. "Guess Mac's blood alcohol."

It was an old game, from when Jules was sheriff.

"Maybe point two nine," he said, trying not to think of the full bloom of Mac's breath. "Maybe point three one."

"Hah!" said Peter. "Point three five."

"Jesus Christ," said Jules. All the little happy cells of the brain, snapping off like Christmas lights in a power surge, or maybe fizzling like a cheap sparkler. The horror of Mac's despair faded a little. A sober suicide was unbearable to consider. A drunken suicide was annoying: fucked-up people fucking up themselves and others.

Ivan strode off toward the junked cars that still covered Jules's survey area. If he was tipsy, he didn't act it; Ivan was always coordinated, efficient, quick, relaxed.

"Anyway," said Peter, "I love your humanity. I assumed you still wanted Mac dead."

"Nah," said Jules. "The issue was always Suzette. And Elaine."

"She caused a bit of a scene at the hospital. She's pushing for his committal."

"I can understand why." Jules lined up burrito scraps on a rock: fragments of cheese, lettuce, meat, tomatoes. Celeste ate all of it, leaving the lettuce for last like a true Montanan.

Peter started looking for a cigarette in his pockets. "I guess he thought she was just joking about divorcing after the anniversary, and when he finally understood she was serious, he decided to blow the whole thing up."

The Selways had been open, even before the lawsuit, about an inheritance that would land on their tenth anniversary, a reward for having stayed married that long. They were planning a big party, but who on earth would come? Jules was torn between wanting to leave the state and wanting to protect their land. Mac had started a grass fire on the Fourth of July, and Jules had seen him unload more fireworks into the garage for this next, presumably last, maybe never party.

"So, spite."

Peter looked amused. They both knew that Mac and Elaine stood to inherit five million, but they kept to a little dance between Jules's role as a private investigator and Peter's privileged legal information. "I guess Elaine also threatened to cut him out of whatever new plot they're dreaming up. But now he's got some clarity. He's giddy at the idea of sleeping with someone else again, or someone again, period." Peter patted more pockets, looking for a lighter. "And you were right—Mac says Elaine is having an affair with the new partner, and he's fine with it. He just wants out."

Jules shied away from a quick strobe of images: the dull gouges on Mac's neck, the rinsed-out edges of the rips on his wrist, the whole concept of Elaine's new lover. All these partners and schemes—Jules didn't want to know. How could he be a private investigator without a fascination for other people's snarls? He let a last gust of hatred for his neighbors swirl through his brain and reached for his shovel.

"Anyway, Mac's getting a new will, and he wants to buy you a new couch." Peter gave a sidelong look at Jules's T-shirt, which had a dirty pink tinge. "You're really a mess, aren't you?"

"Have I acted like I'm miserable lately?" said Jules.

"No," said Peter, watching Ivan walk back from the pile of wrecked cars. "But it's not like the fucking tub landed on you. Everything will be fine with the house now. Suzette's all about peace. They'll have their party, collect their loot, quiet down or disappear." He finally lit the cigarette and turned in a circle. "This isn't much of a graveyard."

"If you couldn't pay your own upkeep, you didn't deserve a memorial. The county says twenty burials so I'm guessing thirty and hoping it isn't forty."

"I wish you luck," said Ivan, packing up the food. "It stinks up there, by the cars. I have something to ask you about, but it can wait. What do you have to deal with up here today? Measuring? Digging?"

"Everything."

"You should have bid per body," said Peter. "At least you don't have to name these people. Or dig them up."

Maybe just a few. Which made Jules think of the reality under the wayward road: caved-in coffins, rotted splinters against someone's cheekbone. It'd been years since he dealt with bodies.

THE ABSAROKA COUNTY Refuge for the Needy, commonly known as the poor farm, first opened on Tokent Flats in 1889, and was burned and rebuilt several times. For the first fifty years, it sheltered hundreds of people in an exemplary fashion. A medical staff, children allowed to stay with their mothers, airy dormitories, gardens, orchards. A milk barn, a mechanic's garage, a ball field, and—Jules's current problem—a burial ground, a potter's field.

The last inmate moved out in 1962, and when fire leveled the complex in the seventies, the county started using it as a car dump. When the road to Marvel washed away in a series of floods, an ad hoc two-track replaced it, and became the route of customary use for wreckers, for Cavendish Clusker, the last inhabitant of Marvel, and for any hikers who braved his NO TRESPASSING signs to reach the national forest trails. The likelihood that the two-track crossed graves wasn't a problem until the neighboring property owners demanded an official county right-of-way.

And so Jules was hired to find a new route or clear any bodies from the current path. Which meant figuring out where the bodies were buried. He knew the endgame would be financial; a couple of the commissioners were already muttering about relocation ("with a memorial!") in the city cemetery and the sale of the parcel. No one wanted this land a hundred years ago, but now most of Orange County and Minnesota seemed to think high and dry were gorgeous. The commissioners made the mistake of saying this out loud, several times, despite Jules repeatedly saying There Are Laws, and the Absaroka County Historical Society (known locally as the Aches, given the members' average age) got wind of the plot. The state of Montana didn't quibble about much—the teepee rings covering this bluff were destroyed long ago—but white people's bodies were different. Even poor, crazy white people's bodies.

Now the commissioners had Phase One and Two cultural resource surveys on their hands. Jules would need to locate every grave and all the vanished barns and sheds and dormitories before the county commissioners would be able to grant an easement for a public road, and sell the parched landscape closer to the mountains.

He'd already roughly staked the structures, but he'd

postponed the dead until the junked cars were hauled away. Monday was the promised deadline, but the cars still covered acres of the flats. A turquoise Cadillac, an egg-orange Olds; it took metal a lifetime to rust in this climate, and now he finally decided to split the potter's field survey in two, on an east-west grid.

For the next hour, he paced it off while his clothes dried on his body and the sun shrank his skin. He sketched the earliest burial ground, the twenty graves he knew, which had a remnant metal fence and some small stone markers subsiding into the ground. No one bothered with such niceties as the populations of both Blue Deer and the plot swelled. Celeste darted between pocket gopher holes, and probably from grave to grave. Why wouldn't a rodent choose a rib cage for a nest? The apple and plum stumps of the orchard—a dead orchard, or an orchard of dead people? Jules used the prod and began to worry. All he had, given the missing county records, were his own first sketches, a rough map of the property in 1900, and a 1916 list of twenty burials. It predated the flu pandemic, crippled World War I veterans, the drought that began almost as soon as the railroad suckered people into dryland farming, the crash, the Depression, which began as early in Montana as it did in Oklahoma. All sorts of reasons for the population to grow, dead or alive.

Jules chugged water and walked closer to the car hulks. During a flyover that spring he'd seen a snakelike mechanics' path between the cars and now he followed it to a ten-foot clearing in the center of the junkers, where someone, decades earlier, had attempted to sort: doors here, mufflers there. The clearing was too trampled down to show any disturbance, and Jules settled on the easiest pickings, three car hoods stacked at an angle. When he dragged away the last, from an aqua Corvair, he stared down at portions of three evenly spaced depressions.

Jules screamed *fuck*, and every rodent in six hundred and forty acres vanished. Celeste shot over and flipped on her back to appease him, poor abused shelter girl. Jules picked her up and sat down on the Corvair hood, thinking of every poor choice he'd made in the last months and what this discovery meant for the fall, thinking of his lost dream career of Neolithic mounds and Silk Road icons and Roman ruins on a blue-skied North African beach.

On their way back through the cars, Celeste stopped at a dark spot, and he dragged her away. Blood, pretty fresh: some gut-shot dog or out-of-season mule deer. There was a fresh stink to the air, to go with all the old death in these cars. Jules hurried, suddenly wild to be out of there, and took a chug of water when he was in the open again. He could see thirty miles of the Yellowstone River, three mountain ranges, a hundred coulees with a thousand hidden cows, the town of Blue Deer proper to the west, much of it unchanged since these people had been alive: schools, the immense railroad machine shops and braided tracks, the Baird and depot and two grain elevators, a dozen modest church spires (wind interfered with heavenly height aspirations), cemeteries for luckier people.

Uphill, toward the south, the forest line was delineated by some optimist's collection of cleared boulders. Suzette Whipple owned this barren patch. Above it, the inholding of Marvel, Cavendish Clusker's private ghost town, was guarded by a wall of fir trees. To the east, a contrail from a millionaire's jet taking off from the county's tiny field and a film of smoke on the blue sky from a fire near Reed Point.

He put away equipment and was splashing water on his face when he heard an engine. It was a black Suburban: Elaine Selway with some new friend driving, a man with sunglasses and white teeth. No one waved. Jules watched the SUV stray from the road, driving over graves.

This was not a surprise. After he took the bid, it felt like fate when he learned Suzette Whipple owned the private land, and that Elaine was the person pushing for the new road. Jules wasn't superstitious, but it didn't do to drive over graves, and Elaine's bad karma would be a little salve for what he guessed now: at least fifty people were buried on the hill.

4 *Ansel*

IN 1986, THE LAW STUDENTS OF THE INNOCENCE Project at the University of Montana chose to review Patrick Bell's death sentence, given in 1975 when he was released from the state hospital in Warm Springs and finally declared fit to stand trial. Bell's medical history was complicated—he'd suffered a head injury years before he shot Ansel Clement and suffered additional damage during arrest. It was a strange case for the Project to pick—Bell never contested his guilt, never really said much at all—but the students determined that Bell's defense was flawed, and his sanity and ability to understand the charges questionable, and they sought to reduce his death sentence to life.

The commutation hearing was Jules's only glimpse of Patrick Bell in the flesh. He drove up to Deer Lodge with his older sister, Louise. Olive planned to go but threw up at the car door, and headed back inside, a relief to all. The first two hours of the hearing were a fuzzy drone. Jules had taken a black beauty, but Louise reacted to stress like a narcolept, and he kept elbowing her skinny ribs to rouse her. The students told the court of Bell's many suicide attempts in the months after his arrest—braining himself against walls, throwing himself down flights of stairs, trying to force a broken plastic spoon into his skull via his ear. This judge seemed no more sympathetic to Bell's damage than Miles Birdland had been when Bell recovered enough for sentencing in 1975, but Jules was shocked by the evidence of abuse on Bell's face. The side facing them was handsome and bland, but when Bell turned his head toward the window—which he did often—Jules could see the misshapen forehead, right eye glazed and ear torn, features drooping as if from a stroke or Bell's palsy. A harlequin.

Louise, who now ran the parks department in Oakland, stood to say that no one in their family, including Ansel Clement, believed in the death penalty. Jules stood to say the same.

Patrick Bell's good eye skidded over the Clements, but he looked at his parents directly. Jules still didn't know how to describe the expression: love, dread, fear. Patrick Bell's father, in a wheelchair, wept and said nothing. Patrick Bell's mother rose to say that if the Montana Board of Corrections freed Patrick, someone would die.

Jules didn't mind that idea. Despite his speech, he wanted them all dead.

"No one is freeing your son, ma'am," said the judge. But he commuted the sentence to life.

5 *The High Ground*

JULES DROVE HOME TO FIND A MESSAGE FROM MAC Selway, saying that his new life was an open flower: he would buy a new couch; he would vouch for Jules with his wife and her new partner. They would still have the party but maybe skip the roast pig; after all, it was another fire hazard! All would be peace and honey. Jules needed to visit the hospital so Mac could thank him properly.

The voice on the landline answering machine was hoarse, either from a lacerated larynx or the trauma of a pumped stomach, but it was still loud and manic. It took a special kind of person to command a visit for the sake of a thank-you, but Mac, of course, was still probably bombed.

Jules, who'd stopped home to drop off groceries, did not call back. "Don't you think you should go?" asked Caroline. "Just to be nice?"

Tommy was eating a lump of peach, fever-free. Jules unloaded a bleak bag of diapers and yogurt and cheap wine. At the store, the kid restocking dairy had given him the finger.

"What's that for?" asked Jules. Though there was always a reason, and the kid had the special skeletal look of a former methamphetamine user.

“You arrested me,” said the young man.

“Did I have a choice?”

“Fuck you, man.”

And so on to home without further incident, along short blocks with small houses that were beginning to sell for too much money. People kept moving here, and the winters were no longer rough enough to scare them back home.

“No,” Jules said to Caroline. “I do not think I need to visit Mac. I’ve had my nice worn out.”

People Jules did need to visit: his mother, just to see if the temporary insanity behind her request had passed; Patrick Bell, if it hadn’t; Deputy Ed Winton, for institutional memory of his father’s case; and Wesley Tenn, the sheriff who’d succeeded Jules, still on medical leave. Wesley needed visitors but sometimes wasn’t up for seeing people.

The previous August, a wealthy suicide in a Big Sky condo allowed his Cadillac’s carbon monoxide to spread to the apartment above the garage, where his longtime housekeeper lived with two of her grandchildren. The carbon monoxide extinguished the pilot light on the apartment’s old gas stove, and when the housekeeper’s husband showed up midmorning, after his two-day shift as a private guard for another rich man, he had a cigarette burning in his mouth.

And so kaboom. It didn’t help that the suicide was a gun-and-ammunition manufacturer and took pride in his display cases. Wesley had been in Big Sky for a middle school soccer game. His children went to St. Anne’s in Blue Deer, which played against the other tiny schools in the region. Between games that morning, the Tenn family drove around, marveling at the new wealth, until a man with a charred face ran down the hill, screaming that his family was burning to death. Wesley seared his hands knocking down the door and suffered more burns in a massive secondary explosion from the gas furnace that finished off the housekeeper's husband. Wesley was airlifted to the burn unit in Salt Lake City, and for two days, in extreme pain, he thought he'd failed to save four people. On the third day, the housekeeper and her grandchildren returned from her ailing sister's house in Idaho. The housekeeper had left a message with the rich man's daughter, who hadn't bothered to pass it on to the now-dead husband and wouldn't bother to apologize now.

Wesley was a mess. Skin grafts on his face, a mitt for a left hand, damaged thumb and two fingers on the right. His wife left him—the marriage had been flawed for years—and he started an affair with a nurse. He asked for six months off, and then another six months.

While Wesley was still in the burn unit in Salt Lake City, Burt took over the big office and had it painted beige. The records room became a conference room, and the county files went into storage. Other officers' desks, in somewhat private carrels, were now clustered in a hellish center, and the perimeter was taken over by lounge chairs (labeled *For Visitors*) and potted plants, and by an information display about guns and tactical gear. Burt loved equipment; he loved the fine new invention of the stun gun. Caroline had taken to calling him Trigger.

But no one else wanted the job. Burt brought two cops with him, Perez and Kruger, but they mostly polished weapons and pulled over teenagers. Caroline certainly wasn't mounting a coup, even now. If Ed Winton's wife didn't wander most nights, he might have stepped up. If Harvey Meyers hadn't been profoundly lazy, he wouldn't have been Harvey. Grace Marble, the office manager, fought her own war—she kept receipts and notes for the union, the state police, and the AG, waiting for the inevitable moment when Burt went too far: brushing up against Sadie, asking a gay defense attorney about sexual practices, withholding food from prisoners, ridiculing Gideon Sorenson, who was biracial, and using excessive force in virtually every situation. Burt didn't protect, he preyed.

The records mess was the least of it, but it was meaningful, because most files from between roughly 1970 and 1985 were AWOL. For Jules, Burt was many things now: the cause of Caroline wanting to quit, the idiot behind the missing poor farm files, an embarrassment to Jules as a former sheriff, and now the reason that tracking down files on a 1972 murder and the 1973 closing of the poor farm would not be a speedy task.

And so, when Caroline needed some files from the office, Jules had an excuse to spread the suffering. He headed first to the commissioners' office, where the assistant, a business-school intern in a golf shirt, refused to say where any of the men—all men, still—were hiding. Three-martini lunch with a real estate agent? Nooky with a landowner? The boy had no sense of humor, and suggested Jules could come back in the afternoon. Jules suggested that he'd come back when the county had removed the car dump. The boy said the county couldn't find the equipment to get the job done. And so it went, on and on.

Jules, who no longer had keys for every door in the building, looped back through the lobby and walked down the hall and to the sheriff's department. There was no getting away from Ansel, who looked down at him from the wall with amused eyes. Jules was up on the wall, too, but Ansel had the big memorial frame, heavy and black, and the central position.

Inside the department, the world kept spinning. Jules sat at Caroline's desk and poked through her scraps. Embezzlement, drunks at bars in Gardiner, the theft of a van, the theft of a small tank from the local armory. Welfare checks, medication thefts, Cavendish Clusker's paranoid calls about trespassers up at the old ghost town of Marvel, trying to steal the last copper roof in town. Jules needed to talk to Harvey Meyers, but he was trapped on a call, possibly double billing with some of Jules's PI work. Harvey had never had any interest in being more than a deputy, always needed money, and didn't mind nights; on a stakeout, he had the birdlike—or maybe catlike—ability to wake when something within the panorama beyond his closed eyelids shifted, even in the deepest darkest alley or on the most banal suburban boulevard.

Grace slammed her phone down. "Tell Caroline that Gideon's off at counseling, so he hasn't managed that welfare check. I think he's having a breakdown."

"Everyone has one," said Jules. "He'll be fine."

"The Burt mess last night at the bar, and that kid case, and maybe still the thing with Suzette Whipple," said Grace, holding out the files.

"Any of them would do the trick," said Jules, grabbing the stack. Grace clearly wanted him to ask what "kid case" meant, but no one was pulling him back into this world, and no one asked Caroline to take kid cases now. He waved to Harvey. "Any of those old county files turn up, the ones to do with the poor farm?"

"Still in storage," said Grace. "Go away."

"No progress?"

"Hah," she said. "Maybe they're in the storage units by the county garage, maybe the old school, maybe the basement. Burt didn't give the moving crew a system, and so they didn't use one."

"I need criminal files from August and September 1972. Olive has questions about Ansel."

He watched Grace's face go slack just for a second. Normally, the topic of Ansel was nearly religious, but now she waved him off. "Go away," she said again. "I'll have Sadie look, before she abandons us completely. You know we don't have little elves back there, digitizing."

He flipped through the call ledger. "The driveway's going in tomorrow."

"You're starting despite the lunatics?"

"Suzette abandoned her lawsuit. Caroline didn't tell you?"

"Caroline is too busy to breathe. You might have noticed."

Jules had years of experience with Grace's little shivs, which he ignored well. "Suzette anticipated legal defeat, and we reassured her about some concerns."

"She can be pragmatic," said Grace, amused. "But do you trust her?"

"Of course not. I just want to get the house built," said Jules "We will coexist."

Grace snorted. Jules walked off toward Sadie, who was slamming things around in the back of the room. Ed's daughter was gorgeous, and efficient, and filled with self-assurance, but she was not the sharpest pencil. Usually, she talked nonstop about her mother's Alzheimer's, her lack of opportunity to find a boyfriend in this small town, her problematic siblings. Ed and Shirley had adopted and fostered a half dozen kids, but Sadie was the one who put in the time now that her mother needed help.

"Have you found anything?" he asked.

"No. I'm finally going through everything with Alice tonight. She says the county dropped off boxes last Christmas."

"Are you really going to quit?"

"I really am."

"To do what? Watch your mother full-time?"

"Hell no," she said. "Mac Selway hired me to help Suzette Whipple a few hours a week. Thank you for saving him."

"Mac?" said Jules. Stupidly.

"Yeah. He's worried about her."

"Her memory? Her heart?"

"Her daughter," said Sadie. "Weirdness with Suzette's medications."

Jules started to form another question, but they heard the heavy, metallic sound of Burt, moving down the hall.

"Bite me," muttered Sadie, shoving her face into the file drawer.

Harvey hung up and limped to the bathroom; Grace started searching for her post office keys. Burt burst forth into the room, chest first. He occasionally sounded like a cartoon, but he did not look like one. Baby-faced, almost pretty despite the beginning of a gut and the gray hair, expensive tastes in western wear when he was off duty and as much bullshit on his belt as he could fit. His eyes passed over Jules for Sadie, then reversed.

Jules, who made Burt unhappy, smiled. "Burt. You finally got rid of your wife, I guess. I remember you wanted to, so congratulations. Man on the town, now?"

Grace's and Sadie's heads swiveled. The idea that Burt was having next-level trouble with his wife was a new thing.

"It's about time I had fun," said Burt.

"Too bad she got to keep the big house," said Jules.

Burt turned to his desk, but there was no paperwork to feign distraction. Grace scented blood. "The deputy attorney general called from Helena about the arrests last night. She wants to talk to you about it. Both men are thinking of filing suit."

"Well, I don't want to talk about it," said Burt, heading for the bathroom.

When Jules left, past the wall of framed, mostly dead sheriffs, he always looked at his father's photo, never his own.

DID JULES AND Caroline believe in coexistence with the Selway-Whipples? Not really, though he rarely thought in terms of good or bad people. He'd always been very uncoplike in his embrace of gray areas, one large reason not to be a cop anymore. Yet now he felt an increasing tendency toward righteousness, toward seeing in black and white.

Suzette Whipple, née Ditteler, the unlikely matriarch, left Blue Deer in the fifties to be a starlet. Instead, she'd married a California land developer and returned to Blue Deer and her ancestral plot a decade later. Jules had no idea where Donald Edgar Whipple was now, but he seemed to be a bone of contention between mother and daughter. After Donald left the scene in the seventies, Suzette became exceedingly outgoing, and eventually famous for being difficult. Which was, of course, sexist.

There was no real age cutoff for AWOL behavior in town—but Suzette's leather-skinned exhibitionism, her celebration of the eternal *I Am*, was impressive. She quieted down when her daughter moved to town—Elaine could suck the happiness out of a room—but Suzette did her best to look as if it was still 1970, and her perfume had an edge of formaldehyde. She was often witty and amusing—she'd played bridge with Olive for years—but when she turned it was an awful thing, a real who-flipped-the-rock nightmare. The fact that she seemed not to remember such episodes made anticipating them difficult, though most people, like Jules (they'd had it out before he'd even bought the land, when Suzette publicly slashed the tires on an elderly Lothario's Ford pickup), retreated to her shit list with something like relief, shattered but free. She'd thrown sets of dishes, told husbands their wives were unfaithful, told children their parents were alcoholics, told bar crowds who was impotent and who wore the wrong kind of underwear, accused half the professionals in town—lawyers, doctors, real estate agents, accountants—of malpractice. Jules and Caroline were not the first victims of a lawsuit, but they would be party to the lawsuit nearest and dearest to Suzette's heart.

She was not boring. Jules did not hate Suzette, or dislike her son-in-law. Mac was goofy and bland with an edge of bipolar tragedy even before the bathtub.

But Elaine, Suzette's daughter, was unknowable and alien. Her righteousness, her prim yet litigious fury, made her repellent. From a distance, before the lawsuit, she and

Mac seemed like an earnest, scrubbed couple who'd moved across the country to selflessly help care for her famously difficult mother. They'd been friendly when Jules and Caroline first introduced themselves back when their land was simply a camping site. Elaine worked part-time for the Chamber of Commerce and wrote community grants. Mac did vague trust-funded things like a money-losing battery start-up business. The mini-mansion they built on Suzette's land was horrific. The family politics were Other.

Jules knew a great deal about the Selway-Whipples, not just for the sake of his own malice. After he and Caroline understood that the land was worth claiming, but before the legal wrangle, he'd been hired by the lawyer for the Selway family trust in Ohio, who wanted to know about the state of Mac and Elaine's marriage. The question wasn't whether the couple had committed a crime or were in financial difficulties. It was whether they were in fact married "in name and deed, according to common practice," and whether they were still maintaining such a marriage at the time of their upcoming tenth anniversary.

"Nice people," said Jules, but the trust attorney had no sense of humor. He said Mr. Selway's grandfather believed in love, and he wanted to know that "his children" worked.

Was it unethical to spy on his neighbors for profit? Cheap shots, cheap thoughts, mixed motives. Caroline, who knew Jules would probably do it anyway, thought this spasm of conscience was amusing, but Jules, feeling the need for a little distance, sent in Harvey Meyers, his tiny moonlight elf. They now knew, through a combination of technology and sheer gumshoe effort, a great deal about Mac and Elaine. They claimed in public to despise each other—the last time Jules had seen Mac at the bar, he'd been calling out for volunteers to break his sexual drought—but they had at least gone through key motions on their couch, curtains open, in front of Harvey's disbelieving eyes just that June. They cohabitated, they sometimes ate and shopped together, and they were involved in some shallow real estate skirmishes in the outlying areas of Bozeman.

Elaine was having an affair, but how did this make the Selways less married? From the point of view of a private investigator, it made them horribly typical. Digging into the couples' financial matters was like punching a marshmallow—to call any of their doings "a business" was ludicrous. They didn't work in the normal sense of the word, no matter how often Mac babbled about investors and land, but Harvey could find little in their names. This new attempt to sell the land Suzette owned between the poor farm and the national forestland was the first meaningful scheme anyone had seen. Back in Ohio, Mac had an office with his family's construction company—he came from a family that had paved most of the state in the early nineteenth century. Not much of interest had happened since. Elaine had a business degree—she was about five years older than Jules would have guessed; the wonders of never going outside, never caring about anything or anyone but yourself—and had worked in sales with a pharmaceutical company. She told everyone that she'd given up her career to come home and care for her mother, but while Elaine might feel duty, she wasn't back home for love. Suzette owned the Selway house, and Suzette owned the land Mac and Elaine and the yellow-haired dude hoped to develop.

This whole PI side gig was a bowl of misery.

Jules poked around for criminal records. Elaine's background was predictably clean, as was Suzette's before Burt charged her with assaulting an officer. Mac had been arrested for public indecency in July 1986, in Ohio. This was a surprise, but really in many ways not one at all. Confusion and denial? Had all ten years been hell? Who lived this way? Jules didn't want to give the trust lawyer any excuse to extend the mess. It was possible that the Selways, having received their inheritance, would vaporize. To that end he told Harvey not to bother writing up Elaine's frolics.

When Jules and Caroline announced that they could legally build on twelve lots (right in town, with a view of the mountains and the water!) within Suzette's fifty-lot kingdom, the shit hit the fan. Suzette hired a lawyer and sued to stop construction, though Jules and Caroline were only at the point of dealing with the Army Corps and house plans. Suzette pulled out a document that hinted at ownership of the same vanished island the Clements claimed. She produced a very old map that showed the town of Doris, with the Ditteler property as a sort of ink blot over everything. No actual markers or legal description, and if Suzette really thought she owned the Clement land, why the hell hadn't she brought it up during the last few decades of camping parties?

The back-and-forth continued through the fall and the holidays. Peter filed a countersuit against Suzette—nuisance, specious claims—with extensive documentation. Jules's Scandinavian family believed in records. Peter wiped the family down a conference table with the chain of title, Army Corps rulings, and the early maps that threw the Whipple claim for any of the area into doubt.

Everyone simmered through the rest of the winter, bitching about five feet here or there on one old deed, seven on another.

At Easter, they hid eggs for Peter and Alice's daughter, Clare, all along the perimeter of the property, and Elaine actually gnashed her teeth at the little girl. On St. Patrick's Day, Jules pissed on the tree that Suzette said she'd planted for her dead husband, and from the Selway house they heard breaking glass. At Passover, Jules eyed the mountain snowpack and wished for another quasi-biblical five-hundred-year flood; for his pains, he ended up helping Suzette get her llama and pony onto the dry land in the middle of the theoretical P Street. Still, the Clement-Fair parcel stayed dry, while the Selway ground floor was covered with a skim of mud.

As one maneuver after another was thrown out, Jules and Caroline assumed that the Selway-Whipples would give up. Suzette's initial change of heart came on a slushy day in June, the kind of branch-breaking, garden-killing day that Jules worried would make Caroline rethink Montana. Suzette went shopping downtown despite the weather. She bought a bouquet of flowers on Main and backed out of a parking place, without clearing snow from her back window, and into another car. Suzette blamed the weather and then the other driver, a stoned, amiable young man whom she poked repeatedly in the chest. When Burt arrived, he said "calm down," words guaranteed to napalm a situation. Suzette clubbed him with her new bouquet of roses. Burt called for backup, and when she clubbed him again, he used his stun gun in lieu of simply cuffing her. She was up off the sidewalk with a bleeding temple and back into attack stance by the time the newest officer, Gideon Sorenson, arrived. Suzette threw the tattered roses and poked him, too, and Gideon, on Burt's command (and ignoring the fact that Caroline was running down the sidewalk toward the group, screaming *Don't*), whipped out his own Taser.

"Gideon just can't bear being touched," said Caroline. She'd gone from despising Sorenson to worrying that he was innately shaky, best kept for minutiae and people who were already dead.

Suzette dropped; Suzette had a heart attack. Caroline gave her CPR and took care during chest compressions to not shatter the frail ribs. A crowd gathered, including the florist, and Caroline learned that Suzette bought the roses for her own birthday. She emerged from the hospital with 60 percent of her previous cardiac capacity and sued the sheriff's department for $700,000, an arbitrary but meaningful amount. Sorenson requested counseling. Burt gave some turgid quotes to the newspaper and Suzette piled on a suit for defamation.

Peter, having been hired by both Mac and Suzette for other, mysterious matters, did not handle these cases, but he did manage the final breakthrough. He and Jules were having their weekly drink at the Blue Bat when Mac walked in. Peter asked Mac what would make a difference. Mac said that for Elaine the land was total war, but for Suzette it was all about that old apple tree. She was crazed by the idea that someone might bulldoze this tree, which she'd planted for Donald Whipple.

Jules and Caroline had never considered chopping the apple tree down. They visited Suzette, promised to keep the tree upright for eternity, to feed it and prune it gently and make delicious things out of its wormy apples long after Suzette was gone, and they watched her cry for a husband no one had heard her mention before, and only Elaine seemed to remember fondly.

The lawsuit evaporated. The driveway would still follow the sixty-foot plat of P Street, mapped in 1895 but never built, but would now curve pleasantly. The garage would go up first, to give the builder electricity and shelter to work on bad-weather days. Jules and Caroline would not allow construction before 8 a.m. or after 8 p.m. They would not use garish colors and they would, as much as possible, build out of sight. A small upper story, three bedrooms and two baths, the kitchen the biggest room, in the center of everything. From upstairs, a sliver of river visible through the trees; from the kitchen, the garden they planned to create in what was now a thatch of rose and dogwood.

In July, they all met on the property lines, in what Jules thought of as the demilitarized zone. The lots were a little like a three-slice pie or a peace sign, with the easement holding the unborn zigging driveway within the platted road as the bottom vertical line, serving as a buffer between Suzette to the east, Jules and Caroline to the south, and Elaine and Mac in the west.

"We can be friends now," said Suzette.

Elaine, who always said "our land" the way you might say "my empire," began to smile, reassured by the joke.

"Really," said Suzette. "They'll leave the tree, and I am at peace."

"What tree?"

"*The* tree. The tree I planted for your daddy."

A fading look of wonder rippled over Elaine's normally

smooth forehead. Why hadn't Suzette warned her daughter? For a second, Jules thought Elaine was going to shriek *What daddy?* but she only said *Mother.* Elaine was always quiet in terms of sheer decibels, though one sensed tremendous mental violence. It occurred to Jules that Suzette might want to lock her doors, hide her pillows, check with her lawyer, or write a nice apology to her daughter. Who, though still quiet, looked yellow green, like tornado air.

Caroline, Tommy bundled against her body, swayed nervously. Their enemies were about to eat each other. Elaine walked back to her mansionette, Suzette to her cottage, and within minutes Jules and Caroline could hear them screaming at each other via telephone.

Post-truce, when Jules saw her, Suzette fluttered vaguely in her yard, rather than darting in beelike line drives. He felt the beginnings of sympathy and drove away the kids who tried to party on her patch of river frontage. He gave her biting llama and Shetland water when he saw their trough was empty, and he shut the gate when he found it open twice. And when someone chalked *old cunt* on Suzette's sidewalk, he rinsed it off with her hose.

It would be safe to assume kids were to blame. But he was sure it was Elaine, who was now at war with everyone on Blue Creek.

And yet here they were on Sunday, August 9, about to dig a hole for a garage and a house, embrace debt and the neighborhood. They'd moved on from the Selway-Whipple wrangle: Caroline and their contractor, Divvy Ott, argued about details—she wanted a small porch on the garage that might eventually be framed in for a greenhouse, and Divvy wanted to use up some cut-rate windows and fill from another job. Tile was bitterly contested; rooflines became the new trench warfare.

Inside what Jules and Caroline called "the old house," Jules threaded through a living room dotted with toys and dropped Caroline's files on the kitchen table, on top of a growing mass of estimates, lumber and window and tile orders, elevations. Tommy's temperature was down, and his ears didn't seem to be bothering him. They watched him fondle a padded plastic book and stare at dust motes, sitting with the occasional twitchy lurch of a newbie or a drunk.

They headed to the land, leaving Celeste at home. The world seemed velvety and green even though it was August. They shook out a blanket under the apple tree and watched Tommy roll around happily in the filtered light and eat Cheerios and lumps of cheese and halved grapes. They wandered around the cleared area that would be their house, and ignored the surrounding thicket of hackberries, raspberries, old fencing, and vines that would someday be their real garden. Divvy said that his crew would have enough room to maneuver, and this battle could wait for spring.

They were here this afternoon to properly stake their as-yet-imaginary driveway to a still-imaginary garage and house. They'd roughly marked out the driveway two weeks earlier, staying as far away from the sacred apple as possible, but half their wooden stakes were already missing. This time they used flagged rebar and a small sledgehammer, and Jules pounded while Caroline followed with a measure. Tommy, up in a backpack, ran his sticky fingers through her hair, and she kept glancing at a moving curtain in Suzette's cottage.

"The witch is in," said Caroline. But she'd also begun to soften. Maybe it was Suzette's birthday roses, or the feel of the tiny fragile ribs as Caroline tried to resuscitate her, or just the enormity of the change, as Suzette walked toward them: her white hair was pinned up in a demure bun, and she wore pants instead of revealing gauze. Her skin was waxy, unoxygenated, and her voice whistled. It was so strange that someone dying of congestive heart failure, someone essentially drowning, could produce such a dry sound.

"Beautiful day," said Suzette tentatively. "But why are those trees marked?"

"We're moving the house site closer to the river," he said. "To give everyone a bit more privacy. If we take them down, we can stay twenty feet away from your apple."

"It's a shame that something always has to die," said Suzette. She seemed to regain her bearings. "Way into the wild area? Are you sure you won't run into other problems? Rocks, or flooding? Donald never talked of building there."

"Well, why not? It's the highest point," said Jules.

"And it's not as if they spend time looking at the river," said Suzette. "Mac still can, from his studio. I'm hoping they'll hang on to each other."

The studio was stacked with boxes. Jules should take a photo for the trustees: the Selways' happy marriage, in one image. "Is that likely with the new friend?" asked Jules.

A pause. "Charlie is an old friend. They haven't told you about Charlie?"

A door slammed and they turned to the Selways' mini-mansion. A man—fit, maybe in his forties, with a helmet of blond hair—walked out to the deck and sat in a lawn chair, sunglasses in place, facing a wall of cottonwoods and the invisible river. Elaine Selway stood with her hands on his shoulders and whispered in his ear.

It was the man from the poor farm, the guy who'd driven over the graves, a smiling Ken doll with yellow hair like a warning sign and black eyebrows, a combination rarely found in nature. A yellowjacket, a coral snake, a tiger. Jules's eyes slid away, the kind of automatic twitch he got when his eyes hit someone with an obvious facelift, the brain saying something is wrong with this picture.

The couple looked fresh in the warm sun, shiny the way a plastic candle looks compared to wax. Elaine laughed, she clung to the man's arm, and the whole thing seemed like a seventies liquor commercial. And then she swayed in their direction.

"What a pretty baby," said Elaine.

"Thank you," said Caroline, clinging to Tommy's feet while he tilted in the backpack to follow a flying magpie, oblivious. She edged away toward the river, rather than staying to protect Jules, and he watched her disappear into the trees.

Elaine was beautiful, almost freakishly so, with a bona fide curl in the middle of her forehead. This slight edge of the unnatural was amplified by her robotic expression and a childhood neck injury that forced her to turn her shoulders whenever she turned her head. When Elaine looked at you directly it was a little like a swiveling spotlight finding you in a prison yard.

"Poor Mac," said Suzette.

"He'll be fine," said Elaine.

"To suffer enough to be willing to end it, though," said Suzette, sticking to mortality.

"He's not suffering," said Elaine. She looked at Jules. "We're divorcing," she said. "Finally. We'll make it to the party and then we're done, aside from business. And we'll both be relieved."

Maybe Elaine didn't understand the town knew all of it.

"Still," said Suzette. "Once they try, they always try again. My daughter may be doomed to go through what I went through."

Some insight into the end of Donald Whipple, Suzette's invisible husband. But your daughter doesn't love Mac, thought Jules.

"Mother, Mac probably won't go anywhere, let alone that direction. He'll probably stay in the studio and peer through the windows." Elaine did a little head cock; she did this when she wanted you to pay attention, and Jules hated this habit more than most things about her. There were so many small ways in which she quietly drilled away at his peace of mind.

"I've heard you're speeding up the schedule. When does my world start to end?"

"The driveway goes in tomorrow. They'll start digging the garage foundation the day after. I'm not sure when you're having your party, but I'll promise to have them quit early that day."

"And the foundation?"

"We'll hopefully pour on Friday."

"My, my," said Elaine.

Now the man on Elaine's deck was doing some weird tai chi maneuver.

"We'll make ourselves scarce tomorrow, then," Elaine said. "Go see friends in Wyoming or check in on Charlie's parents and get a nice hotel room down at the hot springs. You know I'll sue you if the crew touches a daffodil."

Jules looked around. The only daffodils Elaine would find in August were painted on her mailbox. He wondered if she was truly that divorced from what passed for the real world, and now he really looked at her: she was drunk at four in the afternoon, and she had hickeys on her neck. "Well, I'm sure Suzette will protect her property."

"Her" was deliberate—Suzette made it clear that she owned everything, not Elaine—but Elaine didn't go for it. Jules waited for whatever was coming next and so did the watching man, who'd stopped pretending to be a warrior priest.

"My father didn't commit suicide. And Mac didn't really try to, at least not yet."

Caroline edged back as Elaine glided away and kissed the man. "Who is he?" asked Caroline.

"No idea," said Jules.

"I've never seen her touch Mac. But I'll admit this guy is prettier."

"Fuck them all," he said, spooling the tape measure. Tommy was not paying attention; Tommy was leaning back to look at tree crowns, so that Caroline staggered.

"Sometimes I wonder if we really want to be here," said Caroline.

But they did want to, because it was beautiful. Living here would be close to living out of town. They'd have a fence, and the garden would be a buffer. They could carry a kayak straight from their porch to the river; Jules would ask the bulldozer operator to extend a narrow path so that they could even land a drift boat. They wouldn't see a

Selway-Whipple unless they looked, and why would they do that?

Elaine laughed loudly enough to make them turn again, and they watched her lead her lover toward the hot tub on the open deck. Jules and Caroline both looked away, embarrassed, and Caroline reached up and pinched off one small green ball from the apple tree. Two other unripe apples dropped. She looked at Suzette's house in time to see a curtain fall hastily.

"Maybe she'll drown," said Caroline. "I hate her."

"No you don't," said Jules, but if you were a cop, a nurse, even a hospice worker, you gave up judging yourself for imagining evil ends. "No good comes of such thoughts," said almost no one who'd done any of these jobs for more than a month.

"I've seen her flirt with Burt. Maybe they can have an affair next, and she can shoot him."

"You'll never be that lucky," said Jules. "And Elaine doesn't seem like a gun type. Elaine seems like a poisoner. Strychnine in the tea, or deadly Russian umbrella tips."

"Russians again," said Caroline.

6 *Russians!*

STATISTICALLY, WOMEN DIDN'T OFTEN SHOOT MEN, and when one did, it was almost always in self-defense, almost always against a partner. But the woman who shot Merv Galladyce on October 8 at the Blue Bat bar hadn't known him or been in apparent danger. The bartender, Delly Bane, told Caroline that he didn't think Merv had even touched her, though Merv always did try too hard.

This happened during Caroline's last week of pre-Tommy work, two days before the real last day, when the rich woman in the valley committed suicide. Delly couldn't remember a thing about the woman's looks, which made Burt assume that the woman was plain, but Harvey, in the Bat an hour earlier to drink away a car accident, said Merv's shooter was beautiful. He said her lips were the color of blood and when he met her eyes his hair stood straight up. "She didn't shoot *me*," he said.

"Maybe it's because you weren't an asshole," said Caroline.

Merv certainly didn't remember a fucking thing after being gut shot. No one else talked to the woman, though Delly heard her say "driving" and "vodka," and "I've never seen one." She was quick, a shape in the door even as people began to understand the sound of a silenced gun and the man on the floor, before anyone saw blood. The bar was a closed horseshoe on the street-door end, and Delly was no longer capable of vaulting over it. He only saw taillights headed north.

A day later, when calmer, Delly said the woman was thin, with long dark hair, and in fact reminded him of Caroline without the full-term belly. He said she had an accent.

"But you only heard a half dozen words," said Caroline, reading her notes.

"That's enough to tell," said Delly.

"What was the accent?"

"Russian."

Caroline stared at him.

"Something Slavic, anyway," said Delly stubbornly. "My opa was Polish."

"Oh, come on," said Caroline. She was exhausted and past her due date. She felt like a large cake that was about to collapse, and she was relieved when Burt—glory-hogging but citing Caroline's request for nonviolent work—pushed her aside on this case, too.

Four nights after the shooting, two days after Caroline went into labor, Jules and Peter were in the same bar. Jules was weeping about beauty and pain with his hands over his face, undone after one celebratory drink. The only other customer came in out of the snow, kept her parka on for a single whiskey, and left quickly. She patted Jules on the back as she headed out, winked at Peter, and whispered something to Delly, who poured himself a massive whiskey when she was gone.

Delly never drank at work, even to celebrate the birth of an old friend's first child. "What did she say to you?" asked Peter.

"She said I was lucky," said Delly. "'Fucking lucky.' That was the lady who shot Merv and I think she came here to kill me."

They did not call the police. Soon after, Delly sold half the bar to an ex-actor named Tino and left town with his girlfriend on a prolonged holiday in Spain. For six months, all through the winter, they sent postcards of two-dollar verdejo and fried artichokes, snails and sizzling pork.

Acting Sheriff Burt put a feeble amount of effort into the shooting and got nowhere. In the ten months since, there had been a few leads. A woman with an accent had lounged briefly on a couch in the Baird lobby during the May Day caddis fly hatch, making all the fishing guides' eyes pop, and these same fishing guides claimed to have seen her again at the end of July, wearing a bikini and casting from a mysterious drift boat. Was this Volga Vera of the sports car, or the assassin from the bar, or both? The description, bikini aside, was always underwhelming—medium height, medium brown hair, maybe mid-thirties. Nothing, on reflection, was memorable, and yet Russians were on the community's mind again in the summer: drunken Russians herding bison on Yellowstone roads, sinister Russians buying pastries in Gardiner, dancing, nude Russians in Blue Deer's bars and alleys, and that beautiful stripping lady, airing things out over the Fourth of July. Recently, there'd been a cascade of issues in Yellowstone Park, and Caroline and Ed were slated to meet with rangers that week.

Jules didn't think Caroline should have anything to

do with Russians. When she first returned from her six-month maternity leave, she stuck to four half-day plainclothes detective shifts. She'd negotiated the deal with Wesley Tenn and it drove Burt wild: no patrols, no uniform, no twitchy men with guns. Caroline no longer dealt with initial domestic violence calls or child welfare calls, and most important, she rarely had to see Burt. She could avoid arresting a man who chopped off two of his girlfriend's fingers and dropped them into the hamster cage, on top of two halved hamsters, or a hospital administrator who beat his stepdaughter bloody after her abortion, or the husband who left dozens of knives pointed at his wife's pillow. She handled missing persons, cold cases, follow-up interviews, admin, and budgetary tasks. She would be the one to visit Mac Selway before his release from the hospital, helping the county's mostly nonexistent mental health staff suss out if he was a risk to himself or others. She'd recently dealt with a Jack Russell in a violet harness that liked to eviscerate chickens, and a honeybee-carrying-semi rollover, and an old man who imagined bodies in ditches whenever he saw a magpie.

As a detective, though, Caroline was called upon to investigate both crimes and the department's responses, and today the problem that loomed largest was Burt and Gideon's stop at the Bucket on Saturday night. Two men were hospitalized, and Caroline wanted to hear about it before Burt laid a heavy editorial hand on Gideon's report.

At the department, Burt's office was open and empty—of the man, of files, of any sign of thought or effort. Grace, without comment, handed over the freshly typed report, and Caroline tracked Gideon down in the only interview room. It was his favorite hiding place—the door sign was turned to OCCUPIED, but inside all was silence, Gideon and a pile of files, always sitting on the witness-arrestee side.

Caroline sat across from him and started to read: at 8:32 the night before, a bartender named Helga O'Connor called Burt at home to report a disturbance at the Bucket, formerly the Bucket of Blood, the business's name in the earlier part of the century. A group of people were singing, Helga claimed, and they wouldn't stop. Five men, one woman; Helga didn't know them, and they were laughing at her and singing songs that she was very sure were dirty in . . . Russian. She took offense to the language—she was still miffed by vodka prices during the grain embargo, and her father had been a German POW in Stalingrad—and she told them to shut up, but the group said they were singing mourning songs, celebration songs, and they needed to keep going.

Helga was built like her first name, and she was not fond of her clientele—any of them, ever—and she especially despised emotive people. The rest of her customers were similarly mean-spirited and offended on a nationalistic level, but too lazy to address the problem directly.

After the incident with Suzette, Burt was supposed to avoid working with Gideon, but now he ordered him to meet in the alley behind the Bucket. Burt arrived in prime form, bursting with metal bits and masculine hair. He blustered into the bar and rousted the men out to the alley, Helga yelling insults in their wake. He slapped at the men, taunting, and demanded ID, saying he didn't think they were in the country legally. He thought they were mob or selling heroin from Afghanistan. When one of the men said he was from St. Petersburg, Burt called him a liar—he just knew the guy wasn't from Florida—and smacked him on the arm with a baton.

Burt believed in spies, liberal plots, cloud-seeding viruses, the Posse Comitatus. He admired the Montana Freemen. Maybe Burt, like Helga, thought he was fighting Commies.

One of the men was a writer from Tulsa named Wally Sands. He said they were just "unwinding," and no, there was no reason to show ID. Wally asked if they were being arrested, and on what grounds, and asked for Burt's name. Gideon, seeing Burt's outrage, stepped in. Just go home, Gideon said to Wally. No, screamed Burt. Drop your wallets on the ground and put your hands behind your heads.

And when Wally (who was very stoned) asked "Why?" for the fifth time, Burt used the stun gun. It was essentially a cattle prod, not a Taser with a projectile charge. Gideon heard Wally's skull hit the alley pavement and crouched next to him. The woman in the group, who had been standing back, asked Burt to please stop, and one of the other four men, who all seemed to be Russian, stepped forward. Burt zapped him and down he went. Burt said he was going to ram the gun up the man's ass before he slid it down his throat.

This was when the woman used one leg to scythe Burt's legs from under him, picked up the stun gun, and shot him in the ear and in the groin. She said something to Burt, and then she patted Gideon on his shoulder as he was checking the writer's pulse and disappeared down the alley.

Caroline looked up from the report. "And the other men?"

"They followed her."

"What did she say to Burt?"

Gideon, miserable and remote, looked everywhere but at Caroline as she read. "It sounded like a curse—I mean, she was pointing at him—but who knows."

"Why did you think it was a curse?"

"Just the way she said it," said Gideon. "And it did sound like Russian. Maybe she was local, just having fun with him—I heard her talking earlier and she sounded normal. They all sounded normal. It was just the songs and this last thing that weren't in English."

Normal. Caroline looked back at the report and up at Gideon, who was incapable of lying. "I feel like there's a lot you haven't included in here."

"Burt just drove off," he said. "I went to the hospital with the men. Burt followed us and screamed at the ER staff. Those Russians, they aren't bad. The one in the hospital couldn't stop crying. I know Burt will fire me for this."

Caroline knew some of the Russians were staying at the Baird in the old rooms with joint bedrooms, trying to start some sort of travel business. They were a hapless crew, and she'd nearly arrested one of them in June, when he'd been playing a violin near the roof hot tub, swinging his dick to the music in the night air, applauded by a growing crowd. When she pulled up, he bellowed, "I'm going to bed," and she let it go.

"Burt can't fire you," said Caroline. "Just keep your head down and let everyone else deal with it." She drummed her fingers on the table. Burt's stun gun use was getting into class-action territory. "What did this woman look like?"

"I don't know," said Gideon. "The bar was dark, the

alley was dark. Lipstick, not heavy. Not blond. Nice. When she asked Burt to stop, she sounded American."

"What did Burt say when she asked him to stop?"

"That she should make it worth his while. And there's one other thing," said Gideon. "I think Burt knew the Russian kid he stunned. He said something, and it's really bad."

So tentative. Caroline worked on her patience. "I'm listening."

"'I told you to pay up, fuckwad.'"

Caroline's brain buzzed.

"Yeah. He pressed that thing on the man's back to burn him on purpose."

She scribbled for a minute. "Anything else I need to know?"

"Mr. Clusker called to say that he shot at someone again last night. He says we need a first-aid kit and a tracking dog."

Caroline wanted to arrest Cavendish Clusker, but maybe he was making the whole thing up. "Finish the report and go patrol," she said. "Get out of here before Burt shows up."

She followed her own advice, and she'd almost reached her Subaru when Burt heaved out of his own car with a heavy jingle. He always wore more hardware than anyone else: badge and gun, the omnipresent stun gun and a polished club, a certain shine to his mustache and hair, too, though the wind was fucking with the last. He marched toward Caroline, eating a banana.

"You're not on the schedule," he said. "I hope you're not claiming overtime."

"Not yet," said Caroline. "I'm working on the Bucket incident."

"We don't need this sort of thing in the paper," said Burt. "I want a review on Sorenson. He is not adequate backup. I've got the task force in Billings, but I'll deal with it when I get back."

"No," said Caroline.

"What?"

"I will deal with it. You're not to touch the report or talk to anyone."

Burt took another bite of banana. "Little girl, don't even think of raising a fuss."

Caroline looked at him hard, watching his mouth move, the whole foreign Burtness of the armature—the hair that she didn't mind on other men, the weird gummy look of his throat, the spatulate fingers. He jammed in more banana during this staring match, and then he froze.

Caroline had a vision, sudden and vibrant, of Burt choking to death. She waited, but he began to cough, and then breathe. Burt tossed the peel toward the parking lot fence and tried to regain his strut as he walked away, hacking.

BLUE DEER GENERAL was a twenty-bed hospital that also handled the counties to the east and the northwest. More meaningfully, especially in terms of the summer patient load, it was usually the first stop for anyone who had a misadventure in Yellowstone Park. They were legion, and varied: people who played with bison and gravity and every temperature of water; people who had mundane heart and allergy attacks or were attacked by rolling cars; people who put pretty berries and mushrooms in their mouths, or drank or tripped and wandered off. The hospital was full.

At the front desk, Olive was on the phone, somewhat to Caroline's relief. The nurse in charge today was familiar, but Caroline couldn't place her. She wore a headscarf (chemo?) and had a soft face, a comforting face. Her name tag read MARINA, and she smiled at Caroline as if she knew her, too.

"How are you?" said Caroline, trying to bridge the gap between "how have you been?" and "who the hell are you?" She was sure they'd dealt with some mess together. "I need to see Mac Selway, and I also need to talk to the men who were hospitalized after the police incident last night."

The nurse considered her. Caroline, off the clock, wore jeans and a Murray Cheese Shop shirt, but she didn't think that was the issue.

"Mr. Prizikov's doing better, but he's a little fragile. He's an immigrant, you know, but I believe all his papers are in order."

Marina might be an immigrant, too, but Caroline couldn't place the faint accent. She scribbled Ivan Luneau's name and number on a piece of paper. "Mr. Prizikov should talk to this man. He does a lot of pro bono immigration work."

The nurse smiled. "Ah," she said. "You just missed Mr. Luneau, along with Mr. Sands's lawyer, Mr. Gustafson. They were here for an hour."

"Oh," said Caroline. And thought that it was just as well: Ivan always gave her a little flip in her stomach, and it shamed her.

In room 117, it wasn't hard guessing who was who:

the man with wide cheekbones and a boxer's nose, who looked like he wanted to jump through the window when he saw her, was Andrei Prizikov; the other had to be the writer Wally Sands, if only because he was thin and young and looked like he'd grown up with enough money to call himself one.

"Don't worry," said Caroline. "I'm not here to charge you or worry about papers. I need to ask questions about the incident, and Deputy Feckler's behavior."

The Russian looked stricken. This was not the exhibitionist from the Baird roof. "It was horrible," said the writer. "I thought he was sheriff. He told me he was a sheriff."

"No," said Caroline.

"He's a pig and a bully," said the writer, whose temple was grape-colored. "Completely irrational. He said he was going to put that Taser up Andrei's ass. Sicko closet case. But the other officer spoke up. How does a Black guy live in this town?"

Not easily, thought Caroline.

"Andrei and Sergei think they should pay that prick so that they can stay in the country, you know, even though they've got green cards, and a lawyer, and the whole bit. I keep trying to explain that it's bullshit. But really, the only thing that saved us was that witch."

"What witch?"

"The one that Andrei kind of knew."

Andrei had his eyes shut, tears spurting out the corners.

"She put a spell on that sheriff," said Wally Sands. "He's going to die."

Andrei Prizikov covered his face with his hands. Wally said they'd both come in and sign a statement. By the time

Caroline tapped on Mac's door, she'd begun to see his form of crazy as a relative piece of cake, but this really wasn't true.

"Oh," he said. "Oh, beautiful sight."

"You're too kind, Mac," said Caroline. "Is this the manic end of your depression? Do you still want to kill yourself?"

"No!"

"Will you seek counseling?"

"I love counseling! I'll find a beautiful counselor!"

"Okay," said Caroline.

Her expression seemed to sober him up. "Really, I'm fine," Mac said. "Hey."

"Hey, what?"

"You husband won't call me back, but maybe the problem I have is one that should go to you, instead of a PI."

"Just tell me."

"Someone's poisoning my mother-in-law. I believe it's my wife, or her new friend."

"Ah," said Caroline politely. "Actual poison?"

"Screwing with her meds," said Mac.

And then he went wide-eyed and smiled, and Caroline turned to see Elaine in the doorway, bearing cookies.

"There's no need to intrude on this situation," said Elaine.

"We have to follow up on suicide attempts," said Caroline. "But we can talk later."

She retreated to the hall and found the calm, sane nurse, who was talking with a doctor. Maybe not talking with; maybe being talked at, and the nurse clearly didn't like it. It gave Caroline an irrational sense of solidarity. She should deal with the medication theft, but not now, not with this guy. She pretended to study the snack machine, then approached again when the doctor huffed off.

"What do you think?" she asked the nurse. "About these men."

"I can't comment on anything that can come back on the hospital," Marina said. Her headscarf was covered with a pattern of poppies.

"Does it look likely that they'll all be okay?"

"Mr. Selway might have a little long-term damage from that blood alcohol level, or whatever habits came before. Mr. Prizikov is terrified of everything. I believe he had a difficult life before he emigrated from Leningrad. His arrhythmia has resolved but he has two second-degree burns that likely came from Mr. Feckler's electrical stick. Mr. Sands showed no sign of heart damage, but he has had several muscle spasms, and I have trouble believing he deserved a serious skull fracture. I don't think any human deserves to be kicked repeatedly."

But what do you really think, thought Caroline, walking toward her car.

What Marina the nurse really thought, while she finished up paperwork and before she went off shift: She thought that Burt Feckler should find a different thing to do for a living. She thought that Mac Selway should find a different wife. She thought that Wally Sands should file charges, and Andrei Prizikov should finish his immigration paperwork with Mr. Luneau and find a new town. And she thought that Caroline Fair was looking pretty good compared to the last time she'd seen her, when she'd just given birth and had begun to hemorrhage.

THEY BUNDLED TOMMY into a powder-blue car seat that was shellacked navy by sticky fingers, heading out for a last dangling wellness check, one of the tasks in the files

Jules had fetched. An old man named Bernie hadn't been bothering with his mail, his meals, or his lawn, and the person inquiring after his safety happened to be Venus Meriwether, eighty-five, deaf and smart and arrogant, president of the Aches.

"What's his full name?" asked Jules.

"Bernard Aloysius Dinak."

"The old priest? Didn't he move?"

"I don't know. I'd forgotten about him," Caroline said, reading the file. "Father Bernie of girls' basketball fame. Ed really had it in for him. Maybe he gave Sadie a hard time."

Jules didn't need the address. "I don't think anything was ever proven," he said. "I knew where he lived more for the sake of protecting him—people used to slit his tires, throw shit on his porch. I have no doubt he was creepy, but no one ever claimed he touched more than a shoulder."

"I thought it was something financial, too," said Caroline. "If he were a truly horrible human, I doubt Venus would have bothered to check."

Venus Meriwether, who organized the local Meals on Wheels, met them in front of the small frame house at E and McCann, her ancient Tercel approaching at two miles an hour. Caroline helped her out of the car and listened to the full torrent of the story. Jules, waiting with the windows down, caught the gist while Tommy dozed on in his car seat: Dinak had had some sort of hip surgery and recovered poorly. A mutual friend had been concerned.

"When was the surgery?" asked Caroline.

"Last September."

Ugh, thought Jules.

Venus waited on the sidewalk while Caroline knocked

on the doors of houses on either side of Dinak's. Just one older man answered, tipsy and full of theories: Dinak could walk just fine—why did he need meals? The neighbor saw him coming home with clear plastic bags from the grocery and brown paper from the liquor store.

"When?" asked Caroline.

The answer—"Not sure, might have been snowing"—was not reassuring.

"What worried your friend?" she asked Venus back at the sidewalk.

"Sort of a friend hearing a friend was worried," said Venus. "It was enough to call you."

They walked slowly up the sidewalk. No flower beds, and the patches of surviving grass were tall and floppy; if they'd been mowed this year, it had been spring. It didn't necessarily mean anything; some men of a certain age are lawn crazy, but some are too lazy and cheap to spit. No box for a newspaper, and no water or power shut-off notice. Caroline shuddered at the thought of the warm spring, the blast-furnace summer. The mail slot was high on the door: even if Dinak were secretly popular, the slot wouldn't be blocked.

Caroline knocked, and then she pounded. She tried the padlocked gate and hopped the fence into the backyard, showing off. She found nothing but more tidy, dead cement; in the garage, an old blue ragtop Plymouth, a high-profile car for a low-profile priest trying to dodge the pederast label. The wind kicked up, and she steered Venus to the porch, feeling like she might crush the bird bones in her shoulder, and walked back to the Subaru.

Jules popped the hatch for the lock-picking kit. "Do you want me to deal with the door?"

Caroline peered at Tommy. "I'll yell if I can't manage it. Maybe Father Bernie's sitting near a playground in Reno. But we might be late for dinner with Olive."

On the porch, Venus pointed to a mound of dead flies just visible under the blind of one locked window. Caroline turned back to the car, but Jules was reaching for Tommy, who would wake in an ugly mood. She bent to concentrate on the very old lock as the wails began.

"I don't have a good feeling about this," said Venus.

"I think you should go sit in your car," said Caroline, flipping through picks.

"Don't patronize me, Caro."

"All right." She fiddled with the lock, and when it clicked, she stepped back.

There was nothing on the planet like the smell of a freshly unbottled corpse. Venus poked her head inside the door, looked up at the noose and down toward the pile on the floor, then toddled to the south end of the porch to throw up. Caroline headed north, muttering *what the fuck* between waves of nausea.

It's a central demoralizing fact of life that no matter how you leave it, by choice or illness or accident, intact or in shreds, your mortal shell will become someone else's problem. In the case of Bernard Dinak, the delay between the moment and the discovery had been so lengthy, and the temperature in the house so warm, that a scene Caroline had witnessed several times in her short career—a noose hanging from the ceiling (this one from the doorframe and tidy, almost professional), kicked-over chair or stool—shifted toward something temporarily mysterious. Dinak had probably dropped like an overhung pheasant back when there was snow on the ground, possibly back when it was still 1997, maybe even before Thomas Ansel Clement took his first breath. Caroline greeted Bernie Dinak's torso, arms, and legs. By the time she finally found his head behind the couch, she was over the initial body blow of the scene and having to think kept her from being sick a second time.

7 *The Second Morning*

MONDAY

JULES TAUGHT ARCHAEOLOGY AS THE SCIENCE OF what we leave behind, which was almost everything: gold to bones, alphabets to coprolite bacteria. You lasted forever, and yet not. When you were still a discernible shadow on the soil, a chemical imprint, a single silver ring, someone would pave you over.

Graveyards were special, of course: they were universal, and you tended to take them personally. Your life could dwindle to grass within the blink of an eye. If the inhabitants were alive within living memory, archaeologists didn't customarily touch them with a ten-foot pole.

But in case the county insisted on moving the poor farm bodies, Jules cleared the possibility of gravedigging with the department head at Montana State University. Using students for the survey would be thorny—did the presence of the body of a homeless person constitute archaeology?—but it was more experience than they'd get in years as contract archaeologists at more typical sites, sites that only provided bits of chert and charcoal or the broken neck of a patent medicine bottle, and it might winnow out the Indiana Jones element, the glory hogs and drama queens and romantics.

The department head was enthused; someone could

get a thesis out of this. Jules should lead a pattern comparison with other area cemeteries. Jules should talk to the state historic preservation office about a gazetteer for forgotten sites. Jules should . . .

Make a living. Jules, who'd once claimed he wouldn't do divorces, was currently perched on the hill above Evergreen Cemetery, waiting for Gordie Plautz, director of public works, to arrive. He happened to know that Gordie was screwing around on his wife, Tina, who was midway through a second course of chemo at Absaroka Memorial. This was another Olive task: she sometimes sat with Tina during her treatments at the hospital infusion center. What kind of asshole fucked around on a wife undergoing chemo? The answer was Gordie, who pale, quiet Harvey Meyers determined was in the habit of meeting a pretty woman, a jogger, at dawn on Mondays in the cemetery records shack.

Jules drove to the hill above Flanders Creek and backed into the parking area below the soccer field, where he and Celeste were now admiring the view. Conveniently, there were two matters at hand: rarely had fuckery dovetailed so conveniently. Beyond the cemetery, on the far side of the marshy creek that separated it from a new development, Jules and Celeste could see a small beige house with a maroon truck with an NRA sticker in the driveway—Burt's truck, parked in front of the place he'd rented when his wife kicked him out. Jules, leaving the shitshow of the Dinak house the night before, had seen the truck in front of the Bucket bar, Burt visiting his best friend, Helga.

Now there was a white van in the driveway, blocking the truck in. In the matter of Burt versus Burt's wife, who Jules represented, any new friendships were meaningful, which was why he'd photographed the truck the night before, too. He knew he should feel scummy, but how could he when he was dealing with the shittiest cop in the state and a man who had assignations in a graveyard trailer? When Jules loved a woman whose life was made difficult and dangerous by said shitty cop?

The day might hit 90 degrees Fahrenheit but at this point, at daybreak, it was still only 43 degrees. Jules brought binoculars because the marsh below the cemetery was a good place to bird, but he also carried a camera. They settled into the truck, and Jules looked through the stack of files from Grace: the initial call transcript, some interviews with the Bell family, and the scene investigation of Ansel's murder. This last would have photographs, which he'd ask Caroline to sort through. Photographs would be too much.

Celeste moved next to Jules, and he looked up. A woman in a white straw hat was shutting Burt's gate and walking down the sidewalk with a small brown mutt on a leash, Celeste's doppelgänger. Jules took a photo. The woman and the dog were quickly obscured by a hedge.

He opened another file. On some level he wanted to deal with Ansel more than anything in the world; on another, Ansel was what Jules avoided his entire life. He was able to read only the heading—*Clement homicide 8.15.72*—before a truck turned in to the cemetery, lights still on. It passed within twenty feet of Ansel's tall, simple headstone. Gordie, hopelessly geeky in a striped golf outfit, climbed out and walked into the caretaker's building and flicked on the lights.

Jules turned back to his father's last moments while he waited to capture Gordie's indiscretions. The pages were crumpled and covered with handwriting, Grace filling in blanks, correcting words; this was a draft for internal review.

At 4:04 on August 15, 1972, Grace to all: *We have a speeding navy truck with topper at mile marker 28 on Highway 504.*

The incident happened on the old highway, of course; the new, smooth delivery system for Yellowstone tourists wasn't finished until the early eighties. Today Patrick Bell could have headed north toward Ansel like a missile out of Yellowstone Park, but in 1972 he'd ricocheted along a bumpy, curvy, narrow road that veered along the east side of the river, with potholes and hummocks from the springs that oozed out of the mountains. When the road reached the southern mouth of the valley and widened, the Absarokas played out like a postcard to the east, and you could glimpse the Crazies thirty miles to the north. How different was the view, back then? Fewer houses. In August now, there was never much snow on the mountains; hadn't there still been a little year-round when he was a kid? Weren't there still glaciers, glowing pink with ancient bacteria during hot summers? Gone for at least ten years.

Grace's handwriting said *see call log D*, and Jules found the time and the entry: a civilian, an unnamed tourist from Chicago, nearly overrun by the car as the road bent north. The man pulled into a ranch house yard to call the police.

Bunny McElwaine: *I'm on break.*

Another reason to hate Bunny, even though he, too, was dead, murdered and unmourned. Jules imagined Grace's tentative young voice. *I believe your break is over, Officer McElwaine.*

I don't agree, said Bunny.

Give me five minutes. Ed, late to work, was only just getting to the station.

Passing Langley Creek, said Grace. *Male driver, "angry"—I've got a plate number to check.*

I'll do it, said Ansel. *I'm just south of town. I'll loop and wait in the dip by Sylvia Coburg's place.*

That car, said Grace, *is registered to a Patrick W. Bell, age 23, of 131 Coralberry Creek. Does he still live there? 1967 navy Ford truck with a silver-and-white topper.*

Is that the good Bell kid or the bad one? asked Ed.

Good, I think, said Ansel.

You have misjudged, thought Jules. He'd have to ask Ed about *the good Bell kid or the bad one.*

He might have stuck around after the father's accident, said Bunny.

Some fucking accident, said Ed. *I'm out the door.*

I'm past Nesbit, said Ansel.

Then added: *I'm blocking the road. He's slowing. Any record?*

Nothing, said Grace.

Nothing.

Three minutes later: *Come in, Sheriff Clement.*

Had Ansel fallen face up? Could he see anything while he was dying?

After another five minutes, a call from a nearby house: there was a body near a patrol car, and the caller identified Ansel Clement, *clearly dead.* Bunny decided his break was over after all, and whatever Ed screamed into the radio was too much for the young Grace, who typed *unclear.* They sped toward the Bells' house while another deputy—Budge, also long dead—confirmed Ansel Clement's identity and his death.

Celeste nudged Jules and he looked up. The dog was watching a woman in a hot-purple running outfit and a long ponytail, threading through the tombstones at high speed. Jules dropped Grace's file, picked up the camera, and started shooting as Gordie Plautz stepped out of the shed, kissed the woman, and shut the door behind them.

Jules gave Celeste a biscuit for a job well done and shut his eyes. The early-morning sun was flooding into the cab, warming them, and they might have dozed but Celeste shifted again, and Jules lifted the binoculars, though two minutes seemed extreme for a quickie. Celeste was watching Burt's house now, and Jules fumbled for the camera and managed a good shot of a woman, and not just any woman: Tamyra Zinke, Blue Deer's least apologetic hooker. Beyond a couple of 1965 rodeo queens in Big Timber, no one else in the area dared hair like that. She staggered a little on her way to a powder-blue Ford Escort—after multiple arrests, Jules should have recognized the Escort—but the hair remained upright.

He picked up the file again. Ed pulled into the Bells' yard at 4:35 and saw four people: Patrick Bell, flat on the ground in the driveway; Patrick's younger brother, Charles, standing over his brother; Francis and Lucia Bell, watching by the house. Patrick was already unconscious, his brain beginning to bleed while Charles continued to kick his head, and the parents screamed to stop. In Grace's handwriting again, a notation about when the injury might have happened, probably for an internal review.

In the here and now of a summer morning, Celeste perked up again as the shed door opened. Jules was just in time to get a shot of a goodbye squeeze to Gordie's genitals before the woman loped off, ponytail spinning like a failing helicopter blade. She stopped to fix a shoelace near the back gate. Thirty yards past her, on the far side of the lush, birdy marsh, three men left Burt's house, shook hands on the sidewalk, hugged one another. Like people leaving a wedding or a funeral or an AA meeting, thought Jules. One of them climbed into the white van, and the others left on foot. Jules took another photo, and clicked a last time when Burt staggered out his front door, pale and furry in green briefs.

JULES DROVE TO his desk at the Baird along the same route as the morning before. He was not quite as tired, and he saw different things: a grocery clerk who'd lost custody of her children to meth, a gray cat dragging a twitching rabbit, a new plume of smoke, a disheveled woman leaning out of Ivan's window, enjoying the view.

He called Caroline, who was scrubbing Tommy after breakfast, packing him up for daycare.

"I have no time," she said.

"Caroline," he said. "Just two minutes. It's about Burt."

He got disbelief, wonder, joy. "Who would ever? Were they filming porn? Oh my god."

This was probably going to be the high point of Jules's day. On the machine, a bitchy message from Divvy about Jules and Caroline's work at the build site, a hang-up from Ed, two clients wondering if they would ever hear Jules's voice again.

He tried Ed back. When Shirley answered he identified himself, and she said, "Who?" Jules said, "Clement!" and then tried, "I used to be Sheriff Clement."

And Shirley said, "You can't fool me. You're dead." And hung up.

Jules drove to Ed's house, trying for empathy. Ed was dragging sprinklers in the front yard, possibly wetting the house down for the next time Shirley left a burner on.

"I tried to leave a message."

"I gather. It upsets Shirley."

Everything upset Shirley except the things that should: flames, staircases, rolling machines with engines. Today Ed looked seventy instead of sixty.

"Olive has some questions about Dad."

"Jesus. Why now?"

Everyone said "Why now," and Jules found it maddening. "We could just get lunch."

"Fuck lunch," said Ed. "You still trying to be a purist?"

"I'm not a purist," said Jules. "I'm trying not to be a drunk."

"Well," said Ed. "I'm trying to get out of this house, and you're not in charge anymore. Sadie can come by after work to watch Shirley. I'll be at the Bat at eight."

Jules was thus in a pissy mood when he met Alice Wahlgren for breakfast. In the same sense that Ed required a bar to be tractable, Alice required food. They'd known each other for fifteen years, and she was always behind, always scrambling for the pittance-paying Absaroka County Historical Society. Asking her for help was a kindness, given that she and the ladies of the Aches hadn't produced a thing about the poor farm thus far, but today, for once, she was at least not late. He did not mention the smeared child's handprint on the shoulder of her wrinkled blouse, or the crookedness of her glasses, or the slightly desperate way she sucked at her coffee. She did not mention the way his right eyelid was twitching.

After a salvo of questions about poor mummified Bernie Dinak, Alice launched into the exhibit the Aches would put on about the poor farm, should they ever manage to open a museum in the old school. They'd have displays about all facets of life on the hill, committals of the mad and alcoholic and simply forlorn paupers displayed with the things Jules found: combs and coins and maybe dice, spectacles and belt buckles and maybe clothing. Would any clothing be intact?

Alice was an English major, but most people were this clueless. At least Jules knew her well enough to be forgiven if he lost his temper. "Even if I were to dig up any of those graves, you can't exhibit people's grave goods."

"Even if they're just lying around? They're not indigenous remains."

"You know that for a fact? And so the fuck what? What do you mean, just lying around?"

"Cicely Tobaggo claims bones are poking through everywhere up there. Venus said there's a rumor that the supervisors charged the county for casket wood and didn't bother using it."

"Bullshit," said Jules. "No one's poking out of the ground, and no one's poking into it. I only care about where they are. We need to know that none of the graves are in the road, and that none will be affected by development. That's it. Have you found out anything at all?"

He sounded angry, and the waitress glanced over as she delivered mimosas to the couple next to them. Jules wanted a mimosa, or better yet a screwdriver, and asked for more coffee with unnecessary vehemence. Alice ordered a bloody Mary and Jules pushed the 1916 list in front of her.

"That doesn't get you far, does it," she said.

"The commissioners say the city cemetery started taking them."

"I asked the Aches about that," said Alice. "And I went down to the cemetery to follow up with Gordie, just before I came here. The city cemetery did not start taking anyone until after World War Two, and neither did Calvary. They both charged the city full price."

"Oh," said Jules.

She tapped the 1916 list. "I gave the ladies a copy and they went through the county ledgers. All these people died between 1908 and 1916. They went through the earlier death records, keeping an eye on disposition, but it's all pretty fragmented—the state didn't start keeping track until 1907. You're looking for another dozen between 1889 and 1908."

She reached down into her tote bag and came back with a list. Twelve names, beginning with Alvin Mantel, 49, German, dead January 23, 1890, of nephritis, and ending with Margarita Danica, 27, Montenegrin, April 10, 1908, puerperal pyrexia.

"The good old days," said Alice, watching him read. "The ladies also remember hearing that the site began as a burial ground for Marvel. Cicely says she remembers two fenced areas. I guess her mother used to deliver food from the women's clubs."

"Only one fenced area so far," said Jules. "I'm guessing it's from before the First World War."

"Did you try checking any names against the markers?"

"You can only make out a handful of letters. I suspect the county of some destruction."

"Cicely wondered if there might be some Doris bodies,

too, but I reminded her of the 1917 flood article. Still, we should dig," said Alice.

Cicely, not Jules's favorite Ache, was getting on his nerves. The food arrived, and Alice gave a little hop and tucked in. "Surely," said Jules, "the city took bodies during the influenza epidemic."

"Nope," she said. "No planting if you couldn't pay. Before the KKK heyday, but the mayor was not a friend of all those Eastern Europeans who'd come for the mine, or anyone else who wasn't quite white enough. Anyway, Sadie and I found some boxes."

She handed him a sheet with an undated plat, "Annex B": it showed the last dormitory and the fenced burial ground, with ten numbered graves to the southwest, and another dozen sketched in faintly. An Annex C was indicated with an arrow to the north.

"You've gotta wonder about Annex A," said Alice. "And I don't see your orchard. Anyway, we all kept sorting through until 1960, and I believe you're dealing with sixty-five to ninety bodies. It's not just the flu—you have to keep in mind the crop failures in the late teens, all those poor Scandihoovians suckered out by railroad advertisements in the teens. And another drought in the twenties and into the Depression proper, so more homelessness and no other government support."

"Fuck me," said Jules.

"We could continue and go through the death records for the twenties on. Sadie and I found another two boxes that seem promising. The ladies do love opening boxes."

And they found all sorts of things when they did. Jules veered away from the memory of prying open a trunk for Venus and Cicely, and finding a dead man.

"Get us a map," said Alice. "And consider chipping in for refreshments."

"Jesus," said Jules.

"He doesn't hear your prayers," said Alice. "But the Aches might, if you're nice and buy some sherry."

CAROLINE WAS TRYING to type up her Dinak notes when Burt walked in and said, "I'm on my way to that big Billings meeting, but you should know I've been robbed. And I'm being followed."

Drunk, mouthed Harvey. He and Grace and Sadie all nodded. Caroline kept typing the report that would be the end of him.

"Are you listening to me?" Burt was using his movie voice. She noticed he was especially loud today. Maybe being shot in the ear with a stun gun damaged hearing, or the brain.

"No," said Caroline. "Apologies. My head is full of all the reasons you should take a leave of absence. Or quit."

Burt always looked cheery; his tell was that he went pink. Right now he was the color of a cooked Gulf shrimp. "That mess you left me—that pervert priest—you mop it up."

Caroline, who attempted to never agree with Burt, gave something that might be interpreted as a nod.

"It's not worth our time. And talk to the rangers about those Russkies. We need to get them out of here."

Was she supposed to put them on a Greyhound bus to North Dakota?

"I'll be back in tomorrow. I'd appreciate if no one distracted me from this seminar with unimportant shit."

They would lay odds, after he left, and then check to

see if the seminar existed. He headed out the door, not in a straight line.

"What does it mean?" asked Sadie.

"It means that he lost his wallet or his gun in a bar," said Grace.

"Jules saw him parked in front of the Bucket last night," said Caroline. "Did he even look into the priest?"

"Gideon said he threw up," said Grace. "And left."

Caroline scribbled it all down and went back to her memo. No note found, no sign of a struggle, no evidence of Dinak's continued existence after November 2, 1997, the oldest date of any newspaper or piece of mail found within the house.

Doors slammed in time with Caroline's punctuation: Sadie, spending her last hours in the department trying to clean up problems for Grace, shoving furniture back to pre-Burt locations, removing his tactical posters. She loosened one of the casters on his chair. She piled mindless official papers on his desk.

And she'd found most of the files, including a fat pocket folder she dropped on Caroline's desk. The tape on the outside read *Clement, homicide, 8.15.72*. There was something innately upsetting about the label. Caroline made a puffing sound and returned to her Dinak memo. Given the husk-like form of Bernard Dinak's body, other surprises were secondary: the body was found wearing blue plaid pajama bottoms and a black brassiere, size 42D.

This would be Caroline's second autoerotic fatality, fourth hanging. She wished she didn't have this particular expertise. In Philly, she'd found a young man in a tutu, head stuck in a plastic bag with an open tube of glue. Bernie Dinak made even less sense: who, intent on an erotic fantasy, combined an unstuffed black bra with boring plaid pajama bottoms? And who, if such pajamas were part of the dream, would have the bottoms still up around his waist while trying for the exacerbated arousal of asphyxiation? Who in the world jerked off through flannel?

At the hospital morgue that morning, as Caroline waited for the van that would take the body to the state lab in Missoula, she ran through her thoughts with Gideon Sorenson, who was intensely uncomfortable dealing with anything like this. Caroline sent him out of the room while she stared down again at Dinak's trunk and legs, the collapsed bra cups and the little bump of his dried pizzle. Adding to the erotic conflict, the bra was ancient, pointed, and formidable, with a J. C. Penney label.

Yowser, thought Caroline.

They set off for a long day of motley issues, Caroline driving. A shoplifting, a parole violation, a theft at the hospital, Cavendish Clusker playing Charles Bronson, and a fender bender at the fishing access near Nesbit Creek.

As they drove out of town, with the bank thermometer reading 95 Fahrenheit, Caroline saw Jules lope away from the Baird, but he did not see her. He wouldn't have expected her to be in a patrol car—she'd promised not to do this—but she still found it interesting that only two years after leaving the job he didn't bother looking.

The shoplifting proved to be mostly bullshit, a private matter between two warring clerks. The parolee was found asleep on his mother's couch. But the fender bender at Nesbit Creek, a screaming match in a dusty field between a fishing guide and a client, put Caroline over the top: she could hear the river and see it glitter, imagine the way it would make her body feel. She disliked both combatants, and they were both at fault, and Gideon seemed willing to let them argue eternally. The AC in his car was failing, and her breasts were tingling—Tommy, when sick, reverted to wanting to nurse. If she were with anyone but Gideon, Caroline would jump into the Yellowstone.

Caroline was driving again as they sped north while Gideon scribbled notes about the parolee they'd just interviewed and twitched whenever he eyed the speedometer.

Then he said, "Do you see those people?"

Three men in swimming trunks, trudging along the side of the highway carrying inner tubes. They'd clearly gotten off the river too soon and were walking back to their put-in and their vehicle. Caroline so resented their day of leisure that she wanted to flick on the siren and pass at full speed. Instead, she pulled over and told Gideon to stay by the door.

One man, probably only thirty but gray-haired, started to run. "Hey," yelled Caroline. "I'm here to help."

A semi blasted by, barely missing the running man as he wobbled on the gravel, and his tallest companion yelled, "Sergei, *stoy*!"

Holy shit, thought Caroline. Russians. The weeper from the hospital, Andrei Prizikov, stood next to the tall man, his stun-gun burn horribly bright. Sergei, the runner, had a bandaged hand, and the tall man, who seemed uninjured beyond a grade B sunburn, gestured for him to come back. They all stared at Caroline, who was plainclothes, and the car, which was not. Gideon, uniformed and large and innately unnerving, twitched by the passenger door. Caroline noted a complete absence of weaponry.

There was no place to hide it: they all wore Speedo-sized swim trunks. The tallest man caught her looking.

"Not packing!" he said. "Everyone turn and show the lady that you have nothing whatsoever to hide!" And then he started to laugh.

Caroline began to relax. "Mr. Prizikov," she said to Andrei. "I heard you checked yourself out of the hospital. Was Mr. Luneau able to help with your immigration papers?"

He nodded. They all cheered up.

"We can give you a ride to your vehicle. Is it at the Spruce fishing access?"

"It is," said the tall man. He was smiling but the face was innately unfriendly, with a hawk nose and heavy jaw. "Thank you so much for this."

Sergei, the runner with the bandaged hand and potbelly, wore a dirty bandage around his thigh, wrapped with plastic and duct tape. Caroline was sure she'd cautioned him earlier that summer for public drunkenness, just like Andrei. All three men wore red Keds, which made her think of the pair on Tommy's dresser. Andrei's thigh wound was oozing. "Should you see a doctor for that?"

"A scratch," whispered Sergei.

"A flesh wound," said the tall man, laughing again. His eyes were different colors, and a scar on one eyebrow made them even more mismatched.

They all watched her, waiting. Caroline nodded to Gideon, who opened the trunk to reveal guns and ropes and ammo, vests and the creepy tactical stuff Burt kept buying. Hundreds of pounds of death, and the men shuffled in alarm. "You'll need to deflate your inner tubes," she explained.

A wave of relief. Sergei, whose tube was sliced

open—she should ask where he'd found such a vicious piece of metal and have the Forest Service follow up—approached slowly.

"Did you have an accident?" Caroline asked.

The tall man answered for him. "Sergei nearly drowned, but he's all right now, aren't you? We are having a vacation, learning to have fun and toughen up. We want to be one with nature."

"Well, don't make it permanent," said Caroline, walking to the car.

"Shouldn't you check their ID?" snitted Gideon.

"Are you serious?" asked Caroline. "See any pockets?"

He loaded the deflated inner tubes and the men piled into the back seat. Caroline shut the car door, locking them in. Andrei kept sniffling. "Neither of you should get in the water with those wounds."

"They say the cold makes it feel good," said the tall man.

Cold with cow shit, thought Caroline. Cold with fertilizer runoff and fishing-guide piss. And yet she'd jump in this moment if she could. "What's your name?"

"Fred," said the spokesman.

"And your surname?"

"Pushkin."

Caroline snorted and met his crazy eyes in the rearview mirror. He smiled back through the metal cage while Gideon dutifully took down Sergei's last name: Lermontov. Everyone said *eeep* as she did a U-turn. "I remember you from the alley behind the Mint last September. You were with a woman, and I gave you a warning." Shades of VVV, but this was a short blonde, a local girl.

"Ah!" Fred said. "I did not recognize you! We are here

trying to find businesses in Bozeman for investments, or to start something on the computer."

"Do you all spend time in Gardiner?" She and Ed were still supposed to talk to the park rangers about errant Russians later that week.

"No," he said. "I have heard that there are some troublesome types down there by the park, but I believe they have all gone home."

Soft sighs from behind her head. "Why is Andrei still crying?"

"Fear of death," said the man, reasonably. "He found the river very alarming, and he is a city boy, and short some of his medication. We will be doing this in a boat, next."

When Caroline dropped them by a dented Jeep with Wyoming plates, Gideon scribbled down the license. Caroline didn't want to know yet, lest there be an issue; she just wanted to go home. She knew this made her a bad cop. "You have your keys hidden somewhere?"

"We are fine," said Fred. "Our friend just walks her dog."

Far down the river, a skinny, long-haired woman in a bikini with a fuzzy brown dog didn't wave. Caroline could barely make out her features, given the distance, but as she drove away, Gideon watched through the rearview mirror and called in the registration.

"Strato Corporation," he said.

"Sounds like complete bullshit," said Caroline.

CAVENDISH CLUSKER, THE last Marvelite in residence, was a teeth-sucking weirdo. When his older sisters died, one by one, he brought them to town in the front seat of the car. He stored his own urine to cure hides; he mail-ordered bugs to strip deer skulls, and because he received no delivery at the house, given the two-mile-long driveway, the post office dreaded his packages. The stone house with its leaking copper roof reeked of rodents, bleach, and aftershave.

Cavendish was, in short, a true Montuckian. But he did read—the cabin sagged with books—and Caroline sometimes caught him buying cheese and wine and vegetables at the grocery, so some of the mountain-man persona was a schtick.

Cavendish always asked for Caroline when he called the department about *incidents*. There was nothing illegal about firing into the air on your own property, outside of city limits, but it did mark you as an asshole. Hikers could legally follow the easement that ran two hundred feet to the east of the house from the public road to the national forest line, but they tended to veer off the path, and the fact that Cavendish's messy cabin looked abandoned—the yard overgrown, rusting machinery and assorted wood and metal scraps everywhere—made it a tempting tourist trap, despite large yellow signs that said I SHOOT TO KILL and FUCK OFF TOURIST.

Caroline didn't mind driving up, because it was beautiful on the way to Marvel, and she might see Jules at the poor farm on the way. But today there was no truck or Jules, just an impressive amount of survey string and two county guys taking a break by their large machines. Farther up the flats, between the poor farm and Marvel, a black Suburban was parked near the single tree in this bleak acreage, and a man with yellow hair and a lime-green shirt was digging energetically. Posts and a huge aqua sign with orange lettering were tilted against the SUV: VISTA DEL RIO.

Maybe the taciturn new boyfriend and Elaine were planning a shrimp shack out on the sunblasted plain; maybe they were trying for an Outback, Death Valley feel on their bone-dry hundred acres. Caroline, finishing every drop of a vanilla malt, struggled to explain the humor to Gideon, who kept swiveling around to see the view.

They drove on into the trees. Cavendish's stone house, with its once glorious roof, was the only standing structure left of what had once been a narrow cramped town on a ravine—one street through the fir-and-spruce forest, prone to flooding and dark all winter, surrounded by honeycombed hard rock: a little gold, a little more silver, all of it chiseled out of the hills on the way to a very short-term fortune. Ivan Luneau and Cavendish were staring down into the gravel of the road, and they looked up and smiled at the same time. Caroline felt a flush start at the back of her head.

"Good to see you, Caroline," said Ivan. Wide green eyes, sunburned cheeks, a pleasantly messy mouth.

"Good to see you," said Caroline.

"Are you coming to arrest me?" asked Cavendish, who always sounded a little like a bugle.

"Maybe," she said. "Are you looking for blood?"

It was a joke. When Caroline showed up, Cavendish Clusker usually downgraded his account, or said he'd mostly aimed at trees. Today, Ivan looked uneasy. "He used a tripod," he said.

"But I shot for the trees," said Cavendish, avoiding Caroline's eyes.

"A tripod for a shotgun?" said Caroline, trying to control herself. Ivan was showing Gideon a spot of blood in the driveway.

"We found all these things," said Cavendish, spilling out a box: a vodka bottle, section map, an unopened package of condoms, and a copy of *Rolling Stone*. "At least three of them came through, yowling and making ghost noises. Obviously, they want to scare me off my land."

Caroline watched his mouth move. Who was "they" in his mind, she wondered. Rich people? The government? There was a certain Ruby Ridge vibe to the old town site. "I told you to call me first. Not shoot and call me," she said.

"Which would do nothing," he said. "Twenty-minute drive."

"We could catch them on the road, Cavendish." There was only one way in and out of Marvel, short of the death-defying two-track over the mountain; this was the essence of Jules's current hell at the poor farm. "Kill a high school kid and I'll drag you to town behind the car."

"Well, maybe the blood's from deer instead of Russians."

She stared. "They were gibbering in Russian. I told Grace."

Gideon, upset by the dust on his patrol car, was thankfully out of earshot. He found more dots on a burdock bush. Caroline found deer prints, crushed foliage, a cow rib, and evidence that an owl snatched one of Cavendish's many black-and-white kitties, who'd been in Marvel for generations without evolving camouflage. She put the tiny perfect skull, filled with fluffy owl expectorant, in her pocket instead of showing Cavendish, but she looked up to see that Ivan was watching her.

"Speaking of Russians, we just saw your client, Mr. Prizikov," said Caroline. "Floating, on the river, in a tire inner tube. He said he was trying to have fun."

"Good luck to him," said Ivan.

"And on my way in, I saw Elaine Selway's new friend, putting up a sign."

"Haven't met him yet," said Ivan. "But he happened to leave a message yesterday."

"Are they circling Cavendish?"

He thought this over. "Is that a way of asking me what I'm doing here, spending time with Cavendish? You're worried that people are trying to pry his land away?"

"Well," said Caroline. "They are. Who wouldn't want it?"

"We all would," said Ivan. "Because it's beautiful. But he isn't the only owner."

"No," she said. Marvel was founded as a kind of collective. The surface ground, at that time, had been meaningless compared to the mineral rights, and those were held jointly by the dozen families who settled the place and promptly intermarried. Peter was trying to track down Cavendish's cousins and generally sort out his affairs. Peter was a bit of a masochist. "Maybe if people are trying to pressure him, he should let them know that selling is not just his decision."

"Maybe," Ivan said. "I've known him for years, and I'm worried. If you arrested him, do you think he'd stop?"

Cavendish padded closer, looking paranoid. "I'm missing a victim," said Caroline. "The pioneers would wail about property rights. Let's see what happens with the blood samples."

On their way back, after Caroline got Gideon to unload and reset Cavendish's wildlife camera, which had never managed to capture more than a coyote, he talked about the view again, and then the wind hit them just right, and they smelled something nasty, something dead coming out of the junker cars. Poor Jules, working with that over the next few days.

8 *Meeting the Boyfriend*

AT THE RIVER PROPERTY, IN THE SWEET GREEN DAPpled light that usually cooled him down, Jules wandered around retrieving scattered driveway stakes, in a fresh rage.

"These were perfect last night," he said, pointing with the sledgehammer. "Fucking perfect."

"Whatever you say, man," said Divvy, in a sulk again. Now, though, he lost his snark when Jules showed him the pry marks in the sand, at which point Divvy changed theories: teenagers, of course, some male, some female—see how half-assed some of the stakes were. Not dope smokers but younger kids, he thought. Suzette's pretty daughter, she of the perfect lawn, wasn't very nice—he'd heard her scream at some middle schoolers for cutting across the lawn—and look at how the stakes seemed to lead toward her house. It was pretty funny. Stupid, but funny.

Jules and Divvy were redoing the stakes when Suzette floated out her front door. She wore a housedress: aqua with a pattern of daisies, and a little short for comfort. Divvy, who'd already seen too much of Suzette when she sunbathed, skittered to the far end of the unborn driveway.

"Good morning," she said brightly.

"Good morning," said Jules.

They regarded the stakes and the spray-painted apple tree, carefully cordoned off like a museum exhibit the afternoon before. "That's not how I left it," said Jules.

"I know," said Suzette, walking gingerly down her steps. "I watched you two do such a wonderful job, and then I watched my daughter and her friend take it all down and aim the driveway right at my tree. They were drinking, clearly. I think she just wants to slow you down."

"She could have asked for a delay," said Jules.

"She's no good at asking. She says she needs to have her party while the land is "virginal."

There was nothing remotely virginal about either the land or the people in question. Hate-filled people, filling him with hate. "Is it true what they're saying about Bernie Dinak?" she asked.

"Dead," he said, "for a while now."

"Perhaps no one missed him," said Suzette, lighting a cigarette.

Someone noticed enough to pass on the news. Did Suzette have friends? Did her daughter have friends? The misplaced stakes made him twitch. "They're really calling it an anniversary party?"

"Mac's sense of irony," said Suzette. "Did he really nearly die?"

"He really nearly died," said Jules. "He might not have meant to but he came close."

"Do you know their secret? Mac hasn't always been sure of what he wants."

So much character assassination in so few words, but her voice was affectionate. "I don't think it's much of a secret, Suzette," said Jules. "It's horrible that his family set those terms."

"I believe this last snarl was because her friend moved in, and Elaine said she'd back out if Mac didn't give her an extra hundred thousand. Now I think he's finally angry."

Jules could see it. Mac goofy as all get-out, so flaky and panicky and vengeful that he'd kill himself for a big fat bowl of reasons: financial fear, revenge, sorrow for a lover abandoning him. He'd sawed gouges in his wrists and his throat; you couldn't quite describe it as half-hearted and manipulative. What kind of idiot killed himself out of spite?

Divvy was pointing to the road, his eyes pleading. Jules could hear flatbed brakes, slowing to unload the bulldozer on the road. "At any rate, I thought I should try to fix the stakes," she said. "There's no point in talking to her about it."

They turned to consider "her" house. This time a downstairs blind shuddered. The eyes of the house; the mother and daughter were watching each other, and Jules and Caroline and Tommy would be stuck between, acid rain falling on their heads. He needed to get rid of these people.

Suzette watched him, waiting. "Please understand that this last mess is not my fault."

"The driveway?"

She twisted her knotty hands together. "You need to meet her boyfriend."

"I don't want to meet anyone," said Jules. "Did he and Elaine really move the stakes around?"

A small smile. "They really did."

Jules thought it through as he walked toward Elaine's big white house. He did not follow the zig of her brick sidewalk or go out of his way to walk on her black tar driveway; he walked on her perfect lawn and pounded on her perfect door. She jerked it open immediately.

"Hi there! What a pleasure! We were just headed out on our little day trip. How's Caroline?"

He ignored this question; he kept one eye on the man who'd appeared behind her in the doorway. The cloud of Elaine's perfume reached him, something caustic like rosemary and lime and maybe a little herbicide.

He took a step back. "Your mother tells me that you put in some time moving my survey stakes around."

Elaine's mouth made a big cartoon O. She shot, just so we didn't have to watch, out the door toward the driveway, looking down in wonder at the marks. The man, who only followed halfway, seemed fascinated by Divvy's big red truck.

"Did we put them back in the wrong place? I am *soooooo* sorry."

Suzette called out. "Honey, Sheriff Clement just told me that Father Bernie is dead. Remember Bernie?"

Jules was not going to be distracted, but Elaine's eyes widened, and her friend abruptly lost interest in the truck. Maybe he was local after all. "Father Bernie?" said Elaine.

"Dead," said Jules. "Yes. But let's talk about my driveway."

"We were just out there fooling around, and we were a little tipsy, but we tried to do the right thing. Right, Charlie?"

A friendly sort of name though everything else about Charlie screamed aggressive prick. He was weirdly shiny, pumiced and tan, manicured and muscled with every blond hair in place, and in that way he was Elaine's perfect mate: the robot couple. Maybe he was an actor, maybe that was why he looked familiar.

"Yes," said Charlie, back to being interested in the truck. He was wearing a neon-green shirt, and it was sweaty. Maybe Elaine wanted him for a lawn boy.

She hugged his waist. "I'm glad you two have met. You have quite a connection."

The man belatedly held out his hand and smiled. "Charlie."

There was a certain wattage to the smile, and Charlie finally looked at Jules with gray eyes that were, in fact, beautiful. They shook, the usual stupidly hard squeeze. "I wanted to avoid this," said the man. "But I realize it seems rude. Charlie Bell. Of course, I know who you are."

"Bell?"

"Yes, I'm Patrick Bell's brother. I'm not proud of it."

Jules could not speak.

"Isn't it strange?" said Elaine. "That you'd end up neighbors? Just the world making peace."

"Sorry about your driveway," said Bell. "It seemed like a better design."

A toothy smile, no more believable than Elaine's. There was something surreal about the face, everything perfect and yet too much: too blond, the eyebrows too sharp, the eyes too excited.

"My driveway is the least of it," said Jules. "Why are you here?"

Charlie Bell stopped smiling and gestured to Elaine, who looked expectant, like a toddler waiting for another child to cry. "Love and money. The three of us—Elaine, me, Mac—are in business together. I haven't lived here in thirty years. This is just a coincidence."

"Go fuck yourself," said Jules, walking to his car. "My father is not a coincidence."

HE DROVE TO the river and wanted to drive into it; he drove around town. It took him a half hour to calm down enough to head for Bernie Dinak's alley. The back door and all the windows were open, and Caroline stood on the back stoop, looking as if she'd taken a hose to herself. She gave him a huge smile and did not immediately take in the look on his face as he walked toward her. She held up three Polaroids.

"You've got to see this. They were tucked under his box springs."

Jules stared at three torsos of older women with their heads off-frame, all cradling bare, not young breasts. He felt a flash of concern for the women who'd posed. No faces but rings in full view, beauty marks, fabric patterns. How scummy had Father Bernie been? He handed the photos back and shook the thought off. "You're being pretty thorough for a suicide."

"Ah, we just got here an hour ago," said Caroline.

He followed her up the porch steps. The smell was mostly gone, though it might never entirely vanish. Some unlucky future owner would stare at the floorboards, confused, as Bernie Dinak's molecules wafted up, a persistent dead mouse. At the far side of the room, Gideon Sorenson was on his knees in a battlefield of dead flies, near a pile of mail that had accumulated under the door.

"I think that someone's been in here and taken things since he died," said Caroline. "Surgery in September, but there are no pain pills, no meds at all, and most of the bathroom drawers are empty. We found a deposit slip under the couch, but there's nothing else from his bank, even in that pile of mail. I wanted Gideon to see if someone wiped the desk drawers or doorknobs."

"Huh," said Jules, unconvinced but polite.

She took a second look at him and asked again. "How are you?"

Not good: Out of all the men in the world, his repellent neighbor chose to sleep with the brother of the man who killed his father. It was hard not to take this personally. Jules told her about the driveway stakes, about Suzette's goading and Elaine's repeated drunk act, while they sat together on the porch and Caroline patted him, hugged him, tugged on his arm—buck up. It was horrible to have this confluence of events, she agreed, but there was no way it meant anything beyond the idea that maybe it was what spurred Olive to begin with: maybe she'd seen Charlie Bell on the street, seen something familiar in his face.

"They don't look alike," said Jules.

"I know," said Caroline. She'd looked up Patrick Bell's face in the newspaper when she'd first met Jules. "But maybe him saying 'I'm not proud of it' covers the apology. Or maybe Elaine chose him just to get at you."

"Who would do that?"

"Elaine."

"'Not proud' is not enough," he said.

"He's probably been apologizing his whole life. When have you ever blamed a whole family for one member?"

When better than now, he thought. He already saw Bell poisoning their Eden. The horrible people next door were now vastly more horrible.

He raged on about motion-sensor cameras and six-foot walls. And Caroline was uneasy, too; she thought of all the things Jules might do to make Charlie Bell go away. People assumed Jules was kind, sane, and law-abiding, and he was 95 percent of the time, but right now he looked more like a hatchet-faced cop than a homely handsome stoner. She rubbed his knee; she knew he was spinning off to a bad place. "At least consider the possibility that he's a nice guy?"

"I don't like his face," said Jules, borrowing Alice's favorite line.

"You can't afford to get weird about it now. This won't last with Elaine," said Caroline. "Ignore him. You didn't know he existed before, and you don't have to grant him any air now."

"Just like that."

"He doesn't seem like the kind of person who likes to be ignored." Caroline reached for her booties and gloves and stood. "I really am sure someone took Dinak's pain pills and banking stuff. Hard to imagine someone holding it together for a robbery with that thing hanging there, or lying there, but I can't think of another explanation."

Jules pulled himself up from Bernie Dinak's grubby cement stoop and headed to his truck. "Maybe he recovered. Maybe he threw them out."

"Would you toss your pain pills if you were suicidal? And if you were just trying for kinky fun, would you clean up your paperwork beforehand?"

Possibly not. Jules didn't want to say what he could have said to Olive: Why bother spending time on this? You'll break your heart, trying to understand.

JULES TRIED THE river, and he tried Caroline, and now he headed back to his clean but soggy office, with Celeste and an indifferent sandwich. When Jules ate all but one crust, they were both able to sulk, and when he quieted down enough, he called Harvey Meyers, the lifelong friend who hadn't picked up on the last name Bell. Jules loved Harvey, and no one would ever be able to protect Jules from the open wounds and all the claws of the past, not to mention self-inflicted damage and average neuroticism. Still, what a fucking idiot. Jules couldn't quite let him off the hook. "Hey, what's the Selway partner's name? The guy Elaine's sleeping with."

"Ball, I think." Jules could hear a crackle of paper: Harvey also operated with a system of mounded files. "Talks about being ex-military but not so much—military high school. *Charlie* Ball. Or not, sorry. C. C. Bell, formerly of Denver, or Arvada, really, now of Cody. Houses are in his wife's name, but he's a widower.

"Bell."

"Bell." Harvey was oblivious for a few beats before he understood. "It's a common name."

"Yeah," said Jules. "But this is the brother. What else have you found out about him?"

A little: a business degree from Colorado State, after finishing high school at some military academy. A later company bio mentioned military experience, but did a high school count? Harvey thought not, but Charlie married a rich girl, an only child, and worked for her father's manufacturing company, which was somehow affiliated with those spooky Halliburton types in Teton County and Cody. The right girl, the right father (dead the year before), and who knew what a company like this really did: gun parts or rubber gaskets or both, but some part was key in rifle manufacture. Wealth made wealth, and Charlie made a bundle in the eighties on real estate, but it didn't stick: both of Charlie's partners declared bankruptcy two years ago, and a planned ski village south of Bozeman fizzled, and around that time Charlie and his wife sold their Denver house and moved to her family's ranch in Cody. She'd died the year before—Harvey guessed breast cancer, because her name showed up on charity lists—but what Charlie was up to as a widower was fuzzier, beyond helping Elaine shill the family property below Marvel.

"So even if he lost big, he's got a new bundle of money," Jules said. Charlie Bell was married for twenty years, and now the father and daughter were dead inside six months. Did it mean anything? Probably not, beyond the idea that Charlie was a lucky or unlucky man. He didn't look like he was mourning.

"There's some sort of delay in the inheritance," said Harvey. "Relatives have a detective in Denver checking around. I was going to talk to him, but you pulled me off."

Jules had, hadn't he. Fucking maddening.

Charlie had been arrested twice, once after a fight in a Cody bar, and once for taking a golf club to a Saab in Denver. There was passing mention of a juvenile record. Jules thought of Ed's words on the 1972 transcript, as the call came in about Patrick Bell's speeding truck: maybe there'd been no angels in the Bell family.

"I can look for more tomorrow," said Harvey. "Today we're short. Burt showed up drunk, probably all shook up by Caroline's dead person. Is she really going to get Burt put on leave?"

"I think so," said Jules.

He hung up. The previous plan for the day—the sacred driveway, a trip to Bozeman to score some student volunteers, and the lease of a ground-penetrating radar machine—could wait. What he needed to do was to start looking up every bit of obtainable information about Charlie Bell, to discover the facts that would reveal him to be a monster. Should Harvey dig further? Yes, he should.

He started a follow-up letter to the warden of the Montana State Penitentiary. No response in twenty-four hours: rude. Next door, in Peter's office, someone was laughing, telling a punch line that included either *attaché* or *La Tâche*; either term meant that Peter was with Ivan again. Ivan who did not cut his own throat ineffectively or have affairs with joggers in cemeteries like the men Jules was dealing with. On any given night Ivan saw a good friend in his apartment at the Baird, all of them beautiful and relaxed, all of them laughing in the stairwell and coming back for more.

Jules printed and signed the Deer Lodge letter. He was punching numbers into the fax machine when he heard footsteps in the hall, and turned, in dread, to see an envelope slide under his door. Maybe it was a love note from a client angry about delays. Maybe Edie was raising the rent to cover repairs. The workmen stomping upstairs sent little flakes of plaster floating down to his keyboard. Outside, car horns and a passing freight train; Jules's limping brain stopped functioning altogether. He walked to the window and there was Charlie Bell's black Suburban, parked and idling on the far side of the street. One of Charlie's tanned arms hung from the driver's window, but he was canted away: after a moment, Jules realized Charlie was looking at himself in the rearview mirror, baring his teeth, tilting his head. Jules could even see the glint as Charlie examined them, which meant that they both missed Elaine, fresh from sliding that envelope under Jules's door, reaching the SUV. She touched Charlie's arm and he jerked away, and the expressions on both of their faces were not loving.

Jules turned back to the room and ripped the envelope open.

> I know you dislike me, but I have a job for you: I'd like you to find some proof that my father is dead. Not how Mother got rid of him or why, but just some physical proof, some piece of paper, so that when I finally inherit from her I don't have that issue to resolve. If she didn't kill him, if he's still alive, he'll come home when she dies.
>
> Here's what you need to know:

A bullet list of information and ten hundred-dollar bills. Jules struggled between horror and wonder for a full minute before he stuffed everything back inside and let the envelope return to the floor, as if that would solve the problem. More lives he couldn't bear to really think about—would he feel dirty, taking her money, after starting the day with a cemetery stakeout? Did he feel some hope that the zombie father was alive and would return to ruin his daughter's life?

Jules owed this woman nothing. He headed out, stepping over Elaine's envelope as if it were a crack in the sidewalk and he'd break his mother's back

9 *Ghosts*

A VISION, WHEN JULES ARRIVED AT THE POOR FARM at the hottest point in the day: Gordie with a crew, a crane, a front-end loader, and a flatbed, men and machinery trying to untangle forty totaled cars, half of them probably bloodstained from their last automated moments. The crane operator was on his second wreck, a pancaked Honda, and dropped it twice while Jules watched. It finally reached the flatbed and slid off, nearly hitting another county worker.

Jules knew each wobble meant another crushed grave. Celeste, panting next to him, probably heard the underground screams of ten thousand traumatized rodents and at least a hundred rattlesnakes. The crane surged up to the roadbed—the roadbed that now seemed far too close to what Jules guessed was the Depression-era burial area—and the driver got out and pissed. Have a nice life, thought Jules. There was such a thing as pushing your luck.

He turned away, wondering how long he could handle the sound of scraping metal, and decided to walk off one more narrow rectangle. Three burned wooden sheds, one a sort of garage—he knifed down in the soil and found a layer of oil stain in the char—and the other two with a different kind of dark, sheepfolds or chicken coops, pig pens or stables. Fertilizer, everywhere: the depressions with the richest grass must have been privies, one just a few stinky feet from a dormitory side door. Hard to be critical when you really thought about a case of diarrhea during a January blizzard. A divot in the current road was probably there for the same reason. If Gordie got to keep this route, he'd find that shit still smelled when the crew widened the road.

Jules mapped the privies and added three prospective test pit sites for his students, spots where they could find a layer of ash from the wooden dormitory that burned in 1900. In England or Virginia or Veracruz—any verdant place—you could count an inch of deposit a decade, but Absaroka County was high alpine desert. Here you could pick your way down through the skim of lichen and rock to the char stratum only half an inch below the surface. He flagged another test pit site in the multi-use orchard, and a fifth in the earliest graveyard, where the ghosts were neatly aligned, east to west with crumbled bits of broken wood for markers. If you squinted you could make out enough letters to match the list: *E—c- -la-dy* was Enoch Bladdy, very dead since 1913.

Another clear, sharp day, no smoke anywhere. The wind picked up and the brutalized windmills to the east began to whine and squeak in rebellion, competing with the front-end loader and crane and a second flatbed, winding its way up the road to fetch another two of the forty or so wrecks. Six antelope, in the habit of bedding down in the former orchard, skittered onto the ridge to Jules's east and watched the machinery, too. In the town far below, he caught the flash of police lights and pulled out binoculars to survey for smoke, more lights, signs of the apocalypse. He thought about what was new since Ansel: the truck stop and chain gas stations, McDonald's, the new supermarket, the dotted subdivisions that lay too close to the river or the highway or stupidly exposed to the wind. With binoculars, he could even see Charlie Bell's black SUV pull out of Elaine's driveway, just twenty feet from Jules and Caroline's own new road to nowhere, finally heading east to the freeway entrance. And looking uphill, he could see Charlie and Elaine's ludicrous sign for their own subdivision. A raven was perched on it, and Jules watched it take a shit.

Was Suzette happy about Elaine and Charlie putting that sign up on the flats? Vista del Rio—that's all you got. The view, the wind, some rocky clay.

Jules lowered his glasses as an engine cut out. The crane and bulldozer operators were off their machines and conferring in a troubling, we're-fucked-for-the-day kind of way. The bulldozer operator, Trip, waved and Jules walked toward the idling machinery.

"Look what I found," said Trip.

A broken tibia; the break looked postmortem. "Dime a dozen," said Jules. "By the fence?"

"No," said Trip. "Right there, where we're parked. Kind of sticking out of the roadbed. Didn't you say not to worry around there?"

THIS WAS EXACTLY what Jules had said. Wrong again! Now he told the crew to keep clearing the wrecks, fast and carefully; he told them he needed to pick up his kid.

There was the temptation to self-medicate. Jules packed up the playpen, toys, food, et cetera, and headed to the daycare. Tommy, who'd skipped his morning nap, was a weepy mess as they regrouped briefly at home. He fell asleep in his car seat within five blocks.

Back to the land of the living. Jules stood on the new driveway; it was strange how a man-made path changed a landscape, made every tree and clearing and bump look different. Whenever he'd seen something like this before he'd been appalled—logging roads scarring a hillside, crushing the wilderness; roads to idiot subdivisions, clinging to cliffs. His road, his scar, was lovely, but the three-foot-deep gouge alongside it, the route for water and sewer, gas and electric, the juice for what Divvy called "this whole fucking enterprise," was raw and alarming.

Jules parked in the shade and pounded on the Selways' door to be sure the couple were gone. In the garage, he saw only Elaine's convertible Saab and piles of boxes labeled *MAC*.

"They fight a lot," said Divvy. He was holding a calendar.

"Good," said Jules. He explained about Caroline's dead priest and about Charlie Bell. Divvy, who'd known Jules since middle school, understood the full horror of the situation.

"Holy shit. What are you going to do?"

"Something," said Jules.

"How are you going to live next door to a Bell?"

"I'm going to assume he won't last with Elaine, either."

The order of the new world, now that there was a way to reach it: clearing and excavation, forms and gravel, beginning with the garage and later the main foundation; electric, gas, water, sewer line, and grading. Pouring, curing, framing, roofing, flooring; windows, HVAC, wiring, plumbing. Interior trim and finish, paint and flooring! And on and on, until they were institutionalized or housed. Divvy's schedule was on hyperdrive and, pending the arrival of the excavator the next morning, he started the garage excavation with his own skid-steer. Jules tried to pay attention to some of what Divvy was saying about moving straight into the house excavation once they'd killed off the garage, about a cottonwood that happened to have a wasp nest. And was Jules sure he didn't want the garage a little bigger? Didn't want to go for a bigger footprint? Skip the bump out for Caroline's potential greenhouse and save on the fussy roof?

Jules did not want this. The potential greenhouse, just six by twelve, might keep Caroline sane some January. He didn't want to take the tree down, either, but he kept his yap shut. At this point the flayed calendar was a hopeless, zigging mess. Jules knew all of it was inevitable and desired, but he was sweating from sheer contact stress. Divvy's pace was delusional. Maybe he was back to doing speed.

"Maybe give us a little more time for the roof?" Jules said. "For windy days?"

"Fuck the wind," said Divvy, chewing Nicorette. "Anyway, here's to groundbreaking."

Heaven would smite them. Divvy pulled out a bottle of good tequila, and Jules, with Tommy strapped to his front like a bomb vest, tried to demur but accepted half a shot.

"Who would have guessed you'd pull this off?"

Divvy loved beginnings, and progress. He loved momentum. His hair stood high in the wind as he flicked his measuring tape around like a bullwhip.

"Herb and the excavator at dawn tomorrow. We'll start

the garage forms early the next day, gravel in the afternoon. Fuckin A."

These dawns should go over well with the neighbors. Jules eyed the trampled grass and berry bushes and molehills on the perimeter of the apple tree, a doomed rodent metropolis. In the fresh tunnel made by the trencher he caught a glimpse of metal and pocketed someone's lost Zippo lighter. He squatted to peer down into the revealed land, Montana from before the arrival of smallpox, relieved that none of the severed roots seemed to belong to the precious apple tree. He dropped a tiny fallen apple into a mole hole as an offering, then studied the mole's shovelings, a fresh rich pile of good dirt, roots, and small ivory pebbles.

At least he thought they were pebbles. Jules stared at them for a moment, feeling queasy.

I am losing it, he thought. "I'm cuckoo," he said to his child, who loved the word. They straightened up and there, walking down his own smooth, perfect driveway, was Mac Selway, heavily bandaged. Mac bellowed, but his voice cracked. "You didn't come visit me! I've complained to your wife. Can we get together?"

"You sure you should be out?"

"Oh, I'm fine." Mac shuffled toward his door, exuberance already passing, still somehow wet and sad. "I find I need some belongings. Suzette let me know that there was a window of opportunity here before Elaine returned. Sadie's just started work."

"They say they won't be back until tomorrow," said Jules.

"Hah," said Mac. "Sucker me twice." He dropped his keys, bent for them like an old man, gave a wave that was halfway between royal and forlorn, and disappeared inside.

"It's weird," said Divvy. "Even before they split up, they locked their doors. Who does that?"

"I will, with them next door," said Jules.

"You would think that being married to that piece of ass would have made a person happy."

Divvy roared off, leaving Jules to clean up. The beauty of leaning against a cottonwood while giving a kid a bottle; Jules nearly fell asleep himself before he lowered Tommy into the playpen.

He pulled on his gloves and walked into the woods. Through the trees, he could see Suzette out on her deck, and his binoculars were strong enough to focus on her empty cocktail glass and a full ashtray of lipstick-dipped cigarettes. She needed to give that up if her ticker was really taking a shit. She was talking on the phone, gesturing, too distracted to notice much of anything: Jules, the river, her wounded son-in-law periodically carrying a box from the house to his car. It didn't sound like a conversation with the solicitous Sadie, or Elaine: her tone was soothing, with little cackles in between. Maybe she did have friends.

Jules ducked to stay out of her line of sight as he filled bags with trash. Down at the river's edge, Suzette's remnant box-wire fence was weighed down by decades of dead spring grass, braided with high-water flotsam. The sociopathic, wall-eyed pony watched him pick up the crap from the trailer park a half mile to the west, following as Jules got closer and closer, then shied; the overprotective llama rammed the box-wire fence and hissed.

"Fuck off, Fido," whispered Jules.

The llama spat. Jules bent to rinse his hands and splashed water on his face and down his neck. He hadn't wanted to cause an animal pain since his last rottweiler encounter as sheriff, but the llama begged for at least a scare. He scanned the wet gravel and soil edge, looking for something smaller than the smooth ivory rock half-buried in sand, something larger than the green quartzite near it. A marble of limestone was perfect. He threw and missed, hitting the cheerleading Shetland, which brayed and bucked and farted off.

The llama rammed the fence a second time, and the post made a cracking sound. Clearly, it was time to retreat; this thing could kill an infant. Jules lurched back, sliding on algae-covered river rock, and hissed, "Go screw your pony." He searched for another rock, touched the smooth white one, moved on to a perfect skipping stone, then tapped a fingertip against the white one again.

It wasn't a stone.

The llama watched Jules drop to his knees and push the wet sand away, then carefully lift a two-inch fragment of someone's left temple. He bent again to wipe away more mud, trying to determine if the river had deposited the bone or was in the process of freeing it, but there was gravel underneath, no other bone nearby.

The river, the bone, the light. Jules slid the piece of skull into his pocket with a horrible sense of déjà vu and rose to a half-crouch as the llama turned, too, to watch Suzette march toward Tommy, cooing. Jules hurried up the bank, the size of her gin glass in the forefront of his mind, on some irrational level believing that if Suzette managed to touch Tommy, she'd infect him with whatever was wrong with Elaine.

It was too late: Suzette hoisted the baby onto her tiny

bony hip and bobbed him up and down. She smiled at Jules, apparently overjoyed by her own effort. He gave her one full minute before he snatched his child away.

Suzette steadied herself on the playpen: gray skin, bloodless lips, a bruise and a little blood on her temple. She looked ninety instead of eighty; she looked like she was going to die right there.

"Suzette," he said. "Are you all right?"

"I'm not sure what's wrong," she said. "Some new medication. I fell."

"Should you go to the hospital?"

A blank look.

"Should I call Elaine?"

She managed a smile. "Mac."

Jules ran to the big white house, kid bouncing along on one hip, skull fragment pressing against the other thigh. He rang the bell; he pounded on the door. He heard a creaking sound from behind and turned: Mac stood in the open door of his studio, lumpy and pale in striped boxers.

"You need to take your mother-in-law to the hospital."

"I just *left* the hospital," said Mac, peering past Jules to Suzette. "I'm heading for the hotel."

"Please," said Jules.

Mac made popping sounds with his mouth for Tommy. "Does she have that gray look?"

"Yes."

"Here's what's happening," said Mac. "Elaine's hauled her in to the ER three times, claiming she has sudden-onset dementia. Each time they figured out there'd been a medication mishap—Rohypnol in July, and then sildenafil, which can cause heart failure in someone with her issues.

The Viagra Elaine wanted me to take went missing, and now I happen to be missing a bottle of Xanax, so who knows what's going to happen next."

Mac went to find clothes; Jules trotted back to Suzette, grabbing a camp chair in the back of the truck. She asked for water. Another sprint, this time to the cottage—the kid loved the bouncing. Jules turned off the deafening television and took in his surroundings. The interior was dusty but surprisingly spare, with tchotchkes contained neatly in a glass cabinet. Everything was pared down: some stacked magazines, a bowl of earrings and another of llama snacks, a solitaire game out on the table, and on the kitchen windowsill, an old-fashioned, painfully ironic street sign: BLUE ACRES.

He grabbed a highball glass of water and a wet cloth and arrived just as Mac approached from the other direction, buttoning his sleeves over his wrist bandages, the ones at his throat looking like a cravat. "Suzette, sweetie. Elaine mixing up your meds again?"

"*She* does always seem to get them wrong," said Suzette. "I felt fine last night, with Sadie. You're not really leaving, are you, Mac? *She* doesn't love that man."

Mac daubed at her forehead. "Well, she doesn't love me, either. She doesn't love anyone alive, anyone but that man who broke all the bones in your body. Let me grab the pill tray for the staff to check and I'll take you in. Is it in the bedroom?"

"Oh no," said Jules. "Stay with her. I'll get it." Again the run; Tommy learned that if he made any noise the sound would warble as they bounced. This time Jules noticed another street sign—GOLDFIELDS—above the bedroom door. A beaded, belled curtain blocked the way and Tommy gave a little shriek—Fear? Joy? My child, this is your first haunted house—as they went through.

Jules braced for more of the bizarre, but this room was spare, too. Photos of Elaine as a child, Suzette young and beautiful in frocks and California sunshine, not a Mr. Whipple in sight. Jules reached down for the shoebox-sized pillbox.

Next to it, a scribbled note on flowered stationery:

Your daily reminder: I know what you did. I know what you are.

Even Elaine's handwriting combined pomposity and poison.

Outside, Mac peered down at the tray. "She'll kill us all. There's my magic blue pills in your tray, again. Into the car."

"They'll be home tonight. She's trying to catch you taking stuff," said Suzette.

"I know," said Mac, helping her into his car. "You didn't see me."

"All right, darling," said Suzette.

"Usually she argues," said Mac to Jules. "She must be near death. You know what's going on here? Elaine's trying to weaken her, get her to sign over some land, make her feel shitty enough that she thinks she's dying. I'm sorry I didn't warn you about Charles, but the alliance is out of my hands, in keeping with Elaine's style."

"Not your fault," said Jules.

"She'll get rid of him," said Mac. "Not that I give a flying fuck anymore. But I do care about Suzette. I wanted to hire you because I have concerns about Charlie's past, and the way he's in the habit of inheriting, and the people he's in business with."

EVERY CONTACT WITH the Whipple-Selways splintered Jules's brain. He drove home with the skull fragment on the dashboard, the poor farm tibia on the floor below Tommy's small plump feet, now bopping along to a ska CD. Jules tried to sort through what the bones might mean, trying to cling to the pleasure he thought he'd feel when the house excavation began. Instead: that fucker next door and a human skull in his child's wading pool.

Jules slammed into his house and fished through the mess on the dining room table. According to a half dozen admittedly flawed maps, the cemetery at Doris lay on the far side of Mac and Elaine's house. According to a half dozen historical accounts, it disappeared in the flood of 1917. The flood itself was a fact, but here was a chunk of human head. Jules guessed it was at least fifty years old, but the bone was stained white on top from exposure, and the edges were only slightly worn. It hadn't washed far.

Which was an unwelcome thought. Jules plopped Tommy on the kitchen floor and called Caroline without a plan, without wanting to mention the sudden wealth of body parts. Did she have an evidence pouch heading north to the lab?

Yes, if he rushed. "How long do I have to hold the courier? How is Tommy doing?"

"Tommy's fucking glorious. I'll be there in ten minutes," said Jules. "I've got something to add from the poor farm. Actually, two samples."

"All right." She sounded confused. "This is urgent? I need to head out with Gideon."

"I think so," said Jules. "I'll make sure the county bills the right account."

He called Shari Swenson at the state lab. They'd known each other for years, and so when she said she wouldn't look at any of his bones for a week, he said, "What the fuck, Shari."

"What do you care about most?"

"The really old chunk of skull," said Jules.

"Really old?" said Shari. "As old as the dude your girlfriend sent me?"

"It's older," said Jules. "And cleaner. But how long do you think Mr. Dinak was lying around? Caroline's having trouble finding a galloping reason for him to top himself."

"People get sad, Jules."

"I know that," he snapped.

"Months, anyway. He probably missed Christmas. I shut the drawer after my first look, but he's next up. I've still got an unidentified OD from a Bozeman bathroom stall—bucketloads of hospital opiates in his bloodstream and his dick out and no needle—and a Billings fall from the only ten-story building in the damn state. And old people are dying at a wild rate at a Missoula nursing home—someone might be doling out streptococcus scratches. Or not. I'm probably paranoid."

Jules knew his bones and Bernie Dinak couldn't compete, but he pushed. "For this piece of skull, I'm curious about date, as well as where it might have been before it ended up in the river."

"Any chance it could belong to one of your last few floaters?"

"It looks older," said Jules. "The tibia is from a separate site."

"Any context?"

"I'd rather not," said Jules. "Keep an open mind."

"Me or you?" said Shari.

"Please," he said. "Please please please."

Click. He'd have to make it right with Shari. Caroline would eventually look over the list of the people missing from the river, but Jules told himself he didn't want to weigh her down with the idea now. She was already nervous about raising a child within a hundred yards of the Yellowstone.

It was five o'clock, but Tommy continued to pretend to be a perfect child, rolling around on the ground with Celeste, who loved him for his food habits. Jules slammed snacks into a bag and packed his child into the truck again. They dropped the bone package at the station and headed onward and upward to the flats, Jules's own ninety-degree field of Golgotha.

Two-thirds of the vehicles remained, along with the county equipment. After a sunblock–bug spray struggle, as Tommy's big-brimmed hat folded and tugged in the hot late afternoon wind, the parked bulldozer distracted from his suffering, and the mood was soon sanguine. Jules needed to know if the tibia was an animal offering from a far-off location, or part of a new burial field. He found a spot with no deadly plants, sharp objects, or edible rocks, plopped Tommy down on a blanket, and jogged the newly visible part of the field for a lightning survey. The recently cleared area was grooved by old car frames, the flat shale outcrops stained with oil and rust. Dips and divots, stray metal, and an overall pattern of poorly spaced, hand-dug rectangles: he'd found another patch of dead people, probably from the twenties.

A wail—Tommy was ten feet off the blanket with a mouth full of dirt. Jules jogged back. He scooped dirt out of the small mouth despite screams of rage and they made the run for the truck and a bottle of water and a good rinse. Except for trips to the doctor, Jules hadn't made his child this angry before, and it took a while for them both to recover. By the time he realized his keys were missing he'd forgotten his route from the dirt-eating site to the truck. He strapped Tommy in his car seat—doors open!—with a pacifier and sprinted around the hummocky site until he caught the glint of new metal and slowed, wheezing.

The keys lay in a dip near some broken wood and he paused, unnerved by the give of the thin layer of soil under his feet: he was standing on a half-collapsed coffin, ripped open by machinery. The pebbles he saw next to the keys were hand bones: carpals, metacarpals, phalanges.

Fresh shrieks from the truck: a dropped pacifier. Phalanges were so useful. Jules slid one into the bag he'd meant for soil, and covered the rest of the exposed, crumbled hand with a fast cairn of rocks. The hand belonged to somebody's baby once; he shouldn't think of this new field of people as just more work.

10 *Ed*

THE MYSTERIES OF COHABITATION: CAROLINE DIDN'T bring up the Russians or her conversation with Cavendish Clusker and Ivan Luneau. Jules, for his part, didn't mention anything about the bones he'd found. It was just nice having a couple of quiet hours together. It started to rain softly, even though it stayed warm: strange weather, but wonderful. They opened all the windows and ate pizza and watched heat lightning while they cleaned up and took turns sitting next to the tub while Tommy splashed.

Jules headed out again at eight, which was later than he'd left his house for anything since becoming a parent.

"Don't get drunk or angry," said Caroline.

She'd come home with another small box of Ansel files, and when Jules left, and Tommy slept, she poured some wine and brought it outside. She started with the day, the log of events, the witnesses to the truck's progress north, struck by how much was timeless: a man beat his wife, someone stole a bicycle, a train started a grass fire. Car accidents, a loose horse, a heart attack at the market. And then the calls started about Patrick Bell's truck, a dozen of them eventually, but only a few with descriptions. At 3:58, *this f----- was passing, coming at me in my lane.* At 4:07, *didn't even see the truck coming from behind going eighty and there they were right next to me, window all smeared with blood.* At 4:29, with Ansel dead, *if you don't take care of the c---------s, I will. And seeing that poor man in the dust. Can't bear it.*

Like a devil, wearing sunglasses.

She skipped ahead, looking for any witnesses, the usual pile on. Everyone always wanted to claim they'd seen something, with a crime like this, and the later calls would be no more useful than a lineup. But she hit something different: at 10:33 p.m., from the Bell address on Coralberry Creek, a weeping woman:

Our daughter! Our daughter is dead! She's hanging in the barn! Please send Ed!

Caroline's wine was gone, but she stayed in the yard, not wanting to pick up the next file.

JULES WALKED DOWN to the Blue Bat just in time to see Ivan walk out of the bar with yet another pretty woman, making for the only good restaurant in town and undoubtedly thence to bed. Banish that self-pity, he thought, turning away just as the door opened again, nearly hitting him in the face: Peter, very late for his own dinner.

"Are you on a roll?" asked Jules.

"Business," said Peter. "Can I give you some?"

"Sure," said Jules, any instinct for self-preservation once again deserting him.

Peter turned as if to go back in, thought the better of it, and leaned against the windowsill, scribbling names down. "I'm hoping you can find these people," he said. "Or better yet find them dead, with no heirs. I'm trying to track down these last Clusker cousins, Marvel heirs."

He ripped off the notebook page and handed it to Jules.

Mallow, Pinbenny, Zucher, Defoe, Merzik, Choake. "I can tell you that Buddy Merzik is very, very dead," said Jules. "Car accident when I was sheriff. I found his sister, to let her know."

"Well, put the sister on the list. We're playing dominoes."

"Just out of curiosity, what's it got to do with Ivan?"

"Cavendish is a friend."

"Bullshit."

"All right," said Peter. "If anyone gets to buy the land, Ivan would like it to be him, and he thinks you're the right person to make sure Cavendish isn't fibbing. Because we all know he does."

Something was off with the conversation. Peter, his friend of twenty years, was acting squirrelly. "Did you hear who Elaine's shacking up with?" asked Jules. "Do you know how that fucking feels? Tell me Ivan's not in on their land con, all the land above the poor farm."

"Oh god no," said Peter. "That's all Suzette's. And yeah, I heard, and I'm sorry. And Ivan knows some things about the guy that you might find useful."

"Like what?"

"Like he's bad news on every level."

"That's fucking obvious," snapped Jules.

"Just talk to Ivan," said Peter. "He'll pay cash for your time."

He scurried off. Jules pushed the Blue Bat door open, trying to get his head back into an older problem.

He paused, as always, to see if anyone in the room was still a cause for worry. Most people were watching news of the body search after the embassy bombings in Tanzania and Kenya, which was, coincidentally, where Ed wanted to travel before the reality of Shirley's condition kicked in and they settled for visiting relatives. He was explaining this to the other patrons, most of whom thought Africa was a country, and everyone at least pretended to listen, because you didn't ignore Ed.

Jules liked approaching Ed from behind, just to make him twitchy. He'd been a cop since Jules was nine, a constant presence after Ansel was murdered, either in the house or professionally, plucking Jules out of cars and busting high school parties in the woods, on the Clement family's little picnic patch.

"Ask me how we've all been," said Jules.

"Okay," said Ed. "How've you been?"

"Fine," said Jules. "We're all fine. Sad about Sadie leaving."

"She should just outlast that shit. Wesley will be back."

Jules told him about Tommy's ear infections, the abandoned lawsuit and Whipple-Selway intrafamilial warfare, Mac bleeding into layers of the hotel flooring. He did not mention Mac's new partner and Elaine's lover by name, not yet. Ed knew about Suzette's incident but not the lawsuit, or the fact that Burt used the Taser three times for very little cause in the last three weeks. Jules told the whole Dinak story, with the flourish of Venus and Caroline being sick at either end of the porch.

Dinak managed to surprise Ed, who still made it to St. Anne's for Saturday-evening services. "I wouldn't have seen him topping himself; I wouldn't have seen him having enough soul to do it. Maybe he was ill."

"Maybe it was a mistake," said Jules.

Ed's face: incomprehension, the beginning of wonder, but why bother explaining. "Do you know what he did to be defrocked?" Jules asked. "Olive mentioned the girls' basketball team and the parish secretary."

"He wasn't defrocked, they just got him out of the school. It wasn't really those girls—he was an equal-opportunity lech."

"Wasn't there a query a few years ago, something you worked on?"

Ed looked blank for a second time. Shirley was wearing him down. "Oh. Well, while you and Caro were still in the southwest, a young guy who saw Bernie for confession said Bernie tried to blackmail him about being gay, and the guy said, screw you, I'm gay."

"Caroline doesn't know this," said Jules.

"The kid talked to the church and dropped it. I mean, I'm guessing it all went private."

Jules thought of the topless women in Dinak's photos, but it was time to deal with his own dead. "So," he said. "Olive has some questions about my father."

Ed put his drink down. "Why?"

"She says it's weighing on her." Jules drained his glass. "I met the brother, Charlie Bell. He's Elaine Selway's new special friend, now that she's getting divorced. He's staying with her in the house, twenty yards from our property."

Ed, twirling drink straws like his fat fingers were majorettes, stopped moving.

"I recognize that I was bound to run into him somewhere," said Jules. "He might be a nice man, but just having to look at his face is grinding at my soul."

"Do you think he'll stick around?"

"I don't know."

Ed sipped his drink. "Steer clear."

"Because of my temper?"

"Sure. And his. That boy used to be a ball of rage."

"How do I steer clear if he's next door?"

"I don't know, but try," Ed said. "He was a fucked-up kid, and no one changes that much."

"Fucked up even compared to his brother?"

"Anyone picking odds on which of those two would end up a murderer would have bet on Charlie," said Ed. "He nearly beat someone to death during my first week at work, before they shipped him off to military school. What's he do for a living now?"

"His father-in-law died and his wife died and he inherited a business and a bunch of real estate. I don't get the sense that he's mourning."

"He always did make his own luck."

Jules stared. "I know nothing," said Ed. "Just a line."

"Tell me about that day."

Ed appeared to count his ice cubes.

"Olive wants everything."

But Ed's face turned belligerent. "And what do you think I want? My wife is not well. I'm not happy with my knees, or my brain, or the idea of going back to work for that asshole Burt tomorrow. You want details? I don't want to talk about any of this. I might worry about your mother, but I don't owe her anything."

The words settled. Jules lifted a finger for Tino. He'd been so good, for so long, but this wasn't something he was willing to handle on one whiskey, after a day of skeletons. Everyone carried a bag of guilt. Years ago, on the night Ed was drunk and said that Ansel was shot twice, he'd also told Jules that Ansel was patrolling that afternoon because

Ed was hungover and late to report. Sober, he'd said he'd made it up. Either way, who would want to live with a bad movie plot point hanging over their head?

"What on earth doesn't she know? There's nothing to know. He pulled the kid over and the kid pulled a gun. It probably took a second. I mean, they must have talked a bit, because Ansel called in the license. We all listened to the recording later—no alarm, just routine."

"And then?"

"For him? How can I know? Two shots, but the first would have killed him instantly—a shotgun, at close range, and his heart was just gone. You saw. I'm so sorry you saw."

"Did he know?"

"For fuck's sake. Read the autopsy."

Jules, examining the shiny wood of the bar, said, "I will. But I'd rather hear it from you."

Ed aged. "He wasn't shot in the back. Maybe for a moment. Half a second. No gun drawn, no movement away. He dropped right by the car, on the side of the road. The people in the closest house came out and found him."

On an 80-degree night, Jules was cold for the first time in months. He drank some water and looked at the Pabst clock on the wall; the year was locked on 1969. Ansel might have seen this clock over a drink with Ed.

Jules knew the answer but asked anyway. "Tell me how it started."

Ed looked pained. "I was just going on shift. Someone called the truck in—it was speeding—and Ansel cut it off at Nesbit Creek. And that was the last we heard. Grace—she'd just started a few months before—looked it up, and the kid was still registered at his parents' address. And so when the neighbors found Ansel's body we drove to the house."

It was understood that Jules knew where the Bells' family house stood. "Who was 'we'?"

"Bunny and I arrived at the same time."

"And?"

"We found Patrick on the ground of the driveway, more or less unconscious. His brother took him out. The parents were up by the house, yelling."

"And?"

"We arrested Patrick. Took him to the jail, ended up taking him to the hospital in the middle of the night when we realized he wasn't faking seizures. Charlie was a little hard on his brother; like I said, he was a violent motherfucker. Probably still is."

The seizures—from the arrest, or from beating his head against the wall later? Why did he remember this? Maybe the commutation hearing, and now he could see Patrick Bell's face, an El Greco face, gray white and somehow misshapen. Whereas Charlie was a ray of sunlight, a golden boy. "So Patrick arrived at his parents' house and said, 'I shot the sheriff,' and his brother beat the shit out of him? Did they know he was coming?"

"I don't imagine that was the conversation. He was there to kill his wife."

"Just announced, 'I'm going to kill my wife'?"

People did that, though, all the time.

"I guess," said Ed. "That's what the family told us later."

"Well, what else did people say? The parents, the wife? I'll go talk to all of them."

"Not much before the state police showed up. I was

the one who got Charlie to stop kicking his brother in the head. The mother was screaming. I never talked to the father at the time. We were in the driveway, and the house is on the rise—the father was still new to the wheelchair. All we kept in our heads that night was Ansel. I don't remember feeling curious, or patient." Ed rubbed his face. "I'm done with this for now. Don't talk to the parents. They're useless. Read the fucking files."

"I've started," said Jules. "I read the transcript of the call. Grace is looking for more."

Ed lifted his hands, let them drop, reached for a toothpick. "Well, why the fuck not tell me you'd read it? You tell me what happened, then."

"So when you asked my father if Patrick was the good one or the bad one, you thought he was the good one?"

"Absolutely. No way anyone could have expected this."

Jules felt woozy, out of practice, punch-drunk. "Have you ever dealt with the brother since? Or the wife? What was the accident you asked about on the transcript?"

"No idea," said Ed.

"Something like 'didn't he help out after the accident.'"

"Ah. The family claimed Francis Bell fell down a flight of stairs. The hospital told us they thought he'd been kicked, stomped. But anyway, the kid who helped after the accident would have been Patrick. Charlie hasn't lived at home since that night."

One boy cripples his own father, the other kills Jules's. "What was the fight about when Charlie was a teenager?"

"A girl," said Ed.

"Care to elaborate?"

Jules knew this expression on Ed's face; he often got it just before he hit someone. "No, I would not care to elaborate. What people do when they're seventeen is a closed book, even for a prick like that. He's stayed away for years, but I saw him in church last summer with his mother, making a big show about his donations. I didn't say hello, but I feel for them. I will tell you that Lucia Bell's pretty religious and had a hard time accepting that neither boy was any good."

"I need to talk to the parents."

"Neither of them will be any help with what Olive wants. And you—I mean it about being careful with Charlie. Really look at those eyes, and you'll see what I mean."

Jules, blinded by Charlie's name, couldn't remember his eyes.

"Don't use this as an excuse to start another fire," said Ed, lifting his finger.

They talked about other stuff to dull things down. Jules didn't finish his whiskey, because what he really needed to wash things out of his head was Caroline, and for that he needed to be sober. Ed could drink because he and his wife had nothing that way, anymore; Jules and Caroline did, and it was time to expunge a little sadness in bed, where Caroline—found asleep on the couch, without getting far in the files—would afterward make him promise again not to do anything stupid, and Jules would say he was a rational human, and wouldn't hurt a flea.

11 *The Third Morning*

TUESDAY

DIVVY SAID THE EXCAVATION WOULD BEGIN AT dawn, but that was a relative term. By the time Jules got to the site, there was a shallow, garage-sized hole in Elaine's former paradise. She was back to watch the process: the black Suburban was parked in the driveway, looking dusty and drab. The excavator made a massive amount of noise. Jules was very happy.

Ed told him to read the files, and so he drove home, ate a huge breakfast, and walked to the library. He delayed by looking up Peter's Marvel names in old city directories; he read a couple of old *New York Times* issues. Finally, he pulled microfilm for the Blue Deer *Bulletin* from 1968, when Patrick would have been eighteen, and for the weeks after August 15, 1972. A Tuesday when nothing much seemed to have happened, elsewhere—the war ground on, a German airliner crashed, no one was bullish on McGovern-Eagleton.

The librarian, who'd been his high school art teacher, tried to hide her pity when she heard the dates he requested, and the two older people using computers nearby seemed to stare. Did they know, or was he just used to people knowing? He skimmed into 1968: there was Ansel posing by the new department headquarters, a great-uncle's obituary, a photo of Louise with the debate club. An ad for the movies playing that week: *Junior Bonner* with Steve McQueen, *Kansas City Bomber* with Raquel Welch. He didn't remember if he'd gone.

And there it was: "High School Fight," November 11, 1968. It took several teachers to restrain the junior who instigated the attack, who would not be allowed to return. A girl was injured in what Sheriff Ansel Clement described as an attempted rape, and the boy who defended her was still hospitalized with a head injury, and the sheriff scoffed at the idea that the students were outsiders, as the mayor suggested. "Sorry to disabuse you," he said. "But this is what you'd call a nice old family."

Family, singular. Brothers.

Jules threaded the machine with the roll that included August 15, 1972, and as it clicked along he felt sick. The headline ran over the photo of his father in uniform, a different man than the one he remembered. He twisted the knob on the microfilm machine for the fuller account at the end of what was still the longest week of his life. The crime was described as motiveless, beyond Bell's obvious desire to kill his wife. Bell's former teachers, neighbors, coworkers described a kind man and a good student. Talk of unnecessary police violence was shot down. The good-looking, good-natured boy in the school photo—taken before the disastrous fight?—shared a general facial shape with his brother, and nothing else.

Jules's eyes glazed over. The machine whirred to a stop on August 21 and a photo of the packed memorial at the civic center, with a smaller, closer photo of his family.

There he was, a frail little boy with his head bent, so recognizably himself his eyes filled up. Louise was blowing her nose, and Olive was expressionless. His grandparents, his old friend Larry Grand, Larry's crazy mother and his sister Emmeline. Ed was a large blur with a uniform and a hat in the back. Jules knew everyone else in the photo, and more than half of them were dead now. He remembered relatives invading the house, old Swedes pulling him to and fro. In the time between Ansel's death and the funeral, Jules went to the Lutheran church with Ansel's parents and to the Catholic church with Olive's family. When his maternal grandmother realized that the Bell family was also attending that day, she stood and left in the middle of mass, and they all followed her out.

At the library, Jules whirred on. A piece praised Charles Bell for apprehending his brother in the driveway of their parents' house on Coralberry Creek, a few minutes before the police arrived. Patrick ended up in the hospital later that night for injuries suffered at the time of his arrest. He was released for his court appearance, but unable or unwilling to speak.

Jules knew the stone ranch house, and he especially remembered the beautiful old barn that burned in 1975, the night that Jules and his friend Larry drove over the mountain from Marvel and threw some burning charcoal into the Bells' hay mow.

"Smells like fried chicken," said Larry.

They stood on the ridge, watching the flames and one glowing running dot that Jules realized was a barn cat. This was another moment that never went away.

Jules respooled the microfilm but paused when the

name Bell flickered by on an inside page. A death notice, on August 18:

> Iris Talouse Bell, 21, of Salt Lake City, UT.
> No services planned at this time.

Was this a sister, not a wife? A cousin with bad timing? If this was the wife Patrick intended to harm, why did none of the stories mention that he succeeded? Jules felt a blast of anger with Ed—how could he have left this out of his account? Though Ed volunteered nothing, really—tragedy as bare minimum. There was no other mention of Iris in the follow-up about Ansel, nothing at all again about the wife, dead or alive, beyond the information that Patrick was ultimately deemed not fit to stand trial because of "self-injury due to grief." For a death he'd intended to cause, thought Jules, returning the microfilm to the troubled librarian. Fuck the Bells' grief. This wasn't getting him anywhere, beyond a stronger conviction that Caroline needed to quit, so that they never saw Tommy's picture in the newspaper this way or stood on a ridge watching flames rise.

In 1975, Ed was assigned to the Bells' arson case. There were no cameras in the interview room, back then, when he talked to Jules and Larry. As sheriff, Jules thought back to that night every time he questioned someone, and he'd been a better cop because of the memory. He and Larry were released after six hours, bruised everywhere from the neck down; they went to bed for days. Jules and Ed never talked about it, and no one was ever charged for the burning of the Bell family's beautiful old barn.

*

JULES, LEAVING THE coal lump of his past, could have gone back to the build site or worked on the dense thicket that would someday be their garden or dealt with anything in the older PI case pile. He could have printed out the photographs from the cemetery spy session; he could have found out whatever other awful things Burt was up to, dug up something that helped his beloved and her coworkers. He thought of calling Shari about his bones, but it was far too soon, and she would be dealing with freshly dead people, mourned people.

Instead, at home, Jules spread out the county map of the Marvel road and the sliver of private land that lay along its route, fifty narrow acres surrounded by the greater Absaroka-Beartooth Wilderness. The two oldest town sites near Blue Deer could not have been more different. While Doris's people were urban refugees, tradespeople and what passed for the professional class—the butcher, an innkeeper, a doctor, a consumptive university professor—from a variety of ethnic and religious backgrounds, Marvel was settled by Scots-Irish southerners, looking for gold a little late, fleeing the South after the Civil War. The two settlements did not socialize, but they did, eventually, fool around. There was some Whipple in Cavendish Clusker, and there might be some Clusker in Suzette; they certainly shared a devotion to ownership and a particular form of bantamweight aggression. And these links were important, because the people who founded Marvel owned the land collectively, and the original property compact stated that only descendants could own land unless all agreed to sell to some new individual, an impossibility when there were still dozens of difficult heirs involved. Whether you wanted to sell or you died without a direct descendant, your share would go to your cousins.

People traveled up the mountain for years, falling on their knees in front of Cavendish Clusker, who always hinted that he was the last one left. He drove down to the bars, claimed he wanted to sell, accepted gifts. He never sold, because of his dirty little secret: it wasn't his to sell. Peter, after weeks buried in Jules's property issues and now Cavendish's mess, must know that Suzette and Elaine were also heirs. How was that going to work, if Ivan was really interested? Elaine, who wanted to get rich subdividing Suzette's high-and-dry bumper property between the poor farm and Marvel, would want something beyond cash—trees, water—and she would drag everything out in her search for the best possible deal. Worse yet, Suzette and Elaine would have to *agree* with Cavendish and any other surviving Marvelites, and no one involved was agreeable.

Suzette's family, the Dittelers, was one of the few old families that managed to acquire land and hold on to it beyond the Marvel share; now Jules wondered if he could still find traces of Ivan's list of names on the surrounding slopes. He also wondered how much Suzette still owned of what was once a long thin empire, a rectangle of old claims that crossed the Yellowstone, climbed the hill to the poor farm and the empty land above it, and ended in Marvel. Or didn't really end—it crossed the saddle of the mountains and dropped down into the Coralberry Creek drainage on the far side, where Jules's least favorite family, the Bells, lived.

It was time to track down Marvel's feeble, attenuated survivors. At the Baird, he made coffee and called Olive, who annoyed him by not picking up. He moved on to Venus, who only wanted to talk about people's affairs and potential illegitimate children, and Phoebe Yellen, the genealogy fanatic of the Aches, who dumped so much information in a half hour that Jules couldn't remember his first notes by the time he scribbled the last one.

The inbred Marvel telomeres were terribly short: they died young, in unpleasant ways, and they weren't a lusty enough crew to last to the point when the kids might have six fingers. Jules got off the phone with Phoebe knowing the Defoes and the Merziks were definitely kaput. Moe, at the newspaper, cross-checked names against obituaries, and polished off a few elderly danglers: there'd been Cavendish's little brother Frog, who'd somehow electrocuted himself in his bathtub the previous August; an old man in San Jose named Lorne Berniers, from the Zucher family, taken out by a car as he crossed to the farmer's market; and an old female Choake at a Billings rest home who'd eaten the wrong nut the previous July. A brother-sister pair of Pinbennys in Wolf Point died of pneumonia within days of each other in September. The last Skinnock died of sepsis in October. The Mallows were the only blank from Peter's list, but he might be missing some strays, still panning for gold in the gnarlier reaches of the mountains.

Jules headed to the clerk and recorder's office in the courthouse, run by his friend Miranda, to check the plat and mining claims. His head was in a file drawer when someone said his name.

"Mr. Clement."

Jules recognized the soft voice, which sounded nothing like its owner looked. You'd draw Charlie with a zigzag pen line, but the voice was melted chocolate, or at least mud. "Checking up on me?" asked Charlie. "I'm just here to line out a title on a nice little parcel. But I would really love to take this opportunity to try to start over again. I want to apologize on behalf of my family."

Two things occurred to Jules. The first was the weirdly transparent falseness of the meeting, the sense of a movie voice talking in a dusty, mundane place. The second was that for most of the last decade, when someone gave him the skin-shrinking feeling that Charlie was giving him now, it was in police interviews, and he'd been in control.

He wasn't now. He could ask questions on Olive's behalf, but the childish part of him needed to feign disinterest.

Jules shut the drawer and said nothing, not even hello. Charlie plunged on, oblivious. "My brother was not well. He destroyed your family, destroyed my parents."

"But not you?"

Charlie looked surprised. There it was, the small test of a narcissist, along with the lack of worry lines: Charlie didn't think he was like other people, but he knew he couldn't say that out loud. He settled for pomposity: "One life to live. None of us knew he would do such a thing—"

"Despite knowing he was not well."

"Unhappy, yes, but we really had no idea. And we have no interest in forgiving him. He should have gotten the death penalty. It would have given some closure."

Charlie didn't need any such thing; Charlie didn't give a shit about anything but himself.

"I don't want that particular kind of closure," Jules said. Such a stupid word, anyway. He never dared use it when he was deputy or sheriff. It never, even once, felt right.

"I'm sure your feelings are complicated," said Charlie Bell.

Jules thought they were remarkably simple: he'd wanted Patrick dead since he was thirteen years old. But he did not believe in the death penalty, and he did not like people who didn't have the imagination to understand that as a cop he might have considered the matter at some length. His other thoughts: if this man was a better man, a kinder brother from a kinder family, Jules might be having a beer with Ansel tonight. They might be talking about Tommy, or food, or politics. They might be floating down the river together this weekend.

Jules gave up on the errand—he wasn't going to check on what sections the Bells owned with Charlie standing behind him—and bolted, but Charlie followed him, not bothering to keep his place in line. "Please," he said. "Let's talk."

"No," said Jules.

"Please," said Charlie.

The sense that all the good-looking features didn't quite go together was just as strong as the feeling that the constant smile had nothing to do with emotion. How damaged were you if your brother murdered someone? Did Charlie seem not quite human because he felt a need to keep normal stray tics and emotions invisible, or at least tamped down? Jules tried imagining him in any relaxed moment, eating, making love. It didn't work. Fucking, yes, or eating for fuel.

Play dumb, he thought. "Were you there that day?"

"When they arrested Patrick? Yeah. I took his gun away before the police arrived. I didn't want to have my parents see him shot like a rabid dog."

"You just happened to be there, or you were there to meet him?"

"My parents were worried. They needed to see me."

"Because they guessed Patrick was coming to kill his wife?"

"Yes."

"Who died the next day. Or was it that night?"

A shudder over Charlie's face. It was the strangest thing, like a flutter under the skin. "Yes."

"How?

"She killed herself."

Jules waited. "She hung herself," said Charlie. "In the barn."

"Why would she do that?"

"No clue. Horrible thing. She was a troubled woman. My poor mother, finding her."

"And why would Patrick want to kill her?"

"He thought she was sleeping around."

Jules watched Charlie's face and tried to identify what was wrong. The eyes?

"Was she?"

This smile was genuine, flitting right by. "You want me to speak ill of the dead? Admit that she was a piece of trash, a tasty hot tomato? I was raised right. I wouldn't have fucked up like that."

Jules would, someday, beat this man's face in. "'Like that.' Like falling in love? Or do you mean fuck up like killing a cop? Only one killer in your family?"

Jules walked away. But Charlie hurried to keep up with him, immune to insults. "I'm here now because my wife died last fall, and I'm trying to sort things out for my parents. Living wills, powers of attorney, trying to give them some freedom but keep them from giving their money to every grifter with a sob story. I work my way through problems, one after another."

Jules said, "Ah," rather than, "I'm sorry," and tried to feel a qualm. Maybe Charlie was just a blowhard, a widower struggling with business issues and aging parents, blathering on about his sainted mother, who'd loved him despite his troublesome high school years and his difficult wife, despite Patrick's sins and her husband's weakness.

Everything, Jules noticed, was someone else's fault.

"Hey, I have to ask for your professional opinion," said Charlie. "I know Elaine's got you working on a little something—"

"I'll get to it," said Jules, hating himself.

"But I have something, too. I think I'm being stalked."

This surprised Jules, and it pleased him: paranoia, another chink in the armor. He made a show of arranging the mess in the back of the truck. "You have enemies, business issues?"

"Nothing! Some stress over my wife's estate—distant cousins she never saw and never liked, but you know how that goes."

He didn't seem to notice that Jules didn't seem to be fascinated. "No," said Charlie. "I think it's something weird and sexual. This girl who's helping Suzette—I know I've seen her before, and I can remember one party last summer for sure. But I think I'm missing something bigger."

Jules stared at him, confounded by the idea that a man like Charlie would think he could be a stalking victim. "Sadie Winton? She lives in town. It's not a big town."

"But I swear she's been everywhere I go since last summer. I'd like to figure out why."

Jules might have underestimated the man's narcissism. "She waitresses half the parties in the county," he said. "For money. People who really live here—everyone does everything."

"But I mean, what's her story?" said Charlie.

"Ask her," said Jules, getting in the truck. "She'll be spending a lot of time with Suzette."

"Exactly my point," said Charlie. "I don't like the way she looks."

No straight male was likely to complain about Sadie Winton's appearance. "You mean the way she looks at you?"

Confusion, one of the first honest expressions Jules saw on Charlie's careful face. "No. Maybe she worked for my father-in-law, a nurse or something. I'm a very instinctual person and I just have a bad feeling."

He probably had them all the time; predictable that he'd link them to his father-in-law. What did Harvey say about that death? "How do I know you're not stalking her?" asked Jules.

Charlie's face shifted again, sliding and calculating. Charlie, it occurred to Jules, didn't understand that he wasn't believable. Charlie wasn't as smart as he thought he was.

Jules grinned. He turned the key in the ignition. "If you could let your parents know that I need to talk to them, I'd appreciate it. My mother wants some answers, and I'm trying to help."

"Oh no," Charlie said. "No, no, no. My father's been ill for decades, and now my mother is losing her marbles."

Such a great phrase; it made Jules think again of his friend Larry, who'd buried his marbles all over the county, and who was forever linked to the Bells in his mind. "Charlie, I was a cop. I'm used to talking to people about difficult things."

"No," said Charlie. "They can't be bothered. Too much pain."

"I'll tell you about fucking pain," said Jules.

Suddenly the hate was out there, red meat on a plate. Charlie seemed to change shape. That anger—Jules looked down at the crowbar behind his seat after Charlie marched off and wondered what it would feel like to swing. Just imagining it gave him a little release.

He drove around for a bit, decompressing. Charlie Bell, as a known quantity, lost some of his juju. He was a creep, a neurotic, a user. Jules needed to see if any of his money was real. Jules needed to find out the story of the multiple inheritances.

Burt's big truck was parked badly on Main Street again, just down from the Longhorn. It was one of the few bars in town Jules never entered; politics in the Longhorn were never laissez-faire. Burt probably used the back room for poker and attended Timothy McVeigh support group meetings every other Monday night.

Jules photographed the truck. He celebrated Burt's public morning drinking by picking up some of the new experimental empanadas at Rosaria, whose new dishwasher was Argentinean. The empanadas made him happy, and he brought one home for Caroline, who was lying in bed, reading files and scribbling into a notebook. Caroline believed in lists. She said that Tommy was with Olive, off to the museum in Bozeman to see dinosaur skeletons.

"Tommy doesn't know what a museum is. Or a dinosaur," said Jules.

"This doesn't bother me."

They eyed each other. Jules's intention of telling Caroline about the library research and the weirdness of Charlie Bell gave way to thoughts of ridding her of her chaste nightgown. He watched her read his mind and weigh this effort, however pleasant, against time spent sleeping or generally having no one fuck with her, as it were. "I'll clean the house," he said.

"Deal," said Caroline.

Twice in twelve hours; it was like the old days. They fell back asleep for a few minutes, and afterward he told her about his talk with Charlie, about Charlie slagging his old sister-in-law, his parents' mental abilities, Sadie's looks. Caroline wandered into the garden with her cold empanada, in a sunny mood—a morning off, guilt-free—and Jules smoked a joint, pulled out the broom, and kicked in. He dusted, sprayed, mopped. He found books and money and dried orange peels, forgotten phone messages and unpaid bills. He read magazines that he'd left in a pile before Tommy was born. He turned the stereo on loud, started a load of laundry, scrubbed the bathroom. He flipped the mattress and changed the sheets. He imagined packing all their belongings for the move into the new house and decided not to think about it quite yet. He saw every ding they'd have to fix to sell this house and his mind veered off again to more approachable problems, such as the sale price.

But he always came back to ways of making Charlie Bell disappear. Jules would expose him as a scam artist, a real estate con man, a thief. Something, someday.

He was wrestling with the dishwasher silverware tray and running the disposal when Ed's legs appeared. Jules screamed.

"You can't hear a thing, can you?" howled Ed. "Where's Caro? She's not picking up."

"She's out in back. Olive has Tommy."

Ed squinted at him; Jules stared back, with a dawning unease. "Why the house call?"

"Are you fucked up?" Ed reached for a coffee cup, emptied the coffeepot, opened the refrigerator, and emptied a cream carton as well.

Jules was a little stoned, but nothing out of the ordinary. He put detergent in the dispenser, shut the door, punched normal. "What's going on?"

"There's a problem in Gardiner. We were going this afternoon anyway, and she's the park liaison, and Burt has Harvey working on other cases. It won't take long. Nice drive."

Caroline was in the doorway. "We've got a little mayhem on our southern border," said Ed. "Nondangerous but it shouldn't wait."

"I have to finish the priest."

"Burt left a note saying he was doing it, after all."

She gaped. "Why on earth?"

"No idea. Changed his tiny little mind."

She couldn't bear it. She would kill the fucker; she would end him. "Then I have to finish the report and get rid of Burt."

"That's true," said Ed. "But I get the sense that this issue in the park is a big deal, not just people behaving badly, and involves Blue Deer people. And everyone else is busy."

"Jules saw a bunch of people leaving Burt's house yesterday, early. Including Tamyra."

"Why the hell were you watching Burt's house?"

"Wife," said Jules.

"Well, go watch it some more. Caro, the priest will stay dead. Let's go to Gardiner."

The passenger side of Ed's patrol car glowed with Caroline's problematic mood, and when Ed agreed to drive her by Dinak's house, he put the locks down in the car, which was quite funny. A rabbit was sitting on the sidewalk, digesting a first flush of new grass after the nighttime rain, but no Burt. Ed did not try to chat for the first few minutes. He let Caroline get bored with her anger, a tactic he'd refined over a half dozen children and many patrol partners.

Ten miles out of town Ed slid the file on Caroline's lap, knowing she wouldn't open it immediately, and he prepared some lines for when she did, statistics about drinking in Russia, or the article he'd just read about the Brighton Beach–Odessa mob.

Instead, file still unopened, Caroline said, "Tell me what happened to Patrick Bell's wife."

She watched Ed's fingers flex on the wheel. "Why don't we admire nature and talk about these other people or talk about our children."

Nature at this point was the Winnebago going forty-five in front of them. Ed put on the lights and blazed by at ninety. "We can do that on the way back," said Caroline.

Silence for miles. Her mind batted back and forth between the beauty of the here and now—the blue of the sky, pelicans as high as the mountains, the glitter of the river—and what she imagined happened on a road and in a yard close to here, twenty-six years earlier. Blood in the dirt. She jumped when Ed spoke.

"First of all, what is the point to talking about it? More pain?"

"It's not your pain, Ed."

"Says fucking who?"

"Was she the girl Charlie attacked?"

Ed tapped the wheel; his face worked. "The high school attack happened in my first week on the job. Iris Talouse was a sweet and beautiful and unlucky girl who moved into a foster home here maybe in 1967, when she was sixteen. She'd been to a dozen other schools, but she wanted to get a high school degree, and then a teaching degree. And two of the boys she met when she started at Absaroka High were the Bell boys, and they both fell in love with her. In 1968, Charlie—a minor, you should know this—tried to rape her in the school basement, and when Patrick intervened, Charlie beat Patrick badly enough to hospitalize him. But it gave Iris a chance to go for help. That night, Francis Bell broke his back, and though he wouldn't admit what really happened, and we couldn't prove Charlie caused this 'accident,' he never spent another night in the family home. He was sent off to some military-slash-reform school in the East and I bet he'd only been back to town a handful of times until this bunking down with Elaine Selway."

Caroline deigned to open the folder on her lap, but it was a distraction. "You liked Iris?"

"Very much. Everyone who met her loved her. Just not in the right way."

Was that a warble in his voice? Caroline looked away. "So not a bad person, not driving her husband nuts. This morning, when Jules talked to him, Charlie said that she was screwing around."

"Yeah, well. 'Charlie said' is a start."

"Who else gave that motive?"

"No one I can recall but Charlie."

"But how would he know?"

"Good question," said Ed.

They drove past more big gates with tiny ranches, tiny people with big heads. "What was it like when you got to the Bells' house, when you saw Patrick?"

"Will you stop talking about it if I answer?"

"Yes."

They both knew she lied. "You need to understand I was in some sort of altered state. Ansel dead in the dirt—I wanted to go to him because I didn't believe it, and my head was roaring. I wanted to kill, but I got there, and everyone was fucking howling. Charlie kicking his brother—Charlie's big into stomping—mother screaming, Francis dragging himself down from the house to try to protect Patrick from his brother. It turned into a matter of stopping what was happening there, trying to hear what people were saying, trying to understand."

"What were the parents saying to you?"

"A variety of things," said Ed. "Do your reading."

"I have. They mostly say they were there, but at least once they say it was already happening when they got back from shopping." She pulled out a chocolate bar and gave him half. "Tell me what you really think."

"I think that the parents didn't see everything in that yard or understand what led up to it. I think that Charlie must have made Patrick believe that he'd fucked his wife. I mean, I still don't understand it, but it's all I can imagine. Patrick loved that girl, and she loved him. Or . . . I don't know. No one knows why he did it, and Charlie made sure we never would."

"What do you mean?"

"Patrick's eyeball swelled out of the socket. I mean, they lifted a piece of skull out. By the time he could talk, he wouldn't."

"But he can talk now?"

"Yes. I don't know if it's a full recovery. More like he retrained his brain." He slowed for a bicyclist. "I visit him. But he's not going to talk about that day. He won't answer Jules's questions."

She was stunned. "You visit Patrick Bell? The man who killed your friend?"

"A couple of times a year. Sometimes I drive his parents up. A few friends visit, too."

Patrick's friends—a new concept. "Why on earth would you put yourself through this?"

"I'm walking the walk," said Ed. "Some part of me isn't sure."

Ed, believing in the miraculous? She pulled back. "You didn't charge Charlie for beating Patrick?"

"I was just glad no one was charging us."

Caroline studied Ed's face, the pouched eyes, the sloppy shave job. "So, again—if Patrick couldn't talk, who told you what he meant to do? Who told you Patrick was coming to kill his wife?"

"Charlie Bell."

"Didn't you want to dig deeper?"

"I wasn't in charge. And it was all very clear-cut. Ansel told us who he was pulling over, and Ansel died, and we arrived to this shitshow, Patrick supposedly having arrived and admitted the crime and why. There was the truck, the gun . . ."

"Prints on the gun?

"Smeared. Both brothers. Charlie was holding it when we arrived—he threw it down."

A long pause, long enough for Ed to hope that they could start to talk about Russians. They passed a pull-over, a state trooper and an old Ford sedan. Caroline knew and despised the trooper; he did not pull over Mercedes or Cadillacs, and he always searched the car. "So where did it happen? I skimmed the first few files, but I thought I saw mile marker seventeen."

"On the old east side road," he said. "This stretch of 89 wasn't finished until the eighties."

She looked across the valley. "Cut over and take me by?"

"Jesus fucking Christ," said Ed.

"We're still missing a ton of files."

"I'll take you by that spot on the way back," said Ed.

"Thank you," said Caroline, picking up the Gardiner file.

"WEIRDNESS IN GARDINER" was a wide topic. Absaroka County was almost a hundred miles from north to south. Gardiner, with a winter population of five hundred, was patrolled by a deputy named Tina who also made the trek through Yellowstone to Cooke City and Silver Gate. She was out for spinal surgery after getting rear-ended by wildlife gawkers. Gardiner's problems usually involved alcohol or the park. In the summer, most of the press went to brucellosis-carrying bison, toothy grizzlies and wolves, potentially disastrous magma, but the norm was humans behaving poorly and in an altered state, whether tourists or park employees or the carney types and Eastern Bloc students who worked as indentured servants for the concessionaire. Apocalyptic Baptists, fake Native Americans, poachers; the arrogant, the misinformed, the flat-out fucking crazy. Texans and Floridians were a problem; wealthy people were a problem. People who thought they should be able to control their environment were always on the wrong vacation.

Ed and Caroline, who'd planned a general strategy meeting, were now driving because of two incidents, one at a Gardiner hotel and one at Lazuli Pool, a thermal feature near West Thumb in Yellowstone Park. They had no jurisdiction in the park—this was a courtesy call, because the park rangers thought there was a link to Blue Deer.

"Incidents" didn't explain enough to Caroline to justify the 150-mile round trip. "Just take it as a change of scenery," said Ed. "Tina said 'genuinely weird' and 'troubling objects.' I couldn't get a thing straight on the phone."

They got it as soon as they walked into the Yellow River Motel: a man from Maryland had been found in a second-floor room, handcuffed and gagged in a chair, with his penis tied to a forty-pound barbell with a taut string. He said nothing to explain this situation to the owner of the hotel, or to the staff at the urgent care clinic.

Caroline perked up.

The barbell-penis man was long gone; he'd fled the clinic and checked out of the motel. Security camera footage showed the man—a big, fit thirty something—entering the lobby from the bar door with a thin dark-haired woman in a shift dress and kitten heels. Her head was down and the man—strolling along with his arm around her shoulders—blocked any other details. The room was a mess—spilled champagne, cigarettes and an empty pizza box, stained silk ribbons—and Ed groused and avoided looking at the blood and other bodily effluvia on the chair while Caroline dusted. There was no footage of the woman leaving, which was mysterious until Caroline looked down from the room's balcony and saw that it was a short hop to the air-conditioning unit.

The bartender said the man from Maryland was pushy,

but when the bartender checked in the woman said she was fine. Her two friends, one with a bleeding hand, played darts. Each of them drank three vodkas; everyone was dark-haired and well-behaved and "okay-looking."

And Russian, but the only problem, as far as the bar was concerned, came in the morning when the cleaner found a bloody wad of tissues in a trash can, wrapped around a finger that seemed torn off.

Caroline iced and bagged the finger and put it into a cooler. They headed south toward Yellowstone Lake. It was raining, the kind of localized weather that made camping fun. The park was a little less crowded than it would have been even a week earlier—families were back home for school shopping—but the roads were still full and slow in the soft rain, people gawking at bison and a distant speck that was a grizzly feeding on an aged elk. Caroline rolled the windows down and Ed started sneezing.

The morning call to the rangers, reporting a sick man near Lazuli Pool, came from a Baird Hotel cook, who'd visited Lazuli the evening before at dusk, when it was almost dark and rain was beginning. He'd recognized a group from the hotel, three men and a woman. One of the men, who the cook knew as Mike or Mika, was a guest who'd often raided the hotel refrigerators. But tonight Mika was in a wheelchair and he looked almost dead.

"Truly almost dead," said the ranger to Ed. "Slumped in the chair, barely breathing. The more the cook thought of it, the more he wasn't sure the guy was breathing at all. But it was foggy and rainy, like it is now. And almost dark, and the pool was steaming. Not ideal witness conditions."

Caroline didn't believe ideal witness conditions existed.

People saw what they wanted to see. "Did he try to talk to Mika?"

"He was going to but he couldn't find them again for a bit. It's a big area, and they were on the far walkway. Steam, rain—you get these big plumes. He looked for them in the parking lot, and he saw the people loading the chair, but he only counted two men with the woman."

They were walking around a barricade toward the pool. It was a darker blue than Caroline remembered, and she wondered if it seemed light aqua only on sunny days. The ranger said they'd tracked down another camper who'd been there at the same time, videotaping.

"Maybe Mika was lying down in the back," said Caroline. She was trying to think of a polite way to say *why are we here*, dealing with vague witnesses and guesses. "No license plates?"

"No. A white van, or maybe light gray. And yeah, lots of possible explanations, but then Babich came down and found this stuff in the underbrush, along with this pouch."

The ranger named Crowley opened a tarp and stepped back. They stared down at a wool tartan blanket and dirty gauze, all of it soaked in blood, so much blood it was still glistening and liquid. The ranger named Babich asked if anyone could live after losing that much. Caroline didn't know. She reached out tentatively for the dirty black bag—more fingers?—and pulled out an empty hypodermic, a glove, a box of Baird matches, a small medal or amulet showing a flame, and her own name and address written on the back of a hotel postcard in an odd, blocky hand.

The camper with the video camera showed up and they all squinted at the tiny screen. In the foreground, a steaming turquoise pool and some shlumpy people. In the background, moving along another pathway to another water feature, a strange, quick parade: a woman with regal posture and a blue headscarf pushing a wheelchair, followed by three men in baseball caps and black coats. The figures were tiny—the woman turned her head from side to side, but it was impossible to make out her features in the blurred video. What struck Caroline was a sense of sixties Technicolor: the blue pool below the dated but stylish pink raincoat, the red of the man's shoes in the wheelchair, the dark blot of the blanket, the small white face against the green trees.

The camera swiveled: there'd been some excitement, a crashing sound in the woods, and everyone assumed a bear was nearby. "That's why I was aiming that way," said the man with the camera. "They were just standing there peacefully, even though it was raining. The guy looked like he'd fallen asleep and they didn't want to bother him. Very sad—she bent over him and whispered in his ear. You just knew that it was his last time in the park."

"And then?"

"I was dealing with my kids. When I looked back, they were gone."

"Could he have walked? Could he have crawled into the woods?" asked Ed.

"We'll keep looking," said Crowley. "We'll charge them for littering and damaging the feature. Someone was stupid enough to leave the walkway over by that pot, and it's very fragile. People somehow don't seem to understand it's all active. And it looks like they tossed more bandages in there and managed to break the crust a bit."

They followed Crowley along the walkways around the steaming landscape. A flash of color—people littering, even here. Another ranger crouched on a mobile balsa-wood platform to retrieve the trash, trying to spread his weight. Caroline could see a bit of curled, bloody bandage and wondered how hot these pools were, if the bandages would melt, if plastics turned into globules. She walked closer while Crowley explained something about the mineral content to Ed. A flash of red bobbed up; it disappeared, but when Caroline circled back it was on the surface again. The rangers and Ed were behind her now, and they all stared into the steaming water. Bahamas blue. Bermuda blue? "The color's changed, a bit, because of all the shit people throw in. Coins and trash and sticks and who knows."

But surely nothing that red. "That still seems to be a solid object," said Caroline, pointing.

"Huh," said the ranger. "Even the coins dissolve."

The ranger edged closer. The shape was rising, turning gently, white then red. Caroline gradually understood the object was familiar because the object was familiar: a red sneaker, upside down, then rolling on its side, now upright, now flipping again.

"It's a Keds high top," said Caroline. Like the ones on top of Tommy's shabby little dresser. And who else was wearing a pair, most recently? The wet Russians, clutching inner tubes on the side of the highway.

The mood began to change.

The ranger dipped the long handled net. Caroline was right. The shoe steamed, and when the ranger dropped it onto the boardwalk a kind of a gel flowed out in lumps.

Everyone lost it, further polluting the landscape.

YOU MIGHT THINK the discovery of dissolved human remains would change the conversation for at least a day, but

Caroline remembered halfway back to town, and made Ed follow the old curvy road north. The spot where Ansel Clement died was just at the dip of Nesbit Creek. In the silence after they pulled over, the hot car ticking, Ed said stuff like "The trees seem taller," but Caroline took her time. Did Ansel wait with his lights on the right? Or did he follow, and the truck pulled over in the dip? Blocked the road, and Patrick braked. How risky had it been?

Horribly so, in the end.

"The owner heard the shots and a car taking off and came out and sat with him," said Ed. "I mean, he was gone, but she sat with him while her husband ran in to the phone, until we came."

They walked back to the car. Hot smell of pine and spruce, just a trickle of water in the creek bottom, but you could hear someone's irrigation pivot turning. "Where do the Bells live?"

"About ten miles up, on Coralberry Creek. Jules never talked about getting in trouble for going there when he was a kid?"

"No." Caroline wanted to ask, but she wasn't going to admit how little Jules would say about any of it. "Isn't that the back road to Marvel? Let's drive up."

"No," said Ed, climbing back into the car and slamming the door.

12 *Marvelites*

THE DAY, SO UP AND DOWN, SKEWED SIDEWAYS WHEN Tommy and Olive returned. She'd been shaken down—by a child who couldn't speak a word—for a small dinosaur and a furry Siberian tiger hand puppet at the museum store. Tommy, of course, was too young to have any concept of the museum, gifts, or the difference between an animal and a rocket.

"Ready to talk?" asked Jules.

"I've been ready for decades," said Olive. She opened the refrigerator, but she found only a lump of cheddar. "What have you found out?"

"Tell me why now."

"I've been thinking about him," Olive said, which wasn't an answer. "I haven't been able to sleep through the night for weeks, because I dream he's in bed with me, and I wake up and he's gone again. It's like it was when he was first dead. Don't you wonder what happened?"

Not if Jules could help it. Death may have been instantaneous, but the moments before—Ansel's fear, pain, or despair—didn't bear thought. The day's silky feeling of well-being disappeared. "Is this because of your heart attack? The anniversary?"

She shrugged. "Maybe. Does it matter? Have you gotten far?"

"No," he said, pretending to eat Tommy's face with the puppet. "The files are still landing. Did you know Patrick's wife killed herself?"

"I gathered, at some point, that she was dead," said Olive. "Poor little girl. Haven't you noticed that no one tells you anything about all of this, still? We live here, they live here, people know both families, and no one mentions seeing Lucia grocery shopping. They think it's better to avoid. That son of hers, the one she has left—Ansel said he was the one true bad kid he'd ever met."

True bad. "People are talking now because I'm asking. Did you know Charlie Bell is seeing Suzette Whipple's daughter, that he moved in next door to us? You really got this shitshow going because of a dream, Mom?"

Olive pulled some laundry off a chair and sat down, heavy and tired.

"No," she said slowly. "No. I wasn't honest. I saw the brother. He came into the hospital when his wife died, maybe last fall. That was the first thing. He didn't want to see her body, didn't want to identify her. He wanted someone to take a Polaroid—he actually brought in a camera. It was so inhuman—everyone wants to see the people they love. He didn't even look at my name tag. And I started hating him, and I put it on you. Which is what parents do, Jules."

She smiled at her own faint joke and he stared at her, sensing more. "A year later?"

"A couple of months ago, I mentioned it to a friend at work, and she'd heard that he was not so nice, and it all dug into my brain."

"Not nice, how?" he said sarcastically. "Ed says the dude has devil eyes."

"Something about his wife's death. Something that wasn't right."

"Should Caroline be talking to your friend?"

"I don't think so," said Olive, uncomfortable now. "Let me see what I can find out."

He no longer felt sarcastic; if a doctor or a nurse or a lab worker felt any doubt, they usually had reason. "Help me out with a couple of things. What do you know about Donald Whipple?"

"Only that he took off, and that's a good thing."

"Dead?"

"If he were alive, he'd still be making Suzette's life miserable. The police told her he was a suicide, which didn't sound like him, but it was good enough for her. What's your other question?"

"Didn't you have a friend in school, a Marvel person, who was a Mallow? Didn't Dad tell me some story about you getting lost with her on that road, all the way back in grade school?"

Olive stopped smiling. "What are you talking about?"

"I'm trying to track down the last few Marvel families. And getting nowhere with Mallows."

"That's because the name is Mellow," said Olive. "I was friends with Lucia Mellow when we were kids."

"Oh," he said. "Shit. Well, do you know if she's alive?"

Olive's happy mood was gone. "You don't understand, do you? She married Francis Bell."

Charlie Bell was a Marvel heir, just like his partner, Elaine.

*

WHEN CAROLINE BLEW into the house, she was desperate to tell Jules about melted men in wheelchairs, and when the phone rang, Jules was too overwhelmed by the welter of the story—sneakers and fingers ("Remember that's in the cooler, Ed") and barbells tied to balls—to answer.

Ed, who'd followed Caroline inside, picked the phone up and they gradually noticed that he wasn't saying much. He handed the receiver to Caroline, who walked outside.

"What's happening?" asked Jules.

"It's about the old guy."

An inner quiver from Jules as Ed opened the refrigerator door, just like Olive, and pushed containers around. But what old guy? What was supposed to compete with finding a melted Russian?

"Bernard Dinak. Shari is changing the cause of death."

"To what? From accidental to suicide?"

Ed opened a container, seemed satisfied, and put it in the microwave. "Murder. A blow on the back of his head."

They watched the seconds count down. "Not a postmortem injury?" asked Jules.

"No." Ed found a fork.

Through the window, Jules watched Caroline windmill an arm as she talked on the phone.

JULES, IN HIS past life, was sweetly indiscriminate: he'd felt a great deal of affection for many women and stayed friends with most. In Blue Deer, the echoes of his youth were unavoidable. Caroline could survey the crowd at a wedding or a funeral or the rodeo—events that brought people back to town—and pick out a fond look at fifty feet. Jules avoided high school reunions.

Caroline therefore disliked Shari by default. Her

dislike was also behavioral—she hated the way Shari said *hallooooooo* when she answered Jules's calls but not hers, or Grace's, or any other cop's—but she'd begun to understand that Shari wasn't really a happy person. She'd probably just been beaten into pretending by her parents.

"Any chance I heard wrong about Mr. Dinak?" asked Caroline.

"Nope," said Shari, all business.

"He hit his head hard, thought fuck it, I'm falling down all the time, I may as well put on a bra and hang myself?"

"No. I don't think he could have stood on a chair after that hit. He would have been dead in a couple of hours if someone didn't cut off his air first. I don't know yet if the damage to his throat was all from the noose. Kind of hard given the disarticulation."

Caroline could see Jules watching her through the kitchen window. The dog followed her as she paced. "Any other sign of force?"

"He'd been beaten around the torso, too, probably kicked. I started on the head, but I'm working on it."

"The knot—is it suspicious?"

"Nothing I would have looked at twice before the X-ray. Pretty professional for a priest, but not if he'd been in the service."

Gideon learned Dinak briefly served stateside as a chaplain during the Vietnam War—did they teach them knots? But it was irrelevant. This wasn't suicide.

"I think he was still breathing when someone strung him up, but his brain was already hemorrhaging. I explained all this in a message to your fearless leader, but maybe he's planning to break it to you gently. Or, you know, keep the glory for himself."

"No other explanation?"

"Nothing but murder," said Shari. "We'll get Rivers in for a second opinion, but I think one serious blow to the back of the head, first, before the beating, and certainly before the death. Very deliberate."

Murder. Not easy to do, not easy to have done to you, not easy to understand months later. Shari said one blow, a surprised victim, but someone still needed to slide the noose around the stunned head, add the pajamas and bra, winch the body up, watch the physiological jig.

"I mean, it's not like I started the examination looking for trouble," said Shari. "I started it hoping I wouldn't have to look at him long at all."

Shari, a tall blonde with stork legs, approached the autopsy table at a tangent like a wading bird, peering down at horrors. Jules said she'd thrown up in her first anatomy class; she'd stayed only because she was in love with a classmate. She aspired to become an osteologist rather than someone who dealt with soft tissue.

"When?"

"Jesus, I don't know. I'll guess November or December. We could bring in an expert on the insect samples, but it'll take a while, and it'll cost. Mr. Dinak was nailed by something rounded, with a flat bottom."

"A mallet?"

"More like a wine bottle or pitcher, a big pestle. Or a bowling pin."

"Defensive injuries?" asked Caroline.

Shari sighed and Caroline listened to paper rustle. "No, though a scratch wouldn't be that easy to find at this point. He was a healthy guy for a fifty-something-year-old—"

"He was sixty-three," said Caroline.

"Really? Wow, good teeth." A pause. "Burt didn't tell you any of this?"

"Just a memo saying that he's taking the case."

"Huh."

"It's okay," said Caroline. She was trying to make herself feel this way.

"But also, hang on—"

Caroline started back inside as Shari rattled more paper. "Is this going to be good or bad?"

"It's about Jules's piece of skull. It's from the upper left parietal, and I'm guessing older than one hundred, probably 1870s."

Caroline was silent. "And then there's the tibia," said Shari. "That one's been underground until recently, and it's not the same body."

"Let me get him."

Ed was at the table, eating Tommy's leftover *risi e bisi*. Caroline handed Jules the phone with no explanation, and after he'd listened for a moment, he said, "You're joking."

"I don't think so," said Shari. "Maybe earlier, but not much after 1870. This is just fascinating to find at your potter's field. Maybe a reburial? Nothing else makes sense, does it? The skull doesn't look Native American. You don't want to pay for DNA testing, do you? I don't think the bone was in direct contact with soil, at least immediately, so that's an added wrinkle, though you know the Plains tribes were using scaffolding and trees until at least 1900 and maybe the body was wrapped well. These days I mostly see recent, obvious stuff, so I'm out of practice. If the poor farm dig has more weirdness like this, give me a job. I'm sick of sticky bodies."

Shari's mind was a run-on sentence. After some

moments of exhausted silence on Jules's end, she said, "That tibia—that one's maybe 1940. Not old at all. Tall, substantial, probably male."

Jules was still back on "reburial." He'd gone dizzy from all the Shari qualifiers and the confusion of maps and dates in his mind's eye. Because the only early European burials should be in Marvel, or down the valley, in the gold-mining ravines of Rome—a very long trip down the river for a skull that did not look polished—or in Doris. But Doris's cemetery lay in the part of town that washed away in 1917.

"There's not going to be a dig," he said. "I'm just surveying."

"Really? I heard a rumor you'll need to move all of them, one of your huff-and-puffs talking to ours. Anyway, I feel strongly about the skull fragment, but it's kinda early, huh? I mean, obviously we need to consult the tribes, but how many other people were even out here back then?"

One too many, thought Jules, turning off the phone, watching the scene in the kitchen through the window. Caroline was yelling at Ed, whose arms were out, palms open. She spun around and looked for keys, looked for shoes, met Jules's eyes, and sat back down.

"Hey, Ed—you tell her about Dinak extorting the kid?" asked Jules.

"Ah, no," said Ed, walking out the door. "Not yet."

"What kid?" asked Caroline, following him.

They were gone by the time Jules remembered he wanted to ask about Iris Bell.

AT THE STATION, Caroline packed up body parts, peered at Burt's note—*Fair, I'm taking the priest case*—and flipped through the mess on Burt's desk. Napkins, a pizza box, six beer cans, and a soda with a dozen drowned cigarette butts. More than one person lounged around here, late.

Not a glimpse of the man today.

"Has anyone messed with the Dinak house?"

"Burt didn't go inside yesterday, but it looks like he went back. I taped the door when I heard this afternoon," said Harvey.

"What was the last thing that he worked on, do you think? The Bucket mess?"

"I guess," said Grace. "I called his wife. She hasn't seen him, doesn't want to see him, and was filled with hope that her children are fatherless."

Caroline stared into space.

"By the way, Cavendish called again. He thinks he shot two people last night."

"He wouldn't know."

"He said the moon was out and he saw outlines, and two fell."

This was horrible. Caroline should have arrested Cavendish, even if she couldn't hold him.

Grace was watching her. "But then they got up and ran." She started to laugh.

They were all becoming awful people.

CAVENDISH CLUSKER COULD wait. Caroline picked up a kit before she drove to Bernie Dinak's house, cut the tape, and let herself in. She pulled on her gloves, opened both doors, and looked around the garage while the place aired. Neatly arranged screws and measuring tapes, light bulbs and batteries, Christmas decorations.

In the living room, crocheted throw pillows, one

embroidered with the words *He Saves*. In the kitchen, innocuous white dishes and very little cooking equipment. In the refrigerator, Slimfast and withered carrots and oranges, tonic water, cocktail cherries, and olives. In the closets, golf clubs, a bowling ball, an incongruous swim ring.

But upstairs was a pleasure palace: chunky whiskey glasses with a crystal decanter, high-end booze, a demure oil painting of a Victorian nude, a silk robe hanging on the end of a four-poster with good sheets. Bernie Dinak was a clotheshorse from a certain place and time—Hawaiian shirts, concha beads at the bottom of a drawer, a powder-blue cardigan. Old-fashioned swinger stuff, including an actual leisure suit. Nothing like the archaic brassiere Bernie was found wearing or the clothing visible in the torso photos. He'd kept a priest's collar and a robe, and Caroline noted that they hung in the center of the closet, the closest thing to your hand when you opened the door.

The sparse kitchen and that lavish bar. The Jesus art for an audience in the sitting area, goose down and cashmere for Bernie where he really lived.

Caroline's sense of the downstairs as a waiting room, a disguise, increased. In the corner of the living room, she found many pens but no notebooks, no paper. The trash can was empty, as was Bernie's wallet beyond a driver's license, a ten-dollar bill, and two credit cards. Two wooden file drawers on the desk, with real locks, were empty but for a camera bag and a single file with Dinak's birth certificate and social security information, his investiture and small 401k, medical insurance and bills, utilities and mortgage information.

Before, the spare nature of the house spoke to a suicide's intent. Now it was a raid, or a motive. She needed to find out who'd asked Venus to check on Bernie Dinak. She needed to look for anything that might identify the women in the photos. And where was the camera?

Caroline sat in Dinak's kitchen and read Gideon's and Shari's reports. Shari pointed out that no one could have caught the nonsuicidal nature of things until the postmortem, given the degree of decomposition. Because of the way the rope moved up on the neck, she guessed the noose was placed around Bernie's neck and the body hoisted up, pulley-style, through the wide transom above the sturdy fir doorframe separating the dining and living room. The chair was still off to one side, next to the funky spots where the man's bladder gave way and parts of him landed. One person could have done this. Anyone with medium strength and enough anger could have brained the man and hoisted him into the air, let him twitch and twirl.

Caroline photographed a small scuff mark on the chair seat and a scrape on the transom. She felt ill—the house was hot, the smell of Bernie lingered. Back in the kitchen, she hurried to the faucet and let the water run over her face. As she gradually lost the feeling that she was going to vomit, her eyes focused on a gray plastic comb tilted behind the sink, the kind with a wide handle. Had Gideon missed this? She left it where it was and looked around the room, thinking of other places worth dusting, and she concentrated on the pious sitting area. The October St. Anne's calendar meant Dinak was either faithful or cheap, and either he'd died in October, or he was slow to turn the page. This was the wall the women were posed against.

Doctor and rehab appointments were dotted throughout the year, and otherwise the only Xs were on Mondays and Thursdays.

From the armchair, near old double windows on the south side of the house, she could see mountains. She studied Dinak's ordination portrait, the petulant, meaty face, and a photo of him decades later, shaking hands with some white-robed higher-up. All that was left to his looks was the sulk. A token bookshelf with bestsellers and self-help titles, a blue-flowered tea set, the wicker-covered box of tissues, an old-fashioned fainting couch—it was all a little like a shrink's office for housewives in 1950. A cookie tin (very old shortbread), a candy box (mints), a decanter of brown liquor that she didn't feel up to smelling. Who came to talk to Dinak in this corner, besides the torsos in his photo collection? Other priests? She thought not, though maybe he extorted them, too. Female parishioners, having tea before—what? Did he touch, or just look, or was it a matter of everything?

The antique electric kettle was no lightweight thing. Caroline walked over, sat in the chair across from the couch, turned her head to the kettle on the sideboard behind her, and looked down at the chintz upholstery, white with orange and yellow flowers and little red-brown berries she now realized were a spray of blood. She crouched close to the kettle. Two gray hairs and a smear of something were caught in the rough beading at the base.

It looked like Bernie Dinak's last guest volunteered to make the second pot of tea. Maybe, Caroline would say to Jules that night, there was almost as much satisfaction in knowing how as who; for now, it would have to do.

*

GIDEON SORENSON, WHILE largely incapable of human interaction, arrived within minutes after she called from the car radio. He was a great scene-of-the-crime man, with the most recent technical training, the temperament to look for stray hairs and sloughed skin, and the personality flaws necessary to make crawling around a reeking house bearable.

Yet the sight of the bloodstains on the upholstery made him green and fretful. "Tell me about the neighbors again?" asked Caroline.

"They said just the food drop-offs, and a nurse early on."

No information yet from the bank or the home health people—Gideon was no good at the friendly extraction of information. "See if there was a post office box or a storage unit. Check again for a record, maybe in another state."

"All right," said Gideon.

"The people at the church were useless, right?"

"They just said he was very nice. That maybe someone took advantage of that."

Maybe, thought Caroline. But nice people aren't the only victims, and nice guys don't keep trophy shots of older women. Someone added that bra out of revenge, spite, misdirection.

"Eliminate his prints—"

"How do I do that?"

It was true that there wasn't much skin left on those fingers. "The dominant oldest prints will belong to Dinak. And we'll need to run them. Look in closets, undersides of furniture. People don't check undersides enough. Look for signs of wiping."

"But we know who he is."

"No, we don't," said Caroline, pulling off her gloves.

"We don't know where he's been. Get the samples off the chair, deal with the prints. Find his dentist and then we'll go see the kid he was extorting. I'll try the neighbors in the meantime."

"All the cars are gone."

It was true; these were all small houses, without garages. Meanwhile, in Bernie Dinak's yard, his resident rabbit chomped the green clover near the fence, rimmed by the dead foliage of bulbs he'd never seen bloom. The rabbit chewed on as she knocked, in vain, on a half dozen doors.

13 *Thickets*

AT WHAT SHOULD HAVE BEEN THE END OF THE DAY, Jules started out toward his office with Tommy and the stroller and Celeste. He was badly off-kilter, and when he hit a wall of people in the Baird lobby it took him a minute to regroup.

Jules pushed past a dozen Selway-Whipple doppelgängers. They'd arrived on the same flight, and they were all clearly descendants of the people who'd loved the suffix *polis*: vacationing business types wearing pink and green, cardigans and seersucker pants and loafers. Golf clubs and floral bags and barrettes and lots of laughter; talk of fraternities and sororities and grills. He pushed through the line to get his mail from Edie, wishing he could show a badge.

"These fine people must be in town for the Selway event," he said to Edie.

Big, jolly laughter from the big, jolly crowd. Still, Jules was in a pragmatic mood when he followed Celeste up the stairs to his office, bouncing Tommy with each step. All this mellow acceptance ended when he read the note in the fax machine: the warden at Deer Lodge said that Patrick Bell would not talk to him.

Jules wasn't sure why this shocked him. Lately everything seemed to, as if he'd fallen into the habit of misjudging the world. It was four thirty. The warden picked up on the first ring.

"Any explanation?"

"Mr. Bell's a nice guy, but a little troubled."

A new bubble of anger broke through his outrage. "That nice guy killed my father."

"I appreciate that, but the effort is real, and so is the brain damage. Some preexisting, some at the time of arrest, some later, when he kept trying to beat his brains out. So he's unpredictable."

So am I, thought Jules, wishing it were true. "The preexisting injury—that was his brother beating the shit out of him? And what did the cops do to him at the time of arrest?"

"Hah," said the warden. "I believe that was the brother again. No love lost."

"Except the wife's," said Jules, taking a stab.

"Yeah," said the warden. "I was state police then, and when Patrick heard about his wife, that's when he started driving his head into walls. He kept it up whenever they'd lift the drugs just a little bit. Hence Warm Springs. And eventually, he calmed down and they sent him here."

Jules spoke carefully. "Can you explain why a man who intends to kill his wife is heartbroken when she kills herself? I'm confused."

"I don't know where you think this will get you, but he said from the beginning—I mean when he could talk again—that because his wife was dead, he didn't want to live."

"And why won't he talk to me?"

"I don't know, but I guess—why would he? He's still not chatty, but within this world of ours, he's okay. He gets some letters, talks to his parents about once a month, a few other visitors a year."

"Where does all this leave my mother?"

"Still a widow," said the warden. "Try writing him directly. I'm not the bad guy here."

Dial that phone, bounce that knee: one of the few truly difficult things about parenthood, or at least today's challenge, was what to do with anger while dandling a ten-month-old kid. The idea that Jules began to feel relief—he would not have to face the man who killed his father—only added self-loathing and sharpened the mood.

He tried Caroline at the department, but Grace said she was still crawling around Bernie Dinak's house. When she finished, she'd hopefully get rid of the Russian foot and finger, currently sitting in a cooler on Burt's desk.

"What's that supposed to mean?"

"Crazy Russians," said Grace.

A salient fact, left out by Caroline. Jules's mood moved another notch in the wrong direction. "The foot is Russian? I don't want her looking into crazy Russians."

"I'm sorry," said Grace, "But what does what you want have to do with anything?"

His face went hot. Tommy, impressed by the way Jules said *Russian*, stopped crying.

"She's been dealing with them for days," said Grace. "Gideon said they picked up some wet hitchhikers yesterday. Did she not mention them?"

"What the fuck?" said Jules. He tried to keep his tone good-natured for the sake of the child on his lap, but Grace still hung up on him.

Jules tried Ed's home number—maybe Ed would call in, maybe Sadie, babysitting Shirley, would know when he was due back, so that she could move on to her third job of the day—and listened to a series of beeps and heavy breathing.

"Hi, Shirley. It's Jules Clement. Is Ed home?"

"I am alone," she said. "I can't find my coral."

"A coral necklace?" Another stab: "Choral? Your choir?"

"Little Corabelle." She snapped it out as if he were an idiot.

None of Ed and Shirley's six kids were named Corabelle. "I think Sadie's helping Suzette Whipple," he said. "I'm sure she'll be back to you soon."

"It's not safe for her," said Shirley. "She shouldn't be so close to him."

"Him? Mac? Charlie?"

"Donald," she said.

Another vote of confidence in Donald Whipple. He listened to Shirley breathe and wondered if she was concentrating or floating. "Can you leave a note for Ed to call me?"

"Well," she said. "If this is about the priest, he can't talk to you about church stuff."

"I'm not calling about church stuff," he said, trying to track the way her mind worked, or didn't work. "This is about the Bells."

He waited. She sighed. "Don't go patrol," she said. "Go home to Olive and the kids. Leave that poor family alone."

She hung up. Jules threw the phone again, but this time it was a gentle lob. When it started ringing again he tossed a baby blanket on top to muffle it and turned the machine off.

The day had begun so well. Jules moved Tommy to

the other knee, thinking things through, and plopped the little boy down on the floor in a circle of grubby toys. Upstairs in Mac's suite, someone was having something that sounded like sex, and a woman laughed. Mac deserved a little fun, but this pissed Jules off, too.

He typed a note to Patrick Bell, introducing himself—*I am Ansel Clement's son, his younger child; when you shot him, I was thirteen years old*—speaking of his mother's recent health issues, and asking him to reconsider. *Because you owe us, fucker.*

Just joking, thought Jules. He deleted the last line and signed his name and faxed it off. He could have used *was* instead of *am* but nothing felt like it was really in the past. And there was no way he could have typed *Dear Mr. Bell.*

He tried Ivan but the line was busy. The kid was tired, the dog was hungry, but everyone put up with it while he finished the map of the poor farm, with an hour to spare before Alice met the Aches. The overlapping dormitories, some ten outbuildings, one double-duty orchard. First burial ground, 1889 to 1908, twelve graves, all potentially identifiable. Second burial ground, reasonably regimented, twenty burials by 1918, potentially identifiable. But the third burial ground, from the influenza epidemic to about 1945, subplots A through D, looked at best like a dying lizard with a fat, detachable tail. Any pretense of an east-west alignment in the graves—used by all three major Western religions—disappeared with the decades, and the gravediggers also stopped aiming for depth. The last plot, the lizard's tail, was still buried under the cars. Jules could only guess, and he scribbled twenty-three to forty bodies.

And number four: a half dozen random graves, all distant from the rest and one another. Random Marvel pioneers? Suicides buried by superstitious county employees?

Lastly, the privies. He marked them as circles, guessing at the order, with a note pointing out that they weren't good road-building material.

He typed and signed the cover note. Tommy by now was eating paper in the far corner of the room. Jules tucked him under one arm and ran up the stairs, sprinting past Mac's door, knocking on Ivan's. Music, voices: the door opened to another world. Two wineglasses on the table, cheese, and the smell of roast chicken.

"I'm sorry," said Jules. "I tried to call."

"That's okay," said Ivan. "Are you all right?"

More or less. He let Ivan pour him some wine and smear some cheese on a cracker for Tommy. Jules could hear the shower running and a drawer closing in the bathroom; Ivan cracked the door open and said something softly.

"You've got a problem," said Jules. "A big problem. Charlie Bell is also an heir."

"I know about Mr. Bell," said Ivan. "Finding anyone else?"

Jules was stunned. "Several, but all dead in the last year or so. All old, all apparently the last of their families. How is it that no one mentioned the Bells to me?"

"Peter should have, but I can understand him not wanting to bring it up. This is good news, this confirmation that it's down to Cluskers and Whipples and Bells."

"Charlie will make your life hell," said Jules. "Charlie and Elaine together."

"They're actively courting me," said Ivan. "Cavendish,

being an idiot, brought up my interest. He's been stringing them along for months."

"And Suzette and the Bells?"

"Their children claim to speak for them," said Ivan. "We'll be careful."

"Their children"—the phrase was loaded with disgust. And who was "we"? The ethics of all of this for Peter were at best spongy. The woman's shower was over; she was humming on the far side of the closed door. Ivan made Tommy another cheese cracker. The wine was so good.

"Peter said you know something about Charlie."

"I do," said Ivan. "Gossip out of Denver. I think you know his wife's cousins have hired an investigator, which might be a classic case of aggrieved slimeball relatives, but they've succeeded in getting the cops to take a second look at the old man's death. But what I'd heard came before, back when the father-in-law was alive, and the daughter—Charlie's wife—was fishing around for help among Strato Corporation's sales reps."

"'Help.'"

"Help. Not nice people, but one of them was my client, a kid we'd known when we were still aid workers in Georgia, who was trying to start over with a green card. And so I asked him about Charlie Bell, and he passed on this rumor, that Charlie and his wife wanted to inherit early."

"What's his name?"

"Let's call him Fred. Charlie's father-in-law surprised everyone last spring by making it through chemo. Possibly an unwelcome remission for his daughter. He was a bad man, a maker of land mines and guns. I worried that my clients, people who were trying to immigrate and have a life, would do the wrong thing for him. Or to him."

Jules disliked feeling like he'd dropped into a movie that would never play in Blue Deer.

"Charlie's wife wanted her father dead?"

"Yes, and I suggested to a friend, a former coworker from the aid days, that there was money in this desire. Make a fortune, and take down Strato and the whole terrible family, including Charlie. Which was, to me, the point." Another cracker for Tommy; in the bathroom, the woman was using a hair dryer. "Anyway, the old man died, and Charlie's wife died. I don't know if my friend was involved, or my client Fred, and I don't want to know. My goal is the end of Charlie."

"Why?"

"Long story." Ivan took the chicken out of the oven and put two place settings on the table. "I am late in telling you this, and I will deny it to Caroline, in her professional role."

Jules stood. "You're not worried? You're saying just leave it alone?"

"I'm not worried," said Ivan. "But I said nothing about leaving it alone."

BY THE TIME Jules reached the street, he wondered why he'd accepted this explanation. Everything, lately, felt like a fable. Money and murder and tricksters, dead fathers, love, intoxication.

The schoolhouse the Aches hoped would be a museum was only two blocks from the Baird. He could hear the women before he saw them—the windows were up on the second-story classroom they used for meetings, and cigarette smoke and laughter curled out. He bellowed Alice's name and heads popped into view, including Olive's, heckling him. Oh little boy, little boy. Come up here, little boy. Tommy tried to crawl from the stroller.

"Not a chance," said Jules. Alice stuck her head out and he waved the folder.

Cicely Tobaggo's fluffy white head appeared in the window. "Jules," she called.

He ignored her and strapped Tommy down.

"Jules, where are the old bodies?"

More fable shit. "Which old bodies?" he bellowed, over Tommy's wails.

"The Doris bodies. We found a better-researched article about the 1917 flood, and it says only a few graves washed away. What did that horrible Whipple man do with them?"

"Well, the city cemetery," said Alice, who'd reached the street.

"Look," said Jules. "Let's just meet up there tomorrow. Look at the map, look at my notes."

"Hey," said Alice, wiping snot from Tommy's face. "Divvy called here, trying to reach you. No one was answering your office phone. Something about boulders, and how you're going to have to move the house to the thicket."

THERE WERE SO many kinds of panic in his life these days. He arrived to find Divvy and Suzette and Herb the machine operator staring down at a grooved wedge of basalt in the unfinished corner of the garage excavation. It was the kind of monster that lined the river, or more accurately gave the river its lines.

"It's not a boulder," said Herb. "It's bedrock. We've got

three feet; we can live with it for the garage, just a slab on grade. But your house might need to take a walk."

"Just not toward my apple tree," said Suzette, who'd come out to watch.

Divvy was wailing into his fancy satellite phone, rummaging through his truck for a probe, but Jules was underwhelmed by the crisis. He ran inside Suzette's house to call Peter, who went off to find the city building inspector. Sadie, who was there to help Suzette, took Tommy, and Jules began to dig. Within fifteen minutes the visible portions of the rock began to bear an unnerving resemblance to the back of a sperm whale as seen by an idiot tourist in a boat. This particular whale was swimming directly toward the house site. Nothing on any map or river morphology or Army Corps records had made this likely, but it wasn't exactly unlikely.

After an hour, they reached a plan B, a build site twenty feet to the west. The city guy would sign off in the morning. Jules even liked the site better, though it would mean cleaning up a large, dense thicket with Sleeping Beauty–scale thorns. He began to cheer up, despite the burbles and splashes from the happy couple in the hot tub next door, and he jumped into the hole to see the bones of the land revealed, strata and secrets. He could make out centuries of floods, shots of gravel and the pale gray mud from Yellowstone Park, thin black lines of carbon from wildfires hundreds of years ago. It was soothing. He'd missed looking at sediment, tree roots, detritus, silent stories, tactile fairy tales. He'd even missed finding bones, though he didn't want to see them here. The existence of the rock at least meant no human incursions.

At the east end of the excavation, he ran his finger along the scraped edge of an ancient downed stump, fascinated by the roots. They were pale and hard; the cottonwood they'd belonged to must have been born and died in the valley how long before?—1600, 1700?—and floated for years, waiting for burial. He brushed at the top edge and his finger hooked on something stringy, and scraped at the soil until he could work it free: a thin gold chain, a flower setting with tiny empty petals, only one seed pearl left. For one bad moment he panicked, expecting to find a spine, but the chain was alone in old mud, lost.

Across the clearing, Elaine called out for Charlie.

"He's using binoculars," said Suzette, out on her deck. "See the glint in the window?"

Jules peered over crushed dogwood. Suzette with a cocktail and her opera glasses, Sadie sunning herself in a bikini. She made a joke Jules didn't quite catch.

Giggle, giggle, giggle. A door slammed. "Oh god," said Suzette. "He has a bottle of wine."

"Chaaarrrlie," called Elaine. Her voice was singsong, as if she were calling a dog.

"There in a minute, honey," said Charlie.

"He's coming this way," said Suzette.

"Fuck a duck," said Sadie.

Crunch, crunch, crunch. Jules dropped the necklace into his pocket and watched Charlie's naked top half cross the way, carrying a bottle of wine toward Suzette's house. He was transparently sucking his stomach in, and it gave his rib cage the weird look of Hollywood in fifties beach movies. He walked to the deck and Sadie rose, in all her pale young majesty, looking unforgiving. She did not take the bottle, and he put it down on the step. When Charlie turned around, Jules tried to read his face, but there was nothing, at least until a small, tight voice called out again.

"Charles, where are you?"

Charlie Bell looked . . . nauseated? Disgusted? Unhappy, anyway. Jules stayed in his hole and thought about life for a few more minutes.

14 *The Fourth Morning*

WEDNESDAY

CAROLINE, HOME AT MIDNIGHT, WAS SO SOUNDLY asleep that when the phone rang at six, she shrieked and threw a pillow, hitting Jules, who was scrambling for the receiver.

"This is a collect call from the Montana State Prison. Will you accept the charges?"

"Yes," said Jules. His voice creaked; his nervous system jolted back to life. He launched himself out of the bed and down the stairs.

The voice was low and creaky. "Why now?" asked Patrick Bell.

"My mother is not well. You're on her mind. She'd like to know some things."

"I'm guessing you have all the testimony."

Not really, thought Jules. "It's all from other people. You're the only one who was there."

They listened to each other breathe.

"Fine."

"All right," said Jules. He couldn't make himself say thank you. "I'll call the warden and make an appointment."

"No," said Patrick Bell. "Come today. This afternoon. Otherwise, I'll change my mind."

Jules hung up. He walked outside and stood in his

backyard, naked, until the cold morning air slowed everything down.

HE FRIED AN egg but couldn't eat it. This was dread, not alcohol.

"You feel okay?"

"No." Jules was shaving while Caroline dried off from the shower; Tommy was sitting in the open doorway, throwing the rolled-up socks in the laundry basket to Celeste, who ran downstairs to hide each pair. "What would you ask him?"

"Something more than why. I would ask what happened to his wife, why and how and when exactly she died that day. And if you gave me two questions, I'd ask how it was that Charlie happened to be home that particular day, if he'd really been banished. Just to get the whole bug of his involvement out of your head. Neither of the Bells offered a real explanation. Charlie said they were worried about Patrick coming; neither of them said they were worried in the interviews I've read so far."

Charlie's presence: not a bug, but a feature, he thought.

AT EIGHT A.M., Jules and Caroline glided down their beautiful new driveway and parked in the trees. The great rock was metallic in the early light, glinting where the blade of the excavator scraped it. No one was digging this up.

Seeing the rock was the only way Caroline would understand. Jules, hours later, still felt some disbelief. The garage, as Divvy pointed out, was always going to be detached, and now it was going to be a little more so. When Peter followed them down, Jules drew the placement out on paper, and he convinced both of them, and convinced himself, that if a thousand-year flood came their way, the whale might keep the house standing when everything around it, all that Selway detritus, tumbled downstream.

Caroline liked this idea. The site was in fact better: higher, with a clearer view of the river and more privacy from the Whipple and Selway houses.

"Seems like we're blocking the Selways' view," said Caroline.

"Are we?" asked Jules.

"Should we talk to them?"

"Nothing was in writing," said Peter, who started walking across the DMZ, away from his car. "But Suzette owns it—there's no *them*—and I've got an appointment with her anyway. Concierge service. This is a day for all sorts of appointments and rethinkings."

Suzette waved from her deck. Sadie and Mac were behind her, working on the infamous pillbox. Suzette was wearing orange today; she was her own demented construction flag, and the effect was strengthened by the truck reversing down the Selways' driveway, beeping and bearing tables and chairs for the joyous anniversary that would deliver the Selways from each other. Two tents were halfway up, a small army swarming and darting with Elaine while Charlie leaned in the front door, as if he owned the place.

But Charlie was watching Sadie again, not the serfs, and his posture was very Henry VIII: arms crossed, legs spread. He gestured to Jules to come over.

Jules ignored him and walked to his car. He started for Deer Lodge early; he needed to work on his questions for Charlie's brother.

*

THE PLAN OF the day, for Caroline—once she'd agreed to have her house built in a new place, with a new view, on a new timetable—was to learn who'd killed Bernie Dinak, to find a name for the foot in the red shoe and some reasonable explanation for how its owner melted, and to get Burt fired. She headed to the station ready for confrontation, but Burt was still AWOL. She slid behind her desk and typed up a covert note to Shari Swenson (*Could you please send any files you might still have for the 8.15.72 murder of Ansel Clement? I can explain later*). When she looked up, Grace was staring at her.

"No word from Burt?" asked Caroline.

"Maybe he melted," said Grace. "Look for an oil spill. And then deal with the hospital's deadly stolen drugs, please, and your friend Edie's missing guests."

And a final salvo. "You're supposed to call Cavendish. He says he shot at another one."

Bloodletting; so much of it going around. This was Cavendish's third night of firing into the dark, at least, and even if Caroline couldn't charge him, she felt culpable. She thought uneasily of the bloody bandages, the man in the wheelchair in the park, tipped into a miraculous turquoise stockpot. The park rangers were sending a copy of the tape showing the group by the boardwalk, along with a series of half-remembered license plate numbers for a silver or gray van that may have arrived with a wheelchair.

Could these nighttime hecklers at Marvel be the same Russians? How many men were in this terribly replaceable army? Did they all have red shoes? She thought of Eastern European bands, dressing alike; she began thinking of bowling shoes, and *The Big Lebowski*. It was the only movie she'd seen in a theater since Tommy's birth, and she was suggestible anyway—whenever she was tired since having him, she started to see weird shit. She found a caramel, put it all in her mouth. When she opened her eyes, Grace was watching her again.

"Go fix everything. Please," said Grace, handing her Gideon's file.

The preliminary lab report: Bernie died after a last meal of oatmeal (with raisins) and bacon, with a small amount of Demerol in his system, along with some hypertension drugs. And his groin was bludgeoned hard enough to tear his penis and rupture a testicle.

Oof, thought Caroline.

She skimmed through Gideon's report: on his second time through on the afternoon before, Gideon found that *two unidentified sets of fingerprints seem to overlay those of Sorenson (on the back of the tipped chair) and Fair (on the sink tap).* In the downstairs bathroom, *clear prints from three different individuals were found on the bottom of the toilet seat, with Detective Feckler's prints overlaying the unidentified partials. Also, some strands of blond hair were observed in a comb on the kitchen counter, and a fingerprint was taken from the handle, which has not been matched. Sorenson is quite sure that the comb was not on site when Deputy Fair discovered the body. Perhaps the comb belonged to Deputy Feckler.*

Caroline tried Gideon's home number from the kitchen phone while she ate someone else's crackers and read the weekly arrest awards. Harvey won the contest for the first week of August: a drunken Czech who painted the jail with his own feces.

She wondered if it was possible that the Czech was really a Russian.

*

ON THE WAY to Bernie Dinak's house, Gideon filled in the missing bits: Carter O'Donnell was blackmailed by Bernard Dinak when he was sixteen, after his friend Matthew talked of their relationship in confession. The arrangement imploded when Carter, broke after turning over $180, told his parents, who gave him a kiss and went immediately to the police.

Or rather, to Ed, who they knew from church.

In any event, Carter didn't kill Bernie: he'd spent the year studying music in Vienna. When Caroline called him, the boy was sure he and his friend weren't Dinak's only victims. "Think of it—do I seem like the most promising victim, out of all the hundreds of people he heard in confession? All those secrets worth storing, if you're a shit like Father Bernie?"

"Did he try for sexual favors?"

"Not his bag at all. I think he did stuff with a couple of the ladies with the Catholic Daughters. Plus that secretary, plus getting creepy with the girls' basketball team."

Ed told Gideon that Carter's family decided to drop the matter after Dinak apologized and returned the money, and that his misbehavior as basketball coach—peeping Tom behavior, creepy notes, clammy but above-clothes massages—didn't go "that far," and revenge was an unlikely motive in any of these matters. His firing seemed to satisfy the St. Anne parents.

But Bernie Dinak continued to pry money out of someone. He'd used the Bank of the Yellowstone, and his deposits amounted to six or seven hundred dollars every month. Lots of small deposits, regular deposits—twenty, fifty, and one hundred dollars—mostly cash.

"'Mostly'?" said Caroline.

"The bank is still looking."

"Anything else?"

"Just that someone was in Dinak's house after we were," said Gideon. "Someone besides Burt. I missed the toilet seat prints, but I can't imagine how we didn't see the comb. And I found a lipstick print on one glass. Missed that the first time through, too. Dr. Swenson didn't find any traces of lipstick on the body."

Caroline couldn't imagine how she'd missed the comb on the initial search, or the glass either. The toilet seat was easy to explain: Gideon was a complete germophobe.

They parked in front of the house. "Any more from the neighbors? Did any of them make that welfare call?"

"No to the call. Dinak did have visitors, but he did not go out at night—"

"What kind?"

"Women, not young. Maybe a cleaning lady, or home health."

Those photos, thought Caroline. She imagined Burt looked at that bit of evidence. She stood in the street and spun, picking a victim.

The house to the west was vacant. The next-door neighbor to the east was nice enough not to mention Caroline arresting his daughter that spring. The one car that he'd seen several times always parked in the alley, visible from his back windows. It was a 1971 Lincoln Continental, a turquoise blue boat that barely fit between the alley shacks and the city's new garbage bins.

In the tiny cookie-cutter stucco houses across the street, Caroline fell into a trinity of watchers, widowed and widowered, none of whom admitted making the welfare call. Where were the children in this neighborhood;

what explained this awful blight? The grocery clerk in the gray stucco house was a pro: she said Dinak lived on frozen vegetables, burger patties, diet cookies, and bad wine. He looked as if he was in pain and in fact looked like he was medicating for pain. Two or three women a week visited. She'd seen the blue car go by the house and leave the alley later.

The insurance salesman in the yellow aluminum-sided house said that Dinak's regular visitor was tall and elegant. He'd see her cruise by in the Lincoln and hide in the alley: the turquoise flashed between tree trunks and houses in the winter. Dinak closed his drapes when she was there.

Caroline felt argumentative. "Maybe it was a man."

"Well, *it* had a gray old lady poof under the scarf," said the insurance man. "*It* seemed old for cleaning, and *it* kept knocking the bins over when it drove down the alley in its fancy old car."

"Some plumbers did the same thing last night," said the grocery clerk.

"What plumbers?"

"That van, maybe working at the place next door. It stayed after your guy left."

"My guy?"

"Sheriff Feckler, in that big stupid truck."

"All right," said Caroline. "Thanks. What color was the van?"

White, gray, tan, silver. They couldn't agree anything beyond the van's existence.

Her little crew of neighbor-spies tailed behind as she tried again, Gideon scribbling notes into his brown book. Stella Denboos's house was beige, like its owner; Stella sometimes showed at Aches meetings, despite subtle dissuasion: she sucked the happiness out of every meeting she attended.

The door popped open immediately. Stella said she'd despised Bernie Dinak for decades because he could not keep it in his pants. Women came by *all the time*, especially the one in the turquoise car, who was there for hours. Sin knew no age.

"Can you describe her?"

"Of course I can. Tall, dark-haired. I imagine she's about seventy now."

"You don't know your ass from a hole in the ground," said the grocery clerk.

"I shouldn't cast aspersions," said Stella.

"No," said Caroline. "But once you've cast them, you need to keep talking. Who?"

"What family do you hate the most?"

"I don't hate," said Caroline. Hating.

"Fine," Stella snapped. "It was Lucia Bell. Patrick Bell's mother."

You smug cow, thought Caroline. And then: how could something so convenient happen? In a matter of seconds, Caroline's tired mind shot toward an endgame, an idyllic solution: maybe they could lock up the whole family.

"Tell me how it is that you know Lucia Bell well enough to recognize her at a distance."

The grocery clerk spoke up. "Well, have you ever seen her? She's pretty distinctive—she looks like a bobblehead doll. I knew I recognized her, I just couldn't place her."

AT THE STATION, Caroline asked Grace to look up the Bells' address. "Are you sure you should be doing this?"

"No," said Caroline. "But I'm going to."

"You might as well have Ed along," said Grace. "He knows the family, and he dealt with that other bank thing."

"The kid? Gideon told me."

"No, the problem with Mrs. Bell's bank account. Someone was skimming, or scamming her, or something. The son called Ed for help. The good son, obviously."

"Charlie?" asked Caroline in disbelief. "Why didn't I know about this?"

"It was last fall, right after Tommy."

"Skimming . . . ?"

"A couple hundred dollars a month."

"For fuck's sake," said Caroline, heading for the door again.

ANOTHER FAILURE IN the free flow of information in their tiny department, in their very small town. Caroline and Gideon drove to the Bank of the Yellowstone.

"I talked to Deputy Winton," said the bank president, W. E. Anderson. He'd always been called by his middle name, Eldridge, but he'd decided he liked being known by his initials. Jules and Ed now called him Wee, but Eldridge was tall and soft.

Ed would never have normally forgotten this, thought Caroline. Two strikes. "Well," she said. "Now you're talking to me. Can you explain the situation with Lucia Bell?"

Eldridge was given to rapid hand movements when nervous, and in this case, having known Jules since childhood, there was extra reason to fret. The Bell son—the *good* Bell son—called the bank and the police the previous fall, sometime in September or October, when he learned his mother was pulling out money every two weeks, fifty or a hundred dollars in cash. The only sign of where it might have gone was a single check—for the same amount in a monthlong lull between cash withdrawals that May—made out to Bernard Dinak. The bank contacted Sheriff Tenn, and Wesley sent Ed. Mrs. Bell, confronted, refused to talk, and Bernard Dinak, confronted, said she'd borrowed money from him years ago. The family decided to drop the matter.

"Show me," said Caroline. "The Bells contacted us, Eldridge, and it's now a criminal matter. Mr. Dinak is dead."

"Oh! Poor man."

"Not dead naturally."

She'd just ruined W.E.'s day. Caroline accepted a sweaty printout and circled the fifty- and hundred-dollar dribs and drabs for Bernie Dinak. They ended in early October. But what caught Caroline's eye was a new flow out of the account beginning in midsummer. For an elderly hermit couple, the Bells bled cash, with $1,000 and $2,000 withdrawals every few weeks. A sizable deposit in the spring—$92,000—was gone by November.

"Oh," said W.E. "Those are for the son, who takes care of them. Charles. The deposit was a land sale, a few acres of the Coralberry Creek ranch. Charles and his partners are developing the land along the Marvel Road, and maybe even the old town itself. Plenty of buildable lots up there. I can't even begin to think of why I'm a banker instead of a realtor!"

"What's this?" she said, pointing to December 9, a deposit of $150,000, with all but $10,000 of it disappearing the next day.

"Ah," said W.E. "Another few acres. I believe Charles opened a trust account for his parents at a different bank."

"He has their power of attorney?"

"I think so."

Caroline stared at him. "Why? And what do you mean, 'I think so.' Shouldn't you know?"

"Well, his mother was tossing cash out the window, and the husband's been in a wheelchair for years. I'm sure the document is on file."

"I know about his injury," said Caroline. She was beginning to know a lot. "But what does that have to do with his cognitive abilities?" She would ask Peter if this was as odd as it seemed; she would visit the couple and see if they were truly out of it. "I'd check to be sure that you have that POA on file. And is that their phone number?"

"That seems to be beyond the purview of this inquiry."

"Maybe not for long." Caroline scribbled down numbers.

"You can't possibly want to talk to them," said Eldridge.

"Why wouldn't she?" asked Gideon, immune to the subtleties of local history. "Mrs. Bell was extorted, and Mr. Dinak was murdered."

"Bell" meant nothing to Gideon, and the Bells might not recognize the name of Caroline Fair. Caroline gave Gideon a rare smile. She wasn't going on this call alone.

SHE DIDN'T GO alone to talk to Charlie, either. When she and Gideon arrived at Elaine's house, there was quite a crowd. The yard crew was trying to belatedly trim the grass around the off-kilter party tents. Two geeky kids with a blue van with a bad stencil job—THE MOVE-YS—were lounging near the studio, rousing themselves, whenever Mac emerged, to carry another lamp or an open box with books and tchotchkes. He stared blatantly at Gideon and crooked his finger to Caroline, who followed him into the studio. Suzette was inside, wrapping silver and china in newspaper.

"The family jewels," said Mac. "Such as they are. We have a goodbye present for you. I found it when we were building, but I didn't show anyone but Suzie, and you shouldn't show anyone, either. Let's call it a little horsie."

He held out a tissue-wrapped piece of marble, gray and streaked white: a lamb, lying down.

"Not a horse," said Suzette. "Little lamb of God. He knows better but let him joke."

"But," said Caroline, and then stopped for a moment. "But it's from a grave."

"Of course it is," said Suzette. "From a child's grave, and it's all that was left after the cemetery washed away in the flood. It was way over here in what's now the river, so you shouldn't worry. But take it. If we gave it to you at the party, the Aches would talk, and they'd grab it."

"The Aches are coming to Elaine's party?"

"No. They're coming to mine," said Suzette. "I've been disinvited, so I'm going rogue. You come, too. I'm quite sure you haven't made my daughter's list."

Caroline headed across the clearing to Elaine's house. She handed the five-pound lamb to Gideon and knocked with excessive force.

"This is a very busy day," said Elaine, opening just a crack. "The party, our anniversary."

"I know," said Caroline. "These questions should only take a minute, and then I'll be out of Charlie's hair."

He appeared behind Elaine, looking enthusiastic, and pushed past her to stand a little too close to Caroline. "Hey!" he said. "I didn't think you'd ever want to talk to me!"

Caroline smiled. "I'll keep it fast. Just take me through what happened to your mother's bank account last fall. I'm looking into the death of Bernard Dinak, and we gather he was taking money from your mother, and you somehow found out."

"Lucky you!" he said. "What a mess that was."

"Did you go talk to him?"

"I did!" said Charlie. "Of course. I said, 'Why would you take my mother's money?' And he said he'd loaned it to her years ago. Which was unlikely."

It was a strange, mannered voice, almost as if he was deliberately adding vibrato, and it went with the odd way he used his eyes. They had their own weird glow, like the glass of deadly milk in a Hitchcock movie.

"What was your mother's explanation?" asked Caroline.

"Charity." He laughed. "The man was a swindler. How embarrassing that she'd even give him a dime."

"Well," said Caroline. "She gave him considerably more than a dime. The bank vouches for at least three thousand. I'll ask her; maybe she can be a little more specific now that he's dead, and maybe she can help us understand what happened to him."

"Oh no," said Charlie. "No one's talking to my mother. How would she know why he offed himself?"

"The thing is," said Caroline, "he was murdered."

"No," said Charlie. "He was a suicide."

Huh, thought Caroline. As if he could make this true by force of will. Whether Charlie was manipulative or oblivious, he always managed arrogance. She snorted and watched his face turn pink.

"I heard he was a perv," said Charlie.

"I'll let the medical examiner know. And I'll see if your parents have any ideas."

"No," he said again.

She guessed it was all he could manage, and she changed tack. "Do you visit often?"

"Not often, no. Not until going into business with Mac and Elaine."

Behind them, Elaine was asking Gideon to move a ladder and a wheelbarrow. "Gideon," said Caroline. "Please don't." To Charlie: "And when was that?"

"A year ago," snapped Charlie. "But not much in the summer, and things were busy this fall, given my wife's death. When do you think this happened?"

She ignored the question. "Were you here for Thanksgiving?"

"No."

"Oh, that's right. Your parents won't allow you into the house. Christmas? January?"

She was almost positive that he hissed. "I tried to come every month, just for a day or two. I don't remember if I made it in January. I'd just sold the house in Cody. It's easier to deal with my parents now that I'm staying with Mac and Elaine, working on this little endeavor."

Interesting order to those names. And "this little endeavor"—everything was smug about this man. "Which is what?"

"We are developing several properties. And we have another very valuable, very special property that we'll be selling outright. An inholding."

She allowed a pause and watched him. "If you're in some sort of deal with Cavendish Clusker, I'd be careful about the title."

"Oh," said Charlie. "I'm afraid I'm way ahead of you. Cavendish and I have fun together. We tramp around and target shoot and I daydream about millionaires' houses."

"He does love having people daydream before he stiffs them," said Caroline.

"I have an in," said Charlie.

Big smile. Caroline wasn't the kind of cop who normally looked forward to making people grovel, but she was learning new things about herself thanks to Charlie. "Wait," she said. "Are you sending people up there to harass him? Or are you shooting the people who are harassing him?"

A look of disbelief, with an underlying smile. "What people?"

"You tell me," said Caroline. "Do they happen to be Russian?"

"This whole town is nuts for Russians," said Charlie. "I know a few, from my years with my father-in-law's company, and from my military time."

"You were in the military?"

"Yes."

"No, you weren't," said Caroline. "You were at a military boarding school, and then you started at the Air Force Academy but ended up at Colorado State instead."

No reaction beyond the sense that the eyes wanted to kill her. Maybe when something really hurt, he clamped down. Gideon moved an inch closer, and Caroline circled back. "The extortion. Bernie Dinak. Could it have been something about your father? Some awful secret?"

This time Charlie failed to clamp. She watched that face tighten; it was hard not to recoil. But his voice didn't go up. "Never," he said. "Lucia—my mother—is a very religious person, and Dinak played on her guilt. It could have been any little thing, something that wouldn't have bothered me. Or you. She would not explain."

"Was the conversation with Mr. Dinak civil when you visited him?"

"Of course. He apologized and returned the money. We all dropped it."

"That just doesn't seem like you, dropping something. Though I realize you must have been quite busy at that time."

He smiled; he thought this was a compliment. "It was a very busy period. Working out the land deal with Mac and Elaine, other financial duties."

"And your wife," she said softly. "That happened in the fall, too? Not long after her father?"

"Yes." He wasn't going to blush for his lack of grief. "I don't want to talk to you anymore. I'll talk to your police chief."

"You mean our very temporary acting sheriff? I wish you luck," said Caroline, walking away.

15 *Patrick*

JULES KEPT AN INFORMAL LIST OF PEOPLE WHO might still want to kill him, and they made a little parade in his head as he walked through a series of checkpoints and clanging doors at the Montana State Penitentiary in Deer Lodge:

Judah Marks, who raped both his sons, arrested when Jules was first a deputy.

Andy Englander, who killed his wife for laughing at him.

Gary Devoto, whose middle-aged, alcoholic son shot himself after embezzling from the Elks, and who took his grief out on the accountant who turned the son in.

It was enough to put a person in a funk. Other people began to occur to him, but he needed to keep his mind on the one person he'd hated for decades. Even back when Jules was what passed for the Law, Deer Lodge's halls of antibacterial green and the bone-vibrating clang of the doors gave him a scrotal twinge. The prison was split between the high- and low-security wings. Patrick Bell, exemplary, brain-damaged prisoner, may have killed a cop, but he was low security. The low-security side was a grubby beige stroll through purgatory; when he was a cop,

Jules walked past Patrick Bell's cell a half dozen times without looking in.

He sat down at a dented wooden table in a tiled room; very old school, though this prison was only twenty years old. The state authorities did not inform people making calls or interviewing prisoners in person that they listened as a matter of course. Which struck Jules as . . . criminal. He requested no recording.

It took him a minute to be able to look at the face in front of him. The many things that were unexpected: Patrick Bell's curly brown hair was graying and receding, so that nothing hid the dent on his left temple or the stitch scars radiating from it. A raised triangular scar was visible on the top of his head, above a split ear and the thick bridge of someone whose nose has been shattered. And the right eye—Jules hadn't understood the damage. It only opened halfway, and the pupil looked blown, large and dark.

The other eye was sharp, and on Jules. It was letting him take his time, but he still didn't know how to begin.

Patrick Bell sat completely still, cuffed hands on the table. He was taller than his brother, with long arms and wide shoulders. He'd been a good basketball player in high school. He hadn't thickened, though he didn't seem weak, and he was weirdly ageless, as if he'd been kept frozen. He was fifty but looked thirty-five, baby skin on a deformed frame.

"You don't have to stay on my account," said Jules to the guard.

The guard looked at Patrick Bell, and Patrick Bell shrugged.

"I do not mind being alone with Jules Clement."

It came to Jules that he was the threat, not the man in for murder.

"So."

"I am here because my mother wants to know as much as possible about what my father went through," said Jules. "And why it happened."

"I have spoken of my remorse every time someone has allowed me to speak," said Patrick.

"That's largely meaningless," said Jules. "You destroyed us."

And yet here they were. Bell stared at the table.

Jules tried a different approach. "Maybe I should ask, why would you destroy yourself?"

"I expected you to kill me years ago. A man came through here who said he'd bargained with you—he'd trade killing me for a lesser charge. I thought the punch line might be that you'd said yes."

"Judah Marks?" asked Jules.

"Yes," said Patrick Bell.

"Why would I trust a man who raped his children?"

Bell smiled. "And yet you guessed who I meant."

Jules brought a small notebook, but he left it closed. It felt silly now—how likely was it that he'd forget anything this man said? "Why did you agree to talk?"

"People have argued your case."

"The warden?"

"Half-hearted at best. He wasn't a fan of your policing."

"Ed Winton?"

A sliver of unease. "No. Ed comes once a year, like I'm a religious holiday. This is another mutual friend."

"So let's get to it. Tell me about the day," Jules said. "Just the day, without the why."

Patrick's face went blank. That much external damage—there must be some remaining deficit. Jules tried again. "That morning, where did you wake up?"

"Afton," Patrick said. "We were moving to Missoula from Salt Lake. We came through Yellowstone because I wanted to pick up an instrument for my father in Jackson, a cello he was going to use as a model. We usually met my parents in safe in-between places, but my father was in so much pain, having a bad week, and we thought this quick visit would be safe."

"Safe from . . . ?"

"My brother. Charles moved to Denver from Colorado Springs that May. He'd gotten into the Air Force Academy, but it didn't last. He met that rich girl." Bell rubbed his forefinger along the table's fake grain. "I was driving the truck, and Iris was in our Civic, and the truck began to overheat. We stopped at a pay phone in the park, and I called my parents, but I didn't talk to them—friends were over, helping my father bathe. Iris went on ahead, and I added water to the radiator, and eventually I made it to a garage in Gardiner."

"And?"

"And your father pulled the truck over." Patrick looked at his hands.

Jules shut his eyes and tried to slow his breathing. He couldn't bear this, but he couldn't bear Olive's reaction if he gave up; he couldn't bear anything. He wondered how much pain he could inflict before the guards grabbed him, but that moment passed, and his arms and head felt heavy.

"Did he recognize you?"

"Yes." Bell met Jules's eyes and watched him carefully during each question, but he looked away as he answered. "We knew each other. He helped me years before."

"What did you say to him?"

"Nothing."

"What did he say to you?"

"My name."

"Did he know what was going to happen?"

"No. It happened too fast. He was looking . . ." Bell stopped.

"At what?"

"I can't." His voice creaked.

"You can't remember?"

"I can't. It would cause . . . pain."

"Pain to me?"

"No." The guard reentered the room and Patrick Bell pulled himself together. "Your father couldn't have known for even a second. He couldn't have suffered for more than a moment. I don't remember clearly but I am sure of this."

"That's not enough," said Jules, who was shaking.

"I know that, and I'm sorry, but I can't go further. I liked your father. He was kind to me. He understood the situation with my brother."

Across the room, the guard jingled his keys. Jules thought about how much information he was missing, how much better his questions could have been if he'd gone through the notes Caroline gathered, how badly he needed to talk to Ed again. He stared at Patrick Bell's bad eye, and then the good one, and thought of his answers: What he'd done—nothing. Why he'd done it—nothing. Telling the truth about the murder, admitting the murder, was apparently unbearable. Jules was sure, suddenly, that while Patrick Bell wouldn't answer most questions, he wasn't going to lie: if the answer was unbearable, he just wouldn't speak.

They sat in silence. Jules thought of his father dead on the side of the road, the truck continuing on.

"Why did you want to kill your wife?"

"I didn't. I would never hurt her. Never."

"The situation with your brother—he tried to rape your wife, when you were still in high school. Did you feel he was still a threat to her? Or you felt that she was in love with him?"

"I've heard that you've met Charlie," said Patrick. "That would be his take. He'll prey upon you."

"He says your wife was unfaithful, and that was why you wanted to kill her."

"No," said Patrick wearily.

"She knew you'd done something horrible, and decided to kill herself out of shame?"

"No."

Another pause. "Either you arrived and followed her into the barn and killed her, or she ran in and killed herself."

"No."

The hairs on Jules's arms began to lift. He was being manipulated. "Did you see her when you got to the house?"

"I never saw her again, after that morning in the park when the car was breaking down."

Patrick was weeping from his good eye, but the bad one was dry. He stood up and the chair nearly tipped. "I am sorry to have wasted your time."

"Does anyone but you know the truth?"

A flash, and the eye darted onto Jules and off. Bell turned to the guard, who was looking at his nails.

"Would you agree to talk again?"

"Sure," said Patrick Bell. "But you can't get blood from a stone."

"Your wife—" Jules started.

"No. I can't do more today."

"You loved her."

"I still love her."

CAROLINE SAT IN the squad car while she waited for Gideon to fetch Harvey and use the station bathroom. She was convinced that if she went inside, Burt would reappear.

A shape loomed, admittedly a small shape, and she jumped.

"You're kind of paranoid, aren't you?" said Harvey.

"Yep," said Caroline, shoving a file into his hands. "Can you try to figure this out? Bernie Dinak was getting small sums from Lucia Bell, but at the same time their charming son seems to be selling off chunks of the ranch. And none of the money seems to stay in the parents' account."

"What do you want to know?" said Harvey, not eagerly.

"More," said Caroline. "Where it goes, what was sold, who bought it. If Charlie keeps it, what does he do with it? Maybe if you get together with that Denver PI the wife's family hired things might dovetail a bit."

Harvey looked dubious. "Try," said Caroline, as Gideon slid into the seat next to her. "Any word from Burt?"

"Nothing. He missed a meeting with the Headwaters Task Force."

Burt must be dead. He'd never pass up a meeting about weaponry. Should she worry? She thought not.

Caroline and Gideon drove south toward Coralberry Creek. She did not call first, or tell Ed—Ed, withholder of information—and it was just as well that Jules was out of town.

The beauty of the place stunned her. The turquoise Lincoln was parked next to a grubby white handicapper van—she had vans on her brain, along with Russians—in the gravel driveway, near the charred stone foundation of a barn. The yard was filled with piles of scrap metal, bent wire enclosures but no visible animals, an overgrown garden with a peace sign on the gate. She saw neat rows of tools through the window of an attached shed, but the paint on the main house was faded, and the solid front door was grubby, with pulled blinds on the flanking windows. She knocked while Gideon bent to peek under the shades.

"Hello," said a voice. "May I help you?"

Gideon peered around the side of the house and pointed, and Caroline circled to find a handsome old man in a wheelchair, sunning himself near a worktable covered with small bits of wood. And there was Lucia Bell, the bobblehead doll with a skeletal face and massive starry eyes, standing next to him. Caroline flashed on Patrick Bell as some young male version of Lucia, skinny and weeping with a gun on the side of a road.

She no longer wanted to be here. She'd never felt so much sadness in a place of such beauty.

"Mr. and Mrs. Bell? My name is Caroline Fair," she said. "I'm a detective with the Absaroka County Sheriff's Department."

"I know who you are," said Francis Bell. "I recognize your photo from the paper, after that shooting a couple of years back. And we hear a bit, through friends. You're with Sheriff Clement, aren't you?"

"He's no longer sheriff," said Caroline. She flushed; she wanted to deal with these people anonymously. Did they know about Tommy, too? Did they ever think about how their child's crime never stopped mattering, changed everything for generations?

Of course they did, she thought. They might be odd, but nothing about them seemed stupid, and Francis Bell read her face. "We are always happy to hear that he's prospering after all the sadness our family brought into his life. Aren't we, Lucia?"

"We are," the old woman said calmly. She held two woodworking clamps.

Caroline couldn't see much Charlie in either of their faces, maybe because Lucia was so odd, and Francis's expression was so pleasant and curious. Caroline was curious, too—how could you not speak out when someone deliberately crippled you in the prime of your life, even if that person was your son? Would you not want to protect the world from them?

"How can we help you?"

Caroline was losing her appetite for this conversation. "Mrs. Bell, last fall, there was a problem with your banking account, and your son Charles was worried, and the bank and the police found that you'd been giving money to a man named Bernard Dinak."

"The money was for the church," she said.

"Did he tell you that?"

"It is what I believed."

"He told the police that you owed him money."

"No," said Mr. Bell.

Caroline stuck with Lucia. "You and Mr. Dinak are friends?"

Did Caroline feel good about herself, using this tense? No, she did not. But there was no quiver when Lucia answered.

"Yes."

"Did you keep seeing each other?"

"No," she said. "I stopped driving. The car broke down."

Gideon edged toward the Lincoln. "Would you like me to help you find a mechanic? You shouldn't be out here alone without a vehicle."

"No, no, thank you," said Francis. "I drive the van. We've been isolated for years."

"And you have Charlie to help," said Caroline.

"Charles is not allowed here," said Francis.

"I go to town to see him. And we write letters," said Lucia.

One son gone forever, the other a raving asshole. Lucia Bell was staring up at the clouds, and she was miserable. "May I ask why?" asked Caroline.

"You may, but I won't answer." Francis smiled. "Why don't we stick to Mr. Dinak? He's a wretched man. He's not allowed here, either."

"Mr. Dinak is dead," said Caroline. "And has been for some time, though his body was recently discovered. We're trying to determine what happened. When did you last see him?"

A look of wonder passed between them, without a fragment of grief. And then: fear.

"Mrs. Bell," Caroline repeated, "when did you last see Mr. Dinak?"

"I don't know," she said. "It was warm. I think September."

"Charlie has admitted visiting him, after he found out about the money. Do you know anything about that? Does it worry you?"

Lucia Bell went blank, an expression beyond deer in headlights. But Francis Bell laughed. "Of course it does."

"And he's selling your ranch off. Does he have your power of attorney?"

"No," snapped Francis. "We've allowed him to make those sales, to cover his debts. We were told he'd be making the money back on a project with Elaine Selway and her husband."

What else could Caroline ask? More about Charlie's reaction, Charlie in general, but she was sure that it would end the conversation, forever. She looked around at the paved path to the tall cottonwoods of the creek bottom, presumably added for the sake of the wheelchair. "What a shame," Caroline said, gesturing to the stone walls of the burned barn.

Francis Bell gave her an odd smile. Who smiled at such a thing? "Yes, it was a shame."

"It broke our hearts when it burned," said Lucia. She was watching her husband. She was so skinny, outright emaciated; they both were. Old couples getting weird together, but this was far gone, and they were a little grubby, too.

"Many things broke our hearts," said her husband.

The elderly Bells, a gnomic chorus, speaking their own mysterious language. Neither of them asked about what happened to Bernie Dinak, how he'd died. To press or not, and should Caroline try another way of asking if they got enough help? Why should she? The Bells' son killed

Tommy's grandfather, and this family's well-being wasn't in her heart.

Gideon, always restless, paced to her right. Neither of the Bells looked at him as Caroline asked tentative questions about their welfare. It was a strange thing about Gideon: he made himself invisible, even in this blindingly white country. He'd told Caroline that when he was a kid in southern Utah he'd just go still, in the hope that no one would look at him. Now she caught his eye and he nodded to the vehicles. She looped toward them on her way back to the patrol car, where the radio was jabbering. Were all Econoline vans shabby and white? How many of them were in the database when Gideon searched?

The secret of why the Lincoln didn't work was simple. The ignition was jerked out of the dashboard.

JULES WAS SHAKING when he drove away from Deer Lodge. The reaction was predictable, but he was still surprised at himself.

It was just two hours back to Blue Deer, not counting the time he spent at the market in Butte. Most of Jules's mortadella sandwich ended up on his lap when a Winnebago veered into his lane on Homestake Pass; he screamed obscenities and made his own ears ring, and when he pulled over at the base of the hill to pick up the mess, he was shaking again.

He reached the town cemetery with just ten minutes to spare and parked about twenty yards from the shed. An old man named Ollo was on a riding mower at the far end. The mower was the only machine Ollo was allowed to drive: Jules, as sheriff, arrested him for his fifth DUI.

Jules walked into the shed without knocking. Gordie hung up his phone, looking rumpled and flushed, but the shed was about ninety. Jules tried to imagine where the adulterers managed sexual congress. The one bare wall? Gordie didn't seem that athletic, though the ponytail definitely saw herself that way. The desk, he thought. Nice cold Steelcase.

"Long day, Gordie?"

"Ask me anything!" said Gordie.

"Well, I wouldn't go that far," said Jules. "Today I just have two minor questions about the past, about policy. Do you know when you started burying the indigent for the city and the county?"

"That kind of thing wouldn't be in my files. I mean, we don't keep a separate area or file on 'Indigents.' The last person we buried like that was someone the Elks decided to pay for. They still keep a fund, and he drank in their bar, so . . . "

"Okay. How about the Doris burials? We have research that says they were moved here in 1972. Know anything?"

"Doris?"

"Doris, the old town on the river."

Gordie walked ponderously toward the filing cabinets that lined one grubby wall and jerked open *D–F.* He eyed Jules. "We cross-reference."

"Great," said Jules, watching Gordie skip from Domenico to Dorlinga, and then flip through his notebook. "Try Whipple, then."

Gordie strolled on to *W–Z* and pulled out a file with a flourish and a show of deep interest. Grave interest. "First names?"

"Donald or Suzette."

Flick went the pages. Jules walked outside and raised his binoculars. A navy Corolla was putting up the lane toward Burt's fuck palace.

"Well, there you go. Right here," said Gordie, from inside the building.

The Corolla stopped and a woman hopped out, her face a blur. She unlocked the house door, and disappeared so quickly that Jules didn't have a chance to pull the small camera out of his pocket.

"I said, right here," yelled Gordie. "What are you looking at?"

"Birds," said Jules. He slumped back into the sweltering shed and Gordie pointed to the wall map. "And here, in two different sections. Donald and Suzette in number 320, and 'Reb' in 369."

"Reburial?" They marched east until they found themselves facing a massive spruce. Jules circled the hard ground around the tree, whose roots were lifting older tombstones to either side—the Blalocks, gone since the 1920s, and a broken tomb named Fred—and domed the lane in front. "This ground hasn't been disturbed since the tree was planted," he said.

"Says who?"

"I'm a fucking archaeologist, Gordie. And that tree is more than fifty years old. I'm looking for bodies that would have been moved here in the late sixties or early seventies."

"Oh, you know trees, too? Maybe they just did a good job."

And maybe Donald Whipple was still alive, or at least

planted elsewhere. Gordie looked at his documents and snorted. He flipped pages; Jules poked the ground again and hit rock. "Could be a casket," said Gordie.

"No," said Jules. "It couldn't. Let's see the other plot."

Gordie huffed a bit and took off down the lane. Why would anyone want to sleep with this man? He paused twenty yards on, over a metal marker. "Fine. Here. 'Reb' for reburial."

Jules knelt near the indentation. It was so small, not much bigger than the test pits his students would practice. Would Whipple have cremated whatever he found at the town site?

"Definite interment here," said Gordie. "Let me see if it will cross-reference."

"Who?"

Flick, flick, flick. "Baby Whipple, September 17, 1972. Not Reb. This is so sloppy."

Ah god, thought Jules. They stood for a minute before Jules shook his head, as if he could lose a tiny ghost.

"Any other names?" asked Gordie.

"Iris Bell," said Jules.

"No," said Gordie. "If you can't find the poor people, what's it going to mean for you finishing the survey on schedule?"

"Not much," said Jules. Lie, lie, lie. Maybe he should check Calvary for the people of Doris. Maybe Alice was simply knee-jerk negative when she said the Catholic cemetery only took Catholics and whites. Though just four years ago, Grace struggled to get Calvary to take an unclaimed homeless girl. First the church wanted proof that the girl was Catholic, and then that she wasn't a suicide, and the unspoken objection was that she was Native.

Fuck the world, thought Jules.

"If you don't mind, I need to get back to the county office," said Gordie. "I'm having some stomach discomfort, and the toilet out here is rudimentary, really just a privy."

"Don't let me keep you," said Jules.

One of the great things about having done a variety of digs in old places is that it dented your notion of the holy, the beautifully symbolic, the wonderful forever. We might be eternal, in terms of pure carbon and calcium, but our precious last details inevitably fall away. If you'd worked in Europe or Asia or North Africa, you knew that one generation's icons were another's phosphorus, Egyptian mummies ground for the pear trees of Versailles.

He walked around the patch of ground that was his father; he circled grandparents and great-grandparents. He read the headstone for his friend Larry, dead for a decade. All they'd found to bury was his foot. He said hello to Otto Scobey, who he'd pulled out of a reservoir, and Everett Parsons, who he'd pulled out of a crumpled car, and George Blackwater, who he'd found under a lilac bush, and Leon Baden, who he'd shot dead in a hotel room. Jules wanted to be cremated and tossed in the river, washed all the way to the Gulf of Mexico to mix with the rest of the eastern seaboard and way too much fertilizer.

Olive, half joking, said she wanted to finally go to Paris.

At the edge of the marsh, he raised his glasses again. The woman's Corolla was gone, which was fast, even for a man like Burt. And on his way back to the car he passed the privy Gordie disdained and started thinking of funny jokes to tell his class about dumping grounds, and the fallacy of assuming everything would make sense in life.

Where were the people of Blue Deer buried? In Evergreen or at the poor farm!

Where were the people of Marvel buried? In Doris or at the poor farm!

But where were the people of Doris and Marvel buried? Where, actually, were the fuckers? Surely the newspaper was wrong, and they were in the river, or they were in Evergreen. And yet here he was, facing the idea that they must be on the hill, where there was zero evidence of a dedicated reburial.

Suzette's acres on the way to Marvel—could Whipple have planted a few pioneers there? Jules had walked off a few acres up there, aware that boundary lines were fluid, without seeing a glimpse of human intervention beyond overgrazing. Hard, too, to hide something whenever anyone with good binoculars could see you for five miles.

Therefore, his mind turned to practical solutions. If a real estate developer wanted to clear a pesky burial ground, and could access other sites, what would he do? Dispose of the burials. And if there was no evidence of such a reburial, what might it mean? Exigency! And what would anyone do to get rid of something fast? They threw it in the trash. Or flushed it. Or in the pre-flush days, they threw the bones in a privy—always the perfect place to dump broken china, old clothing, empty cans. They might cover it with a quick road, to keep it forgotten.

Suddenly privies seemed very, very important.

THE WOMEN WANDERING around the potter's field looked like a mirage: all of them wearing dark clothing, all but Alice and Caroline with canes. It was windy and Caroline pulled a blanket around Tommy's head, bringing on equally timeless screams of rage. Still, throw up a broken temple and take away the eyeglasses and jeans and it could be Greece in a different millennium; add a little green and it could be Ireland, at least until you finished coming over the rise and saw the last few junkers by the western edge and Bob in a pink T-shirt and a hard hat.

"What's up?" asked Jules.

Alice looked nervous. "Well, it was a good meeting." She turned to Venus.

"You should continue, Alice," said Venus.

"Go ahead," said Alice.

"No," said Venus.

"All right, then. We think we've led you astray. After we found the article about the last few bodies going to the town cemetery, Cicely found a note from the trustees saying no dice to reburial, because Whipple couldn't identify each body, and they were uncomfortable with the list of potential names. It looks like he tried to give them a different list afterward, but they didn't buy it, and so Whipple said he'd take them to the poor farm. This would have been in the summer of 1972."

A busy summer. Dead fathers, dead babies, disappearing businessmen. "Who knows where he was keeping them in the meantime," said Cicely.

"But here we have your wonderful map, and we've been walking around, and we don't see anything you haven't accounted for. So where could he have put them?"

"We're very worried he might have thrown them away," said Venus. "He was a horrible man. I wish Suzette would allow people to tell the truth about him."

"Maybe the cemetery took them after all," said Alice nervously. "On the QT."

"No," said Jules. "I just came from there. Whipple purchased a plot, but not for Doris."

"For the baby," said Venus.

"For the baby," agreed Cicely.

Alice was wild-eyed. "What baby?"

"Let me show you what I think happened," said Jules.

It wasn't far, but thirty yards took a while with this crowd. Jules paused by a round depression in the hard-packed mud of the road. Alice was impatient. "Whipple was hiding them?"

"Maybe," said Jules. "See those divots? Those are privies. That soil will keep subsiding, and so will the road."

"He put in that road to reach Suzette's acreage," said Venus. "But she wouldn't let him sell it."

They waited. In the old days they would have been flirtatious. Today, though, Jules was just another contractor who might disappoint them. He held his hands out, palms up. "Voilà."

"Oh no," said Venus. "Tell me no. Why would he do such a thing?"

"It sounds like that's just the kind of guy he was," said Jules. "Cheap? Pissed off? You'd think that he might have dumped them in a grave with someone else, but maybe the burials ended by then. I'll find out for sure when classes start and I have a crew to help."

"In September?" asked Alice. "We're just going to leave them?"

"For another month, after twenty-five years? One hundred years? Yes, we are."

Alice's expression changed. She was having an idea,

which meant that Jules was having dread. "Have you found anything on your land?" she asked. "Anything consistent with a cemetery?"

"Cemeteries are awfully inconsistent," said Jules. "Especially in flood zones."

"No, really. Have you?"

"Some detritus."

The other women waited. He felt Alice's eyes, and his neck began to flush. Caroline was out of hearing, dealing with their snitty child, who was very tired of the view from the poor farm. "What kind of detritus?" asked Alice softly. She was reading him, she was guessing, she didn't really want him to answer.

"One necklace, and one bone fragment. The fragment was half-buried in the riverbank, and the lab's trying to figure out how far it traveled."

Was it a lie? Not really, but not the whole truth, and here he was, hoping to find the town's oldest inhabitants buried in shit.

THE WHOLE TRUTH: Jules didn't know it, but he was a curious boy. He'd never gotten inside the clerk's and recorder's files on the day that Charlie waylaid him, and now he wanted to know many things: was all the land between the poor farm and Marvel still Suzette's, or now in Elaine's name? The same question applied to the river land. And the Mellow-Mallow land—how much did the Bells still have? How much of his parents' ranch was Charlie selling off, and who was buying it?

The answer about Suzette's land—it was all in her name, Elaine's efforts and sign notwithstanding. Vista del Rio, Goldfields—both father and daughter thought they could own the moon by putting a flag on it. Elaine and Donald Whipple, aiming for empire.

The Bell parcel was never huge by western standards, but it was choice—six hundred acres stretching down along the creek, widening as it went. When the Bells sold the lowest forty-acre parcel in 1974, they'd probably needed the money to pay for Charlie's military school. Jules did not swim in empathy. And then nothing until the summer before: forty acres last May, fifty-five in November, ten key acres west of the homestead just last week, all sold to Cello Partners, of Garrison, New York. Jules wrote down the name, even though he already knew it: he'd seen it on every check Ivan Luneau wrote to Peter.

JULES CAME HOME through the alley and remembered, too late, that he'd heard Caroline invite the Aches over. His backyard was full of old women. He twitched his way through a beer until he realized that Olive, at the other picnic table, was telling everyone that he was researching Ansel's death, that he was going to talk to Patrick Bell, that he, Jules, was going to finally clear her heart of confusion and grief. Jules met Caroline's eyes, shook his head, rose, scooped up Tommy, and made for the car. He wasn't ready to talk about his day.

Everything he'd done since Olive's call seemed ludicrous and small, chickenshit and evasive, but something was breaking. He had things to find, things to know, questions to ask.

The mile marker was scribbled on a note in his pocket. Jules knew this road by heart, and for some reason he'd always assumed—when he didn't manage to block out the thought—that the place Ansel was shot was a high, flat section closer to the Bells' house. Instead it was tucked in and green; he pulled off and walked a few feet from the car, turning slowly in every direction, trying to see what his father saw that day: mountains, cottonwoods, clouds, the glimpse of a tractor. Maybe in 1972 Ansel would have heard the creek, but maybe water greed was eternal.

When a car passed, he turned his back to it. He wondered how long blood was visible in the gravel, if he was standing on a little bit of Ansel. A hot sunny day, ticking engines, overheated patrol car and truck. Ansel might have blocked Patrick and put his hazards on, or he might have pulled up behind Patrick and walked north along the verge, with the river visible on his left between bottomland cottonwoods. Turning to face Patrick and the end, he would have been facing both the gun and the most beautiful slopes of the Absarokas.

Jules got back in the car and did a U-turn to head north, following Patrick's path. Was he revved and triumphant, ready for his real goal? How fast was he going before he braked for his parents' house on Coralberry Creek Road?

Jules drove this stretch slowly and pulled to a stop at the top of the driveway. The house was tucked out of the wind, midway between the road and creek. An old man—white hair, thin at fifty yards—read a book in a wicker chair on the upstairs sleeping porch. He watched Jules for a moment, and then he waved.

A woman called out and the old man turned to his open door.

All right, thought Jules. Do it. He drove down and parked near the stone footprint of the barn that he and Larry burned when they were sixteen, the river rocks and cement of the foundation still showing char.

He knocked on the door, but no one came. The windows were down and pinched tight with curtains, and he could hear no voices. When he backed up to see the porch, the old man was gone, and the door behind him was closed.

16 *The Fifth Morning*

THURSDAY

CAROLINE READ ALL EVENING, AND SHE READ AGAIN in the morning. She wasn't on the schedule, and she had no morning daycare. Bernie could stay dead a little longer, because she could not rid herself of the Bells.

Tommy was not easy. Bananas yes, eggs no, and beans were projectiles. She dodged them while she read Shari's files: Ansel's autopsy, interviews with the other officers on the scene, the attempts to interview Patrick in jail and in the hospital. *More to come!* said the note.

She kept turning pages while Tommy was sitting in his bath ring, rolling aimlessly on the floor, getting a little weepy about the cat's lack of desire to be fondled. She put the files down whenever she dealt with him—it was one thing to examine the face of a dead grandfather when she wasn't touching Tommy, but going back and forth too quickly did not work.

When he slept, and she read in earnest, she missed the buffer. Ansel died instantly, two shots to the chest, no defensive injuries. She studied his peaceful face, his forehead and his ears, his hairline and his chin. She could see Jules, and she could see Tommy.

She couldn't find the ballistics report or forensic

evidence from the 1967 Ford truck. It was hard to get a handle on the absences, the things that were missing, that might bring understanding. She sorted together all the interviews with the parents and with Charlie, to read in one go. She couldn't find any of Ed's or Bunny's testimony.

Small confusing notes in the file, in Grace's handwriting: *call social services* and *need restraining order.* Who was left to restrain?

Caroline skimmed a day-two interview between Ed and Bunny and Francis Bell.

> EW: Why would she have done such a thing . . .
> *[inaudible; FB unable to talk]*
> EW: I'm confused about the timing here . . .
> FB: We thought she'd left with the car. Maybe she did leave and came back.
> EW: I understand why she might not want to see your son. Either of your sons.
> *[inaudible]*
> BM: Just fucking leave it, Winton. Fucking waste of time. We'll try again in a half hour.

For Iris, there was no ambulance record, no incident record, no coroner's report. The file was labeled *investigation into the death of Iris T. Bell, female, age 21, probable COD suffocation/strangulation*, but Caroline could find no autopsy or evidence of an inquest. The file held a birth certificate—Iris Lorraine Talouse, born in Lewistown, Montana, in 1951, mother Bette Talouse, deceased, father unknown—and a marriage certificate: Iris and Patrick before a Dillon justice of the peace, in 1970. Death certificate, 8.15.72, suicide by hanging, next of kin Patrick C. Bell.

If Iris's husband was rushing home to kill her, why did she commit suicide after he was arrested? Because she felt at fault from Ansel, from all of this happening? Whatever happened, the context was clearly that she was unfaithful. All her fault, this Trojan War.

Something new under the sun: Caroline wanted to talk to Shari Swenson. It was the lunch hour, but she got a voice, rather than a recording.

"It's quiet here at lunchtime," said Shari. "Everyone else is out using up their puny hour. And why would I want to eat, after that person from the park, red tennis shoe person—holy fuck buckets."

Caroline was so far inside a very old tragedy that she'd forgotten Shari might be dealing with the melter. "Yeah, sorry about that. Did the rangers warn you?"

"Well, they tried, but I can't say there's ever been anything like this before. It takes a lot to make me want to throw up these days. Anyway, couple things—I got the toxicology early on your priest, and there was nothing in his bloodstream beyond a trace of codeine. But I took another look before I shipped him back for his funeral, and I am quite sure that he lay on his left side for at least a day, maybe longer, before he was hoisted. All that dried-out blood's pooled, and there's a trace of a pattern on his arm, like a seam, or a sweater cable."

Caroline remembered a stack of thick hand-made sweaters in Bernie's upstairs bedroom. She imagined little old ladies knitting for him, maybe topless, while he told them all about their sins.

"And get this," said Shari. "I found a piece of fingernail in the back of his neck, right at his hairline. I think he was beaten and choked manually. Killed in anger, costumed and hiked up later."

Caroline made a puffing noise. Did she need to get a sample of Charlie's nails? They'd had no progress finding Bernie's other victims; Gideon just wasn't the man for talking to compromised matrons or the spouses who might have been angry enough to kill someone.

"What can I do for you? Tomorrow I'll send back that skull fragment Jules found in a riverbank, plus that bit of tibia—"

"What skull fragment?" said Caroline. They'd only talked about Patrick Bell the night before. Was Jules billing the department for the poor farm? And then she thought, What riverbank?

"Well, if you can't keep them straight, I certainly can't," said Shari. "Final guess on the cranium is 1880 give or take a decade. Tibia is tubercular, maybe 1920."

Caroline happened to be looking at the windowsill, where she'd tucked the marble lamb. It looked back at her. Maybe she should hide it from Jules. Their various worlds were melting into one mess.

"The Ansel Clement files—thank you. Did you happen to find any scene forensics, or anything about the interior of the truck Bell was driving?"

"We did!" said Shari. "On their way down. But what's Jules got in mind, looking into this? Crazy-making, after all these years."

Yes, it was. Caroline hung up and spent the next few seconds choking herself, seeing where her nails hit the back of her neck, but of course everything was upside down. She reached for the next interview:

Interview with Lucia and Francis Bell, 07:00, 8.16.72, conducted by Deputy Stanley Budge

SB: What made you go to the barn?

FB: We were very worried. We thought she would have called to tell us where she was if she was all right.

LB: I walked out when the police left, and her car was behind the barn. And so I went inside. It was very dark. And then I saw a shape moving.

SB: I'm sure it was a horrible shock. You moved the chair . . .

LB: The chair was several feet away. I tried to get her down.

SB: Sometimes people kick.

LB: [inaudible, crying]

SB: So you assume that Mrs. Iris Bell saw her husband, and ran off, and then later decided to hang herself?

FB: We don't think that at all.

BEFORE JULES DRAINED his first cup of coffee, a call from Gordie: they'd finish removing the wrecked cars today. Bullshit, thought Jules. At ten, a call from Divvy: a little slowdown, but they'd be ready to pour the garage the next morning. At noon, there would be an ultimatum from Caroline, who'd spent her waking hours since the Aches left reading files: Jules needed to go through them, because she thought there was a different way to see what happened to Ansel.

"Different?" he said. "How's that possible?"

"Just read them, Jules. Shari's sending down another batch. You can't put it off any longer."

Oh yes, he could.

Today, when Jules drove to the office, he smelled smoke, the kind that was close, that still smelled like wood, and the light was a filtered rosy gold. In a normal week, he'd have talked to someone about whether or not the county was going to erupt in flames. But not these days.

In the Baird stairwell, the smell shifted to aftershave. Mac, newly energized, out late and up early, was perched on the windowsill facing the office. A barrage: he was waylaying Jules in case they didn't get a chance to talk that night. He would be traveling, and he needed to line things out, because he'd changed everything: withdrawn from Elaine's attempt for a real estate empire, changed his will, changed the automatic routing of the check that would land at 4:45 today from the trustees. He would leave money for Suzette, because he believed Elaine may have gutted her accounts, and enough for Elaine to pay for the caterer and six months of their extremely large construction HELOC, with a bonus contingent on Charlie leaving. The world was clean and new. He'd go to his own party, try to not to get too weird with his fireworks aim, and then leave it all behind. Jules or Peter could keep the pig roaster. "I've got all my fireworks," said Mac, "but I forgot to buy a pig to roast. Hard to see Charlie or Elaine using it. I'd worry they'd put Suzette inside. I am, in fact, worried about Suzette."

"More dosage issues?"

"Give the day time," he said. "This is all about Elaine trying to have Suzette declared incompetent so Elaine can take charge and have the Marvel sale. Charlie is doing the same thing with his parents. My role, more or less, has been to fink on them. Sadie's been very careful, and I hired a firm to put in surveillance equipment at Suzette's and in my apartment. All sorts of things are going to make Charlie and Elaine unhappy after tonight. Peter's requesting a restraining order against both of them, but Suzette wants to wait until after the party, just in case people feel mystically loving. We'll see. Suzette thinks she'll be protected by her new will."

Peter appeared in the hallway and let himself into his office, looking uncomfortable. As well he fucking should; his client was not the soul of discretion. Jules felt compelled to ask, without wanting to know. "Explain."

"Suzette's disinherited Elaine," said Mac. "Elaine has no recourse but to convince her mother that she loves her, after all."

"People aren't always rational," said Peter. "I worry."

"Well," said Mac, smiling. "It's satisfying for now."

Jules and Peter watched Mac swan out the door. "So much going on," said Jules. "Who knew?"

"Not my story," said Peter. "Not my secret."

"Like Ivan buying the Bells' property?"

He didn't say this in a friendly way. "I'm sorry," said Peter, "but yes. It's not what it seems."

"Ivan's not buying the whole mountain?"

"I can't talk about this," said Peter, turning away. "You'll understand, and I can promise you'll actually like it."

Jules, who no longer believed anyone, got on with his day. He called Deer Lodge to request another interview with Patrick Bell. The warden sounded dubious, put him on hold, and a moment later returned to say no, Bell already expected a visitor. Jules could try a phone call around lunch.

"Just ask if he'll talk now. Please. Who is visiting?"

Silence from the warden.

"It's public information, right?"

"His old friend Ivan."

"Old friend?"

"Yeah, old friend. I've been here fifteen years, and he's the first visitor I remember. That doesn't rate with you?"

It rates, thought Jules.

Upstairs, in Mac's apartment, a woman's voice—possibly Sadie's voice—and laughter. A little lull, and then the bouncing began again. This new rhythm was one result of Mac heading out every night since the hospital. Another was an expanding guest list to the Selway anniversary party. According to Caroline, via the Aches, Mac, braying about endings and new beginnings, was inviting everyone—Divvy, Ivan, Edie, the county attorney, his plumber—while Elaine, trying to catch up, disinvited anyone of a lower economic order (many of Mac's bar friends), or anyone she disliked (any of Suzette's acquaintances). Caroline said Suzette was going to throw her own simultaneous party. Why waste someone else's fireworks? Caroline wanted to go: Tommy might love the show, and they'd be at a safe distance.

Jules didn't think anyone or anything was safe.

The warden came back on. "He was apologetic, but the answer was no. Lots of family phone calls lately."

"The brother?"

The warden laughed. "That fucker? No. He still sends letters, though. I allow Mr. Bell to burn them."

Jules hung up. He walked to the window and leaned his head against the glass. Sadie emerged from the hotel in time to see Ivan coming up the sidewalk toward her with a bouquet. They hugged each other, and Ivan gave her something like a noogie, like you would to a little girl, to someone you'd known for decades. He climbed into his car with the bouquet.

Ivan really got around.

Tommy was at daycare that afternoon. Jules drove home and carried the box of files outside and settled into a lawn chair with the top folder. On Caroline's copy of the day's log, the entries about the truck were circled, and the times highlighted. Maybe she thought he'd been avoiding things. He skimmed the names of people who'd seen the truck moving north, before and after the shooting. All these people who'd known more than he'd ever asked, Caroline among them now. Ansel was still alive for the first two encounters; when the last witness reached a phone, Olive was running to the hospital. August 15 was a busy day, even before heartbreak, and who knew why Ed was running late, why Bunny was especially foul. Ansel might have begun the day distracted and hungover from his anniversary. A small fire on the north side in the morning, a domestic call, tourist fender-benders, a lost car, a lost grandfather, a lost horse. Did anyone find the time to follow up on an assault at a gas station in Gardiner at 3:00, a buckshot cow at 6:00, a woman screaming at Coralberry Creek at 10:30?

This last was probably Mrs. Bell, finding her daughter-in-law's body. All the different explanations for where Iris was when Patrick entered the yard, what she'd done to herself and why—Jules felt no closer to understanding.

When Ed and Bunny drove into the yard on Coralberry Creek, Charlie Bell was standing over his brother, and said his brother had confessed to shooting the sheriff. Francis Bell told the deputies that his son Patrick couldn't have done such a thing.

> Present: Deputies McElwaine and Winton; P. Bell, C. Bell. Cty Atty Axel Scotti. 8:05 8.15.72.
>
> BM: Why were you driving to your parents' home?
>
> PB: Iris.
>
> CB: He wanted to kill her. He was coming to kill her.
>
> PB: Kill you.
>
> BM: Where is she?
>
> CB: Who the fuck knows. Ask my parents.
>
> BM: Mr. Bell, why were you driving here?
>
> PB: Iris.

That was the last intelligible thing Patrick said for months. According to Ed, each time Patrick tipped out of his chair, Bunny began to beat him, until the seizures were so violent that the deputies mutinied and Patrick was dragged to the hospital, and on to the psychiatric facility at Warm Springs three weeks later.

Jules found no interview of Iris Bell, no mention of her being on the scene. Iris drove into the yard that afternoon and still seemed fine and happy when the Bells left to do shopping. No one admitted to seeing her again until she was found hanging that night. When he pushed his luck and reached into the evidence box again, he wondered what Caroline might have removed to protect her frail flower of a mate. He came back with a list of effects from the body of Ansel Joseph Clement and his squad car, checked as claimed by O. Clement: a bloody uniform, shoes, undergarments. Sunglasses, pocketknife. In his wallet, a driver's license, a Master Card, photos of his children, receipts, handwritten notes, aspirin tablet, twenty-three dollars cash, an envelope with small pearl earrings. A change of clothes, a box of Wheat Thins, a bag of books—*The Day of the Jackal*, *Hawaii*, *The King Must Die*. Olive left behind the uniform and the earrings; Jules could understand the former but not the latter. On his last day, Ansel stopped at Fryer's Stationery to pick up sex and violence and hopped-up history to lure the young wastrel and his sister into reading. The Renault book would have been for Louise, but Jules read that, too. Olive must have slipped the books onto the coffee table at some point, without explanation.

Jules flipped through other files. Caroline left notes: "Check page five," "Please don't open this one," "Why did it take so long for someone to murder Bunny McElwaine?" She'd been right to suggest that she be the one to deal with all of this. Each time Jules reached inside the box he felt like he might find a snake, a real dead body.

Her sticky note on the next read: "What a prick. Flag all the sociopath markers."

Interview with Charles Bell. 8.15.72 22:08.
Conducted by Deputy Edward Winton with
Acting Sheriff Basil McElwaine also present,
as well as witness's attorney.

EW: This was the first time you'd been home in how long?

CB: Several years. You must remember.

EW: So why were you home now?

CB: My parents called. They were worried—Patrick was coming, and they thought he'd hurt someone.

EW: Them? His wife?

CB: Everyone.

BM: Is there a point to this? We know what happened.

EW: I'm confused. Patrick and his wife set out to move together to a new city. They were fine that morning. The parents have no clue what went wrong. The people who helped them with the car say they acted like a normal couple. What changed?

CB: I guess he found out she was fucking around.

EW: How?

CB: I'm not sure. Maybe she confessed. My mother said Patrick called the house just after she arrived, said Iris was worried after she talked to him.

EW: Why?

CB: Well, wouldn't you be worried, if someone was going to kill you?

EW: And what did Iris say to you?

CB: Nothing. I never saw her.

EW: Charlie, your mother sometimes says something completely different.

CB: My mother is a hysterical mess.

EW: Your father does, too. I believe them.

Jules looked up at a blue sky, white zeppelin clouds heading east. A beautiful sunny day, two days to go until it was exactly twenty-six years. Exactly the same weather he remembered from that day, maybe a few more contrails in the sky. He was just a few blocks from Olive's house; he'd been lying in a lawn chair then, too, reading a James Bond book—could it have been *From Russia with Love*?—ignoring an equally shabby lawn.

And Olive answered the phone, and made a sound, and ran, and Jules ran after her. When Caroline was in labor and wanted a blanket from home, he'd covered part of the same route, running through a strobe of memory.

AT THE STATION, Caroline's first call was from a custodian at the high school in Gardiner, who wanted her to know about a wheelchair with a bloody cushion, found abandoned in the parking lot behind the gymnasium. Her second was Crowley the park ranger, saying she'd found a bag with more bloody bandages in the shrubbery, along with "some other things."

Given the context of the body in the hot spring, there was a *Monty Python* ring to "shrubbery." Caroline watched the bouncy, blurred footage of the park video again. The color gave her the sense that she was watching a home movie from 1965: the bright blue of the woman's headscarf, the brutal, deep red of the blanket on the man in the wheelchair. He might have been a mannequin, and the whole group—the woman gliding along, turning a birdlike head from side to side, the wheels turning on the chair, the three men following with identical strides, in identical shoes—a complicated wind-up toy. Had the woman already used the hypodermic?

Caroline put her head down on her desk for a bit, and Grace patted her back. "Hey," said Caroline, snapping to, "what was the deal with the restraining order against Charlie Bell?"

Grace stiffened. "I have no idea what you're talking about."

"After Ansel's murder. You left a note about calling social services, too. Did Charlie hit or threaten his parents?"

Grace headed for her desk. "I've wiped that day right out of my memory. Ask Ed."

"Fine," said Caroline. "Where is he?"

"Domestic in Clyde City. Anyway, Gideon's looking for you," said Grace. "Something about fingerprints. Again."

Gideon, maybe not believing that Burt might be gone for good, was still hiding in the windowless interview room. "Gideon, Burt is not coming back. He will no longer work here."

"I'm just here to concentrate."

"On what?"

"Prints," he said. "It's very confusing."

She waited. "Give me an hour or so," he said.

"I have to go to Gardiner, because they've found a wheelchair. Let me help you sort it out when I'm back."

"If it isn't the one you're looking for, maybe it's the wheelchair that was stolen."

"What wheelchair?"

"The one that Harvey is investigating."

Caroline waited, her right eye twitching.

"The one that was stolen from the Bells," said Gideon tentatively. "Harvey says their van was taken, too, but returned. I guess that van we saw."

She took a minute. “How did we not know this earlier?”

He shook his head.

“Tell me.”

“Harvey said the name is hard for you, and how on earth would they be connected?”

When Caroline blew, she usually blew big, but today she let the flush go over her cheeks and out her eyes. Gideon held up his hands. “I just heard about it this morning, when I got coffee.”

Caroline suggested that he search and print the van, and closed the door to the interview room gently, letting him stay in his cocoon, and headed for the kitchen. Harvey was pouring milk into a bowl of cereal speckled with flabby blueberries. She smiled and sat down across from him. “What are you working on, Harvey?”

“I’m looking for a stolen wheelchair. Along with a van, but that was returned.” He took a first bite. “And I’m digging into Charlie’s in-laws, and I’ve found some weird coinkydinks.”

“A wheelchair?”

“It’s not what you’d call a full theft,” he said, concentrating on his cereal, not meeting her eyes. “The people who owned these items wanted to hold off on a full investigation. They just wanted us to keep an eye out.”

“You didn’t hear about the melted guy in the park? We have video of the man in a wheelchair before he disappeared. So maybe if Francis Bell is missing a wheelchair, it’s worth mentioning.”

Harvey finished chewing a bite and cleared his throat. “Look, I admit that I didn’t think the timing or the van through, but we all thought there was no point to bringing up the Bells. Are we supposed to follow you around saying

Bell Bell Bell, or let you two get on with your life. How is this possibly related? How many wheelchairs do you think are rolling around this county?"

"I don't give a flying fuck, Harvey. I care about this one. Why don't you tell me about it?"

Harvey considered his sogging cereal. "The Bells think it was taken by Charlie's employees. I guess he uses some Russian guys for some chores and stuff."

Chores, she thought. "Some Russian guys. Like maybe the guy who got stunned, or the guys who are missing from the Baird, or missing a finger? Or maybe the man who left his sneaker behind and nothing else? Like maybe the people Cavendish is shooting at?"

Harvey stared at the ceiling.

"Can you find time today to check the goddamn footage from his security camera?"

"Yes," said Harvey, pushing away his bowl.

THE WHEELCHAIR LAY on its side by the high school gym entrance. The initials *F.B.* were engraved on the rail and she found some bloody bandages, a note in Russian, and a box of Baird matches in the back pouch. *Carolina* was written on the matches in blocky letters; she found them vaguely Cyrillic. She took prints, got it all wrapped and loaded, and took the old highway north. She couldn't give the wheelchair back to the Bells before Gideon went over it, but it gave her a good excuse to talk to them again.

As she'd driven south earlier, she'd thought of Charlie Bell, employer of Russians. Now, as she headed north toward Blue Deer and home, she imagined Patrick Bell passing the same drainages she passed: Strawberry and Langley creeks; Silber Creek near Chandelier Rock. Soon

Nesbit Creek, where Ansel died. *They were right next to me, window all smeared with blood.*

Caroline slowed and thought about this. She wanted to go home and read the log, but she was close to the Bells' place now. She'd just taken the Coralberry Creek road when her radio blasted: she needed to go to the poor farm.

Her heart blew up.

"Not Jules," said Grace. "Jules called it in."

Caroline did the math and blasted up the old road to Marvel, every bolt in the Subaru squeaking in agony. She clapped on the lights and smiled at Cavendish's stunned face as she sped through Marvel, knowing that this could be the end of her car, and wondering if the county might buy her a new one.

BIG BOB THE crane operator, who worked at a pace of about five cars a day, took snack breaks on the step up to the cab of the machine, admiring the view around the poor farm, commenting—when Jules was in earshot—on the beauty of the day. Who knew what else he thought as he untangled ancient metal fuckups. Sex, chicken-fried steak, the horror of the Balkans.

Today what Bob talked about was the smell, which Jules agreed, as he headed toward the privy site farthest upwind, was a torture. How the big man could eat with the surrounding funk was a mystery, and Jules suggested that Bob keep an eye on the car interiors for a dead dog, a tangled deer running from hunters. It was all a reminder to dread the actual search of the privies for the bones of Doris. The graduate students would understand that buried shit never stopped smelling.

In hindsight, some part of Jules knew earlier and

looked away. Birds meant something; birds led him to his first murder when he'd just become sheriff, only ten miles from the poor farm on his uncle's ranch. Crows and magpies everywhere, a big raven that seemed fascinated by the crane and flatbed, a kettle of turkey vultures making the most of the hot wind, which also kept the smell away from Jules.

The sound came just as Jules finished marking the first test pit. It was the kind of high-pitched unearthly siren Alice and Peter's small daughter unleashed when she saw her first life-sized Santa Claus, but these banshee wails came from Bob, who ran ten yards toward Jules before he dropped on his face and began to flop about. Because he didn't seem to be dying, Jules ignored him and ran toward whatever it was Bob saw.

Jules stopped a few feet short of the old Plymouth, as if that might make a difference. He was out of training, and his eyes kept jerking away from the face, black wounds staring straight ahead through the lost windshield, the mouth equally dark and gaping. The man's abdomen was crusted with blood, and so was one leg.

Jules took a half dozen steps back, keeping his eyes on the body and the car as if they might start rolling toward him. Bob's howls slowed, then picked up force, and when Jules ran over he understood: Bob's leg was trapped. Out here by the ragged end of the old road where Jules never considered looking, Bob was knee-deep in a grave.

"For fuck's sake," Jules said weakly. When he helped Bob pull out his bloody right leg, he saw broken pine and more color: dark hair, dirty pink cloth, a fragile collarbone: a girl, probably a child, lost, trampled and alone on a hill.

Doris? he thought.

Of course not, but somebody's darling. The pink was a modern-era synthetic coffin lining; a girl, left alone in a windy field, probably within someone's memory.

CAROLINE BLEW DOWN the hill in a cloud of dirt and gravel, and barely talked after Jules led her to the man. She asked questions about dates while she pulled on a polypropylene suit and shoe covers—when did Jules first notice the smell?—and then she circled the ground near the car and climbed inside to examine the body. She could handle the smell better than most people. She didn't act angry, but he knew she was enraged and horrified. This was on Cavendish Clusker, winging people in the dark, and that meant it was on her, for not arresting him. But when she made it back out of the car and walked upwind and poured half his bottle of water over her face, it wasn't so clear-cut: Cavendish owned popguns, small-gauge bird-hunting guns. All his taxidermy came from clients; Cavendish was always claiming to be a Quaker (or a Buddhist, depending on his audience at a bar). The other times he'd admitted to shooting out his window, he said he thought he was aiming at poachers.

But maybe Cavendish lied about this, too. The stomach wound—if a shotgun was used, it would have been point-blank, and the wound to the man's knee also looked like a rifle shot. Cavendish couldn't have done all of this, Caroline thought. And she began to think again of Charlie talking of having fun together. This frolicking among assholes took on greater significance; this dead man, currently being pried out of the junker by Gideon and Harvey and Perez, didn't get much love out of the deal.

No ID, but also no sign that anyone might have taken it from him, or that anyone but the crows and ravens and vultures had interfered with his body. Even with the bird damage, she was sure this man was shot with a rifle, at least twice, abdomen and leg. If he was on Cavendish's conscience, it seemed clear that he'd made the long, brutal crawl down from Marvel on Sunday or Monday night.

"Do you think this is one of the Russians you've met?" asked Jules.

"Maybe. But maybe this guy was already dead when Gideon and I met the inner tubers on Monday. Maybe he's one reason they were so unhappy."

CAROLINE HEADED UP the hill to confront Cavendish Clusker, who was wearing a suit, napping in his porch hammock. "Who died?" he said, smiling. "I've already been to my lawyer today."

This mood ended soon enough. Cavendish wept and wept: when he learned where the dead man was found, when he realized that going in with the police was necessary, when Caroline got a warrant and Harvey and Gideon began to search his mess of a house. They pulled out a .410, a 20-gauge, a very dusty 30.06 with a broken trigger, a Confederate sword, some nunchuk-type items, and about $30,000 in gold bars, kept in Cavendish's grandmother's hope chest. Caroline suggested Cavendish call Peter for a criminal attorney recommendation, but instead he called Ivan, who didn't pick up.

The old man sobbed the whole way to town. By the

time Caroline stowed him in the interview room, Gideon working the tape machine, Cavendish jibbered out most of the story: for the last month, as Charlie was courting an agreement on the land with food and booze-filled visits, Cavendish began to be tormented by the intruders' voices. They'd growl, and sometimes they'd say, "Old lonely man, sell," and then last Saturday they'd started a fire in the yard. Which was terrifying. It was reassuring to have company; it did get lonely up there, and Charlie Bell was interested in the glorious history of Marvel. But Caroline was all *craaazy* to think Cavendish's 20-gauge, his little bird gun, could have done this horrible thing. If this was one of the intruders, if this was something that happened in Marvel, the problem was that Charlie decided to help by taking shots, too. If something happened, it was just accidental. Charlie did like to show off with his rifle.

Caroline thought of Sergei's lost finger, the story it told: an explosive near-amputation and the final separation from a pocketknife. Unless the shot was taken at point-blank range, only a rifle would take a finger off, or go straight through a thigh, without peppering the perimeter. Those bandaged Russians—what painkillers were they on that day on the river?

She wanted to talk to Charlie but she knew she should wait. "We need to look for his prints," she said to Gideon and Harvey. "In the Marvel house. And for a rifle in Charlie's house in town. We need a search warrant; we need to not give him any warning. Doing it tonight would be a nightmare."

It was almost six o'clock, and Cavendish was still

weeping, eating away at her brain. "I can't see getting anything more out of him, tonight," said Harvey. "But he can't go back up there."

"Maybe I can stay with Suzette," said Cavendish. "I usually visit most weekends, anyway, and she planned to have me for the fireworks. We like to barbecue when Elaine isn't around."

What a clusterfuck, thought Caroline.

JULES LEFT THE hill when Gideon and Harvey and Perez drove up bearing equipment, Burt's precious satellite phone, and a search warrant. He picked up Tommy at daycare and took him to the city pool. Olive met him, and they sat in the shallows, dandling Tommy, hoping he didn't shit his swim diaper. It was very nice.

A skinny man with an extravagant nose was watching them. He was tattooed; though they weren't cook's tattoos, or navy tattoos, Jules felt no sense of threat, or the creepiness of a lurker. The man stuck to the deep end with his two companions, who seemed damaged. Bandages, exhaustion—all of it could have been the result of a classic bad Absarokan camping experience, though they didn't look outdoorsy. Jules lost interest while he tried to get Tommy to relax on his back, and when Olive waved to one of the men, he was only mildly curious. "Who are they?"

"One of them is Marina's friend. You know, the nurse who saved Caroline."

Did he know? Should he write a thank-you note? This train of thought disappeared when Tommy went underwater for a moment and screamed in protest. When Jules checked again, the men were gone.

*

JULES POURED HIMSELF a beer, put Tommy in a playpen, and sat at the picnic table to cold-call Patrick Bell. This time the call went through.

"Your parents are selling pieces of the ranch."

"Charlie's selling it. Charlie needs money. I gather he's incurred new debt."

"Why don't they stop him?"

"Fear. Someone is trying to help."

"By buying away their ranch?" said Jules. "What is Ivan Luneau, the third son?"

A pause, and then a joke: "Well, obviously the first two haven't panned out."

Jules waited for more. "It's fair to describe Ivan that way. My parents took him in during a bad time, years ago, and he helps them now. He's a good man."

"Why does Charlie owe money?"

"Lots of very bad reasons, I hear."

"From Ivan? I hear he's visiting."

"Yes, from Ivan. The father-in-law died and Charlie's wife inherited. She overdosed and Charlie inherited. He owes someone a thank-you."

Again, the worry that he was being played. "I know nothing," said Jules. "And that's fine. I'm missing everything. I am trying to understand why you won't speak about the actual shooting."

"I can't."

Not "I don't remember." "Why don't you tell me your version of the truth?"

Patrick said nothing. Jules rephrased. "What would it take to tell the truth?"

"My brother's death."

"So that he couldn't defend himself?"

"So that he couldn't kill my family."

"Does he threaten to hurt your parents?"

"Yes."

"If they what?"

"If they tell the truth."

"Charlie says no one should talk to them, that he's protecting them."

More amusement: "Do you think Charlie's ever protected anyone but Charlie?"

"Does he say things about Iris in the letters he writes to you? Did he think she was his?"

"Always."

"If what you're saying is true, if he wanted to harm Iris and harm you, why would your parents have told Charlie you were coming?"

"They didn't. My mother told a friend, and the friend's child happened to pick up the phone when Charlie called her father. She was excited to see . . . us. I don't blame anyone."

A child. "Did he hurt Iris that day?"

"I was lying in the dirt."

Jules, feeling around: "That day, did he tell you he was going to hurt her?"

"Yes."

"When?"

Patrick didn't answer, he didn't bite. Jules felt something form and pushed it to one side.

"Why is your wife dead?"

Silence on the line. In the long lull before Patrick answered, Jules watched a squirrel run along the fence with one of Caroline's cherry tomatoes.

"Because of my brother."

"Is your brother dangerous?"

"Yes."

"To whom?"

"To everyone."

17 *Party Time*

AN OLD JOKE: WHAT SHOULD YOU TAKE TO A WASP picnic? Martinis, and whatever food you bring, make sure it isn't enough. But throw a fully catered party with a loaded bar in Blue Deer, and they will come. Elaine was opening her perfect front door to a hundred people, from bank presidents and Los Angeles expats to most of the town's white collars, all vaguely familiar from glimpses at fundraisers. Caroline's book club friends, people from the hospital administration and the courthouse, and a part of Blue Deer—stable, conservative, churchgoing—that Jules didn't deal with often now.

Jules and Caroline left for the party at seven, once she showered off the smell of the man in the car. They parked behind Suzette's garage, and came around to the deck from the back of the house, taking in the chaos cautiously. The Selways' driveway was already filling up. Mac was playing Earth, Wind & Fire, and a breeze was kicking in, cutting the heat; napkins were already fluttering away. He wore a turquoise Hawaiian shirt and was surrounded by a half dozen women, the largest peacock in the middle, overseeing a troop of kids with small-gauge fireworks on the part of the Selway driveway closest to the Clement property, the middle of the peace sign. Before the bloody bathtub, Mac's fireworks were his only bit of local fame.

Elaine's piping voice made it through the music, the leaves, the people, burrowing into Jules's head again. Charlie, meanwhile, leaned against the door of the house as if he owned it, staring across the clearing toward Suzette's deck, where the older woman was a blaze of magenta and Sadie, in a very slight sundress, was a vision of loveliness, Helen of Troy or at least the closest thing Blue Deer offered this summer. Caroline sat down with the Aches, who were trying to hang on to both their drinks and their cards in the sudden wind.

Divvy and his crew were sitting on stacked boards, drinking beer and admiring the show. To one side, the fully prepped forms for the garage, just waiting for liquid cement; behind them, a gaping hole: the house foundation was dug, and a huge pile of dirt lay to one side.

Jules yipped and sprinted toward the site. "I didn't finish clearing."

"Eh, we figured it out," said Divvy. "Went like a charm. The cement guys might show in the morning to pour the garage."

"That quickly?" Jules stared at the spoils pile, a twenty-by-twenty-foot mound of rocks and dirt filled with who knew what horrors.

"What, you want to wait until Monday? We'll get that pile hauled away."

"Oh no," said Jules. "No, no. Don't touch it. We'll use it for landscaping. Nothing weird? No old fuel drums, river barges, buried treasure?"

"Didn't notice a thing," said Divvy, which was not

much of an answer. "If you want to keep the dirt, you'll have to clear out that thicket and make some room for the wood and the trusses. It's hard to maneuver in there. And if you want them to start on the house forms tomorrow, get down there and clean up the stray bits. The shovel's there waiting for you."

They turned to watch Mac shoot off a screaming rocket with a parachute. It landed on the bar tent, and was still smoking when three children started to climb the poles to retrieve it, making the tent sway and Elaine shriek.

"Or maybe these fuckballs'll just burn your clearing clean," said Divvy. He headed for the Selways' overwhelmed bartender.

Jules circled and poked the spoils pile, seeing only rock and clay, sand and tree roots. He jumped down into the hole that would be his house, again loving the feeling of being hidden, and saw a little charcoal, some discoloration from some old foundation-style timbers, but nothing awful. Everything was going to be okay.

He picked up the spade and started scraping up the last piles.

ON SUZETTE'S DECK, where the average age was seventy-five, Caroline plopped Tommy on Olive's lap, made herself a drink, and took in the apparently peaceful scene. Ivan's car was parked near the Clement garage site, and Caroline picked him out near the bar, Cavendish attached by an invisible cord. Elaine and Mac nattered with their Ohio guests; a plump woman in a fuchsia dress who seemed familiar talked with Charlie, who looked sulky in a jade-green asshole shirt. Another belated recognition:

this was the rich friend of the woman who'd overdosed in the valley, just before Tommy was born. She met Caroline's eyes and smiled. Charlie met them and frowned.

Caroline moved to the far end of the deck, where Alice was sussing out the crowd.

"Who's that?" asked Alice. "He's interesting."

A man was leaning against the Selway house, midway between the tents and the hot tub. He wore jeans and a white T-shirt, but what caught Caroline's eye was a flash of red: sneakers.

"Guy's got a face like a weapon," said Alice.

There was a lull in the music, and someone called Charlie's name. Two other red-sneakered men were pulling off their shirts near the hot tub. Caroline stood as her inner-tubing pal Fred Pushkin called Charlie's name a second time, and Charlie's head jerked around.

Caroline chugged her drink and headed over to Jules, glancing back at Charlie's face as it listened to whatever Fred was saying. Jules was a sweaty, cheerful mess; Peter was sitting on a nearby log, and she saw two empty glasses.

"Anything burning yet?"

"Not quite," said Caroline. "Though Mac is drinking tequila."

"Well, fuck it," said Jules. "Look at this beautiful hole in the ground."

"Hey," she said. "You should keep an eye on Charlie."

"Fuck Charlie," he said. "Jump down with me."

"Not right now," said Caroline, watching Charlie scan the crowd.

He tugged and she relented. "Did I tell you I went to see the Bells?" asked Caroline.

"Fuck the Bells," said Jules, kissing her. "But why?"

And then Charlie was standing at the edge of the excavation, blocking the low evening sun, a living metaphor.

"How dare you let that woman go near my parents."

"Run that by me again," said Jules after a moment.

"That bitch harassed my parents."

Jules scythed the shovel under Charlie's feet, jumped out of the hole, and held the blade against Charlie's throat. It was over in a minute, but people were running their way, notably Elaine, who was screaming, "No trouble! No trouble! Charles, think!"

"Are you thinking?" asked Jules.

"Should I call the police?" Peter asked.

"No," said Jules, stepping back and lifting the shovel.

Charlie got to his feet and dusted off his pants. "No."

Charlie and Elaine walked back to the party, hand in hand.

UP ON THE deck, Suzette made Jules a big fat whiskey. The party was devolving in other ways, too: the Russians were in the hot tub, apparently naked, while Charlie pretended they didn't exist; Mac's fireworks were getting larger, his aim a little looser.

Cavendish and Ivan came up on the deck, Cavendish schmoozing the ladies as if nothing at all was wrong or new in his life. Ivan greeted Sadie and Caroline with a kiss and sat down between Caroline and Jules, forestalling a quarrel about how little she'd told him about her day, or her week. "I hear you're going up to Deer Lodge," said Jules to Ivan.

"I am," said Ivan. "We could go together. I need to give a better explanation, but it's not really my story."

People kept saying this. Ivan turned to Caroline. "Cavendish tells me—tells his lawyer—that Charlie has been visiting with a rifle, shooting into the dark at intruders. Which is interesting, because those Russians"—he pointed to the hot tub, where Andrei and Sergei were lolling—"tell me that they've been hired to harass Cavendish. By Charlie. And they tell me they are here because they haven't been paid, and they've suffered."

"He's shooting his own employees?" asked Caroline.

"Maybe he's trying to get out of the bill," said Ivan. "I hear he has some serious bills."

"You hear a lot," said Caroline.

"I do."

"Maybe we could have a more formal questioning," said Caroline.

"All right," said Ivan.

Charlie was watching them while Elaine shimmied back and forth in front of him, as if to block his view of Suzette's house and the people on the deck.

"Charlie will be back for more," said Ivan. "I'm quite sure; look at his face. He doesn't know I'm the buyer of the acreage, and he won't understand when he finds out. The Bells took me in. I'm buying the land back to thank them."

"Patrick Bell told me you were kind to them," said Jules.

"Did he? I'm impressed that he would say that much to you. I'll protect them now, when Charlie gets wind of everything."

"Maybe it won't matter to Charlie who comes up with the money."

"Well, there's more," said Ivan. "He won't be happy. I booked the Bells into the Baird to keep them out of range."

Mac lit a larger rocket and the crowd, sashaying around one another like mating cranes, shrieked in a flurry of embers. Caroline headed down. "Be a little careful?" she said to Mac. In the background, the Russians were hurrying into their clothes.

"Ah," he said. "It's so hard! I'm not a careful person. But I'll try."

She wasn't quite back to the deck when he fired another, larger rocket. Most of the guests, especially the out-of-town ones, thought this was funny, but Jules watched Charlie walk over and poke Mac in the chest.

Which wasn't something you did if you wanted to avoid an escalation. Mac moved a cake of nine shots a little closer to his former home and lit the fuse. It couldn't start raining soon enough. As the last embers fell, people began to roar: a blow-up doll with bright yellow hair hung from the upstairs window. It wore a noose around its neck and a bra around its torso above a tiny, deflated penis, painted bright red.

Caroline saw a shape slide out the back door by the hot tub: Fred Pushkin, with his crazy killer Bowie eyes. He smiled, and waved, and disappeared into the trees toward the river.

The music stopped; the doll bounced in a gust. Mac aimed a rocket straight for it, missed, and scorched the house's siding. Elaine began to scream. Someone said they were calling the police, and Caroline heard Jules ask Olive to take Tommy into Suzette's house.

Charlie studied the doll, Mac, the guests, his screaming lover. Elaine ran toward him and he pushed her away; she fell but popped up and followed when he walked toward the peanut gallery on Suzette's deck.

He can't quite give it up, thought Caroline. But Charlie pointed at Ivan, then at Jules.

"You shouldn't talk to this man," said Charlie. "This man's wife has abused my parents, who are frail, and elderly, and not in their right mind."

"You're protective now?" asked Ivan.

"Of course I'm protective."

"But you're selling off their ranch."

The ladies on Suzette's deck sucked in their breath.

"Well, you should know that rumor is mostly a lie. But anyway, if you want to be in business with me, avoid Mr. Clement."

It was like a dog offering its stomach and biting at the same time. Ivan smiled. "I don't want to be in business with you," he said. "I have no intention of being in business with you."

"You don't want Marvel? You'll let some other asshole buy Marvel?"

"I own Marvel already, as of this morning. I bought it from Suzette Whipple, Francis and Lucia Bell, and Cavendish Clusker."

A pause; even Mac was listening. "I think not," said Charlie. "Because tomorrow morning, my parents will sign paperwork giving me their power of attorney. And tomorrow morning, Elaine will present evidence that her mother is incompetent. And Clusker is my partner."

This was a little like the time he told her Dinak hadn't been murdered, thought Caroline. Charlie wasn't reading the crowd. Suzette's face was fascinating: watchful, vengeful.

"It's over," said Ivan. "Done deal."

Cavendish Clusker, who'd been sticking to the Selway

bar table like a remora, began to creep closer, asking people what was being said. Charlie wasn't paying attention; Charlie was having trouble comprehending. Elaine grabbed his arm and he shook her off again.

"What are you talking about?" said Charlie.

Up on the deck, Suzette finally put down her cards and waved a crumpled hand. "I'm sure a share will come to you eventually, Charles. And I'm fine with you and Elaine taking a cut on the dryland parcels. But it was quite silly and hurtful for you two to try to diminish your parents in this way." She held out her glass. "To Ivan, the new owner of Marvel. To our old home finding the right home."

"It's my fucking land!" screamed Charlie.

Elaine tried to grab his hand one more time and he swung an arm out, smacking her across the face and dropping her to the gravel. Caroline, moving toward Elaine, heard sirens. By now everyone was watching—Mac, the Baird guests, the book club, Eldridge the banker.

"I know what you are," said Suzette. "Give me a point or two for not telling the world."

"Mother," said Elaine.

"What, honey? What would you have done?"

Something worse, thought Jules. Peter was looking simultaneously smug and worried. And Charlie's eyes were a strange new sight.

"I warned you," said Charlie to Jules. "I warned you to stay away."

It was such an odd voice, a warm, toasty voice. Did it lull people? How could a monster have such a voice? How could someone with hair the color of a fucking banana have this voice?

"Stay away from what?"

"Everything. You've belittled me. You've helped people cheat me."

"I'll admit it's all making me happy, but I didn't hang the fucking doll up there."

Down below, Mac fired a rocket directly at the food tent, and the streamers caught fire. Charlie pointed a finger at Suzette. "You murdering old bitch. Stop talking to my mother."

Jules, who in the past knew better than to insult a man with a habit of kicking while leaning back in a chair, feet on a deck rail, said in a moment of drunken glee, "I'm enjoying talking to your brother; he's a nice guy. Did you dye your hair so you wouldn't look like him?"

He saw the foot coming. Jules went down fast, his face blown open, making a weird noise that was almost a laugh. A flash of Caroline's stunned face; nothing but a car accident could have been faster. But he was ready when Charlie hopped on his chest, both of them on top of the broken chair: jab to the throat, fingers in the eyeballs, and once Jules flipped him, a knee to the genitals.

Blood was bursting from Jules's nose, and his head roared, but he'd rarely been so happy. He took a step back and waited.

"Look what you've done to my deck," said Suzette.

Jules gave Charlie credit: he was vomiting but still crawling forward, like a George Romero extra. Jules grabbed him by the back of his head, slammed his face into the deck, and then held it to the side so that the prick didn't choke on his own vomit. Someone pushed him and Ed was suddenly there, without fanfare—it was always surprising, how quick he could be. Jules met his eyes and jumped off at the last possible moment. Charlie got to his feet swinging and tried to kick Ed. Gideon, just a step behind, flipped Charlie and cuffed him.

"Time for jail," said Ed mildly.

Elaine wailed and Jules turned to stare, and looking at her agonized face, felt a drunk conviction: she was doomed. He didn't care in most ways, but anyone shied away from doom. He felt pity, and he didn't want to.

IVAN AND JULES faded into the trees on the far side of the house and got stoned and watched Peter reassure Gideon that Mac was done lighting explosives. Only now did they notice they were just twenty feet from Mac's prize possession, the Caja China pig roaster he'd planned to use that day. This was Peter's sell job—he'd wanted someone to buy one because he wanted to borrow it. But now Jules felt a little horror: something was mounded on the four-foot box, covered by a tarp. Did Mac buy a pig, forget that he'd ordered a pig, and leave it out to rot for the day?

This was more or less what Jules said. Ivan eyed the mound and the tarp and handed him the pipe. "Jesus. What a waste. Was this here when the party started?"

No, thought Jules, trying to become an alert human one more time that day. Getting kicked in the face took it out of a person. There was, for instance, a truck parked on the edge of Elaine's perfect back acreage, half-crushing some faux-Greek planters—was it here earlier? Did it occur to anyone that such planters began their design life as sarcophagi? No, of course not. Had it occurred to Jules that this truck belonged to Burt?

Only gradually. He walked over. The cab was empty, the tailpipe was cold, and the curtains were pulled tight on the camping shell windows, though he could hear a radio playing. He banged on the back and called Burt's name. Nothing. He peered into the front seat, pushing his face close to cut down on the glare of the sun, and there was Burt's service revolver, baton, and handcuffs, piled on the seat. They lay on top of a stack of hairy nudes, evidently Burt nudes, and a spray of candy bars and gram cocaine packages and bags of pot.

To Jules, even stoned and bruised, it seemed gratuitous. Ivan muttered about not wanting to be someone's lawyer, and Jules felt a moment of suspicion and decided to dismiss it. This was, at the very least, not a pro move on Burt's part. The window was down a bit, but neither of them could get an arm in to unlock the door. Jules waved to Suzette's oblivious, ancient, bloodthirsty deck party, and bellowed, "Caroline!"

She looked annoyed—the tenor of the night was now giddy, and Tommy was sleeping peacefully on Suzette's bed—until she focused on Burt's truck. She trotted over and they circled it together. The music inside was gospel; Caroline thought she heard someone hum, out of tune. He boosted her up and she managed to reach the door lock.

Jules and Ivan both stood back when Caroline opened the driver's door. Burt's truck keys lay on the floor of the cab, under a pile of his clothes. She extracted them gingerly—she didn't have gloves, and she was dodging white envelopes. They stood for a moment before Caroline turned the key in the camper's back hatch. When she opened it, a flutter of printed photos on cheap paper swirled out. Another dozen heavier Polaroids stayed where they were on a stained camping pad, next to IV bags and syringes and adult diapers filled with shit and urine.

The battery-powered tape deck warbled on: *didn't it*

rain, children. Ivan started to gag and Jules turned back to the tarped mound on the pig box. Now that he really looked—now that he was sobering up at relative rocket speed—there was a shimmer of movement to the blue plastic. Maybe it was his head injury, but the tarp seemed to vibrate, to hum.

Caroline, always quicker, trotted over and ripped the tarp away, and there, revealed, was the acting sheriff of Absaroka County, trussed with a small apple in his mouth and a clown sock puppet on his penis. The thing protruding from his ass would prove to be his stun gun.

No one knew what to say, but they all moved to cover him.

In the background, Mac, now wearing a long dark coat over all his Hawaiian brilliance, shot a last rocket and finally managed to set the caterer's tent on fire. He stepped back into the smoke, a Cheshire cat in the trees, only the smile left as he faded away.

18 *The Sixth Morning*

FRIDAY

SOMETHING ABOUT CHARLIE BELL BEING IN JAIL, about a couple of whiskeys and a little physical trauma and some sloppy late lovemaking, allowed Jules to sleep like a rock. They all slept like rocks, all three of them, while elsewhere in the town crimes were committed, fires were set, guns were fired, people were unkind to one another. He remembered the sound of a cat running over the roof, and Celeste baying once. She never barked, and in his sleep, he worried.

When Tommy woke them at six, Celeste and the cat were with them. Jules opened the front door, saw the open gate and the tall box on the porch, and decided to drink a cup of coffee before he opened it. He was thrilled when it was a bouquet, with a block-lettered note. *Beautiful Caroline: I have information. This horror, this murder, must be stopped. Have you not matched the prints of the fingers?*

"For fuck's sake," she said, peering at the note and the flowers, a whatever-survives-in-an-alley-in-August collection of hollyhocks, birdseed sunflowers, invasive campanula, and someone's prize gladiolus. Nicely arranged, though. Fred, you shouldn't have. Let's talk about Bernie Dinak's Polaroid camera.

"I don't know. I think this is pretty upbeat," said Jules. "Gift horses, and all."

Caroline did feel kind of upbeat: Charlie was in jail and she might be able to keep him there. She shot out the door, leaving behind a file she knew Jules needed to finish. He didn't see it until he was stuffing Tommy's fat, writhing feet into socks:

Please read this again, Caroline wrote on the log, the record of Ansel's last minutes ticking by:

> 3:58—Well it was just five minutes ago. I was headed south, just about to Shandley's Ridge, and this f----- was passing, coming at me in my lane in this f------ truck. I just about s--- myself, nearly rolled in the borrow pit.
>
> 4:07—I was coming up from Sabine and I was pretty tired—what time is it now? Then I'd say this happened at four maybe, but you know I've been shaking since then. Didn't even see the truck coming from behind and there they were right next to me, window all smeared with blood.
>
> 4:29—My wife is still shaky. If you don't take care of those c---------s, I will. And seeing that poor man in the dust. Can't bear it.
>
> 4:31—Like a devil, wearing sunglasses. Hoping he managed to drive in the river or some such.

Twenty-four-year-old Grace, earnestly counting out hyphens for obscenities (Jules couldn't resist checking *c---------s*), whispering the letters as she typed).

A sticky note at the bottom. *Do you see what I see?*

No, he didn't.

UNTIL THE PARTY, Caroline thought of Charlie as a kind of malign Ken doll, but seeing his face in the light of the burning tent, seeing his rage, shifted her thinking, and so did the mention of him bringing a rifle along for target practice at Cavendish's house. She'd arranged for a second search warrant by seven a.m. and followed Gideon and Perez to Blue Creek.

It took a full minute for Elaine to come to the door. She was wearing a pink bathrobe, but underneath it her legs were scratched and dirty and bloody, as were her hands. Her hair was a rat's nest, her nose swollen, and her right eye a bloodshot slit from the back of Charlie's hand.

Caroline held up the warrant. Elaine shrieked and fell to her knees. She began hitting her head against the floor.

This was not the reaction Caroline anticipated. Elaine got in a half dozen thwacks before Caroline grabbed her shoulder and rolled her on her side. The woman wasn't acting—she didn't try to cover herself as she rolled, and the robe parted to show more scrapes, more blood, no underwear. Caroline leaned over her and said, "Elaine, stop it. Did Charlie tell you he'd shot those men? You don't have to go down for this, too."

Elaine stopped, stared blankly at the floor for a minute.

"Tell me."

Elaine stood up and cinched her robe. "I don't know what you're talking about."

And that was all she said to the next dozen questions. She sat primly on a couch as they scoured the downstairs, but she screamed when Gideon started for the stairs. Caroline went up with him and left Perez to babysit. Charlie's very prim corner desk in the bedroom held bank statements, an address book, an envelope of gel vitamins, and workout magazines. In the garage, they found a remnant pile of boxes labeled *Mac*, and a rifle, a .308.

Which was disappointing, because the cartridges they'd found in the Marvel house were for a .30-06. Gideon found bullets for both rifles in the Suburban.

Inside the refrigerator, Kruger found a thousand dollars in a crumpled manila envelope, puffed out like it once held more.

Caroline left Gideon to it and walked across to Suzette's house, where Cavendish was staying while his house was cordoned off. He wept again, but this morning the reaction was automatic, a self-preservation technique. Tears fell as he buttered his toast.

"We didn't find any evidence of a fire you said the intruders set," said Caroline.

"Charlie said they started it on a gas can lid. Good thing it wasn't a windy night."

"I'll look for the lid, see if it squares with what you're saying now. And you can bet we'll talk to Charlie, but I don't buy it. The thing is, Cavendish, all week you've been claiming you hit someone."

"Not possible."

"It's very possible," she said. "It's the likeliest explanation."

"Charlie joked that he was hunting," said Cavendish. "But he wouldn't want me to say that."

"How upset will he be with you, about the sale? I imagine Ivan offered more money."

"Well, he did, and he was being nice to all of us. How could I screw my childhood friends? I know Suzette is a little up and down, but those pills her daughter was giving her—it's just not right. And Ivan says he won't chop our town into little pieces. He loves the Bells, and they love him. He said I could keep the house, and he added a few grand. And you know, I could die any minute, like my poor brother Frog, the idiot. Who listens to a radio in a bathtub?"

She remembered hearing about that death; she should ask Gideon about it. All this blather, these tears—a week ago, Cavendish was willing to cut out friends and family, a night ago he was pickled in remorse, and today he was back to blind indifference for a man who'd been shot, crawled down a hill, and died alone in a wrecked car.

"Right," said Caroline. "Let's go back through it. What nights?"

"I don't know. I always called you after."

"Cavendish, please concentrate. What nights did Charlie use the rifle? Did you actually see or smell the fire Charlie said he'd found? Could he have lied to you?"

"No, but that really freaked me out. I don't want to die in flames in that house."

"Where do you want to die?" asked Caroline.

But Cavendish didn't get the joke. "I'm going to get a little place in Costa Rica."

Caroline walked back to Elaine's. Gideon whispered about pills in envelopes and empty cocaine wrappers in the hot tub, but Caroline couldn't get enthused about wrappers. Find a full one, she thought—the judge was terrified by every drug but alcohol. It would be the least of Charlie's sins, but enough to lock him up for days, weeks, years.

"Elaine," she said. "I'll ask again. If you don't answer,

I'll be tempted to charge you as an accessory. Do you know if Charlie went up to Cavendish Clusker's to scare away intruders?"

"Oh," said Elaine. "I don't pay attention to Charlie." She tilted her head, the old gesture, and appraised Caroline.

As a couple, Elaine and Charlie were not short on ego; now Caroline hoped it would do them in.

And she was rewarded. Elaine pursed her lips and spoke. "But he did. Three times, I think, late last week and on the weekend."

Under the bus, thought Caroline, rubbing her aching neck.

"He was very mysterious, you know. It can't have been for long, because we are always together. He really can't stay away."

Gideon's seized items included an envelope with a pill and a note inside (*For sexy times, Sweetie*) found shoved under some wool socks, and another note, in Fred's distinctive handwriting, pinned to a pair of Charlie's dirty underpants: *Pay up, tiny man, for the blood on your soul.*

The dead man's friends were unhappy. Dead men. The wounded boy in the wheelchair, the compassionate injection before a final hot bath in Lazuli Pool—that was probably down to Charlie's rifle, too.

JULES'S ENEMY SOMEWHAT vanquished, it was time to clear the fucking decks, to finally deal with Donald Edgar Whipple, chiseler and fraud. DOB 6.13.30 in Dayton, Ohio, last seen in Blue Deer in October 1972, last seen in San Clemente, California, later that same month. Elaine wanted *at the very least, his death certificate.* She'd given Jules family names, marriage dates, full addresses, her parents' social security numbers. Her father was about six feet and skinny, with dark hair with a little gray. She believed he fought in Korea but she'd never seen any uniform or documentation.

Elaine expected Suzette to say Donald Whipple walked into the Pacific in the fall of 1972 but *that is so very impossible.* Her father wasn't interested in the out-of-doors. He was a businessman and he made money and Elaine knew she took after him. She wasn't sure what worried her more—that her father died in some horrible way, or that he wasn't dead at all, and he'd come back after Suzette died. When he first disappeared Elaine remembered a dream of her mother bloody on a bed. At least Suzette said it was a dream, before she told Elaine it was her own blood, a miscarriage, and the miscarriage was Donald's fault. *But she was drunk and she makes everything about her. The bullshit the hospital is trying now—that I've poisoned her, that he broke her bones—she's a drinker. You know that.*

Harvey's notes were thorough and professional. A pickled retired cop in San Clemente who'd dealt with the case said that Whipple was sleeping with his secretary, scamming his partners in his California real estate office, forging his wife's signature to sell some of her land in Montana. In terms of blood, Blue Deer police records showed that neighbors reported screams at Blue Creek several times over the late summer of 1972, but Mrs. Whipple never pressed charges.

Nor, thought Jules, did Bunny McElwaine or anyone else in the sheriff's department give her much support. Ansel was dead by the date of the first call.

Jules, typing fast, did what he could to answer Elaine's questions. Whether Donald Whipple was dead or not, he'd been declared so; if walking into cold water was impossible, then he'd staged his suicide. There were no absolutes, but Jules could provide five pages' worth of facts. Elaine could still believe whatever she wanted to believe.

He left the Baird as the lobby filled with the Selways' bleary guests, all of them very eager to check out.

WHEN JULES PARKED in the DMZ, he saw Divvy surrounded by workers to the west, Elaine's tattered and scorched Field of the Cloth of Gold to the east. Trash from the party littered the clearing. Jules wanted to see Elaine crawling around with a hangover, picking it up with her shell-pink tongue. He also saw police cars, and he was relieved they were in front of Elaine's house, not Suzette's. Even pleased, though he buried the thought like a good Lutheran boy.

Kruger, whose first name Jules could never remember, was shoving bank boxes into his car.

"All of that?" said Jules. "For the shooting?"

"Motive," snipped Kruger.

Indeed, thought Jules. "Where's my friend Caroline?"

"Court. We're just finishing up."

Upstairs, in what was probably the master bedroom window, Jules watched Gideon bring the lynched blow-up doll inside and stuff it into a bag. The Russian guys loved their hints. Jules itched to know what Gideon was seeing and possibly not understanding in the Elaine-Mac-Charlie bedroom, but he turned back to his own life.

Divvy stood by a beautiful garage-sized expanse of cement, a gorgeous thing, shimmering in the sunlight as it dried. He was keeping an eye on his felons as they tempered the slab.

"Wow," said Jules. "They really came. Dawn."

"I dunno about 'dawn,'" said Divvy. "But holy fuck, your face."

"No problems?"

"Nah. We only needed to rerake the slab gravel before the pour."

Jules swiveled, alarmed. "Kids?"

Divvy grinned. "Or a dog or deer or neighborly drunks. I mean, we're finding glasses and bottles everywhere, and a few other found objects." He fished in his pocket and dropped a large button, a small turquoise earring, and a Baird Hotel key into Jules's hand. "It wasn't bad, just a ten-minute touch-up. Perfect temperature to pour, perfect weather. Everything's perfect, but you'll need to clean up a little more to make room for the trusses."

Jules gave a sidelong look toward the apple tree.

"The tree will be fine," said Divvy. "Just deal with the prickery shit, and all that metal. I don't want the boys getting tetanus or thorns in their fingers. Fucking whiners."

"All right." Jules watched Celeste, boozehound, lick some gravel near the foundation. Partygoers, dumping their bad margaritas on Jules's precious ground. "What's up in the wars?"

"She"—Divvy nodded toward Suzette's house—"was taken to brunch and a funeral by the lovely Sadie Winton. And she"—a nod to Elaine's house—"you can see there've been some interruptions to her beauty sleep, even though the prick is downtown."

They watched Gideon stuff the doll into the back seat of his patrol car and drive off.

Jules dodged party cups as he returned to Elaine's house. He pounded to no effect, even though she was transparently home—her car was in the garage, Charlie's in the driveway. Jules found an evidence bag and a staple gun in his truck, wadded the report about Donald Whipple in the bag, and was about to staple the thing to Elaine's nice wooden door, like Luther nailing up his theses without the hammer or the Devil, when it swung open. Elaine looked so awful it was alarming. He averted his eyes, but she blatantly studied his cheekbone and enlarged nose and bloodshot right eye. "Do you have good news or bad news?"

"Hard to tell, given that I don't know what you want to hear."

"Come with me, then, and wait while I read it. A very odd-looking police officer pawed through my personal things, and I need to relax."

Odd-looking, thought Jules. He followed her around the side of the house, where perfection gave way to dinged-up garbage cans, broken lawn chairs, more piles of stuff labeled *MAC*. Elaine scooped some leaves and bobbing plastic glasses out of the water. The hot tub was draped with dirty towels and a tiny, tie-dyed Speedo.

The mind boggled. "Charlie's associates," she snapped. "Do I have to pay you more so you don't talk to the trustees?"

Clearly she didn't understand that Mac wasn't planning to follow through on their agreement. "Of course not," he said. "I want you both happy and off the fucking block."

She started to take off her robe. "You don't have to look at me."

She was wearing a demure one-piece, but Jules looked up at the cottonwood crowns swaying above. Some of the branches held bits of confetti and plastic. When Elaine settled into the water, he handed her the memo and watched her read. When she concentrated, she almost looked human. Her lips parted, her breathing slowed, and he could see—at this moment when she was wasn't moving, wasn't openly antagonistic—a scar on her neck, the deep pucker of a tracheostomy.

When she looked up, there was no animosity. "Do you know what I remember about him? I remember him holding me so tight that it hurt, and I remember him being very angry. I think he hated her and wanted to take me with him when he left. Do you think she'd tell you? She likes you."

"I think she's likelier to tell Mac," said Jules.

"Mac wouldn't ask her. He's failed me. He's left me. That dream I told you about—maybe it's my father's blood. Maybe Suzette killed him."

"I can tell you, after talking to a detective down there, that the secretary who identified the clothes left on the beach was having an affair with your father. And I can tell you that money seemed to be missing from his Long Beach account but your mother decided not to have the secretary investigated."

"Was his wallet found?"

"No, but would you expect a wallet left out on a beach to be found?"

"Would you mind talking to the secretary, for your money?"

"She died of cirrhosis in 1980. She never worked again,

so she may have managed to take quite a bit of cash." A pause. "You see how this looks."

"I see, but I also know he wasn't the kind of man who'd walk into cold water. He wasn't the kind of man to kill himself, period."

You can't walk on water at the bottom of a lake, thought Jules. He could question her faith in her child's memory, but he knew, better than most people, how cruel that would be. *You can't possibly remember your father*, over and over. *Oh yes I can*, he'd thought.

"In 1978, Suzette asked to have your father declared dead, to receive social security benefits for you, for college. It went through in 1980."

"Why not have him declared dead back in 1972?"

"I can't guess. Dealing with the system. Maybe she really didn't want to know."

But he thought: dread, inertia. Not rocking the boat, not being sure what would be found.

"Or because she did know," said Elaine. "She knew because she killed him, and she knew no one cared but me. Without that woman, my daddy would still be buying me lobster. She told me he wanted to put her in a loony bin. How great would that have been?"

Lobster. She wasn't hiding her crazy eyes today. "Did you know he beat her?"

"She was beatable," said Elaine. "My face was an accident. I won't let it happen again. And I'm not going to defend Charlie or ask that charges be dropped. He might not have meant to do it at the time, but I didn't get the sense it made him feel bad. Did you?"

"No," said Jules. "I didn't."

People were, of course, fucked up, which was one big problem with being a civil servant. Jules decided to head to the poor farm, where no one needed a shrink but him.

AT THE STATION, Caroline was relieved to learn the morning's arraignments were delayed—the judge hit a deer on her way in and needed X-rays. Grace and Harvey were both dealing with calls, and the dispatcher was wild-eyed—the Billings NBC affiliate was calling about the Burt story.

Harvey belatedly made prints from Cavendish's wildlife camera. Hikers and coyotes: Caroline thought she could pick out Fred's and Sergei's and Andrei's faces. The car man surged past the camera, dark-haired, burly, and handsome, and she recognized a face from the summer, her drunk violinist of June, who she guessed was the melter. It was heartbreaking—he was a boy, with soft curly hair and very wide eyes.

None of them were captured leaving. Caroline imagined them running through the woods, losing their way, losing one another.

Edie, when tracked down in the laundry room of the Baird, peered at the photos and said that yes, they'd all been guests. She thought the car man's name was Paulie, Pavel. He liked to quote poetry; quite a flirt. The melter's name was Mika, Mikael. Sweet boy, very musical, bad drunk. He wasn't going to age well, she joked.

Well, no, he wasn't. Caroline decided to put that conversation off for a bit.

Edie, who was a little depressed—Mac and Ivan both missed a morning meeting of condo owners—also recognized Sergei and Andrei and Fred, who she said, "just kept trying." The lady who'd booked the rooms paid cash. She was a kind of office manager—they were trying to start a travel service—and she'd booked the same rooms for a different, smaller crew, just her and two men, the fall before. Those men were not as pleasant, and when Edie found a bag of suspicious medications in their room and complained, the woman said it would never happen again, and the men would never come back. Fred was the only repeat—he'd only been in briefly the fall before—and he wasn't bad. The rest of this crew were sweeties, but if they were gone, they were gone. Edie couldn't afford to keep the rooms vacant anymore. Caroline must know the fingerprint powder wasn't easy to clean up. Did Caroline want the suitcase they'd left behind?

Caroline scribbled down names. She needed to start thinking of the car man as Pavel, and the foot as poor Mikael. Sergei, missing a thumb, with a hole in his thigh—another rifle shot? Andrei of the scorched back and leg and brain; Fred, the jokester, apparently the only undamaged one out of the five men. Russians sliding toward injury and death, like bugs to zappers, inner tubing between strange funeral rituals. They didn't seem like murderers—were they just mop-up men, with a penchant for taking photos with a dead priest's camera?

Down in the basement, Caroline opened the forgotten suitcase. Folded shirts, jeans, no sneakers, band T-shirts, a scribble in Cyrillic. A Polaroid of a bison, taken over the shoulder of a woman wearing a deep blue scarf—the same scarf from the Yellowstone-melter video—and an envelope addressed *to Carolina.*

Caroline got some prints from the suitcase, took the Russian note and the envelope, and she left her own: *call me*, and her number. She told Edie to let her know if anyone showed up for it.

SHE OPENED THE envelope at the office. Fred Pushkin's list showed dates and figures and read like a rolling invoice. "Services rendered," "partial payment." Fall, spring, total outstanding, interest. These last two were boggling: $363,000 and $89,000. Of the total charge, $114,000 was marked paid. Caroline worked through a timeline of information, and she thought of what it all meant, the scrambling land sales and big payments. None of the amounts on the note (thank you, Fred—promise you don't kill people) exactly matched the sales or the withdrawals, but if she gave it all to Gideon, maybe his beautiful spectrum brain would come up with an algorithm.

"I wanted to follow up about the other prints," said Gideon. "The Dinak prints. There were matches."

He sounded jittery. "To whom, from what? And don't get your hopes up. Remember that Burt screwed up the scene, and he might have been with other people."

"I know, and his prints are all over the place, but some are matches between Mr. Dinak's toilet seat and the Baird suite where the Russian people were living."

"Wooo," said Caroline.

"I've got a match for the guy who left the finger in Gardiner, presumably Sergei with the bandaged hand. Plus another match to the Baird room they rented—possibly one of the dead men. But all these prints, as well as Deputy Feckler's, are on top of a layer of dust. One print matches a man who died last fall, a bit of a John Doe—that one was on a brandy flask, *under* the dust, along with another individual you'll find interesting. This last person also left a print on the underside of the toilet lid."

Caroline, grasping and losing the John Doe comment: "Interesting?"

Gideon beamed.

"Tell me."

"Guess!"

"Gideon, you're having a great day. I'm really not having a great day."

"You are now. Charlie Bell. I grabbed his prints from the jailer."

It was sweet, truly. She leaned against the wall. Charlie might have admitted going to see the priest, but you didn't threaten someone and then go piss in their toilet. Not unless you'd taken the time to beat them or kill them.

Should they charge Charlie? They should not; they needed more. They needed to understand how he linked up with the Russians; they needed to find the Russians. Try the neighbors again, try St. Anne's, track down who called for the welfare check. Gideon was still taking apart the van for prints and blood.

"Get Charlie's mugshot, too, for the neighbors. Let's get this tied a little tighter." Something would stick.

CAROLINE HEADED TO the courthouse just in time for Charlie and his orange-suited jail mates to climb the stairs from the windowless jail and enter pleas. The judge was wearing a cervical collar and looked as if she might take her day out on everyone. Caroline sat toward the back on the aisle: she was hard to miss, and she knew Charlie, stewing in his own juices up front with the night's other sinners, saw her. He was swiveling his head like a weathervane, presumably looking for his beloved Elaine. Caroline saw no evidence of other friends, not even Fred Pushkin.

Today the judge flipped the alphabet, and Charlie would be last of nine defendants. Peter, up near the front as moral support for two clients, winked at Caroline.

Caroline watched Charlie fidget, waiting for his turn, looking like a human flare. She could see him confronting Dinak, and after Ed's story of Charlie beating his brother, she could imagine him causing the injuries they'd found on the body, but why kill a man for the theft of a few thousand dollars, when all this other money was in the offing? Why incur more debt by inviting people to come in and mop up? What secret was big enough to warrant a staged suicide, and if it was Lucia's secret, was Charlie protecting it or trying to discover it? Caroline needed to back up, one more time. Someone made Bernie Dinak dead. It didn't have to be Charlie—Caroline and Jules should be so lucky—because Bernie was in the habit of extortion. There were other people out there who were at least happy that he was dead. They might even go to Bernie's funeral, due to start at three.

But, she thought, none were likely to have lynched Bernie postmortem, leaving prints.

In the courtroom, one man, up for a DUI, shrieked "Guilty!" Charlie picked his nose, and Caroline tried not to think of the jail toilet.

When it was finally Charlie's turn, he smiled at the judge as if they were meeting for a cocktail, and he pleaded not guilty to assault as well as a partner–family member assault charges. The second was a stretch, but Charlie, at his peak the night before, seemed capable of killing a baby, a puppy, a pope. Caroline needed to remember that look on his face. Now, as he headed back to jail to retrieve his belongings, he did not meet her eye.

Caroline left the room and waited outside on the sidewalk. When Charlie walked out he looked around, at a loss. Just a flicker of alarm when he saw her.

"Hey," said Caroline. "Let's talk."

He smiled; he took this as a sign that all might be forgotten. "I apologize for my behavior."

This was a phrase he'd probably learned after he drowned his first kitten at age five. The words were correct but the eyes were elsewhere. Caroline led him down the hall and into the interview room, where Gideon waited.

Charlie sat down and said, "What's up?"

"I'm a little concerned about your relationship with Cavendish Clusker and Suzette Whipple and your parents going forward. You seemed to feel that they've done you wrong."

A magnanimous flick of a very dirty hand. Charlie Bell needed to check a mirror. Despite having been given a jail uniform, there was splashed piss on his pant leg, with a dark stain on the seat of his pants, and his fly was slightly stained. Did he know? The dark roots were growing out in his bleached hair. One eye was blood red with a blown vein, and there was dried blood on his chin, dried mucus under his nose. He smelled like booze and shit and the sour odor of fear sweat. It probably didn't happen often to him—in Charlie's mind, he was an apex predator. A night in a cell with tweakers would have been fraying.

Caroline couldn't wait to pin the booking photo to her new refrigerator. "You and Cavendish were friends."

"Oh, I don't know if you'd call us that," said Charlie. "I needed his land. Now he no longer owns it. I'm not holding his hand anymore."

"Holding his hand against all those scary intruders on his property?"

"You would think he would have been thankful."

"I don't know what he thought he was going to achieve, with his popguns," said Caroline. "Beyond shooting someone's eye out."

"He did need help. A man has the right to protect his property." Charlie chugged his bad coffee. His teeth were scummy, lacking their usual shine.

"So you'd bring your rifle and some food and booze and try to talk him into signing off. Did it take weeks to talk him into the deal? Months?"

"Months," said Charlie. "It's okay. Elaine and I have other properties to sell, and to buy. Her money from Mac would have landed this morning, and my inheritance has finally been cleared."

"She'll still want to be in business with you?"

Surprise. "Of course."

"She looked like shit when we searched your house this morning," said Caroline. "Nice shiner. She wasn't very concerned about your well-being."

She watched him work through this.

"We saw her when we executed a search warrant for a potential homicide charge. We found a man's body yesterday afternoon, a quarter mile from Marvel, and we've been looking into another death, as well. We've searched Cavendish's house, and we'll see whether the rifle we took from Elaine's house matches the cartridges we found on his floor or the bullet in the man's stomach. You'll be provided with a full list of what we brought out of the house, and you're welcome to call your lawyer."

Charlie's eyes settled on the middle distance. "I think I'll just leave."

"Good idea," said Caroline. "We don't want to keep you, yet. But aren't you curious about who's been killed? We've got two Russian John Does, and we think they've been working for you. Not very kind of you, to shoot these men after you paid them to scare Cavendish. What else have you asked those Russians to do for you? And where'd you stash your rifle?"

"You're insane."

"Pretty weak," said Caroline. "I'm also wondering about the coincidence of someone hanging a blow-up doll with a bra by its neck, from a rope. Kinda like Bernard Dinak. And your use of a Polaroid camera when you identified your wife's body. Mr. Dinak's camera is missing, and there are suddenly dozens of Polaroid photos flying around the county. Maybe your surviving employees grabbed it, for the side hobby of humiliating Deputy Feckler. I'm not trying to put that one on you."

Charlie smiled and stared at the ceiling. Gideon started to tap his pen, and for once Caroline didn't mind. "Go home, wash up, relax," she said. "We'll be in contact. There's a phone in the lobby if you'd like to call Elaine for a ride. But don't go far, Charlie."

He slammed out and they evacuated the reeking interview room. Gideon headed off on patrol with Kruger. Caroline washed her face and checked her calls with Grace: Jules, Shari, Ed looking for Jules. When she walked out into the lobby, Charlie was standing near the pay phone.

"Elaine not picking up? I could take you partway. I'm just leaving now."

"Thank you," he said.

She led him through the warren of hallways to the back entrance by the jail stairs. Someone was screaming for a cookie. Outside, in a hot, sand-blasting wind, she held her Subaru door open.

"Hop in," she said.

He smiled as if they were flirting. Everything washed away, everything was all about him—nothing dented that ego, because there was nothing in there besides ego. But she smiled, too, and he climbed in.

"Seat belt," she said.

"Really?"

"Really," she said.

His belt clicked. She allowed herself a small sniff—*what is that smell?*—and watched Charlie clock it. She'd clean the car later.

"Do you always get angry when you drink?"

"I will admit I prefer to remain in control."

"I noticed a couple of incidents in Colorado," she said. "Including a partner–family member charge that was dropped. An accident, like that one with Elaine?"

"Yes. My wife was quite excitable, very manic-depressive. I was trying to restrain her."

"But you loved her, you were faithful. Is it true that her money came from rifle parts, or land mines, or some such?"

"All true," said Charlie. "Why is it your business?"

"I'm making it mine," said Caroline. "On top of wondering if you've shot a couple of men dead, I'm wondering if you're a habitual abuser, a controller. Obviously, whatever you did as a juvenile stays out of a legal equation, but it's hard to not have it in mind, after meeting your father. Such a gentle man, crippled for life. And clearly your wife was unhappy, to kill herself. You were selling off your parents' land, and telling people they'd signed a POA to you, which wasn't true, while you're living with a woman who is trying to have her mother declared incompetent, possibly poisoning her to make this possible. And yet you seem to need cash. I mean, selling off your parents' beautiful ranch—who do you owe money to? Are you in trouble?"

"No trouble." Gritted teeth. "It's gone to my many investments. It all stays in the family. And as I've said, the inheritance is finally coming through."

"Ten months later. Your 'many investments'," she muttered, pulling up to the curb. What was she doing? She didn't have a gun.

"Someday, I will make you pay for this." His hands were claws on his kneecaps, and he didn't notice that she'd pulled over.

"I'll let the judge know," said Caroline. "You stink, Charlie, in every possible way. Get out of my car."

He finally looked around. Ahead of them, the St. Anne's nursery school class was crossing the street. "Why have you stopped?"

"I thought I mentioned—I'm only going a few blocks. Sorry, but you've just got a short walk to Elaine's now. This corner okay?"

He stared at her, and then at St. Anne's. "You're going to mass?"

Caroline smiled. "Bernie Dinak's funeral. It's

customary to go when you have a murder victim. To show you care. Want to come along?"

The bastard tried to slam the aged Subaru's door to death when he got out. Caroline pulled away a little quickly, making Charlie jump, and turned into the parking lot. People were just beginning to arrive, and she drank water and looked for anyone who seemed especially happy. She'd watched a dozen older women, all potential Bernie friends, limp into the church by the time a mustard-yellow Mercury Monarch glided into the lot with Sadie Winton at the wheel. Suzette popped out, opened the back door, and a tall, spectral woman unfurled, wearing a gauzy black headscarf: Lucia Bell. Suzette bent to talk to Sadie, checked her watch, and headed inside, holding Lucia's elbow. Caroline watched Sadie lean back in the driver's seat and waited until the older women were inside before she sidled up, startling Sadie badly.

"Hey," Caroline said.

"I get it," said Sadie, rubbing her face. "You're here to see who reacts oddly, and you'll guess which one is the murderer. But no one in there is putting their honest face on."

"I know," said Caroline. "But I have to ask—Lucia Bell and Suzette are friends?"

Sadie paused. "Lucia said you'd come by. She's a nice lady. I understand why you wouldn't want to know her, but she's kind, and sweet. She and Suzette went to grade school together."

"And your family knows her well, too?"

"I took music lessons from Mr. Bell. I know it seems odd. I've known them since I was a baby."

"I'm curious—do you know Ivan Luneau?"

She laughed. "I do! I've known him forever, too."

"And how is it that he came to know the Bells? Ivan isn't local, and they don't go out . . ."

"He lived with them when he was young and having a hard time. He was kind of an apprentice as a luthier or at least a carpenter, but he helped them with everything—groceries, the animals. I was just starting music lessons then, maybe only seven or eight. He was such a help for them, but I think they really helped him, too. Screwed-up rich family, but he didn't have any money then or act like it."

Caroline thought it over. Sadie shut her eyes again and leaned back. "These are nice people. Unlucky people. Have you ever seen Suzette's X-rays?" she asked. "That nurse Marina told me Elaine's father beat her. That's why her hands look like claws. Lucia and Suzette have been through so much. Me, I've been lucky."

Caroline screwed the lid back on her water bottle and followed the ladies inside. The priest looked tired, sounded indifferent. Lucia and Suzette whispered to each other throughout. They'd probably whispered together in this church for sixty years. Two old women conspiring, for cause: their children were trying to strip away their rights.

Caroline found it inspirational.

Sadie, lucky girl, was sound asleep in the driver's seat when Caroline walked back outside. She wanted to ask her if everyone in town knew and liked the Bells, if everyone just didn't want to mention it to her or to Jules.

19 *Iris and Doris*

JULES, WHO WANTED TO ENJOY CHARLIE'S BRIEF IMprisonment, went out for a late lunch with Wesley Tenn. They'd met the week before, too, without telling Caroline: Jules was determined to talk Wesley into returning to work, because otherwise Jules was sure that Caroline would become sheriff, and become unhappy, and as sheriff would be forced to work full-time, and run a higher risk of violent death. And so he winnowed away at Wesley's newfound enjoyment of inactivity. Rina, the nurse who'd brought him back to life, needed to take care of her mother, and lying around alone during a Montana winter with half-healed hands was no one's recipe for happiness.

Usually, in the midst of this kind of pep talk, Wesley mentioned his reluctance to deal with meth addicts and Burt, but now there was more proof of the miraculous in the exit of Burt. Rina, who was very into the power of positive thinking, had gotten Wesley to make wishes when they first met in the hospital. Keeping his hands was number one, bed with Rina was number two, and the disappearance of Burt was number three. Presto! Maybe Wesley should make another wish.

Wesley was a little goofier than Jules remembered,

but he was happier, too. Rina was leaving her dog, a cute brown mop, to keep him company.

"I'll make a wish for you," said Wesley. "I'll wish that Charlie Bell stops breathing. I'll tell Rina. Maybe she can pull that off as well."

After a sedating chicken-fried steak, Jules picked Tommy up at daycare and drove up the hill to deal with the open grave, and to think through—now that he knew who owned the easement—where the road to Ivan's kingdom should run. He'd only been up there for a half hour when a plume of dust headed his way and resolved into Ed in the county's aging Ford pickup.

"Get in," said Ed. "I'm abducting you."

"Ha ha," said Jules.

"Seriously," said Ed. "There's not a lot of time. Please."

Jules, all his life, was in the habit of trusting Ed, who looked like he'd been crying.

The three sizes of man, stuffed into the cab of a half-ton pickup. Tommy fell asleep within the first two miles. They followed the Marvel road past Cavendish's tarnished roof and the crumpled woodpiles of every other lost house, through the beautiful ribbon of clearings Jules had been blind to when he came with Larry, carrying gasoline, past scree and over the almost treeless pass, and down along the beginnings of Coralberry Creek.

"I apologize for lying to you," said Ed. "But there are some things you need to know."

Jules didn't say anything as they closed in on the Bell place. Which lie, when? Some horrible truth was about to be revealed, some pain, something about Ansel his son shouldn't know, something about Olive. Keep it buried, he thought. I don't need it, after all.

Francis Bell sat near the burned-out barn foundation with Ivan, who was loading suitcases into his car. Francis spun his chair around to face them and waved.

"So you're close friends?" Jules asked bitterly. "Just get together and shoot the shit?"

"We are," said Ed. "I've brought Sadie down here for cello lessons since she was a tot. They didn't stick, but we kept visiting."

"What's with the suitcases?" asked Jules.

"Packing for town. Ivan got them into a room last night. The bank and legal work is done—Charlie can't touch the money or property anymore—but there's no easy way to get a protective order, and what good would it do out here, anyway?"

He turned off the engine. Tommy began to wail but stopped once they were out of the truck. What was Jules supposed to say to Francis Bell—nice to meet you? They shook hands.

"This must be Thomas," said Francis. "Lucia loves the newborn photos when the hospital posts them in the paper."

Babies with faces like unrisen buns were easier than the reality. So much for the small talk, but the intensity with which Francis Bell was watching Jules was paralyzing, and he tried to imagine the conversation in Deer Lodge if Patrick Bell still had two working eyes. "Why did you want to see me?" he asked.

"I need you to understand some things, and it was easier to talk while Lucia is away and Charlie is in jail."

"He won't be there for long," said Jules. "Caroline is digging, but she can't charge him yet."

"For which crime, might I ask?"

For which crime: Jules limped through an explanation while Francis rolled away from him, making for the ruin of the barn. Ivan and Ed stayed behind, by the cars.

"Do you mind following me down to the barn? It's less windy, and your son will like the balls I keep down there, and it gives me room to roll around when I'm edgy." Francis was moving remarkably quickly. "I'm nervous. You're probably nervous."

"Yes," said Jules. "I am."

The old barn's stone central path to the lower stable was still intact, with a dirt foundation to either side, all of it dotted with tennis and racquetballs. Maybe Francis Bell played a kind of wheelchair handball. Jules put Tommy down and they watched him scuttle off.

"This shooting at Cavendish's house—Ivan thinks Charlie was killing off his creditors."

"I know this might not be the point today," said Jules. "But what do you think he owes all this money for?"

"Ivan says Charlie hired people to help him kill other people," said Francis. "And Ivan is no angel; he would know. When I say which crime, I guess I'm thinking of the deaths of Charlie's wife and father-in-law and the priest who blackmailed my wife. And then we can go back to the point of this visit, which is my daughter-in-law Iris, who was a fine, sweet, lovely girl. Utterly blameless."

He rolled a ball and Tommy wriggled after it.

"You need to know that we lied all those years ago, or at least Lucia lied, on the day your father was killed. We drove back from the store to find the truck here, Patrick unconscious in the driveway, Iris nowhere to be found. We were not here when our sons arrived, and if Patrick was speeding to get here, it was to keep her alive. It was to save her."

Jules's mind danced away from "if." He understood denial, but decades of anger were hard on empathy. "I don't quite understand what you mean."

"We drove up as Charlie was walking out of the barn. He was flushed, and smiling, and relaxed. I have always believed he killed Iris, and since the priest died, Lucia accepts this. Ed has some evidence that could help us prove it."

Back by the house, Ivan was patting Ed's shoulder. This secret group of friends; Jules pushed down his anger. "Is that what Charlie wanted to know from Bernie Dinak? Whether his mother suspected him?"

"Well, I imagine he wondered whether Lucia confessed her doubts about Iris's death," said Francis. "He clearly didn't trust him to not talk. But apparently Mr. Dinak did not tell Charlie every secret Lucia confided in him. We would know by now."

Jules was back on "doubts." There wasn't much room for them in Ansel's case. "How could Ed not tell the truth?"

"Patrick asked us never to speak of it, and there are things you don't understand yet. Ivan talked him into allowing me this conversation with you. If your wife can lock Charlie up for good, then things might change. But Iris—we need to do the right thing. We allowed this thing to happen, we could not mourn her, we don't even know where she is buried. I know he killed her. She saw him arrive, and she ran for the barn to keep him out of the house."

"But I don't understand. Wasn't he here waiting? How did he arrive at the same time?"

Francis threw the ball a little farther. "We don't know

but we can guess. His car was not here. If you press him, he might say that someone dropped him off. I did not press him; I have not spoken to him since he broke my spine, except for on the day your father died. Lucia, who cannot fully accept the situation, sees him occasionally."

"And Patrick is aware of all of this?"

"Yes. He said nothing to us, for so long. Charlie asked his mother to lie, and she begged me. And to my shame I did not volunteer my guesses at the truth, because I worried that Charlie would harm the family."

"So why now? Why are you telling me any of this?"

"Because now we think you can help put Charlie away." He smiled. "For at least thirty years I've prayed Charlie would go away. It's very hard, when you know something's wrong with your child." He looked at Tommy, covered in dirt and mud yet fresh and new, trying to pick up the ball without falling over. "You would know already, if it's that basic of a problem. Not drugs, depression. Really wrong, like Charlie has always been very wrong."

Bullshit, thought Jules. "Tell me what you're getting at."

"We don't think Patrick killed your father."

Tommy pitched forward on his face and began to shriek. His high fragile forehead bruised in a second, but there was just a little bit of blood.

"Let's take him inside to clean him up," said Francis. "It's important you see something."

In the kitchen, Jules cleaned Tommy's face, then plopped him down on the floor with yet another ball. He looked around the room, thinking of the children who'd come out of this house, thinking of the fire, the poor burning cat. All the sadness, and yet here was a cello perched on the old-fashioned stairlift and a bowl of ripe tomatoes and some dusty yin-and-yang stained-glass circles hanging from guitar string, spinning every time someone moved through the room. Tommy kept forgetting the ball for the sake of staring.

And photos, everywhere. Small school portraits of each boy, but nothing of Charlie—brown-haired Charlie, but still with wrong eyes—after about the age of fifteen. Instead, Jules saw Sadie Winton: Sadie in a kindergarten portrait, Sadie on a pony, Sadie in a baseball uniform, a bikini, a prom dress. This couple who'd lost two sons, torturing themselves with a borrowed daughter.

Francis reached for a baseball team photo and pulled the frame apart. A stack of other images lay under the top photo, and he handed Jules one of Sadie in an old-fashioned pinafore dress, a dark jumper. This photo was bleached more than the others, and it took Jules a moment to see that the photo was old, that the baby was Sadie, not the woman. Her cheekbones were higher and wider, with a pretty gap between her front teeth, and she wore a thin gold necklace with a dangling violet flower.

"Iris," said Francis. "Do you understand now?"

No, thought Jules. But a second later, yes. Sadie, everywhere in the house: baby, child, graduate, bikini babe. Iris's daughter.

Jules felt drunk; he felt like his skin would explode. He felt, horribly, as if he were thirteen again, and he wanted another barn to burn down.

"Charlie never knew Sadie existed. Iris hid her in a closet in the house. He still doesn't know. That is the point. He killed her mother and he would kill her."

Ed was in the room now, and Jules wanted to hit him. "How could you keep this from me?" asked Jules.

"The truth," said Ed, "is not worth the risk. We kept it from everyone. No one was going to listen. Bunny McElwaine hated your father, and we think Donald Whipple paid him off to let Iris's death lie."

"Why?"

"Charlie gave Whipple some acres his grandparents deeded to him—this isn't the first time he's sold the family ranch. Whipple was already giving Bunny money to keep his abuse of Suzette quiet. And Charlie seemed like such a golden boy. Whipple took his side on the high school fight, put him up until he was shipped off to school."

"We tried to speak out when McElwaine was off the force," said Francis. "We tried talking to Patrick's doctors, before he was at all cogent, and before Ed agreed to show us the files. But once Patrick could think again, he said to do nothing, to protect his baby. It made sense to us at the time."

Ivan came back through with a crate and packed the photos on the table. "If Charlie comes into the house, they don't want him to understand. If he decides to burn it all down."

Charlie, staring at Sadie, saying he didn't like her face. Jules was in no position to say he wouldn't do such a thing. In the truck, Ed said, "She got them through it. Do you understand now? We all needed to protect her."

"Does Sadie know?"

"No. And you can't tell Caroline until she does. Until we deal with Charlie," said Ed.

CAROLINE WALKED INTO the station to a complaint from Charlie Bell—he'd arrived home to find a giant yellow penis painted on his Suburban—and a message from

Charlie's attorney, saying that his client would be traveling to Cody for some paperwork relating to his wife's estate, should Caroline need him for further questions. It was almost impossible for her to believe that Charlie wouldn't lash out at Suzette or his parents or Cavendish. Harvey watched Charlie and Elaine pack and leave, and Caroline gave the police in Cody the plate number and address.

The files from Shari waited on her desk, and she worked through a list of questions as she dialed the medical examiner's office.

"Have you gotten a bullet out of our last patient?" asked Caroline. "The man who sat in a wrecked car in a sunny field for at least a couple of days, feeding crows? The working theory is that he was winged by a homeowner and bled to death. No ID."

"I peeked and decided to wait until it was almost time for a drink," said Shari. "Maybe we should just move the lab to Absaroka County."

Please don't, thought Caroline. "I'd really like to know if you can retrieve a bullet from his leg or his abdomen. I have someone I'd love to arrest. But for now I have another favor to ask. Is it possible to test the foot for painkillers, or other drugs?"

"Ah, no," said Shari. "We're not really dealing with solids in that case. But the hypodermic you sent up along with the foot held enough fentanyl to drop an elephant, a whole circus. But really—so many bodies! You're way out of proportion to your population."

"Would that it were otherwise," said Caroline, stuck on Mikael in the wheelchair, the conviction that he was a mercy killing. "The eyeless guy can't be as bad as the foot."

"Oh, high bar! Don't forget the headless guy or the

finger! But really, think through the last few months in your batshit area."

The disarticulated human: were they anywhere close to a full assemblage in the last week? Caroline thought, *This is not my fault.* But she was so tired, and she was interested: what was she forgetting, what did she miss during maternity leave, or lose to Tommy and the neighbors and fatigue? Shari was going to tell her.

"Some natural stuff last summer—a fall and a bear attack. Of course they weren't letting you out on search and rescue, and these aren't rarities. August, that explosion that crisped a guy named Suarez—did anyone care enough about him?—and burned poor Wesley."

"Not our county," said Caroline. But did anyone care about Mr. Suarez in Gallatin County? All the press was about Wesley and the rich guy who'd gassed himself. Was the name Jones? Smith?

"Awfully close, though, eh? Also, in no particular order: a lady choked on a cherry at the Elks Club. A couple of old people died of sepsis at the hospital. Happens all the time, but always worries me. That OD in the valley in October you worked on. Old guy named Frog electrocuted last August in Jasper. Your little dried-out guy in the cone bra, who probably dropped in November. Those bones from Jules. The foot. And now this poor guy with the tattoos on his penis. I was just joking about not looking at him. Rifle shot through the knee, another to the abdomen that pierced the stomach and the liver, probably from a .30-06 Springfield."

A skirmish in Caroline's brain. "The OD's name?"

"Rich lady with enough opiates in her to drop her five times over. Suicide."

And now Caroline saw the room and the body, the woman she'd dealt with on the same day her own body started to transform. Maryellen. "Where was she from? How old?"

"No idea. I don't recall the name now, but I knew it—when her father died there was some possibility of hinkiness. That was the Wesley mess, when he burned his hands. Old guy, running car, garage, boom, poor dead Mr. Suarez. Lemme look."

Caroline was experiencing a level of confusion akin to Algebra II, circa 1980.

"The old rich guy was named Thornton Smith. Daughter Maryellen Cassandra Smith Bell, DOB 4/1/57."

"Bell," said Caroline, stupidly.

Shari was tired of making her point and flicked through her stack as noisily as possible. "Spouse was Charles C. Bell. Body released to him on October 23, 1997. No idea of disposition."

Mop up, follow up. Caroline was sucking at it. She did not blame her child or Jules or any single element of her life; she did blame herself. She'd seen Jules's notes about Charlie's wife months ago, but the bland name never clicked.

Caroline hadn't done right by Maryellen Cassandra Smith Bell. "What did she overdose on?"

"Opioids."

"Anything more specific? Pill, injection . . . ?"

"Liquid, I think," said Shari. "I'll send you the file. There was some conflict—I think you people said hydrocodone but the lab said fentanyl, so maybe there was a hospital connection. My only deaths from fentanyl have come from you lunatics. It's a new surgical drug—"

"Some went missing at the hospital last fall," said Caroline, thinking: and again last month.

"I was surprised she could even crawl or vomit. I told Burt all of this. You people in Absaroka County are allowing your citizens to gack at an incredible rate."

"Please send the files," said Caroline.

She was given a full minute of mindlessness before Gideon padded through. "I forgot to tell you—the welfare check on Dinak was called in by Suzette Whipple."

Naturally, thought Caroline. Lies, all lies. Sadie was in to grab something for Ed, slamming around the office, fast because she'd left Shirley in the car. "Have you seen a file on a Percy Mays?" asked Sadie. "I guess Dad has to testify Monday and he's drawing a blank."

"He throws stuff in that deep bottom drawer," said Caroline. "Good luck."

She rooted through Shari's latest files, intent on finding the forensic report for Patrick Bell's truck, but when she opened the top folder, she flinched. Dead Iris Bell, her face beautiful and young and horribly bruised and bloody, a bale-twine noose deep in the flesh of her neck. Caroline made herself read: Iris had been twenty-one, and she weighed only ninety-six pounds. She'd been beaten, badly: one cheekbone was shattered. Defensive injuries to her hands, a broken rib, bruising on her stomach. Her neck was broken by the noose, but the coroner did not specify murder or suicide. Body temp down to 70 degrees Fahrenheit, full rigor by the time she was found, no time specified. Caroline skimmed the toxicology report—nothing.

Sadie rabbited on. "I can't believe this mess. Suicides from the eighties, green juvie files from the seventies. And oh my god, here's a stack of stuff about Ansel Clement. *Bell vehicle search*; *Bell vehicle inventory*; *Bell, C., custody*; *Bell, C., restraining order*; *Bell, P., interview 1973.*"

"Give it here," said Caroline.

It was a big pocket file marked *Clement homicide, miscellaneous*. Caroline took everything to the kitchen, where she grabbed the last stale doughnut in the bag. She slid the file contents onto the table.

On top, a memo in Ed's handwriting—Charlie Bell was not to return to the ranch—and a number for a man he'd stay with, a Donald W. She skimmed an inventory for the items in Patrick's truck—he'd been carrying tools and various fine woods for his father as well as suitcases for the move to Missoula and normal household stuff like pots and books, toys and toiletries. She skipped more interviews and a juvenile file marked *C. Bell, 1/5/71*—someone's mistake—and reached an evidence bag labeled *C. Bell clothing 8/15/72*. She put on gloves to pull out a bloodstained Oxford shirt and pants, and two sets of bagged handcuffs.

She stared at it for a long minute, thinking about witness statements, oddities and timing in the log, the plurals, searching for another lost thought beyond the witnesses who'd said *they* instead of *he*, something from before the body in the car, before finding Doris. Something.

"Blood on the passenger window," said Caroline. "How did that happen?"

Caroline reached in again and pulled out *P. Bell vehicle forensic 8.15.72*. She read the hospital notes on Patrick Bell, and she read the day log again, and everything changed.

"Are you okay?" asked Gideon, passing through.

"Will you send this to Shari for me?" asked Caroline,

handing over the handcuff bags and *C. Bell clothing 8/15/72*. "Ask her whose bloodstains."

Those c---------s. There'd been two men in the truck. Charlie driving, Charlie with a gun, Charlie on his way to kill Iris, with Patrick half-conscious and handcuffed to the passenger door.

EVERYTHING WAS HAPPENING, all at once. She tried Jules again, but he still didn't answer at home or the office, and Olive hadn't heard from him. Caroline found what she could about the incident that injured Wesley. Searching online was making life easier but a search for Smith already brought a gray wash of bullshit, thousands of hits. How many Smiths died in the last few years, just in Montana? Too fucking many. Caroline's only horse thief was named Smith. Jules's last fatal car accident was a woman named Smith who tried to get her cassette deck to work on a curvy road.

She called the Gallatin County Sheriff's Department and decided to be direct about Thornton Smith. The medical examiner had, after all, used the word *hinky*.

Yes and no, said a detective. Law enforcement concerns centered on motive—a considerable fortune—and a few wrinkles. The timing was off—when the car began spewing exhaust, how long the old man could have moved given the painkillers in his bloodstream. And he was found on the passenger side—people didn't often do that. "But it's not enough to get far, especially given the terrific damage to the body in the explosion. And anyway, the daughter's dead now, too."

"And the son-in-law?"

"He was definitely in Cody."

Caroline dug up the Maryellen report and walked down the hall to the evidence locker, guessing that it hadn't been cleaned since the spring the year before, when she'd taken the chore on between bouts of morning sickness. Burt's notes were maddening: "the wife," "the husband," "the suicide"—breezy and without detail. There'd been no coroner's jury. The couple who'd hosted Maryellen, the Cattons, didn't add much: "complete surprise," "heartbreaking." "We didn't worry when she didn't come to breakfast because she only liked healthy stuff."

Caroline remembered collecting Xanax and hydrocodone in the Catton guesthouse; she remembered a fancy lip balm, the kind of undereye cream that probably contained ground pearls or unborn rabbits, a common bottle of aspirin. She remembered some special-looking liquid vitamins; she'd just read an article about rich people tailoring their mixes into empty gel caps and ampules, and she was annoyed by this evidence of a different lifestyle. It still annoyed her.

She put on gloves, feeling a little silly. Usually personal goods were returned at some point, but while Caroline was AWOL, maybe no one in the family asked for the last bits of Maryellen: earrings, rings—a yellow diamond, worth a fortune; surely Charlie must remember—vomit-encrusted sheets and a nightgown and the clothes Maryellen had worn during the day, which were in the path of her final struggle toward the phone. The Smythson journal; a paperback copy of *Bridget Jones's Diary* (what a reading choice for a suicide), a silk-lined toilet kit with pills and balms, toothpaste, Tampax. Caroline smelled the toothpaste, stared into the prescription bottles. The vitamin bottle she remembered, with fancy handwriting on the label—*Youth Blend*—held a half dozen gelatin capsules, some leaking. Which brought alarm—was the evidence cabinet overheating? She reached into the bottle with her gloved fingers and pried one capsule out of the goop, turning it in her fingers. On impulsc, she squeezed it, and a tiny worm of goo squiggled out. She went back to her desk to find her magnifier.

Gideon was looking at a list of Russian visa holders and Grace was typing up the final, exceedingly crisp report on Burt, who'd been released to his sister's care. Caroline brought the capsules up to her eye, one after another, and bagged them again carefully.

She found a small hole in each. She drove too fast on the way home, but when she got there, she found Olive smiling placidly in front of Tommy's highchair. Jules needed to deal with the thicket, and so she'd come to help.

But this wasn't Caroline's story to tell Olive.

AT THE HOUSE site, Jules was so intent on privacy that he cut his engine as he rolled down the driveway. By the time he shut his door, Suzette was waving from her deck. "Can you help me?" she asked. "Sadie needed to spend some time with her mother, and Cavendish went to the bar, and Mac doesn't answer the phone, and my daughter is away. Thank God."

Suzette's broken hands could not open a prescription bottle of codeine. She was feeling a bit shaky today. "Will you feel safe down here, when Elaine gets back?" Jules asked. "Peter told me about the will. Maybe now that there's no incentive Elaine will stop screwing with your meds."

"Ah, but if I *tell* her I've flat-out disinherited her she'll kill me out of anger. I worry about you, too. You know, Lucia is my oldest friend. We know everything about each other, all the secrets, and you should know that Charlie tried to kill his brother about once a year from the age of four on. He used a fork, and a rope, and he put bluing powder in Patrick's pancakes. Charlie threw an electric shaver at him in the shower, but the cord was too short. They tried counseling—they were way ahead of their time that way—but nothing took. No difference in the way the boys were raised, and I know Lucia somehow believed Patrick egged him on, but I think it was all Charlie. At least he didn't harm animals or other kids, until that day in school."

A naturally occurring psychopath. Jules didn't usually believe in them.

"He was just so pretty," said Suzette. "It was hard to believe that anything bad was going on in that gorgeous head. It was almost amusing, the way Donald liked him. But the girls still liked Patrick, because he was and is a fine human being."

"I visited Patrick, and I'll see him again, but this is hard for me to believe. I should send cookies."

"I'm sure," said Suzette. She put the codeine lid back on with her broken hands, and then tried and failed to remove it again. "Lo, how the mighty have fallen. I'm old, I'm sick, I'm alone."

"Oh, Suzette," said Jules. "No one gets out alive. I went to the cemetery looking for the people of Doris, the people who your husband said he'd bury there."

"Did Donald make that promise?" she asked. "I stopped listening to him at some point."

"He did. They didn't end up there, but I saw another grave."

Another wave of the hand. Suzette was embracing the art of letting go. "Do you ever wonder what happened to Donald? Do you ever worry?"

"No," she said. "I don't worry about Donald."

"Have you seen Mac today?"

"No," she said. "Maybe he's at the Baird, maybe he's on a plane. Last night I was worried—I saw him standing by the apple tree, staring at the moon, and then he walked down by the river. Now Suzette struggled to open a tab of foil-wrapped Nicorette. "Would you be a dear?"

He peeled open the packet and handed it back. "Did you really plant a tree for a man who broke your bones?"

"I really did," said Suzette. "I planted it as a tribute to the happy time of our marriage, having Elaine, being in love. Sometimes you need a reminder."

JULES SAID HE'D feed the spitting llama and the biting pony; he said he needed to work. Back to destroying Eden. Part of the reason he and Caroline delayed clearing the area was that the wildness was the point. They wanted this buffer. Divvy didn't realize that every sprig of dogwood helped shield them from psychotic neighbors, curious dog walkers, rampaging stoned teens.

Anything Jules did would be gentler than Herb with a bulldozer. But now that he tried to wade into the thicket, Jules realized the truth was somewhere in between. They didn't know the thicket was fifty feet deep *because* it was fifty feet deep, thorny and impenetrable.

He backed out, panting, and went back to his truck for an overshirt and bolt cutters for the thick wire tangled in the grass and brambles. He worked as quickly as possible and despite his suffering drifted into delusional plans of espaliered fruit trees, rhubarb, raspberries, peonies. They would need a deer fence. They were going to tame nature, at least in the short term, pending floods and bugs and freezes and fires.

After another hour, as the light dimmed, the burn pile, with a separate stack of wire, rotten fence posts, and a small horsehair mattress, was chest high. He found a black coat button and a turquoise earring and a pretty shard from a bowl. The ground in the patch closest to Suzette's fence and the apple tree proved to be uneven. He lurched about, wondering about the old ice plant, wondering if the dips were just old slash or manure piles. He headed to the truck for the halogen light, which immediately caught the glint of a prize, the corner of a crumpled iron bedstead, probably four feet wide and seven feet long, hammered rather than cast, buried under a crumbling tree. He couldn't understand why someone would leave such a thing. Even after a flood, wouldn't the neighbors have scavenged something so lovely and timeless?

He was sweating even though the night air was cool. He cleared more of the frame, thinking he could use the bedstead for a trellis, or part of the garden fence. The pattern was bizarre, diamonds with flowers inside, or maybe little faces. He dragged the halogen light closer and squinted down.

Angels and skulls.

Jules rocked back on his haunches, and the blood roared in his head. Any idiot could see that this bedframe was too large for any bed but the eternal model. The Doris graveyard didn't wash away, hadn't been moved. It stayed where it was born, on the outskirts of the first and the current town, here in his own backyard.

Suzette's lights were out. Jules detached the halogen head from the stand and circled the mound of dirt from the foundation, peering through the gloom at suspicious sticks, rocks, anything organic and ivory-colored. Then he slid the light back into the stand, aimed it east, and started crawling through clawed shrubbery, feeling like a true supplicant. He dug with his hands in one soft wallow until he touched a shaped stone, a rough raised cross. The other graves would hold more lambs, sheaves of wheat, wood crosses. Babies, wives, worn-out Eastern refugees, murderers of the first peoples. These were the men and women he'd been looking for up at the poor farm; these were the inhabitants of Doris, never moved. Their garden was a graveyard.

WHEN JULES CAME home, he put the earring and the button and the shard into the bowl on the windowsill, next to the returned skull fragment, the necklace, a Zippo lighter, and the poor farm collection: a bullet, a belt buckle, a marble; the end of a comb, a scrap of leather, a bone ice pick, a tooth. The lamb he hadn't wanted to ask about perched next to the bowl, looking out into the yard.

He told Caroline about what he'd found in their garden, and wondered why she took it calmly. He told her about his afternoon standing within the foundation of the barn with Francis Bell, but she still seemed impatient to talk, to barely pause over this experience that rocked him. She was polite enough to wait for him to finish, and then she spread out the log for August 15, 1972, and the forensic report of Patrick Bell's truck, which showed that Patrick's blood was on the passenger window of the truck.

"This is what I wanted you to see earlier," she said. "*They. They. Cocksuckers*, plural. Both Bell brothers were in the truck. That fight at the gas station in Gardiner, that no one could investigate—that was Charlie hijacking Patrick."

"Put it together," said Caroline, and Jules did: a second set of handcuffs, not Ansel's, with Patrick's blood. More of Patrick's blood on the passenger window of the truck, but only Ansel's on the driver's window and door. Patrick's and Charlie's prints on the truck interior and on the gun. The fight at the gas station in Gardiner, the absence of Charlie's car at the Bell ranch. Lucia and Francis's testimony that they returned from the grocery to find Patrick on the ground and Charlie walking out of the barn, relaxed and smiling.

Plural: Charlie, learning of the visit from a little girl who didn't know better, Charlie waylaying Patrick, beating him, cuffing him to the passenger door, and driving home to kill Iris.

Ansel was simply in the way, in the old version and this new one. Charlie killed him.

"Are we sure?" asked Jules.

"I am," said Caroline.

JULES DID NOT tell Caroline about Sadie. Later, in the kitchen, she stood in front of a vitamin E capsule poking it with a push pin. "Do we still have needles left over from Zaida?"

Zaida was Caroline's diabetic cat, dead for a year. Jules

dug around in the drawer. “Two unused but I donated the insulin to the animal shelter. What’s up?”

He watched Caroline squeeze out some of the pill liquid, fill the hypodermic with water, and inject enough water to plump the capsule up again. As soon as she removed the needle the liquid leaked out again.

“Still,” said Caroline. “I think this is doable with a thicker suspension. Maybe some fast-acting epoxy would keep it sealed. I think this is how it happened.”

“What?”

“Maryellen Smith Bell’s overdose. Remember the woman who overdosed in the valley, the day I went into labor with Tommy? She was Charlie’s wife.”

He barely remembered, but he certainly got the point now.

“And remember the guy who gassed himself, when Wesley was wounded?”

He did, of course, but he didn’t get the point.

“He was Maryellen’s father.”

20 *The Seventh Morning*

SATURDAY

JULES WOKE UP THINKING: IT IS THE ANNIVERSARY of my father's death, and I have someone I can destroy now, on his behalf. And then he thought: My yard is full of dead people.

THE FIRST CALL came from Alice, and neither Jules nor Caroline touched the phone. She'd found volunteers to help dig up the privies—why not do it this weekend?

The world would shatter, and Alice would still roll on like a demented Energizer bunny. She'd find everything they didn't want her to find about Doris's missing bodies, and more. The only thing that would make her stop was the truth, but it was hard to look forward to the conversation: we fucked up, but you fucked up, too, and now we're building our home on dead people.

"Not on," he said to Caroline. "Near." At least they knew they weren't on top of the burials. They should think of Rome, think of Butte. Living people lived next to dead people all over the world. It was ever thus.

The bank would love this line. They needed to find a way to delay discovery until the house was up. They worked through such thoughts in ugly gouts of talk, trying to ease into the tragedy of the day, and in between

Caroline pulled the pillow over her face. She was no longer quite so sanguine about the people in their garden.

He felt the nausea that comes from doing the wrong thing.

It was a Saturday, but Miranda, the county clerk, was an old friend (yes, that kind of old friend) and she gave Jules a key to the clerk and recorder's office. He decided to carry on as if his property weren't filled with dead people, as if his house wasn't slated for demolition before it was even roofed. He would temporarily ignore their new reality.

In the archive, he pulled out all five maps of Blue Deer before 1900. In the winter, they'd put two aside as grossly inaccurate. Now Jules ignored the unlikely shape of the Yellowstone, the relocation of mountain ranges—Crazies, Absarokas, Bridgers, beautiful bumps like Sheep Mountain—and focused on the scribble that marked little Doris. The ferry landing, the squares marking stores, and two small thatches of crosses, one to the north, the other sheltered by an island to the south near the river. Two cemeteries.

Religion struck again. They were the victims of the Crusades, the Reformation. Even in Doris, even with two hundred people, they'd split up the dead. Who knew which one they'd used for Johannes Rosenfalter, or where they'd plopped the Black Henry family. Who knew who was in their garden.

Donald Whipple, who'd proposed to build a Whippleville in two places, one on flood land by the river—Blue Acres—and another on high—Goldfields—with a view of almost everything, hadn't followed through on much of anything but blowing town. Jules went back to the maps they'd thought were reliable, his half-assed regression, trying to understand how they showed the town of Doris and its dead everywhere but on his building site. In an 1890 map, abandoned Doris, no cemetery marked at all, was a half mile to the east; in 1905, Doris was a faint X a quarter mile to the south, in an area now under the landfill dog park. In 1921, in the first attempt to map the post-flood river, someone put a historical star a quarter mile to the northwest, under the Selway mushroom manse. But it didn't matter. From a sketch to a fable, mistake compounding mistake on each successive effort.

Jules straightened up and stared blindly at the shelves of ledgers. Offhand, there were three choices:

They could tell the truth immediately, stop construction, and come clean with the town and the county.

They could destroy or disguise the truth permanently.

They could disguise the truth temporarily and tell it later. After some time to think.

Jules confirmed the previous night's choice of option number three and congratulated himself on feeble optimism.

CAROLINE TALKED TO Cavendish again. Could Charlie have hidden the rifle somewhere in Marvel? Did Cavendish know about any storage lockers, other houses or offices?

He did not. He was a worthless lump, settling right in at Suzette's house.

"Take me through it again. What night did you start taking potshots at your prowlers?"

"Tuesday I heard them and shot in the air. Wednesday I was half-hearted. Thursday, Charlie brought a bottle of Chivas, and saw the fire. Friday, we got serious."

"And on Saturday?"

"No Charlie. No one really bothered me that night. I mighta just shot in the air once or twice. There were people around calling for a dog that morning, but no one after dark."

"Why'd you think it was a dog?"

"They were calling *Pavel*, or *Pavlov*. Isn't Pavlov a dog's name?"

Calling for a man who was dead or dying in the car. This was horrible, but maybe someday it would be funny. Caroline needed to tell Jules, if only to get it out of her head. "And then?"

"Charlie came out again on Sunday."

Getting serious, Friday matched up with Pavel-Pavlov crawling for the shelter of the car and a mourning song at the Bucket on Saturday night. Enter Burt with the stun gun, and Andrei was maybe lucky to end up in the hospital, while the curly-haired kid, Mika, and his sneakers headed up on Sunday night to harass Cavendish for another pittance and a mortal wound. Maybe this was when Sergei was shot in the hand. On Monday, when the Bells' van and wheelchair were called in as missing, the crew floated down the river in inner tubes to *relax, learn to have fun*, and headed down to the park in the evening for Mika's last injection and liquid funeral, just at curfew. They unwound that night in the bars and hotels of Gardiner: Sergei gave up on his finger (or Fred, Mr. Decisive, gave up on it for him) and VVV got her yayas out on the guy they'd found tied to the barbell.

And on Tuesday, Mika once again a part of nature, they returned the van (Gideon, searching it, found hair dye, a hiking guide to western Montana, as well as guides to mushrooms and animal tracks) and disappeared.

But where did that leave Burt? This must be the same crew, but where did he fit in? On Saturday night, Helga the bartender called Burt to the Bucket, and Andrei and the writer Wally Sands ended up in the hospital. On Sunday night Burt headed out again and was burgled and possibly doped. On Monday, the crew—floating and heading down to Gardiner—probably left him with Tamyra as a sitter. On Tuesday, once Mika was deposited in his bubbling grave, the survivors played with Burt, exacted a little retribution.

Gideon confirmed the timing when he noticed a news banner in the background of one unmentionable Polaroid. He could not find the Russians.

Caroline drove to the Catton house, one of those mysterious homes of the very rich, tucked high above the valley in splendid isolation, and she marveled at how little she remembered of her previous visit. Flora Bamfert-Catton—the name was ludicrous, but Flora said her family made asphalt roofing shingles in Kansas—wasn't the average flake; two laptops scrolled big-board numbers while they talked. It was barely lunchtime, but she offered a glass from a bottle of wine that was entirely beyond Caroline's means. There was a telescope in front of her large and very clean windows. Flora apologized for not recognizing Caroline, who pointed out that she'd dropped forty pounds rather drastically and was no longer bundled up in a turquoise parka.

"How strange to meet again at a party! How is your neighbor Charlie?"

"No idea," said Caroline. "The evening didn't end

well, did it? You were friends with both Charlie and Maryellen?"

"Well, Maryellen and I went to school together. She had buckets of family money, all about rubber bullets and some gasket thing they use in guns, so she would just say 'armaments' and talk about getting caviar straight from Russia. Asphalt is not so interesting," Flora said glumly. "My husband is wary of Charlie—he's constantly asking people to invest in one thing or another. But that weekend he dropped her off—he was going to see an insurance agent about the mess with his father-in-law."

"She was depressed after her father's death?"

"No, not depressed at all. Maybe a little guilty—she'd been with her father the morning he died—but she was quite relieved about it, the father dying, and she couldn't quite hide it. Like a weight was gone. I guess he'd been sick for a while." Flora leaned forward and tested Caroline again on the wine, filled her own glass. "She said she was leaving Charlie—he'd already run through all the money she gave him for an investment after her father died."

Caroline tried to decide which tangent to follow, but Flora wasn't the type for long pauses. "What depressed her—I mean, honestly, she didn't *seem* depressed—would have been the last miscarriage, but I thought she was over that, too. Shedding things, you know. Husband, father, baby ideas. She could be a rich, free woman. Charlie wasn't exactly adding value at that point. He's never been a good businessman, one crackpot plan after another. So good-looking, but she didn't need to deal with his anger issues. I've wondered and wondered—he must have been having an affair. I mean, why else would she do this? How depressing, you know, to be cheated upon, and she wasn't a very logical woman. Maybe she dipped when she talked to him that night. He said they talked and she sounded fine, but maybe he was cruel."

"Can I see the cabin?" asked Caroline.

"Of course," said Flora. "No one's stayed in it, since. It's been cleaned, of course—my cleaning lady was the absolute best—and what a mess it was. But no one since—my husband is very into security. Cameras, the whole bit. We gave the tape to Sheriff Feckler," said Flora.

"Deputy Feckler," murmured Caroline, wondering if Burt enjoyed watching a woman die on video. Nothing was in the notes.

They walked down, and Flora blathered on about Charlie claiming he was going to own a mountain while Caroline felt through the drawers and thought again about what a happy name Charlie was, how goofy "Charlie Bell" sounded. That charm, on and off, sunshine followed by a sucking black hole. No dial tone on the phone; she followed the line to the wall and found it was cut at the carpet level, as was the camera. She took to the floor while she asked about Charlie's mountain project. A resort on an inholding, a ghost town; twenty-acre parcels with sweeping views, exclusive town houses in tall trees along the Yellowstone.

Back up at the main house, Caroline no longer turned down the Chablis. She took a long sip while Flora rattled on about how they might have misled the deputy, while Caroline was dealing with the scene. Flora's husband, Stan, told Burt that Maryellen was a neurotic mess who loved her husband. Flora, to her later shame, drank heavily and said nothing. But what did it matter?

Not once did she ask why Caroline was investigating

now, nor show much interest when Caroline showed her the capsule she'd pried out of the carpet. "I'll have to take this back with me. Could you give me the number for your cleaning lady? Just in case she remembers something?"

"She's long gone, home to care for her mother. I'll never find her kind again."

"What's her name?"

"Mari!" said Flora. "She came my way via Maryellen, all too briefly. That's what Charlie was asking about, at the party—he was trying to find her. But tell me about Elaine. You know he was having dinner with her the night Maryellen died? She just seems so . . . mean."

"Maybe I can track Mari down. Where's home?"

"Berlin."

"Your cleaning lady is German?"

"Half German and half Russian," said Flora.

CAROLINE WENT BACK to the station. Gideon was off searching the woods of Marvel and Blue Creek for rifles, and radioed in to say that there was human shit floating in Elaine's hot tub. Clearly the Russians hadn't gone far.

"Leave it," said Caroline, cheering up. She'd stowed Ed's files in her own deep desk drawer, and now she pulled out the last C. Bell file, the juvenile file for a man who was twenty-two when he shot a sheriff.

Except this file wasn't about Charlie at all.

THE COURT-APPOINTED LAWYER for the infant had been Manny Walls, probably fresh out of school then, now a pickled munchkin in a toupee, with some alcohol-related dementia. You'd think Manny would remember a murder and a suicide, even if it was almost thirty years ago, but he was a blank. "Well, of course I remember Ansel, and what happened. But a dead girl with a kid?" He floated. "So many sad kids. Everything's in storage. Let me think . . ."

He agreed to meet Caroline at the Bat. "I'm confused about the situation," she said. "The daughter-in-law was found hanging and the family wouldn't take in the baby?"

"Hah," said Manny. "Fucking people; they just break your heart. I think this was the little boy in the straw. Moses in the bulrushes. Actually, no—a little girl, so make that Mosette. And not straw—they found her in a closet."

Caroline realized she was gaping. Manny noticed. "The woman hid the baby in the closet to keep her safe, and then . . . I don't know what really happened. She was kind of dehydrated when the old couple found her."

"A newborn?"

"No, no. Older. Over a year."

"Why would the family not keep her?"

But even as she asked, she thought of Charlie, and how he'd feel about Patrick and Iris's little girl. They couldn't keep her.

Manny flipped through the file. "It was all so sad, family just destroyed, father crippled. Seemed to feel it was for the kid's own good that no one know, and that they find another home for the baby. It's not fair to judge when something so horrible has happened."

He took a drink. "Though as I said, I don't remember much of anything. But there was definitely a baby. Ask Ed Winton."

"I've talked to Ed about the case. He didn't mention the kid."

"Well, that's odd," said Manny. "Because he and his wife were named as the temporary foster parents."

When Caroline found Jules at the house site, arguing with Divvy about what to do with the cracked greenhouse slab, she pulled him away and handed him the papers she'd copied from Manny, papers missing from Ed's file: a declaration that Iris Talouse Bell had died intestate with a single heir ("her daughter, Coral Lucia Bell"); the termination of Patrick Bell's parental rights; the adoption paperwork for the infant, who'd been renamed Sadie Louise Winton.

Jules didn't confess to knowing; there was no point, and they both understood the Bells' fear. The Bells still had someone to lose, something Charlie could still take from them.

JULES AND CAROLINE said they needed a little time alone, which was true enough, and Olive agreed again to babysit.

They parked in the lane to the river, next to the new box wire and fence posts for their garden. Sadie was just locking Suzette's door, and they all stared sadly at the cracked pad attached to the garage while the theme music of *E.R.* bellowed out of Suzette's open windows. Hospitals, her home away from home. Caroline refused to give up on the greenhouse project; Divvy would have to pull this slab and pour another.

Another war, thought Jules.

The iron fence came out in undamaged sections, with minimal digging. They laid it carefully to one side and covered it with a tarp and some rebar, marking one end of the new garden location. In a nod to delusion, Jules staked out corners and two gate locations. The plan was to fence the garden without hitting bones, blocking as much as possible from Divvy's digging machines. They'd discover the cemetery later, when they dug planting holes for fruit trees on each corner, once the house was safely up. They'd make the discovery, go public, and donate this chunk for a walking area that could link to the dog park with a little bridge, work out something with the city and the Aches. A second garden could go closer to the DMZ, and truly block the Selway view.

Unless, of course, they sold the place instead of confessing, and let it be bulldozed into concrete eternity.

For the first hour, Jules felt smug—a certain edge of deniability could be maintained—but he knew he'd have to keep tamping down the underlying ooze of self-loathing. He'd never in his life done anything this unethical, at least as an archaeologist. He worked on lines: *We're not moving anyone, we're not dumping anyone, we're not destroying anything. We're living near, not on. It's an issue of timing.*

At eleven, working under the halogen light, the posts were stable, and they'd hung bull panel fencing and a temporary gate. The enclosure was entirely covered by a tarp, ostensibly to kill the weeds in the area they intended to plant. Jules finished wiring the fencing in place while Caroline added some bricks to the tarp, piled up tools, and finally flopped down under the apple tree. Fruit lay on the grass after the wind and rain on the night of the party, and Jules watched her search for an unbruised, unwormy apple.

"These are getting tastier," she said. "Applejack. Cider." Silhouetted against the light, the apples looked like cartoon bombs, and the city of molehills looked like Cappadocia. "Do the moles harm the tree?"

"No, but they might be bad for us, depending on what they bring up."

"I should look for ribs? More jewelry?"

"You should."

He was searching for the bolt cutters when Caroline hissed his name. She was crouched over one of the larger rodent exit holes under the apple, and her expression was not good, not happy. He dropped the bolt cutters and walked over, and she held up a small patch of fabric, something faded and striped. Jules bent to study it, and she handed him something else from the pile, a tiny white bone. "Is it a fingertip?"

"Could be," said Jules. Of course it was—he was haunted by phalanges. But he found the fabric even more unnerving.

"Should I push it all back down into the hole? This is making me feel like a complete creep. And look at this."

Another bit of fabric, with a rusted snap. "Geez," she said. "When were snaps invented? The thirties?"

Certainly not the 1880s. "Fuck," whispered Jules. He felt like his head was going to explode, and he lunged toward the light and turned it off.

They crouched in the grass and waited for their eyes to adjust. "Did you ever look at that lighter I found over here?" asked Jules. "That Zippo I put on the windowsill?"

"No," said Caroline. "Did you?"

"Donald was always losing his lighter," said Suzette. "Please don't worry about it."

Neither of them screamed. Old woman standing in the moonlight, holding her animals' feed bucket in one hand, a gin and tonic in the other. Caroline covered her face with her hands.

"Please," said Suzette. "There's just no point to digging anyone up. But did you notice that part of your garage pad was cracked? Maybe the gravel wasn't prepared correctly."

"Divvy's replacing it in a couple of days," said Jules.

"It's endless, isn't it?" said Suzette. "You want it all so badly, but you never stop worrying."

BACK HOME TO the voodoo altar: bones and toys, treasures and ammo. Jules dropped the crusty Zippo into soapy water while Caroline perched on a stool. He turned the wet lighter so that she could see the engraving: DEW. Donald Edgar Whipple was feeding Suzette's apples, providing a rib-cage mansion for the moles who'd brought his lighter and boxer snap and finger bone into a new decade's air and light. They both thought of the hospital report, the dead baby, the timing of Suzette's trip, and the finding of a suicide's pile of clothes on the Pacific beach. Elaine's dream of Suzette covered in blood, Suzette promising them paradise if they left her apple tree alone.

"Are we sure she killed him?" asked Caroline.

Jules looked for a corkscrew. "Wouldn't you have?"

21 *Marbles*

JULES AND CAROLINE, SEPARATE YET LYING IN BED together, began to sort out just what to do about so very many issues. He saw them (with a headache, sliding in and out of sleep at four a.m.) as a writhing, interconnected ball labeled *cemeteries*. That would be problem number one, the end of things becoming the beginning of several nightmares. Too many people, in too many places, being ignored by too many other people for the sake of profit. This category unfortunately included him, and it included his beloved.

Caroline thought of two trajectories, spiraling around each other on the way down: Charlie's finances and the Russians' life spans. They must be getting annoyed. But she mostly thought of Russian men, losing body parts, losing everything, to Charlie's cascading financial panic, his killer instincts. She needed to understand causation, the chain reaction, the beginning and end points.

You can't see everything simultaneously if you're a marble in a Rube Goldberg machine.

BY MIDDAY SUNDAY, Caroline still came up lacking. No rifle turned up in the woods. Prints on a priest's toilet seat weren't enough, leaking fentanyl capsules weren't enough, circumstantial evidence and Charlie's financial motives for the murder of his wife and father-in-law wouldn't get it done. There was no paper trail between him and anyone who might have helped. There were no stray prints that might have belonged to the maid in the Catton guest cabin—VVV in a uniform, how kinky—though they did find a single small print on the wheelchair, right where a person might have wanted to hold it to tip out a dead load.

On Sunday morning, Charlie and Elaine returned from Wyoming like bad pennies. Charlie sunned in the yard, reading *The Wall Street Journal*, while a cleaning service removed the shit from the hot tub, and he let the pages blow toward the building site when he wandered off. He brayed into his satellite phone while Harvey, the watcher, tried to nap. He went to the grocery and on his return chased a shrieking Elaine around the yard with two live lobsters. They frolicked in the hot tub that evening, cooing to each other, dovelike.

ON MONDAY MORNING, according to Caroline's contact in Denver, Charlie got the news that a motion to intervene had again been filed in Maryellen's estate proceeding. The disaffected Smith heirs were regaining traction. The news came Charlie's way via Elaine, who stalked out to where Charlie dozed in the hot tub and apparently gave it to him loudly, with gestures. Caroline, just pulling up to warn Suzette and Harvey that her neighbors might get touchy again, started running as Elaine hit Charlie with the newspaper. Charlie jumped out and began to throttle her on the lawn, simultaneously driving his hips against hers. Harvey tried and failed to pull him off, and Caroline used Harvey's stun gun on Charlie's wet back. He flipped around like a fish on the lawn; she admitted, later, that she felt pleasure at his pain.

To jail again, bailed out that afternoon. By whom? Caroline didn't know. Charlie went directly to the bank, learned he lacked access to his parents' account, and lost his shit. Ed and Gideon were on that call; Charlie quieted down quickly.

THE NEXT DAY, Jules was back at the poor farm, having thus far put off dealing with the pink-lined coffin that Bob the crane operator stepped into. He was reluctant to proceed with an exhumation, but moving one person was better than moving three, and this grave was half on private land, on Suzette's property, and could be a learning moment for the grad students. When a dust cloud approached, and Charlie's Suburban appeared, Jules stood by his truck and tried not to flinch. Charlie barreled through, coming cross-country over dead people, the yellow dick on the side of the Suburban not quite scrubbed clean. He kept going until he reached the new locked gate on the road to Marvel.

Karma, man. All the devils buried with these people will seize you and rend you to small bits, thought Jules.

He watched Charlie flail at the new locked gate, climb back in his car, and head for Jules, needing a target. He braked about twenty feet away with a spray of gravel and climbed out. He was drunk, and he held a small pistol.

What a way to go, thought Jules. There was a certain freedom in being fucked. He hoped his father felt the same way on another August day long ago; he hoped he didn't need to, now.

"I was going to drive up there and kill Clusker," said Charlie. "But here you are."

"True," said Jules. "I see you."

"But if you stopped existing, it'd be like a tree falling in the forest."

"Except for the fact that everyone knows you want to kill Cavendish," said Jules. "And me."

Charlie tapped his teeth together. "Everything," he said, "is temporary. I'll find a way through. I always find a way through. Or I'll burn the place down."

He gestured to the twenty-mile expanse, then seemed at a loss. "What are you doing up here, anyway?"

"A dead woman," said Jules. "An afterthought, somehow. Not aligned to the east, not . . ."

"Nineteenth century?"

Still pompous, still trying. "No," said Jules. "She's only been up here thirty years or so, I think. Very sixties clothing and jewelry."

"I don't like to see dead people," said Charlie.

"I hear you wouldn't even identify your wife," said Jules. "Someone you knew and loved."

But this dig didn't seem to hit. Charlie stared at the hole, turned to look at the landscape around him, and gripped his head like a bad actor.

Tapping teeth, ticking eyes. Jules watched him take a step back and calm himself. The hell of being Charlie, but you really needed to dig to find some empathy. "Did you have even a moment of doubt, when you shot my father?" asked Jules.

"No," said Charlie, relaxing. "It was just so good to do it. The only people I'd wanted to kill before were in my own family. So, you know, it was something new."

He looked around as if he'd just remembered where he was, lifted the gun, and shot the tires of Jules's truck.

"Go make like prey," he said. "I'd like a little fun. I'll give you a running start while I take care of some other business."

Charlie took the Marvel road toward his sign, once again driving over the dead. Jules guzzled some water and looked around the open flat. Some dips and swales, but nothing bigger than a boulder to hide behind. An uphill mile to the mountains, but that would mean running toward Charlie. A mile to the river dropoff, but then he'd have to slow down, and Charlie would have plenty of time to pick him off, drop him into rocks and water. Jules pulled out his binoculars: four hundred yards away, uphill and to the south, Charlie was using a long shovel to dig under his already tilted VISTA DEL RIO sign. A half mile to the north, still soundless but approaching fast, Jules saw the Bells' dirty white van skidding toward him. It stuck to the road; no graves for these boys. It accelerated past Jules, heading up the mountain to Charlie.

Jules couldn't have told anyone, should he have wanted to, who was driving, or how many people were in the van. Everything felt ludicrous and operatic, especially as Charlie began to run. A swarm of men—white T-shirts, red sneakers, men at the end of a vacation—jumped out, clubbed Charlie with the shovel, and bundled him into the van. They scrabbled in the dirt a bit, then bumped on up the road toward Marvel, unlocking and relocking the gate before they disappeared.

After Jules walked down the river ledge to the nearest ranch and called for a ride from Peter, they drove to the uprooted sign, where they found a half-buried rifle and two remnant thousand-dollar bills ground into the dirt, not yet freed by the wind, which was picking up. As was its wont.

A mortgage and a dinner out, said Peter, patting his pocket for a cigarette while Jules finished taking down the sign and smoothed the dirt. They'd order Ivan-style bottles of wine, too. They would not mention the incident immediately to Caroline or Alice.

Peter drove him to Blue Creek; Jules was due back at four to oversee the removal of the cracked pad. He'd neglected to mention the return of machinery to his neighbors, but as they came down Lewis Street, Elaine took the corner from her driveway at something close to forty miles an hour. She nearly T-boned Peter's car, and only the weirdness, the strange joy, of the last vision of the van and Charlie on the hill kept Jules from wanting to chase her down.

"This was not how I imagined Elaine trying to kill us," said Peter, continuing down the driveway. Herb was about to lift off the flawed, cracked pad. They climbed out of the car, and Jules kissed Caroline (without getting into why he was so relieved to be able to kiss anyone). Then the cement moved up in the air and they all reeled backward at a wall of smell, a swollen, blue ankle. Jules saw the flash of a turquoise Hawaiian shirt in the gravel, and he understood that Mac was never going to get his vacation. Jules's missing sledgehammer, lightweight and fourteen inches long, lay in the gravel next to the body.

ELAINE WAS ARRESTED at the airport in Billings, trying to get on the next flight to anywhere. Caroline put out an alert for Charlie, despite his very good alibi for Mac's death: he'd been in the Blue Deer jail during the only window of time when Mac could have ended up under the gravel, after the last firework on Thursday night and before the seven a.m. cement pour on Friday morning.

When Shari saw the body, she said Mac probably didn't feel a thing.

ON TUESDAY, CAROLINE heard from the Denver police that the stay was lifted on Charlie's inheritance, and the money was already in his account. An hour later, Charlie Bell climbed out of a blue Toyota Corolla and walked into the Bank of the Yellowstone. When Caroline looked at the black-and-white exterior camera footage later, she could see only the nose of the car, no plate. On the interior footage Charlie seemed tired, even with sunglasses, and his ear was bandaged. He wired money to Berlin and New York and Delaware. All the stateside banks immediately routed the money on to Freeport, where it would disappear in days. He tried to get into his parents' account one more time and claimed to the nervous teller that he'd just mixed up the numbers. The Bells were old clients, from an old, good family.

In the footage, Charlie did not look as if he was under threat, or worried, but no one saw him again. A navy blue Corolla, driven by a woman with remarkable talents but an unmemorable face, was eventually declared abandoned at the airport in Billings. The van turned up in Butte, parked near the Bell Diamond headframe. From the van, there was a beautiful view, but only a glimpse of a river, the Silver Bow. Without knowing the city's history, you wouldn't undertand all the tunnels below, or imagine the things that might have been thrown into them.

22 *Finds*

A DAY AFTER ELAINE WAS ARRAIGNED AND CHARGED for Mac's murder, Caroline was sitting cross-legged at the shallow end of the city pool with Tommy on her lap. Nothing else on her mind, at least until a man with a snorkel got closer and closer, and she thought, *I must know this goofball.*

He lifted his head and took off the mask. It was Fred Pushkin. Caroline didn't scream.

"Shh," he said. "Isn't this nice? We used to come here often. But we are leaving, really this time. The internet is just not good enough for our business in a town this small, and we have maybe worn out our hello, or whatever you say."

Tommy cooed and marveled at the snorkel mask. Fred put it on and took it off, on and off. Caroline hoped this talent with children meant he was an uncle, not a parent.

"I am to say to you that Marina is gone, and she apologizes for misleading you. She needs you to know that we are not so bad, just a cleaning crew, she says. And you shouldn't blame Mr. Luneau, because he couldn't know what she was going to do. She gives an apology for the poor extra man blowing up last summer, and the injury to Wesley Tenn. She just gave her clients pills, said what to do and say, was the devil in the ear, and yet they still made a mess. The priest was not her doing. As I say, we were cleaners, making sure we left some things for you to understand."

Caroline blinked. Fred was having trouble not looking at portions of her skin, the wild eyes drifting over an ankle or a shoulder blade, then jerking away.

"Anyway, all is good now. You must know she did enjoy Wesley. She loves being a nurse; she's a good nurse. He was very happy, wasn't he?"

Caroline marveled at the idea that Fred was dwelling on this, rather than his own sins. "Wesley? He was," she said. The girlfriend Rina, the nurse who'd gotten Wesley to smoke weed, cook on his own. The nurse who'd saved Caroline's life, stolen medication from the hospital for people whose business she disagreed with, ethically, and for her dying Russian friend. Who sat next to Olive during their shifts, who also cleaned Flora's house. Who'd ended up with all the Smith family's money. For fuck's sake.

"You mustn't blame us, or Mr. Luneau. Just the bullet-making family and Charlie fuckwad. He never did pay us everything, and now he can't."

"He can't?"

"No. He can't. Really and truly, there's no worrying about that man anymore."

"And where is Marina? With her mother? In Berlin?"

"In Berlin? Oh no. Marina's very Russian. I think Novgorod, but I may be wrong."

A very large child dropped into the water next to them, swamping Tommy, who screamed. "Anyway," said Fred. "A good life to you."

"And to you," said Caroline.

He snorkeled off, jumped out, and shot off through the gate and into a rental Chevy. The men inside waved, one of them missing a finger, one of them no longer weeping.

Caroline did not call the authorities. Whoever they might be.

ALICE INSISTED THAT they deal with the privies sooner rather than later. How could they tell the town that they'd known its oldest inhabitants were lying in shit, and left them there?

Now that the last of the cars had been removed, and the road route was finalized, the county began to mumble about memorials. Jules had lined up three students. He wanted to prove to the Aches that this would, in fact, be a shitshow, and they convened on the flats for a ceremonial groundbreaking.

Alice said that the ladies would help; she said Caroline would help, and Caroline, who'd worked for Jules on one historical Tucson dig, laughed in her face. But she showed up, too, as did Ivan—neighboring landowner—and Sadie, who was thinking of going back to school. She brought along Suzette.

Olive, who'd gotten her truth, was there, too. She'd driven up with Caroline and Tommy and Jules and talked about how boring it was at the hospital without her friend Marina, and how sad it was that the hospital was losing its good nurses.

Jules got out the maps and gave a little spiel: the city fathers might fluff about their holy resting spots, but the great thing about archaeology, just like medicine, just like being a cop, was that it got you over the rah-rah quickly.

How much land does a man need? As if these students had read their Tolstoy.

But Ivan said the title out loud, and the graduate students all eyed his Land Cruiser and thought *hmmm*. They eyed Sadie, and Sadie eyed them back. The students were complete geeks but tanned and fit, committed to a life of poverty and yet not interested in a monastery.

Jules picked up a shovel and was about to start when Suzette plucked at his elbow and whispered: he did know, didn't he, that Donald helped bury some people up here? Jules said that he knew better than anyone in the world, and she shouldn't worry. He dug in, and Alice popped the first bottle of champagne. Another shovelful and the smell of Depression-era shit rose in a puff that was almost visible. The ladies scattered upwind, laughing, and the students reeled in regret.

Jules led a short tour to allow some aeration and provide context: here was the first burial plot, the second, the third. The orchard, the dormitory, the barns, the older privies.

"What about this?" Sadie asked, pointing to the collapsed grave Jules covered with a tarp, the one Bob stepped in after discovering Pavel of the crow eyes. Jules hadn't returned to the task after his last encounter with Charlie. This was where the road would be placed, finally, disturbing one body rather than three.

"We're not sure," said Jules.

"Can I see?"

Jules paused. Why this reluctance when he was planning to dig other bones out of the privy? The loneliness of the dirty pink lining, the shallow hole? He pulled back the tarp and told the students to scrape and brush carefully. He put on gloves and lifted the boards.

And he was sad, again: a blue silk dress, a fine-boned skull. Jules wanted to cover her quietly.

"Can I see that thing," said Sadie. "What is that?"

A tiny bit of gold and violet glass, an odd little flower jewel. An earring, he said, pulling away another bit of broken board. They saw the dress was torn from the chest down, gnawed by rodents. The students talked about how the soil had discolored the woman's vertebra but not her clavicle.

It was a woman, not a child. Jules could see that now. Sadie was saying that the tiny piece of jewelry was a necklace, not an earring. A flower. Jules abruptly replaced the boards.

"Let's leave this for now. If I need to move her, I'll get you back out here."

"She makes me so sad," said Sadie. "That pretty little iris necklace."

An hour later, after the class left, after Ivan and Sadie drove away, Jules looked around the barren field, and in the wind, under looming clouds, it felt like he was hearing an opera, that in this field of sadness, this girl with a broken neck was the crescendo.

Ah god, he said out loud, and he sat down on the mound of fresh dirt next to Iris Bell, who had been dead almost as long as Ansel Clement.

THEY'D ALL DISAPPEARED, like doves in a magic trick.

What tips the scales, what wakes up bad things? Olive, missing the living for the dead, talking to her friend

Marina at the hospital, Marina who was always trying to fix problems for the people she liked, and rid the world of people she didn't. Who caused Ansel's death? Only Charlie. Who caused Charlie's death? Volunteers to spare. Jules began to give up what-ifs: what if Ansel had got the call too late to stop the truck? He might have had a good hungover day after his anniversary, the normal arguments with his children that night at dinner and over the next decades, been annoyed when Olive didn't like the earrings. He probably would have retired early and joined the Forest Service, and Jules wouldn't have become a cop, and maybe never would have moved back. His parents might have visited him in New York, or in Morocco, or in the Altai after the wall fell. Jules wouldn't have met Caroline, unless she pulled him over on a visit home.

Jules was all right with no longer being oblivious. The hole in the sky, the central tragedy—Jules could finally bear to see it, felt like he would finally understand. Ansel falling to the ground, looking up at the clouds, flying into the infinite blue.

Acknowledgments

Many thanks to my family and friends for their patience, humor, proofreading, and love. Thanks, also, to the people at Counterpoint Press, who are pretty much the best people in the world.

I was lucky enough to begin this book at the Ucross Foundation, one of the most beautiful places to think on the planet.

None of the people, places, and stories in this book are quite real.

JAMIE HARRISON has lived in Montana with her family for more than thirty years. She is the author of the Jules Clement novels as well as the novels *The Center of Everything* and *The Widow Nash*, the winner of a Reading the West Book Award and a finalist for the High Plains Book Award. Find out more at jamieharrisonbooks.com.